Lost Rider

THE COMING HO

HARPER
SLOAN

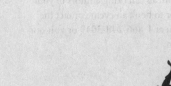

POCKET BOOKS

New York   London   Toronto   Sydney   New Delhi

Pocket Books
An Imprint of Simon & Schuster, Inc.
1230 Avenue of the Americas
New York, NY 10020

This book is a work of fiction. Any references to historical events, real people, or real places are used fictitiously. Other names, characters, places, and events are products of the author's imagination, and any resemblance to actual events or places or persons, living or dead, is entirely coincidental.

First Pocket Books paperback edition May 2017

POCKET and colophon are registered trademarks of Simon & Schuster, Inc.

For information about special discounts for bulk purchases, please contact Simon & Schuster Special Sales at 1-866-506-1949 or business@simonandschuster.com.

The Simon & Schuster Speakers Bureau can bring authors to your live event. For more information or to book an event contact the Simon & Schuster Speakers Bureau at 1-866-248-3049 or visit our website at www.simonspeakers.com.

Interior design by Bryden Spevak

Manufactured in the United States of America

10 9 8 7 6 5 4 3 2

ISBN 978-1-5011-5519-2
ISBN 978-1-5011-5520-8 (ebook)

To my sweet daughters.
Never stop chasing your dreams.

Lost Rider

1

MAVERICK

"Traveller" by Chris Stapleton

I wince as a sharp ray of sunlight strikes my windshield just so and beams into my eyes, making me curse and briefly swerve before course correcting and picking up speed again, my truck blazing a path down the 35. The highway is barren, no other cars to my left or right. It would feel lonely, but luckily I have a son-of-a-bitch hangover and a stinging sense of hurt pride to keep me company right on through.

It's been eleven days since the doctor told me my career was over. Eleven days of pretty much drowning in the bottom of a bottle. I did the one thing that I swore I would never do—become the man that raised me.

Everything I've worked for, gone.

Everything I had ever dreamed of, vanished.

I had every single thing I ever wanted in the palm of my hand. Riding was all I ever needed, and now that it's gone, the only thing I have left to show for my broken dreams is a fat bank account, buckles thrown carelessly in the backseat, a duffel bag of clothing, and one fucked-up body. Everything I own shoved into my truck, one measly cab's worth of belongings.

Over.

Just like that, Maverick "The Unstoppable" Davis was, in fact, stopped, and every second that I've pushed myself to reach the top might as well have been for nothing. Ten years of living my dream, gone like it never existed.

You haven't lost the only life you've ever wanted. The small voice in the back of my head just pisses me off even more. Like I need another reminder of what my chasing these now lost dreams cost me. That voice is right, though, riding isn't the only life I wanted for myself . . . not that I have a chance at the other now though. Not after I made sure to destroy every chance for it.

My head starts pounding even harder. Adjusting my hold on the wheel, I grab my Stetson and place it beside me on the passenger seat, resting my head against the headrest as my mind starts to wander, again.

Bull riding is one of the two things in my life that bring peace. I was meant to ride just as I was meant to draw air in my lungs to live. The drive I felt to ride beat alongside my heart. Without it, I wouldn't be me. Since I was old enough to walk, I would climb on the back of our ranch's sheep and pretend I was fighting for that perfect eight seconds on the back of the biggest, baddest motherfucking bull on the circuit. The fearless streak has never left me, and it's always been the driving force for me to take on any beast that was in the way of me claiming the championship.

I left home before the ink on my high school diploma was dry. All these years later, I'm not sure what pushed me to hightail it out of town: my need to chase my dream, or to escape the life I had that I was barely surviving. Deep down though, I knew I couldn't stay, no matter how much I wish I could have. I had already burned the only bridge that meant something to me in that town, because I believed that I couldn't have anything pulling me back, tying me down. I knew for certain that if I couldn't have it all, at least I was going to make sure everything I gave up wasn't for nothing. I vowed from that day on I would rule the world.

And I did.

For almost ten years I've been the biggest name in professional bull riding. There wasn't a beast I couldn't conquer.

Until I met Lucifer.

One hundred and four consecutive buck offs, and his hundred and fifth was the one that took everything away from me.

Too many head injuries, the doctor said, shaking his head at my scans. One more and I'll be leaving the arena in a body bag, he warned. I would be a dead man riding if they cleared me, he promised.

So just like that . . . it was gone. That dream vanished right along with the only thing I had left in my life that didn't cause me fucking pain.

I slam my palm down on the steering wheel as the doctor's words come back to me again, running in the same continuous loop that I had been trying to drink out of my mind for days. Haunting my memories and reminding me that I'll never be able to get back what I had.

My phone rings, breaking into my self-loathing thoughts, and I know without looking at the phone or my truck's dashboard that it's Clay, my older brother, probably calling to ask me—again—what time I'll be in Pine Oak.

I press the hands-free button on my steering wheel.

"What?" I snap.

"Well, well . . . seems my always pleasant little brother is excited to be headed home," Clay responds to my short-tempered greeting with sarcasm dripping from his words.

I reach over and pull a pack of smokes from my cup holder, putting off responding so I can light up and take a deep drag, blowing the smoke out audibly. My headache ramping up another notch at my brother's annoyed, scornful tone.

"You smokin' again, Mav? Thought you gave that shit up."

"I've got a lot on my mind, Clay."

"Yeah, you and me both, brother. What time are you gettin' here? Quinn's wantin' to wait for you before we leave for the church, but if you're not close, we're going to have to just head on over."

"Don't wait for me, Clay. I'm not really sure I want to go."

"What?" His voice is hard, unforgiving, and it fucking kills me that I'm letting him down. Again.

"You heard me, Clay. What's the point? The old man didn't want me around ten years ago, so makes sense he wouldn't want me there now either."

"Roll your goddamn window up so I can hear somethin' other than your fuckin' tires," Clay demands.

I take another long drag before flicking my cigarette out the window and rolling it up, switching the AC on before the thick Texas heat kills me.

Clay's silent for a beat. I hear his boots striking the ground through our connection, the heavy tread his tell that he's pissed. "Here, asshole. You're thinkin' of not comin', tell Quinn that, and I'll talk to you later."

He says a few words that I can't make out before my little sister's voices takes his place, coming through sweet and sorrowful over the speakers in my truck.

"Hey," she says softly. "You almost here, Mav?" She sniffles a few times and I silently curse Clay for playing the Quinn card.

"Hey, hell-raiser," I say with a sigh, wishing I wasn't driving and I could go to the nearest liquor store and spend the next few hours blissfully drunk. "I'll meet you guys at the church. I'm still an hour or so out."

"Okay, Mav. Love you."

"Love you too, darlin'."

I wait, knowing Clay isn't going to miss a chance to get back on the phone after getting what he wanted by using our sister.

"I'll see you there, Mav." He lowers his voice, probably so Quinn won't hear him laying into me. "Don't fuck this day up. You don't want to be there, I get that, but things weren't like they were when you left. You didn't want to hear it before, but it's time. Get over your pride and make sure you show up, if not for him—do it for Quinn. Don't let her down when she needs you the most."

I don't respond, instead disconnecting the call, shutting off the stale AC, and rolling the window back down. The steady hum of my tires against the hot asphalt is the only thing I hear as my thoughts consume me yet again.

It's been a decade since I last stepped foot in Pine Oak, Texas. Other than Clay and Quinn, there was nothing left for me there.

That's a lie.

My foot jerks on the gas as the whispered thought floats through my mind. I can't let myself go there. Not when there is so much unknown in my life. Not since the one way I've been able to find peace in my mind is now gone—and the other is the one thing I can't allow myself to hope for anymore.

I kept in touch with my brother and sister over the years, but Clay's right—I didn't want to hear shit about the goings-on. There was only one person other than them that, at one time, I would have soaked up any mention of, but pride stopped me from ever asking, the regrets eating me alive too much to bear. Not for the first time, I wonder how things would have turned out had I not been so hell-bent on escaping.

With every turn of my tires, the dread in my stomach multiplies and the pounding in my skull grows louder. My skin flushes hot then cold as my breathing speeds up. All this time away, and just being close to home makes me feel trapped all over again, which makes not a damn bit of sense seeing as the one man who held the keys to my metaphorical cage is dead.

I told myself all those years ago I would never look back. Nothing would ever make it worth coming back to this hellhole.

That's a lie.

"Goddammit!" I bellow, the sound harsh and a little panicked even to my own ears.

Yeah, I used riding as an excuse to get away from Pine Oak. It wasn't a lie, per se; the need to ride has always been an inch just below the skin, something I couldn't ignore. It was what I used to leave, my excuse to escape. But there was one thing I might have actually wanted *more* than even riding—and, because I ran away from it, I've spent every day with the ghost of regrets licking out of the shadows.

I left to chase my dreams—but I also left to escape him, knowing that after the hell he put me through my whole life, leaving to do the one thing I knew he despised so much would be a giant fuck you to him.

Ironically enough, the same man that helped push me out is now dragging me back.

Looks like the old man was right when he said one day I would be crawling back with my tail tucked between my legs. A failure that would be begging him to take me back when I couldn't make it out on the circuit.

"Well, laughs on you, ain't it," I grumble, reaching out for another smoke.

I might be crawling back, but it damn sure ain't to beg him for shit. I can still see his face when I said my parting words to him.

Over my dead body.

Only it's not my dead body, it's his.

The thing I'm struggling with the most, though, is the deep regret that's filled me since I found out he died. And fuck if that doesn't piss me off more, because if I was honest with myself, I would know that it isn't the loss of my career that has been eating away at me. Instead, all I can focus on is the fact that, even at my peak, I wasn't good enough for him to be proud of me.

No matter what, the silence from him over the years said it all. He couldn't give two fucks what I accomplished out there on the circuit.

It took me a long time to realize that I had been pushing myself for so long to prove to him I was worthy, but even when I fucking knew it wasn't worth it, something inside me still wanted to matter to Buford Davis.

All those lost dreams and unmet goals will die right along with the little piece of hope that I've been carrying around for years, unknowingly, but fuck if that little piece didn't make itself known in the past few days.

So, like it or not, with no career left and the summons from home that I couldn't ignore, I'm headed back to Pine Oak. A town that I always feared would suck me back in. The same town that is now the only future I can see in front of me, since the dreams I left to chase are just as dead as the man that drove me from my hometown in the first place.

Irony, ain't you just a bitch.

- ★ -

Ten Years Ago

I should have known she would be here. Hell, if I'm honest with myself, I came here *because* I knew she would be. Right or wrong, I can't help the pull I get when it comes to Leighton. She's the only thing that can calm me when I feel like I'm spiraling out of control and fuck it's so selfish and unfair of me to put that kind of unspoken pressure between us—especially now.

My heavy booted feet take me from the wood edge and into the clearing at what I like to think of as our pasture. The flowers are blooming bright this time of year, the bluebonnets that her mama loves so much surround her as she lays gazing up into the blue cloudless sky.

She looks like an angel.

Even from the distance between us I can tell she's upset. Leighton is always happy, it's something that used to annoy the hell out of me, but in the same breath, it was something that calmed me in the oddest ways.

When I decided I was leaving Pine Oak—leaving her—I knew that I would mourn that part of her. I didn't understand it at first, but it's also a big part of why I know I have to break away clean. The feelings that I've come to realize are a lot bigger than she's ready for—*I'm* ready for—aren't something I can deal with. Not when escaping this town—my father—is right within my grasp.

"Hey, you!" Leighton says with a smile, lifting up on her elbows and turning her head in the direction that I'm trudging through the flowers, careful not to harm any of them on my path to her.

I'm silent as I drop to my ass on the blanket next to her. I can feel her eyes on me, but I focus my attention on the fields around us. There's a slight breeze, the flowers blowing and flowing in the gentle flow of air.

"What's on your mind, Mav?"

"Nothin', Leigh," I mumble, my mind back at the ranch and the hateful words that my father threw at me when I told him I wouldn't be changing my mind and sticking around. That was before he threw his full bottle of beer at the back of my head. Thank God I had just taken off my Stetson. If he had ruined this hat—the one that meant a whole hell of a lot—I probably would have killed him.

"That's a whole lot of nothin' to be frowning about, cowboy," she jokes, reaching out one dainty hand to grip my wrist in a stronger hold than she should be capable of. "Talk to me, Maverick. You wouldn't have come out here if you wanted silence."

"Just got in a fight with my dad, it's nothin' new, Leigh."

She makes a noise in the back of her throat and I look over to her, her gaze hard and angry. "About you leaving?"

I nod. Her anger isn't something I'm used to, but on the rare occasion that she knows I got into it with my dad, it's something she has no trouble showing me.

"You know, he isn't the only one that doesn't want you to leave, but he's the only one that wants it for the wrong reasons. I know Clay and Quinn want you here, but like me, they know you're meant for greatness. Don't let his options on the matter sway you, Maverick. One day, years from now, you're going to look back at the moment and know that, regardless of what he said, you did the right thing. Even if I wish you weren't leaving."

She adds the last almost as an afterthought, her eyes rounding the second the words slip through her mouth and I *know* she didn't mean to say them out loud. I'm not stupid, I know she's had a crush on me for years, but I always knew this moment would come—me leaving—just as certain as I was that Pine Oak was the place Leighton never wanted to leave. She's always wanted to stay here. To grow old and raise her own family on the land her family has owned for decades.

And it doesn't matter one lick that if I close my eyes and think about that future, I could see myself right next to her if I stick around here—the same town that my father's nasty words can reach me—I know it will kill me quick.

"I leave in a week, Leigh," I mumble, twisting the arm that she's still holding and shifting slightly so that our hands are linked tight. "I leave in a week and I honestly don't think I'll ever come back. You know that right?"

She blinks a few times, clearing the moisture that had started to gather, not letting the tears fall. "I know," she whispers, looking down at our hands and giving a squeeze. "I'm going to miss you, Maverick."

"I'm gonna miss you too," I tell her, honesty dripping from each word.

Then, as if my mind had given my consciousness a giant middle finger, I let go of her hand, lace my fingers through her hair, and pull her lips to mine. I feel her braces press against my closed lips at the same second her squeak of shock fills the air around us. I ignore it all and open my mouth, using my tongue to coax her own. She follows without delay and before I know it, I'm panting with my forehead against hers and her swollen lips just a breath away from mine.

Those tears that she had done so well at keeping at bay fall in slow succession now and I know that kiss managed only to fill her with a little hope when I had done so well to make sure that never took root.

Fuck.

Without a word, I get up and stomp back to the woods, taking me from my heaven and back to my hell.

One more week.

One more week and I'm free.

I'm just not sure now if I'm really going to be escaping or running into another prison—one that keeps me from the peace that only Leighton can give me.

Fuck.

2
LEIGHTON

"Cowgirls Don't Cry" by Brooks & Dunn

"**H**e'll be here, Q. He will." *I hope,* I add silently. *God, he better be here.*

I shift on the unforgiving wooden pew and wrap my arm around her shaking body. She drops her head onto my shoulder and I look over her head to see Clay's jaw clench and his nostrils flare. I meet his eyes and hope he can read my silent question about his brother's whereabouts. He just gives his head a hard shake in my direction before returning his focus to the front of the church. I have no idea what that means, but I have a feeling it isn't good.

There's no way he would let his family down today . . . right? I mean, sure things have been strained—and that's putting it nicely—but there is no way he would leave his siblings to mourn alone when they needed him.

I lean my head against Quinn's affectionately and rub her shoulder. Quinn Davis, the youngest of the Davis siblings, has been my best friend since we were babies. We were both born in the same week, and since our dads had been friends their whole lives, it was just natural for us to grow up together. I don't have a single memory from my childhood where Quinn isn't in the forefront. Twenty-six years later, that hasn't changed one bit. Whether it be knee-high, snot-nosed, and full of mischief or buck-toothed, muddy as hell, chasing goats, and riding horses through the fields, I love her like my own sister.

Clayton, her oldest brother, is six years older than we are and has always been the overprotective brother—even toward me. He's the rock in both of our lives and has been for years. He always looked after me like I was family, but when my parents passed away right after I graduated from high school, leaving me with a ranch I couldn't and didn't want to run by myself, Clay stepped in. He knew I was in over my head, drowning in grief and responsibility, and made sure I kept my head above water. Since our prop-erty backed up to the Davis ranch, he bought the land, no questions asked, and allowed me to keep living in my family home, something I will forever be grateful for.

With Quinn and Clay, I've felt like I wasn't alone in the world because they loved me enough to fill the void my parents left behind.

And then . . . there's Maverick.

I haven't seen the middle Davis since that ill-fated night before he left town. A night that has plagued me ever since. It's hard to forget the pain of the past when the memories still shine bright. He might be long gone, but his shadow will never leave this town.

Quinn sniffles again, bringing my mind back to the present. I shift in my seat again, checking quickly to make sure the skirt on my black dress hasn't ridden up with all my squirming around, before I turn my head slightly and let my eyes wander around the packed church.

Again.

I have to fight with myself not to think about the missing Davis boy, but as my eyes roam, I know exactly what I'm looking for. Or, I should say, who.

Focus, Leigh. Today you need to stay focused on Quinn and Clay. And hopefully, if he does show up, Maverick won't make an already hard day for them even worse.

"He's not comin', Leigh. Why would he?" Quinn whispers brokenly, her soft voice breaking through my thoughts, drawing my eyes from the crowd as I scan her tear-streaked cheeks. She's looking toward the front of the church, but she knows me well enough to guess what I was just doing. I don't say anything, allowing my eyes to drift up to meet Clay's gaze. His handsome face looks as if it's carved in stone, the anger clear as day in his stormy eyes. His sister's hushed words obviously not missed and, if I had to guess, just amped up his already simmering anger at his missing brother to a full boil.

"Maybe he's just stuck in traffic?" I hedge, knowing damn well he's not, not if he really was an hour away, like he told Quinn earlier. An hour would put him already off the interstate, and everyone knows there isn't a lick of traffic to be found between here and there. Unless he got stuck in some rouge cattle escape, there's just no way.

Clay lets out a gruff sound deep in his throat. "Doubt that, sugar."

"He'll be here," I whisper again in Quinn's ear, praying that I'm right, but honestly I have no idea if he will be.

The old Maverick, the one I grew up crushing hard on my whole life, wouldn't have let his siblings down. But the new Maverick, the one that left so easily, well . . . I'm really not sure what he's capable of. I've seen him a handful of times over the years when the rodeo would come to Cedar Park, just outside of Austin, and the very few times I joined Clay and Quinn, even from a distance I could tell that he's changed.

His smiles no longer came easily. His laughter didn't ring out over a crowded room. If I had to guess, he escaped what he thought was the prison of a small town life only to find himself locked away in one of his own solitude.

I turn my attention to the front of the church once more and will my mind to clear when I hear the pastor start to talk. My eyes gloss over the deep mahogany stand directly in front of where he's standing. The one that holds the silver urn on display. Pastor John's voice carries over the room as he delivers his message about a long life lived and a forever promised with our Father. I keep my arm around Quinn, her soft sobs breaking my heart as he continues to speak.

I hear someone crying behind me, pulling my eyes from Pastor John as I look around the room again. I'm shocked that so many people are here. Knowing that everyone around here most likely had to close up their stores or halt their already busy day of farming to be here. In my case, to close my bakery, the PieHole, down for the day.

To pay our respects to Buford Davis.

The hard as nails father that ruled his house with an iron fist.

The one man that everyone in this room, at one time, would have been happy to see gone. Myself included.

Regardless of the fact that Buford Davis was a hard—at times, nearly impossible—man to love, Clay and Quinn did, albeit in their own way, and his loss is one that's hit them to the core. They didn't have a conventional relationship with their father, but it didn't matter to them that mutual love was something that they didn't find until the recent years. He was disliked for so long that I honestly thought that it would just be us, the family, but I should have known that just like Clay and Quinn, Pine Oak has a forgiving heart and Buford had been working hard to make up for all the wrongs he had done throughout his lifetime here when he passed.

He was a man who commanded respect, if nothing else, being that his ranch kept a fair share of the townfolks employed, not to mention the fact that the Davis family owned the only auto detail shop for a fifty-mile radius. The Davis family is *the* family in Pine Oak, and even though Buford had come a long way in earning back the town's regard, I would best my last slice of hot apple pie that the majority of the people in this church are here for Clay and Quinn.

I give Ms. Marybeth Perkins a smile when I meet her eyes, her weathered face giving me a winkled smile in return. My eyes float over the room, looking at the stoic familiar faces, before I start to move my gaze back to the pastor.

And that's when I see it.

Or rather, him.

It takes every ounce of control not to react, but my heart pulls tight before it takes off in a quick gallop that could give my horse, Maize, a run for her money.

Standing in the back of the room, black Stetson pulled low on his head, shadowing his face from view. His black dress shirt nestling snugly against his muscular build, the pearl white buttons standing out against the darkness. My eyes trail down his trim torso to the round silver belt buckle shining bright against his tucked-in black shirt and pants. The tight black Wranglers hugging his narrow hips . . . and good grief, I snap my eyes back to his face when I realize that I've subconsciously been staring at his crotch.

I don't need to see those emerald green eyes to know that the face shadowed from view belongs to the only man I've ever craved more than Nanny Jo's famous chicken and dumplings. I would recognize him in a pitch-black room.

Well, I'll be damned.

Maverick Davis has finally come home.

3

LEIGHTON

"Fire Away" by Chris Stapleton

Ten Years Ago

"**L**eighton Elizabeth James! I won't wait a second longer for you to get out of that dadgum bathroom. It's time to pull up your britches and open the door."

"I'm not sure I'm ready for all this, Quinn." I look over at the mirror again and pull at my top, vainly willing it to meet the waistband of my cutoffs. The plaid shirt that usually looks mighty respectful now makes me feel like a floozy, thanks to Quinn. I dress for comfort on a normal day, but I also hide the body that looks more like a boy's than a growing girl.

Somehow, Quinn's managed to make it look like I actually have some cleavage, not much, but it's a lot more than I normally have on display. She's tamed my overly frizzy hair into sleek and silky curls, something I will never be able to figure out how to do on my own. The makeup she so skillfully applied makes me look a lot older than sixteen. I never wear makeup. so anything more than some mascara is drastic. I look so far from the awkward teen that I hardly recognize myself.

"Come on, Leigh! You know I went through a lot of trouble to get my brothers to let us come tonight. If you're closed off in the bathroom all night it's just gonna prove them right."

"Gosh darnit," I huff and turn to open the bathroom door. Quinn almost falls into the bathroom, her arms flailing around like a windmill trying to catch her balance before she falls ass over elbows into me. I quickly hook my arms to catch her before she hits the ground.

"Jesus Jones, Leigh, you could have hollered out a little warnin' that I should stop resting my tail on the door you've been refusing to open for the past half hour."

"Sorry, Q," I say with a laugh, giving her a shove. "At least I caught ya."

She mumbles something under her breath and turns to face me. Regardless of the fact that I know she would never judge me, I still fidget with the shirt and pull down at the shorts that feel like they're being eaten by my butt cheeks.

Quinn lets out a low whistle through her teeth. "You look hot, Leigh!"

"Yeah, I don't, but thanks."

Her green eyes narrow and I know what's coming. Quinn hates it when I put myself down and isn't afraid to throw a whole lot of sass when I get started.

"Seriously? You're gonna stand here, in front of me, and feed me that pile of horse shit?"

"Uh, yeah. I don't dress like this, Q. You know this. I feel like I'm naked."

"Well, you aren't," she snaps and smacks my hand when I try to untie the knot she's made in my shirt so I can tuck it into my shorts.

My whole stomach is bare. The tails of my shirt pulled up and tied right under my very unimpressive boobs. I look at her top, the tight red material of her halter covering her chest—the much more impressive chest than mine. She's got a jean vest on over it, making it so that she's pretty much covered. Well, except that she's wearing the same ridiculously short jean cutoffs that I am.

I turn and point to my ass, the one thing I know I got lucky with, then down my leg as I huff in exasperation at Quinn when she rolls her eyes.

"You look great, Leigh." She ignores my protests and rolls the long sleeves of the shirt up to my elbows, straightens the knot under my chest, and reaches down to hike up my shorts.

"Dangit, Q. I already feel like I've got a massive camel toe. They don't need to be inside my vagina."

She laughs, bends, and hands me my red cowboy boots. "Here, these will look great with that shirt. Your purple boots would look better, but not with black-and-red plaid."

I pull my boots on, reluctantly, and hold my arms out for Quinn's inspection. She gives me a nod and bends to pull on her own brown boots. I stop myself from pulling at my shirt, again, and remind myself that every girl at the party will most likely be wearing less than I am, but that doesn't do a lick of good to ease the feeling that something bad is coming my way.

"So, tonight's the night?" Quinn asks, excitement about to bubble out of her.

"I guess so," I tell her, an ache in my stomach.

"How are you goin' to do it? I mean, I know the plan, but what are you goin' to say?"

"I reckon I'm just going to be honest with him."

"Yeah?"

"Dangit, Q, I don't know . . . I haven't thought that much about it. I've gone over it time and time again, but everything I can think of just sounds stupid. He's never even given me the impression that he sees me like that. Plus, I saw Mindy Anne yesterday at the dollar store and she said he was dating Krissy Thompson. I know I told you not to let me back out, but really . . . I'm okay with being the only sixteen-year-old we know that will die alone. And virginal." I don't mention the kiss. I haven't told anyone about *the kiss*. I'm not even sure I understand it, so I couldn't say that was his way of showing his interest. But God, it sure felt like it.

She gives a small sigh and wraps her arms around me. "A little dramatic, Leigh, don't ya think?"

"I'm terrified down to my bones, Q. Of course it's a little dramatic. All I've been thinkin' about is that I'm quite possibly going to make a huge fool out of myself tonight. I know you said you noticed him watchin' me the last few times we were down at the lake, but this is a huge step. I just know if I don't tell him now, he's goin' to leave town and who knows what will happen. If I let him leave without sayin' somethin', I just know I'll regret it."

She leans back, her hands staying planted on my shoulders, and gives me a soft smile. "It's a huge step, I know, and I'm here every step of the way. No matter what, at least you're going to try. Come on, let's get out of here, it's time to party."

Ready or not.

We both jog down the stairs, calling out to my mama that we're leaving, and rush out the front door before she can see our outfits, the screen door slamming against the house in our wake. Thankfully Daddy had been mending a fence back in the west end of our ranch, so he wasn't here. He's a lot harder to dodge than Mama. She had been working on her famous pies all day so I knew she wouldn't be coming out of the kitchen to check on us. Not with the county fair a day away.

Quinn jumps up into the cab of her truck and turns the key. The deep rumble of her exhaust echoes around us when the engine turns over. Placing one booted foot on the running board, I grab the "oh, shit" handle and pull myself up into the passenger seat. If it wasn't such a long walk through the woods separating our families' properties, we would have just walked, but I also know she's eager to show off her truck.

"Did you have to jack this thing up so high?" I huff when I settle in and buckle up.

"I was thinkin' about addin' another two inches, that way I could get those thirty-seven- inch trail grapplers I've had my eye on." She looks over at me before turning out of our driveway and onto the street. "What?"

"You know I don't understand a thing you say when you start talking truck, right?"

She shrugs and I laugh, the nerves letting loose a little. Ever since Quinn got her license last month, she's spent every second fixing up her 2001 Silverado; the first thing she did being to jack it up and add mud tires. I swear she would live in Davis Auto Works if she could. She's been begging me to let her mess around with my Jeep, but I'm perfectly fine without it being jacked up to high heaven, thank you very much.

We spend the rest of the ride over to her family's back pasture singing along to the radio and laughing as Quinn goes out of her way to hit every muddy patch she can find in the dirt road. It had rained the past two days, finally letting up for the bonfire tonight, which means that today Quinn's spent every second behind the wheel trying to turn her black truck brown. I don't even bother trying to see out of my window anymore, not with the good inch of mud coating it.

"I hope Jenny Fisher isn't here. I can't stand that uppity bitch," Quinn grumbles as she pulls her truck in line with her brother's, backing up so that their tailgates are all in line with each other. I laugh when I see Elliott Parker, one of her brother's friends, jump in front of the truck waving his arms like one of those airport workers directing flight traffic.

"Hey, El!" Quinn yells, shutting off the ignition, jumping down, and running over to give him a hug.

"Hey Quinn," he says, giving her a big bear hug. "Oh, howdy, Leighton," he says when I open the door and jump down. "Didn't believe Clay one bit when he told me he was finally gettin' his baby sister come to the bonfire. Hell-fire, this is gonna be great. He's gonna shit a brick when he sees what you're wearin', Quinn."

She laughs, swatting him on his shoulder and giving him her best innocent smile. Predictably, Elliott blushes from the roots of his red hair all the way to his freckled chest. I'm not sure he ever wears a shirt, which is ridiculous since he spends the summer months burned to a crisp.

"Jesus Christ, Leighton," he grumbles and his eyes travel down my body. God, I knew this outfit was a mistake.

"Does she look good or what, El?"

He nods, his eyes on my legs. "Or what, for sure, sugar. Damn, Leigh, you've been holdin' out on me." He reaches his hand down and adjusts his crotch. "You've got how many years until you're eighteen?"

"Oh, gross, El!" Quinn laughs and smacks his arm, reaching over to grab my hand and pull me behind her as we walk to the back of her truck to pull the tailgate down.

"Two years, Leighton, you come find ol' Elliott in two years," he calls out after us, his laughter trailing off as he disappears into the woods that line the Davis's back pasture.

Quinn rolls her eyes. "God, he's such a pig. Ever since Jamie O'Neal broke up with him he's been like a bull in heat."

I laugh, but don't respond. Quinn jumps up and sits on her tailgate. Not wanting to look like an idiot, I just lean back and cross my arms over my chest and take in everything around us.

The bonfires that Clay has become notorious for have always been off-limits to us, but then again, we just recently turned sixteen, and Quinn decided it was high time we find out whether the rumors are to be believed. Since Clay graduated almost four years ago, a lot of the crowd is his age. The rest are friends of Maverick. They let some kids our age come, but for the most part, everyone is eighteen to twenty-two.

The Davis family owns almost two hundred acres, so it's easy to get away with these things. No one ever comes out this way since the entire east end of their property is mainly tree-lined, with the exception of this field. I know Clay comes out here with the tractor and clears it out just for the bonfires, and he personally cleared the trail for trucks to get back here himself. Then again, his father is usually passed out drunk by dinnertime anyway, so even if he knew about these things, he wouldn't do anything to shut them down.

I look around and see coolers scattered throughout the field, at least one every other truck or so. All the trucks are parked in a circle with the blazing fire in the center, tailgates down and people either sitting on them or in chairs closer to the fire.

Clay and Maverick's trucks are on either side of Quinn's, a spot they clearly left open just for her. Both tailgates down, but empty. I push off from where I had been resting and walk over to the cooler next to Clay's truck and grab two Bud Lights, handing one to Quinn before I pop the top on my own and take a huge swallow.

"Don't even think about it, Quinn."

I laugh to myself and bring the can back up to my lips, but end up wearing the swallow I had been about to take when the can is ripped from my hands and foam sprays all over my face. "Hey!" I yell and turn around.

"Hey to you too, sugar." Clay laughs and brings my stolen can to his lips, downing the whole thing in one go before crunching the can in his hand and throwing it over his shoulder into the bed of his truck. "Just because I said it was cool if y'all came doesn't mean I'm gonna let you two get drunk. No fuckin' way." He gives me a brief hug before moving to give his sister one, kissing her forehead on a laugh when she gives his gut a weak punch.

"One beer isn't gettin' drunk, Clayton Davis," Quinn snaps.

"You aren't drinkin', babe. End of story."

"Whatever, *Dad*," she snaps, knowing he hates it when she calls him that. Doesn't stop him from acting like it constantly, though. Clay is more protective of her than her own father anyway.

Quinn jumps down from her truck and pointedly turns her back on her older brother. "Come on, Leigh, let's go dance."

I look over and give Clay a shrug and wave as Quinn drags me over to where Brant Weaton is parked. He's got all the doors open in his truck and the music is blaring, creating a little makeshift dance area in front of it.

I'm not sure how long we dance and laugh with the others around us, but when we stop the sun has long since disappeared behind the trees and everything around us is lit by the fire only. The crowd has grown considerably since we arrived, topping out around a hundred or so. Probably because graduation was yesterday, and people are looking for a party.

That sobering thought takes all the lighthearted fun right out of my sails when I remember the whole reason that Quinn pushed her brother into letting us come.

"Hey, Q! I'm going to go to the little girls' room!" I yell over the Toby Keith song that we've been dancing to.

"Kay, I'll be here when you're done. Make sure and grab the bathroom stuff out of my truck."

I give her a nod and take over toward her truck. I'm no stranger to peeing in the middle of nowhere, but it still sucks to be clomping through the woods in the middle of the night and not being able to see where you're going.

I smile as people call out my name, giving a few waves, but keep heading toward Quinn's truck. The groups of people talking, laughing, and drinking are now edging from the circle of trucks surrounding the bonfire and taking up almost the whole pasture.

"Where are you headed off to, sweetheart?"

I stop dead in my tracks.

"He-hey, John."

He steps out of the shadows by Quinn's truck and walks over to me, tugging at the collar of my shirt. "You sure do look pretty, darlin'."

Thank God it's dark. I can feel my cheeks heating and I just know that my blush is turning every inch of my skin bright red. John Lewis is one of the most popular boys in school and I know for a fact that he's got a girlfriend. But I also know he's got a reputation for not staying true to his girlfriend. That being said, he's never exactly shown attention to a girl like me, so I'm about to come out of my skin I'm so nervous.

"Tha-thanks."

He laughs. "Where you headed?" he asks again.

I clear my throat. "Pit stop in the woods." God, this is mortifying. I hate how I turn into an awkward mute full of nerves any time a hot boy talks to me.

He steps closer, I can smell the beer on his breath. "How about you come find me when you get back down here?" He gives me a wink before walking around me, leaving me gaping at the empty spot where he just stood.

Holy. Crap. I turn, seeing his retreating back and let a nervous giggle escape my lips. That *did* just happen. Yeah, no way am I going to search him out. Judging by his drunk stumbles, that would be the worst idea ever.

I grab the toilet paper out of Quinn's truck, one of the empty grocery bags, and hand sanitizer before heading over to the side of the field that seems empty enough. Walking a few paces into the tree line before I stop and push my shorts and thong down to my knees and squat. Making quick work, I wipe, toss the used toilet paper in the bag, and tie it off before cleaning my hands.

My shaking fingers make it hard to right my clothes, but after making sure my shorts are buckled, I head back out of the trees and toward Quinn's truck again, but I stop in my tracks as butterflies take flight in my belly—right next to the bed of her truck are Quinn's brothers, leaning against Clay's Chevy.

"You see what Leighton has on tonight?" My jaw drops

at Maverick's question. I look down, the firelight casting a glow on my outfit. He noticed?

"Did *you* see Leighton?" Clay retorts as he brings his beer up to take a long drink. "My guess is Quinn got to her and wouldn't take no for an answer."

Maverick is silent for so long, I'm half convinced he isn't going to answer his brother, but I hold my breath anyway—waiting for what he'll say. The flutters in my stomach going into overdrive. "Hard to miss when she looks like she's naked. What the hell was she thinkin' wearin' that shit?"

My cheeks flame as those stupid butterflies wither and die. No longer feeling the excited flurries because of the burn that's taken over my gut as Clay laughs, slapping his brother on the back, and shaking his head. "Not that I need to point this out, Mav, but my guess is she's trying to get noticed tonight. She looked pretty hot to me."

Maverick lets out a laugh that doesn't sound even a smidgen like a real one. It's deep and almost spiteful. "Yeah, kind of hard not to notice. She looks like a little girl tryin' to play dress up in her mama's clothes. The only thing people are goin' to notice is a kid tryin' to play with the big leagues."

Clay stops his beer on its path back to his mouth at his brother's harsh words and looks over at him, the glowing light from the fire highlighting his deeply furrowed brow. "You see the same shit I saw, brother? I know I ain't losin' my mind and I know for a fact I'm not the only one that noticed how good she's lookin'. Elliott already said something and I'm pretty sure I saw John talkin' to her not even ten minutes ago."

My heart is about to beat right out of my chest. I'm not even sure that I'm breathing as I listen to them talk about me. As I listen to Maverick tear into me, each lashing of his tongue feeling like a physical whip to my soul.

"Jesus, Clayton. It's kind of hard not to see when she's been paradin' around like a whore. She's fuckin' sixteen and has the body of a ten-year-old boy, for fuck's sake, so I'm pretty certain we didn't see the same thing. All I saw, brother, was a kid desperate for some attention. Tell me you weren't actually lookin'?"

I couldn't stop the sob that erupts from my mouth if I tried. And of course I tried, so it came out like a gargled, wet gasp. Hearing Maverick voice all my insecurities so harshly brings a shame over me like I've never known. Here I was trying to get *him* to notice me and he thinks I look like a little *boy*? Tears fill my eyes as both of them turn sharply at my choked cry.

"Shit," Clay barks and pushes off the truck to walk toward me.

I just stand there holding a tied grocery bag with my stupid used toilet paper. Tears roll down my cheeks while my heart breaks, my eyes never leaving Maverick's face. He's turned away from the fire now, so I can't make out his expression in the shadows, but there is no doubt he can see the hurt in mine. I might have lost faith in the power of my crush over the years, but that doesn't mean that my heart doesn't still yearn for the man it will never have . . . but hearing what he thinks about me, even though I always guessed it, well, it just about nearly *kills*.

Clay stops in front of me, his hands clasping my shoulders just like his sister had earlier, and dips his head down to look in my eyes. "Shit, Leigh, I'm so sorry."

Clay continues to talk softly to me, but I don't hear his words, my focus completely on the person that I grew up imagining some grand love story around as he shakes his head a few times. I was right to give up on that stupid fairy tale, but that realization doesn't ease the burn his words left behind one bit. Maverick is staring intently at the ground in front of him. He looks up, tosses his beer in the cab of his brother's truck as he lifts his Stetson off his head and runs his fingers through his hair.

He looks over to where we're standing and I jolt, my body going solid in Clay's arms when Maverick makes the move to start walking over to us. I look back at Clay, my eyes meeting his sympathetic gaze before I return my focus in his brother's direction. He's maybe ten feet away, but the second he takes the first step I jump. Clay's fingers tighten around my shoulders when I let out a strangled sob. Maverick's booted foot makes another move closer and I don't waste a second. The grocery bag, toilet paper, and hand sanitizer fall from my hands as I rip free of Clay's hold and take off running toward the trees.

"Goddammit," I hear Maverick snap. "Give me one of the flashlights."

I run.

The tree limbs strike my bare legs as I flee, but the searing pain doesn't slow me down. I keep going as quickly as I can.

If I can just keep going, I'll break through somewhere around where my family's property butts up to the Davis's.

It might take me an hour or so on foot, but the way I'm running, I'll be home soon enough.

"Fuckin' stop, Leighton!"

Maverick's voice booms out around me and scares me so much that I turn my head around and blindly search through the moonlit woods, searching for him while continuing my quick pace.

That is until I smack right into a tree I hadn't seen coming because I had been too busy trying to pinpoint his location so I could run in the opposite one.

"Shit!" I cry out when the rough bark scrapes against my thighs and left arm, bringing me to my ass before I know what hit me . . . or what I hit. I yelp when my palms scrape against the rough ground.

Judging by what sounds like a herd of elephants crashing through the woods, I know they're close. Shame from Maverick's words now mixing with the embarrassment I feel over my tree collision.

"You all right, sugar?" Clay questions me in concern. He drops to his knees beside me, the light from his flashlight hits my body, and I quickly kick my leg up to knock it out of his hand. "God almighty, Leigh, let me look at you."

"No!" I scream.

"Let me look, Leigh," he tries again and I just shake my head, pulling myself up off the ground and brushing my palms on my shorts.

I take a deep breath and push down the hurt, ignore the pain, and look to where Maverick is standing. The moonlight helping me see him, but his Stetson makes seeing his expression impossible.

I'm so sick of this. Feeling like he's completely unreachable. Untouchable. Closed off. He hasn't always been like this and I think part of me is still hoping the old Maverick I used to want to run off in the sunset with is still somewhere inside this cold person in front of me.

I've got nothing else to lose right now, might as well just let it out.

"Shit," I mumble to myself before clearing my throat and speaking up—directly at Maverick. "You were right, you know?" I tell him, looking to where Clay is still kneeling in the dirt before moving around him and stomping over to where Maverick is standing. "You're right, I tried my hardest to get noticed tonight. I was so sick and tired of just being 'stupid little Leighton.' Stupid Leigh, who has to listen to all her friends talk about their boyfriends, their first kisses, all of it! Funny enough, it was *you* I wanted"— I yell and jam my finger into his hard chest—"to notice me. All I've wanted since I was some love-drunk kid was for you to see me and *notice*! I never in my life thought that when I finally got your attention, it was because I look like some . . . some . . . what did you call me? That's right, a prepubescent boy playing dress up!" I scream the last words so fiercely I would be surprised if they didn't hear me over the music echoing around the darkness. "I've thought you hung the moon and all the stars around it my whole life, Maverick Davis. I've imagined you to be some Prince Charming that would come sweep me off my feet when you finally saw *me*. Pity me for not realizing that all you are is the villain determined to knock me on my ass instead. You know what's funny? In all those years that I foolishly crushed on you, I never once imagined in all of the time that I've known you that you would be capable of breaking my heart. That's on me, though. All of this is on me."

He doesn't move. No words are spoken from his lips to stop me when I turn and start to walk back in the direction I was running, but I stop a few feet away and whirl back around to face him. "Maybe I *was* desperate for you to see me more than just the little tomboy next door, but you're leaving and it was now or never. So, here you go, I've loved you for years, Maverick. There, now you know and now *I* know and at least I tried, so no sweat . . . this is on me, not you. You can leave like you planned and I can go on with my life knowing for sure where you stand."

With a deep breath and more strength than I ever thought I had, I push down the hurt and turn back around. I started this night with a smile on my face and hope in my heart. I should have trusted my gut.

"Hey!" Clay calls as he falls in step with me, his arm coming around my shoulder as he keeps pace with me. "If you want to go, let's head back and I'll drive you? It's too dark to head through the back gate, not when I know your dad has the bulls in the north pasture tonight."

I nod, letting him turn me until we're headed back to the bonfire. Clay's light hits Maverick's face and I hold his eyes, letting him see the hurt in mine when Clay and I pass through his flashlight's path. When we pass Maverick, still standing in the same spot, Clay checks his shoulder hard enough that his arm falls from my shoulders, but Maverick doesn't move an inch.

I keep walking as I leave my heart behind me.

If I would have known that was the last time I would talk to Maverick, I might have done things differently. I may have held my hurt and rationally told him how I felt. Who knows? But in that moment, I lost a little of myself in those woods. I should have known that when the love you have for someone is bigger than you can understand, it's better to leave that to your dreams.

As we make our way out of the clearing I promise myself never to let another man hold this kind of power over me. What's the point if this is the kind of pain that is waiting for you in the end?

4
LEIGHTON

"Step Off" by Kasey Musgraves

Present Day

I should tell Quinn and Clay that he's here. But one look at him and it's like the last ten years have never passed and I'm back at the bonfire, the awkward high schooler uncomfortable in her own skin. Marching away from him in the woods. It was the last time I saw him.

How is it possible that he can affect me this much after all this time?

He hasn't noticed me, not with his head bowed, so I quickly turn around and focus on Pastor John as he finishes up his prayer. Him being here means nothing. I should be happy that I remember the pain from that night so well, it will make keeping my walls up around him so much easier.

"On behalf of the Davis family, I want to thank everyone for coming today. At this time, the family has asked for some time alone as they say their good-byes. They wanted me to remind everyone that the PieHole will be opening up for a few hours tonight starting at five for anyone that wishes to join them."

I keep my arm around Quinn, not looking back to where I saw Maverick. I can hear the church slowly emptying and I feel a frown pull at my lips. I had hoped that when everyone started to leave that he would have come up front to be with his family, but so far, the pew we're in is still empty save for the three of us.

We sit and wait for everyone to leave, something that Clay had asked Pastor John to make arrangements for in place of the customary recessional, knowing that no one in this town would really mean a word of it anyway. Plus, I know Quinn is having a hard time. Regardless of the fact that she wasn't the closest with her father, she was really counting on this—Maverick home. She's still shaking in my arms, but when I look over at Clay I realize his silence isn't because of the heaviness of Buford's death, but instead anger over his brother's absence that has started to build to a boil. I fear that he's seconds away from tipping over the edge.

I stand when Clay and Quinn do, but hang back at the edge of the row we had been sitting in as they meet Pastor John and gather their father's ashes. I can't wait to get out of these heels. If it would have been acceptable to wear my boots, I would have, but Quinn would have killed me. As it is, I feel like I can't take a deep breath with how tight my dress is against my chest. I never wear tight shirts. I haven't since my boobs became beasts of their own right.

I'm too busy fiddling with the straps of my dress, trying

desperately to get some of the pressure against my chest to ease up so I could take a deep breath, when I heard Quinn gasp.

"Mav!" Next thing I know she's running past where I'm standing, her black hair streaming in the air behind her as she speeds forward right into her brother's arms.

Clay moves to stand next to me and I look up to meet his green eyes, the questions he isn't vocalizing dancing in their emerald depths. He's not stupid and I'm doing a crappy job at hiding the memories haunting me right now. He gives me a small smile, shifting his hold on the urn to wrap his free arm around me and pulls me into a strong hold.

"You're shakin'," he says against my temple and I just nod.

"I'm good, Clay. Go see your brother."

"I'm fine right where I am, sugar."

I keep my eyes to the ground, focusing on his worn boots instead of looking up, hating myself for making this moment about me when I should be focused on them. Like it or not, I can't fight the feelings that being near him bring me. I'm that stupid, naive sixteen-year-old all over again.

"Let's get out of here," he says after a few silent seconds.

I look up and give him a smile, hoping that it looks a hell of a lot braver than I feel. Inside I feel like I might puke.

"You think I could have a second with my family?" My head shoots up at the coldness I hadn't anticipated in Maverick's voice. He's not focused on me, though, instead looking at his brother with a hard expression and one brow raised upward.

"Mav!" Quinn gasps and he moves his attention from his brother to her.

"Sorry, Quinn, but I'm thinkin' that Clay's lady friend would understand that this should be a moment for our family and give us time alone."

"I'll just—"

"Don't you dare finish that sentence, sugar," Clay all but spits through clenched teeth and drops his arm to take a step forward. "You've got something to say, Mav, then say it."

"Nothing to say, Clayton, I just think it would be nice for your girlfriend to give us some space."

"My girlfriend," he parrots sarcastically, his deep voice vibrating in anger.

"Mav." Quinn attempts to butt in, but stops when Maverick leaves her side and turns to stalk out of the church. I should find it comical that he obviously didn't recognize me, or hell, maybe he did and he's just picking up where he left off ten years ago in the middle of the dark woods.

I take a deep breath. "It's okay. He's right. Y'all need some time as a family. I'll head over to the PieHole and start settin' up for tonight."

Quinn brushes a tear from her cheek and just shakes her head. I look at Clay to see him staring in the direction that his brother just left.

"You're family," he finally says, not looking in my direction.

"Clay, really, it's okay. It's been a long time since y'all were back together and I don't need to be there for that reunion. It sucks that it takes all of this to finally bring him home, but he's here and y'all need to make up for a lot of time lost."

"Shut up, Leighton."

"Don't, Clay."

"Don't what? You've got every right to be here. You're just as much a part of our family as he is. Hell, maybe even more so than he is at this point. So just shut up, come with us, and ignore him."

I shake my head, the fight instantly leaving my sails, knowing I would be arguing until the end of time if I pressed this issue.

"I can't believe he doesn't even recognize you," Quinn whispers.

"Or he did and that's why he wants me gone. You know we didn't part on good terms back then. It's really no big deal, Q. I'm good and the last thing I want is to let him cause you more pain today. Let's just get you home and changed. Don't worry about me. That's the last thing you should be doing."

We move, the three of us together, out of the church. Everyone has cleared out and there are only two huge trucks and the pastor's Honda sitting in the gravel lot now. Maverick is leaning against the black Silverado, his Stetson pulled down again as he takes a drag off his smoke.

"Gross, when did he start that again?" Quinn asks her brother. I watch the smoke puff out around his face, wondering why I find that so sexy.

"No clue, darlin', figured he quit a long time ago."

"Still here?" Maverick asks without looking up from the rocks he's kicking up with the toe of his boot.

"Shut the fuck up, Mav," Clay snaps.

"Yeah? Who's gonna make me? You?"

"Jesus, how old are you two?" I ask, finally finding my voice. "Maybe you two could stop actin' like kids long enough to keep your shit to yourselves and be there for your sister."

"The hell you say?"

I look up, finding the backbone I had seemed to lose at my first glimpse of Maverick Davis in one long ass decade and cross my arms over my chest, cursing my boobs when I notice his eyes drop to where I'm sure they're spilling out the top of my dress.

"My eyes are up here, cowboy," I snap and drop my arms to point to my face. "Have a little respect."

"Well, darlin', if you didn't want someone to look, maybe you should cover yourself. You put it out there, I'm gonna look."

"You're an asshole," I fume.

"I'm surprised you let her dress like that, Clay, she's just beggin' for the attention."

"Just when I thought that you couldn't be a bigger fuck-ing ass, you just keep goin'," I respond, interrupting Clay before he could speak.

"Darlin', you don't know me a thing about me, so why don't you keep your opinions to yourself."

"Jesus, Mav," Quinn gasps in shock.

I look at Quinn, giving her a smile before walking the two steps forward that will bring me toe-to-toe with Maverick.

"You, Maverick Austin Davis, haven't changed one bit. You would think that in the years that you've been gone from Pine Oak you would remember what happens when you treat a girl like the shit stuck under your boot, but let me assure you that I stopped dressing for attention a long time ago. Ten years ago to be exact and honestly *darlin'* I couldn't give two shits if you noticed me when that notice is neither wanted nor desired. Get your head out of your own ass long enough to stop being a massive prick and have some respect for your brother, sister, and your father."

His hand comes up and he tips his hat back so that he can see me better, but I don't give him a second to try to figure out what I'm talking about before I turn and walk over to Quinn.

"Come on, babe, let's get back to the ranch so you can get changed. Clay?" I ask, holding out my hands to take the urn before moving with Quinn to the truck's door. I open her door and wait for her to sit down in the front before handing the urn to her and shutting her door. I take a deep breath before moving to the back of the crew cab to open the back door. I look behind me, give Maverick one long, hard, hateful gaze before hiking my skirt up way past respectful levels, placing my heel on the running board and with a small leap, jump into the backseat, and slam the door behind me.

"Holy shit," I gasp in the silence around us after the door shuts.

"I *really* can't believe he didn't recognize you, Leigh. Hell's bells, that was intense."

"It's been a long time, Q. I've changed a lot since he last saw me."

"You were at the rodeo in Vegas not even two years ago."

I laugh. "Quinn, you know damn well that I went out of my way for him not to see me."

She was silent for a while, probably trying to remember that night. "You skipped the bar after, didn't you? Shit, Leigh! You've always skipped goin' out with us after every rodeo, haven't you."

"Ding, ding, ding," I sarcastically tell her.

"How did I not notice that before now? My lord, Leigh. I know you didn't come to many with us, but now that I'm thinking back, you really did vanish any time we went to see Mav."

"Because I didn't want you to. It's not a big deal, Q. I've only been to a few and it was easier for me to beg off than make you guys suffer through the awkwardness that would follow if I tagged along. You didn't get enough time together as it was and there was no way I was going to take away from that. Judging by how all this just went down, it would have ruined the time you did have together for sure anyway."

I look out the window as Chris Stapleton's voice sings through the speakers and see Maverick and Clay in a heated discussion. I can't hear them, not since Quinn turned the truck on while we wait, but when Maverick's head snaps up to look in my direction, I know Clay just spilled the beans.

Yeah, it sure does looks like Maverick Davis has come home.

"Shit," I whisper.

5

MAVERICK

"Nobody to Blame" by Chris Stapleton

"**Y**ou're a goddamn asshole, Mav, you know that? First you're late when you knew Quinn wanted you—no, *needed* you—here with her. Now you're showin' your ass when you have no right."

"Show my ass? You're the one having your newest piece sitting front row and center with my family. Looked like Quinn didn't need me one second, brother."

"Goddamn, Mav!" he exclaims and steps closer into my space. "Could you be a bigger fool?"

"Excuse me? You've got that tramp up there with my family, dressed like some two-bit whore, in a church, no less. She's probably got nothing but dollar signs in her eyes now that the old man's kicked the bucket. I wouldn't be shocked if she starts baiting you for a ring after the will is read. Make sure and get a real good prenup, Clay."

I need a drink. I can't control my words if I tried. Too

much shit swirling around in my head long before I even rolled over the town line, especially after everything that happened in Vegas. When you add that on top of why I even came home, yeah—I definitely need a drink. Just being back in Pine Oak is making me feel like I'm going insane. A caged animal desperate to break free of its confines. I know I'm being a prick, but I can't seem to make my mouth stop spewing shit.

Clay let out a low growl. "If I didn't think it would upset the girls, I would beat your fuckin' head in for that."

I cross my arms over my chest and stand to my full six-foot-four-inch height and hold his heated gaze.

"Your intimidation bullshit won't work on me," Clay heatedly says with a dry laugh as he walks closer. "Let me help you out here, little brother, since as you've been gone a lot has changed around here. A lot. That woman you seem so sure in your judgment over there is the furthest thing to a whore you could find. She's the one that's been by our side daily. When Quinn and I had to leave Pops alone after his first stroke, she was the one that stuck around to make sure he was okay. Closed down her bakery for hours while she sat there and read to the old man." He takes a deep breath, letting it out in a rush. "She was the one that dug her knees into the hardwood for forty-five minutes and did CPR on him even though she probably knew he was well past the point of help. She did that until someone found them. Too afraid to stop her compressions and run for a phone to actually call for help because she refused to give up hope that she could do somethin'. Forty-five minutes she never once gave up.

Sat there until her knees were bruised tryin' in vain to save him."

"You left her there with him? Damn, Clay . . . for all you know she could have been fuckin' her way to his money the second you turned you back."

"I should fuckin' deck you," he says, seething. "I really fuckin' should."

"How well do you even know her? You haven't said one word about having a new piece of ass so she must not have been in the picture long. Best I can tell, I'm not too far off the mark."

"How well do I know her?" He laughs bitterly. "I'd say pretty well, considering she's been Quinn's best friend for twenty-six fuckin' years. Why don't you let *that* sink in, you fuckin' asshole?"

My eyes leave his instantly and I look over to his truck, trying to see past the black tint that hides her from my view. No fucking way. It couldn't be.

"Yeah . . . see you're connecting the dots just fine now. Congratulations, Mav, not even back in town an hour and I'd say you've managed to hurt Quinn and give Leighton some more pain to add to the last dose you dished out. Shit, brother, it's like you never left."

He slaps my chest, shakes his head, and walks over to his truck. Before he rounds the bed, he looks back over and meets my stunned gaze. "You fucked up, but that doesn't mean Quinn isn't going to want you close. All she's wanted since the day you fuckin' left was for you to come home. Do what you need to in order to make it up to *both* of them."

He doesn't wait for a response. I look back at the darkened window when it rolls down a few inches. Clay reverses out of the parking spot, that crack in the window taunting me as it gets closer to where I'm standing, and right when he shifts into drive, one dainty as fuck hand comes out—middle finger pointed straight up and fuck me, I couldn't stop the burst of laughter that shot out of my mouth.

Looks like little Leighton James is all grown up.

The last time I saw her, I know I hurt her deeply. It's a moment I'm not proud of and has popped up more often than I'd care to admit over the years. A regret I will always have. The look on her face when she walked away that night held me stuck in place for almost an hour. I tried everything I could to justify my actions. To find a way to right what I already knew was wrong, but I knew then, just like I do now, that if I would have given in to the truth to my feelings about her, I never would have gotten out of this town.

Leighton James isn't a woman that you can have and let go.

I knew exactly what I was fucking doing when I saw her heading our way that night of the bonfire. It's the same thing that I've done to everyone else in my life.

Push them away before they push me away.

"Fuck!" I shout, pulling off my hat and running my hand through my sweaty hair. Settling the hat back on top of my head, I look up at the blue sky above me and wonder, not for the first time, who the hell I pissed off up there so badly that I keep finding myself in these positions.

Whipping the people I care about when the only thing they've ever done was care back.

Leighton's words come whispering back through my mind and I squeeze my eyes shut, remembering the look of hurt on her face.

"You would think that in the years that you've been gone from Pine Oak you would remember what happens when you treat a girl like the shit stuck under your boot."

"One would think . . ." I mumble to myself before giving my tire a kick.

"Maverick? That you, son?"

I look up, searching for the voice. When I see old Ms. Marybeth Perkins, I give her a smile. One that comes easily when I remember the sweet lady that would bring over home-cooked meals when Pops got too drunk to cook for his kids after Mama left.

"Well, I'll be. It is you, sugar. Just as ornery as you were the day you skedaddled out of here faster than Jim Bob's last win at the hot dog eating contest. Mind you, he had a little snag when he thought he could eat three of those dogs at the same time, but he still finished in just shy of two minutes. Mighty fast, if you ask me." She ambles over slowly, her walker's little tennis balls hitting the ground softly.

"Hey, Miz Perkins." I give her a smile, feeling some of the tightness in my gut ease.

"You sure are a sight for sore eyes. About time you got your tail home. You here for good this time?" Her weathered hand comes up and she gives my cheek a few pats.

"Yes, ma'am. Just got back today."

"Good, good, honey," she says, still smiling and patting my cheek.

I'm about to open my mouth to speak when her smile slips and she gives me a look cold enough to freeze hell. The soft hand that had been patting my cheek lovingly gives me one more pat, a helluva lot harder than the last. She lets go of her walker with her other hand, brings them both to my chest, and balls my shirt in her hands, jerking me down to her level with a strength that I never would have thought she possessed.

"You young'uns always actin' like you know everything when you really can't tell a horse's ass from your own. Dreams always too big for your own head, Maverick Davis. You had a wild air about ya, even as a young buck. Sowed those oats, I reckon, and now you're back home. Where you always belonged."

"With all due respect," I start, but snap my mouth shut when she reaches up and pinches the top of my ear.

"I remember the day you left. Those back wheels of yours spinnin' up so much dust it took years to settle back down. I might be old, but I ain't senile. Watchin' that sweet girl follow you around like a lost pup lookin' for a scrap. Hurt her good when you left, but I reckon you meant it that way."

I open my mouth, wishing she would let go of my ear, but she just gives it a twist and pulls me down so my back is hunched over her walker while she looks directly into my eyes.

"She's been through too much pain in her years for you

to add more to it. Leave that poor girl alone if you can't get that stick out of your ass, you hear me?"

"Yes, ma'am." Fuck, is she pulling my ear off my goddamn head? I'd agree to just about anything if it meant she would release her hold.

"Good. Now I'm going to tell you somethin', young man, and I hope to high heaven that you take mind. Your old man was a sorry bastard, God rest his soul. Did no good by you three as far as I could tell. After that no-good mama of yours ran off, coldness settled inside of him that was just pure evil. You take mind of that, Maverick, and don't repeat his mistakes. Not everyone has it in them to up and leave you. You left just like your mama, thinkin' you were bigger than your own roots, and just like her you didn't think one second about that cloud of dust you left in your wake. It's time to come home, not just your body, but your soul too. Open that stubborn mind of yours and take a good clear look around you."

"Miz Perkins, I appreciate what you're sayin', but I really mean no disrespect when I say that it's really not any of your business."

She hums softly. "Yes, I reckon you would think that, but you've been gone a long time, boy, and like I said, I'm not senile. I'm old, but not dead. When that no-good daddy of yours got sick it was like somethin' snapped inside of him and he's spent the last couple of years makin' amends with your brother and sister. Tore them up when he passed, but you? You act like just bein' here is too much to ask. You won't see it now, maybe not anytime soon, but

I've lived a lot of days and I know a stupid fool when I see one."

"It's not stupid when you're makin' sure you don't repeat history, Miz Perkins."

"Ha! Like I said, stupid fool. Wasn't that you repeatin' history when you kicked up that dust cloud? Now you're back and just like your daddy, you're hurtin' those that love you."

"Jesus Christ," I mumble and pull my hat off, again, to wipe at the sweat on my forehead.

"You watch your mouth, young man. I've got my eyes on you. You remember that the next time you want to act like a little turd. Now give me a hug and go apologize to your family, Leighton James included."

Fucking hell, I forgot how she always saw everything.

I give her the hug she demanded and kissed her wrinkled cheek.

"That's more like it. It was good to see you, Maverick. You be a good boy and come by one night soon for dinner, you hear? Now be a dear and walk me over to Johnny's car," she says in a sweet voice, no sign of the old hellcat who just handed my ass to me on a big steaming platter.

I look up, seeing Pastor John Lewis leaning against his car. I give him a small nod as I help her walk over. He doesn't say anything, instead climbs behind the wheel, but I don't miss the smile playing about his lips. I help her get settled in the passenger seat and stand back so they can pull out.

Clearly that last buck off knocked all the sense right out of my head, because if I was a smart man I would have gotten back in my truck and hightailed it right back out of town, but with my ear still burning from Marybeth Perkins's wrath, I pull out of the church lot and head to the last place I want to go.

The Davis ranch.

Home.

6

LEIGHTON

"Better in Boots" by Tyler Farr

After leaving the church, Clay heads toward my house. The ride is silent, but my mind isn't, and for that, I am thankful. It means I'll have some quiet time before I need to be at the PieHole. I have a feeling that they need that as well. Right now, the last thing I want is to head over there, which has me feeling even more out of sorts. Normally, you couldn't get me to leave my bakery, but after this afternoon I just want to stay home, pour a hot bath, and get lost in a good book.

With a deep sigh, I climb the steps to my porch, waving good-bye to Clay's retreating truck as I go. I had planned on spending some time on one of the many rocking chairs that line the wraparound porch after Buford's funeral, but I know any time I allow myself to be idle will just kick my mind into full speed down memory lane, and that's the last place I want to be.

Kicking the package at the door with my toe, I bend down and lift the mat to grab the key, pulling back the old screen and unlocking the door. My mind continues to churn as I bend to replace to key and pick up the box— judging by the logo-printed tape, another impulsive Amazon purchase that I didn't really need. Stepping inside, I quickly kick off my heels and settle my feet down on the cold hardwood, letting my arches have a moment of bliss. As much as I love the way my legs look when I wear those beauties, I would much rather be wearing boots or chucks.

I wasn't kidding earlier when I told Maverick that I stopped dressing to impress years ago. Even though now I actually have a body worth showing off, I still feel like that little girl playing dress up. I would much rather just be me.

"Hey, baby," I coo, a smile hitting my face when I feel the comforting furry caress against my shins. Bending down, I pick up my beefy cat, Earl, making sure to scratch him behind his left ear. His purrs greet my ears, breaking through the silence around me. Earl is the only thing that makes living alone bearable. I hate the silence that suffocates me when I'm home, which is probably why I spend so much of my time at the PieHole.

At the PieHole the only thing we serve is pie, so it isn't your typical bakery. It's so much more than that. Over the years, I've been able to turn my obsession with making pies into one of the best specialty shops around. It started as a way to keep my mama's memory alive—to feel like she was still with me—and to ease that ache I felt daily with her absence. I wouldn't say that owning a bakery is something

I always dreamed of, but it was her dream, and when I lost her, I found my happiness in making her dream a reality. I've been lucky, and now people come from all over the South just to grab some of my famous pies. Quinn jokes that it's my secret "recipies," something I won't even tell her about, but I like to think it's just my mama looking out for me from above—giving my creations a little dash of herself that make them so memorable everyone craves the feeling they get with each bite. We get people from all the way over in Georgia and all the way up to Canada.

Leaving the entryway, I move from the front door, around the love seat and coffee table, trying to decide where I want to settle; I finally choose the deep-seated couch. Earl's purrs intensify as I cuddle him close and continue to scratch behind his ear. He's a beast, but I love holding him close to my chest, or as close as you can get a twenty-pound Maine coon. He looks more like a small bobcat than a domestic house pet, but I love the little fur ball.

With a deep sigh, still petting him softly, I look around my home.

With the sudden appearance of Maverick back in Pine Oak, I can't stop my mind from playing loops upon loops of old memories. Not just of him, but of my parents too. Because our past is so interwoven, I should have seen this coming, but the pain the memories bring is greater than I could have ever anticipated. I feel the loss of my parents like it was just days and not years since they've been gone. My eyes roam over the room, looking for subtle hints of them.

For the first year after they were gone, I couldn't even stand to be here, the pain of their loss too great to stand. We had lived comfortably my whole life, and my father's thriving horse breeding business meant the house I grew up in was paid off. I was left with more money than I would ever spend in my lifetime because of their planning, but it was money I would have gladly given away to have them back. After selling our land to the Davis family, aside from the ten acres that my house sat on, that money grew even larger. It was Clay's idea to remodel my childhood home. I had never felt right spending that money, but he reminded me that my parents had worked hard to make sure I would always be taken care of—even if they weren't around. It was his idea that made it easier for me to be here, because once the house no longer resembled my childhood home, it stopped being a constant reminder of what I'd lost.

The first thing we did was take two of the back bedrooms and knock out some walls, turning my old en suite into a bathroom fit for a luxury spa, complete with a tub of my dreams. Big enough to fit two people—not that I've had that opportunity in a long while. By freeing up what had been one of the two guest rooms, my room now had a walk-in closet that I would probably never fill completely. We took my childhood bedroom and made it into a woman's dream dwelling: white-and-lavender accents with the palest of purple walls completed the look, giving me a soft, feminine room that looked nothing like the teenage cave it had been.

The other guest room we left alone, but gave it a fresh

coat of light yellow paint and new furniture. It was simple but cozy.

It was another year after we finished those rooms until I was ready to clean out my parents' old bedroom. Since their room took up half of the front of the house, opposite to the large family room, we decided to turn it into two rooms. It took awhile, since we were taking the old bathroom and converting it into a smaller guest bathroom that attached to one of the newly framed guest rooms. The rest of the space was turned into a library, a small one, but one with shelves lining every wall with two huge cozy chairs, separated only by a small end table in the middle. There was no doorway, just a double-wide arched entryway.

It was—aside from the PieHole—my favorite place to be.

Since Quinn spent more time here than she did at her family's home, she had taken over the drawers and closet in the front guest room. I didn't mind because when she was here, she made the silence disappear.

With the bedrooms all on the right side of the ranch, the left side was left for a welcoming open floor plan of the living room that feeds into my kitchen. My kitchen would probably give Paula Deen wet panties. Aside from my library, this room is where I spend most of my time—well, when I'm not at the PieHole. I make sure that I can bake here and transport so that I'm able to break up a normally very long workday at the bakery. There really is no smell better than all four ovens in my kitchen cooking away and my ten-foot island covered in delicious pies.

It took a lot of money and tears to completely change what was once my family home. Now the only things left from my childhood are little knickknacks and family photos. But even with all the changes, that ache still roars loud on days like this when memories assault me.

"I miss them, Earl," I murmur, and give him a good scratch next to his tail.

It's been almost seven years since they passed, but I still swear I can hear them sometimes. The click of Daddy's boots when he would come in from a long day working the fields, Mama's pots and pans clinking in the kitchen, or even their soft laughter and kisses when they didn't think I was around to see. Not that I ever minded.

When I lost them, this place stopped feeling like home. Even after the remodel, it's just a house, a shell of the happiness that used to hang thick in that air. It doesn't matter how many bright and cheerful coats of paint are thrown on the walls, sometimes you can't force the light when there are too many shadows blocking the way.

"Come on, old man, let's go get changed," I tell Earl, tired of feeling sad and sorry for myself, standing from the couch and walking toward my bedroom.

"Meow," he purrs and I look into his green eyes with a smile.

I continue to pet him as I walk through the house, talking to him in soft tones as his purrs respond to my words. Not for the first time, I realize I'm turning into the crazy cat lady.

"I really need to get out more, Earl," I muse.

"Meow."

"Yeah . . . first chance I get Mama's getting out of the house for some human time."

"Meow," he calls out again.

I place him on the end of my bed and he immediately circles a few times before laying down in the middle, like he always does, the king of his domain.

"Maybe the first thing I need to do is get a bigger bed to make up for all the space you take up," I say with a laugh, reaching behind me to awkwardly unzip my dress. The second the zipper is released, I feel like I can finally take a deep breath. I turn to the mirror and take in my full chest.

Getting a boob job when I turned nineteen was probably the worst idea I ever had. Not only was I dealing with the loss of my parents, but also the depression I had sunk into made me think only of every other heartbreaking thing I had ever experienced.

My lifelong battle to love and accept my body, for instance.

When it became painfully obvious that my boobs would never look more than mosquito bites on my chest, I let a weak moment after the end of another failed relationship convince me *I* wasn't enough, and before I knew it I was lying on my back in an operating room getting silicone stuffed into my chest. To be fair, it probably had very little to do with getting dumped and more to do with the grief I hadn't been able to shake. A person does stupid things when she's stuck in the fog of painful hurt.

Of course, as luck would have it, I was one of those girls that finished developing in my early twenties. Taking that boob job and doubling it, leaving me with an E cup that was the bane of my existence. Hell, I never even knew there were letters past D in the breast size alphabet until mine morphed out of control. It took me a year with those bad boys before I was back in the operating room. I still have implants, but they're nowhere near what they were, leaving me with a full D cup. Still, even though they're not as big, they are big enough to be a pain in my ass . . . or shoulders, neck, and back, rather.

I bend and twist, trying to work out the kinks. I reach behind my head, gathering my thick blond locks together as I grab a hair tie off my dresser. I open my top drawer and reach for the bright red lace bra, covering my naked chest before slipping out of my thong and pulling the matching lace boy shorts over my hips. Just because I choose to dress for comfort doesn't mean I don't love looking and feeling all woman with my lingerie. Even if I have to go to extraordinary lengths—and costs—to have sexy lingerie in my generous cup size.

Checking the clock hanging next to the door, I curse myself for getting so lost in my own head. As it is, I'm going to be rushing to get everything warmed up in time.

I wriggle into the first pair of shorts I can find, not even paying attention and I step into them and button them up.

I pull my red PieHole T-shirt off the hanger and yank it over my head, cursing my haste when my ponytail loosens, allowing my thick hair to escape in places.

"Lord have mercy!" I shout when I almost pull my ear off trying to rush yet another ponytail. I feel like the underside of a turnip green with the way my nerves are bubbling over.

And I know exactly what—or, should I say, *who*—is the cause.

Earl eyes me when I step out of the closet and exhale in a huff of frustration. "What? Quick lookin' at me like I'm lower than a snake's belly in a mud rut, Earl! It's been a long day; I'm allowed to be a little frazzled."

He just stares a beat before lifting his leg and licking himself.

Grabbing my red cowboy boots off the floor, I sit on the bench at the end of my bed and pull on some socks before pushing my foot inside the worn leather. A vision of sixteen-year-old me, nervously pulling at the knot in my flannel shirt, flashes in my head when I catch my reflection in the mirror in the corner of my room and I quickly beat it back. I've had enough of tripping down memory lane and I refuse to give Maverick any more power.

"Love you, baby boy," I call to Earl and rush through my door, snatching my purse off one of the island chairs in the kitchen.

I start digging inside of my bag while stomping through the kitchen and living room, looking down as I pull the front door open, and cursing the fact that my Jeep keys always seem to go missing inside my purse's depths.

"Damn it all to hell!" I shout when I collide headfirst into a hard chest the second my boots hit the threshold, knocking me back until my ass painfully hits the floor. "Son of a bitch," I breathe as a sharp pain shoots up my back from where my tailbone painfully smacked against the unforgiving hardwood just inside my door.

I look up and gasp when I see the reason for my tumble before quickly getting my face under control to something resembling calm and collected, despite the scene I've just created, and raising a brow in question. He doesn't speak, but takes a step closer and bends slightly to offer me his hand.

"You should learn to look before opening your door," Maverick says in a voice that's deep and rusty, making me fight off a shiver of arousal.

"If that's an apology, you really need to work on your execution."

His mouth turns up on one side, his full lips mockingly saying without words that an apology was not his intention.

Agh, that good-for-nothing, arrogant, stubborn asshole.

"You know, while you're at it, you should add workin' on your manners too. You really seem to be lackin' in that area," I retort sarcastically, ignoring his proffered hand and climbing to my feet, rubbing the sore spot on my ass.

"Guess I'll add that to the list of other shit my mama never taught me," he drawls.

I bend over and grab my purse before standing straight, squaring my shoulders and meeting his eyes. His expression doesn't change as he brings up one tan hand to tip his hat back slightly, allowing me a better view of those bright green eyes the Davis kids are known for.

"What are you doing here, Maverick?" I ask on a sigh. "I'm runnin' late and need to get out of here."

"Figured I needed to stop by," he says in way of an answer.

That's all? What in the hell does that mean?

"Then I would reckon we aren't on the same page, because I'm not sure I would agree with you there."

"You gonna let me in or what?"

I let out a humorless laugh. "Or what." Pulling my purse over my shoulder, I reach out and press both palms against his stomach and give him a shove backward, mentally screaming at myself not to enjoy the way his rock-hard abs feel against my hands. Nope, not going to enjoy that one bit.

Christ, he feels like hot stone under my skin.

Focus, Leighton!

He allows me to push him back a step. I shut the door hard enough that the sound rings out like a gunshot. When I turn back, I notice he's been holding the screen door open with his leg, and I raise my brow in question as he continues to prop it open.

"Mind letting go of my door? I've got places to be," I snap, pretty proud of the fact that my voice sounds a lot calmer than I feel—well, if bitchy is calm.

He moves his leg, letting the screen crack against the door frame, but doesn't make another move to let me walk past him down the porch steps he's blocking.

"Are you going to speak?" I heatedly complain when it becomes clear that he's either become mute in the past few seconds or is intentionally being an even bigger ass.

"I was out of line earlier. Just wanted you to know."

My jaw drops as I stare up at him dumbly. Are we serious right now?

"You were out of line?"

"That's what I said, darlin'," he responds, crossing his arms over his chest and squaring his stance. I look down, seeing the fabric of his shirt stretch against his thick biceps. The long sleeves are folded and pushed up to his elbows, making the veins in his forearms stand out as they pulse thickly. It takes one hell of an effort on my part not to lick my lips at that sight.

Who would have thought that veins could be sexy? I bet if I ran my tongue up their length, he would taste delicious. Wait—no! Shit, he hasn't even been back long enough for his engine to cool down and I'm right back where I was ten years ago, lusting after him even though I sure as hell know better now.

I tear my eyes away from his forearms—those sexy, hot, lickable—*dadgum, Leighton, snap out of it!*

"I'm not your darlin'. It's Leighton, and you best remember that, cowboy," I harshly whisper before poking him in the chest. He needs to stop calling me that or I'll be putty in his hands. Is there anything sexier than a deep southern drawl uttering the word "darlin'"? Nope—there isn't, which is why he needs to stop that immediately.

"Cowboy?" he questions, unfolding his arms to swat my hand away. "Jesus Christ, would you stop doing that shit?"

"Look," I huff, taking a page out of his book and crossing my arms over my chest. "I don't know why you felt like you needed to come out here. So you said some callous things earlier, whatever, I'm over it."

"You ain't over shit, darlin'," he says, laughing.

"Leighton. You don't know me well enough to be dropping those 'darlin's!'" I yell, fighting the urge to stomp my foot and have a conniption fit, ignoring the way my body is burning with arousal. He has *got* to stop calling me that; just hearing that word spoken in his deep velvet voice is enough to make me want to start dry humping the air.

"Yeah. Like I said, you ain't over shit. I was out of line. We need to put it behind us so I can go back to the ranch."

His words hit me, the meaning clear, and I'm suddenly even more pissed than I was just a second before.

"So you can go back to the ranch?"

"That's what I said."

"Why, you good-for-nothing jerk. You didn't come over here to apologize for showing your ass, but to what? You get put in time-out by Clay? Or Quinn? You could have saved us both the trouble and just driven around in that flashy little truck of yours for a red-hot minute before heading back and reporting to them like a good little boy that you had done as ordered."

"Now, you listen here—" he starts, stepping forward, our chests just a foot apart.

"Oh, I don't think so, mister. You might think the sun came up just to hear you crow, but I assure you that I don't need your cocky ass lighting my doorstep. How's this? Go on back and tell them that I accepted your 'apology' and agreed to let bygones be bygones."

His brow shoots up with my air quotes and I watch the anger flash in his eyes, turning the bright green into a murky storm.

I don't give him a second longer before I edge around him and stomp to my Jeep. One booted foot on the running board later, I'm behind the wheel and turning up dirt as I whip the wheel and speed down my gravel drive.

Who the hell does he think he is? And what in the hell

was that back there about? And more important, how do I convince my body that it's a bad idea to lust over Maverick Davis again?

Shit, I'm screwed.

If I thought my crush on him when he was just a teenage boy was strong, it has nothing on the force of desire for which I crave the adult Maverick now. When I was four, Maverick six, I thought he was the most beautiful boy, wishing he'd chase after me and pull on my long, swinging braid like all the boys who liked the other girls at school did. When I was ten, even his awkward preteen stage couldn't disguise his rugged good looks. When I turned fourteen, he started filling out his shirts, and my dreams changed into fantasies.

I learned how to beat it back when I turned sixteen, him eighteen, and I realized that the ugly duckling I was would never be able to compete with the girls he was always with, but just because I ignored how much I wanted him doesn't mean that the feelings died. Which is probably why his words hurt me as much as they did back then, because they told me I was right: I would never be what he wanted.

Best to remember that now, because the man he's become sets me ablaze hotter than an out-of-control wildfire, and if I don't beat those flames back, he might have the power to consume me until nothing but ash remains.

And I, Leighton James, am better than that.

7

LEIGHTON

"Crash and Burn" by Thomas Rhett

Jana Fox, the best employee in the world, is already at the PieHole when I speed into the back lot and slide into my parking spot next to the Dumpster. Her hot pink VW Beetle is pulled up to the backside of the building, and she's holding the back door open with a small smile on her pretty face. Jana's been with me since the day we opened the doors at the PieHole. I honestly couldn't imagine walking through these doors without her being with me.

"I told you when you called five minutes ago not to rush, Leigh. I've been here since before the service let out. Everything had already been put out, except for the pumpkin. Apple slices are already dished, and in the warming shelf, pumpkin has about a minute left before I can pull and slice, then shelve. You needed a second, honey, and I have it under control."

"What would I do without you?" I ask before giving her a hug. She came into my life at the perfect time, filling that motherly role that I had been feeling the void of for way too long. Not only that, but the woman can whip up a damn good pie, and she's played no small part in putting the PieHole well on the map.

Her arms come up and I breathe in the familiar and soothing smells of my bakery mixed with her perfume and I soak up the comfort she's offering. I really don't know what I would do without the quirky older woman in my life.

She rubs my back for a few treasured seconds before pulling away. "Come on, little one, let's go get finished."

We walk through the short hallway and I toss my purse in my office before entering the large kitchen area. The smells swirling around the room bring the first unforced smile in days to my lips. Yeah, this right here—this moment of lighthearted happiness is exactly why I spend so much time right here in the PieHole's kitchen.

Walking over to one of the four industrial refrigerators and two huge freezing units, I smile when I see them.

Twenty of Buford Davis's favorite pie greeting me.

I can't remember when I started putting my TIC, Twix ice-cream pies, on the shelves, but I will never forget the day that grumpy Buford called my shop and demanded, "Get your hide over with a slice before I'm forced to go graze with the fillies." They started off as something I was playing with. I had been looking for a way to make some frozen style pies and they just kind of happened by accident. From that moment on, whenever I would go over to their house, I made sure I had a whole pie just for him.

He never thanked me. Never offered anything other than a wink before grabbing the whole pie, a fork, and sitting back down in his chair for hours of watching the Game Show Network.

It wasn't his thanks that I was after, though. It was times like that, when he forgot how angry and bitter he was, when he would give us the rare glimpse of the Buford people rarely saw. The one that carried his regret-filled life like a battlefield of anger. He showed his frailty in those moments. His fear. His loneliness. And his guilt. He worked damn hard to change things around before the end of his life and, while two of his children had forgiven him, no one ever forgot.

I swipe at the tear that escapes and pull two pies out before moving to the stainless steel island in the middle of the room. Jana gives me a sad smile before pulling some of our purple plates out of the cabinet above the island and lining them up for me to place slices on.

"You sure you don't want me to pull the cookie dough pies you made this mornin'?" she asks, methodically moving the plates I had already placed a slice of the TIC pie on, before shuffling the empty ones in their place, the two of us moving in sync like a well-oiled machine.

"No. Tonight is just about the Davises, and the only pies I'm servin' are their favorites. No one will think to argue. Not today."

Little wrinkles pop up between her brow, but she nods, her gray curls bouncing with her movement. "You're probably right, honey. Plus, ain't a soul around that doesn't know those Davises love their pies. I think Clay has apple staining his shirt at least once a week." She lets out a soft laugh, the sound like bells chiming around us.

"Maybe I need to have a bib made up," I joke.

We finish plating thirty or so pieces of the TIC pie and start to move them to the chill box display in the main room. I look around, seeing the lavender walls, black round tables scattered throughout the floor, vases of daisies perched on each one, and smile.

When I first opened the PieHole, I had a tiny shop right off Davis Street, not far from the center of town, but it was perfect for what I needed. Until the word started to spread about my pies, and the next thing I knew, I had to turn people away because I couldn't keep up with the demand.

Having been wise with the money that I inherited over the years and living a frugal life, apart from the house remodel, I turned an already healthy chunk of change into a mountain of it. After being open for two years, I was able to move into one of the empty, larger shops on Main Street. You couldn't go anywhere in Pine Oak without driving through Main Street, and it turned my already thriving business into a monster success.

The kitchen took up a good bit of space, but when I renovated the old BBQ restaurant, I made sure to use only the necessary amount of space for my kitchen, leaving an office that felt more like a large closet at times, but it was important to me that the main area be large and welcoming.

The back wall is lined with specialty made cooling and heating displays that lead to the register in the middle. At the end of each display there's a small swing door that allows us into the dining area. The black hardwood and black tables are the only things in the room that aren't a shade of purple.

It looks crazy, purple walls, plates, utensils, but when I decided to name my place the PieHole, I knew this was the only way it could be.

My mother taught me everything I know about pies. When I was little, one of the best pies she made—and her favorite one—was her purple sweet potato pie. When we would finish that last slice, I always begged her to let me lick the pie hole, which was what I always called the empty pan. So when it came time to create my own place, it was never a question that my purple home away from home would be called the PieHole.

I smile to myself as I move around the tables scattered around to go unlock the front door. The heavy wood is painted the most vibrant purple shade in the whole shop and never fails to brighten my mood.

"Leigh, honey?" Jana calls out from behind the counter.

Turning from the door—and my thoughts—I smile over at her. "Yeah?"

"I just wanted to ask you one more time if you were sure about the cookie dough pies. I can go dish them up lickety-split."

"I'm sure. What's with the sudden worry over the cookie dough?" I laugh.

"Well, Leigh, honey . . . well, I just figured . . . never mind, honey. My old mind sometimes just gets stuck a little."

I cock my head to the side and furrow my brow in confusion. Old mind, my tail. I know for a fact that Jana's got all her wits about her, and I would hardly call fifty-three old. "What are you trying to ask, Jana?"

She starts to fidget with the business cards near the register and I know I'm not going to like whatever has been on her mind.

"I just figured, well . . . with Maverick home and all, you might want to add his favorite too."

Her words are like a punch to the gut. Cookie dough was always his favorite when we were all growing up. It was always one slice of pumpkin for Quinn, apple for Clay, and Maverick and me . . . always cookie dough. It was just another one of those stupid things I used to convince myself we were meant to be together. Young and dumb, I actually believed our shared love of cookie dough pie meant something.

"I doubt he'll even show up, Jana. I didn't make it for anything special. I guess I just let memories of us growing up together get the best of my mind this mornin' and didn't even notice I had added his to my prep. Plus, they always sell well when we have them out, so we can just use them tomorrow."

I hate the look of disappointment that flashes in her brown eyes, like I'm doing something wrong, but I wasn't kidding when I said I doubted he would show up.

I let out an audible sigh and reconsider. "I'll tell you what: *if* Maverick shows up and asks for a slice, feel free to run back and pull some. But I wouldn't hold your breath."

Her face lights up and she gives me a small nod.

We continue our prep, making sure all the shades are

up and the display cases are fingerprint-free. At a quarter till five, the front door opens and Quinn walks in. I rush around the counter and to her side.

"Hey, you," I greet and give her a warm smile and hug.

"Hey, Leigh. You need any help?"

I pull back, clasping her shoulders in my hands like she always does when she's offering comfort or support to me, and shake my head.

"Come on, Leigh. I'm going out of my mind today. Just give me something to do before people start showing up and pile me with that 'I'm so sorry for your loss' shit when we both know ain't a damn soul in this town that's really sorry he's gone."

God, my heart breaks for her. One thing Quinn Davis hates the most is when people are fake. Of course, she's also dealing with a lot. I think she and Clay both are glad the old man is gone, but that doesn't make the loss any easier. They worked hard to give him forgiveness, but after his first stroke, things just became strained. You can forgive easily, at times, but forgetting is a whole different ball game. It was hard to watch such a larger-than-life man crumble. I think that, in the end, his death just reminded them of everything that they never had growing up.

"I know, honey, I know."

"I hate this. I hate feelin' like this, Leigh. I shouldn't be this sad he's gone."

Wrapping my arms around her again, I pull her close as her soft sobs break my heart a little more.

The door opens again and Clay walks in, pulling off his hat and dropping it on the hook by the door before running his hands through his thick black hair. He looks over, his eyes going soft when he sees his sister in my arms. Not wanting to see the pain in his expression, I look away from his face. He's changed out of his black dress shirt, traded it for a brown button-down shirt that's tucked into his Wranglers.

His boots tap heavily against the floor as he walks over to us. "Sorry, I was on the phone with Drew," he says. I know the only reason his foreman would be bothering him today is if there was a problem on the ranch. I know he's been having trouble with his stable manager, Jimmy Wheat, but other than that I can't think of a single thing that would be wrong at the well-oiled Davis ranch.

"Everything okay?" I question, rubbing small circles on Quinn's back.

"It will be when I fire Jimmy's ass. He didn't place an order for feed last week, so imagine Drew's shock when he noticed on the log that none of the horses had been tended to this mornin'."

Shit. If there's one thing that Clay doesn't stand for on his ranch, it's lazy employees and neglect of his horses.

"Do you need any help?" I ask, not really sure what I could do for him since I never had any interest in running my own family's ranch, but I know my way around the ways of ranch life, and if they needed help, I wouldn't hesitate.

"Nah, sugar, don't you worry your pretty little head over it." He leans down and gives me a kiss on my forehead.

"Well, don't you all look cozy," a sharp voice says and the three of us turn toward the door.

Maverick.

Just lovely.

So much for him not showing up tonight.

"If you can't keep your mouth shut, little brother, then leave now."

Quinn lets out a soft whimper and I hug her tighter. She never did well when it came to her brothers fighting.

Maverick holds his hands up and a wicked smile crosses his face. Arrogant jerk.

"Maverick, honey. Well aren't you just a sight for sore eyes," Jana calls as she comes through the kitchen doorway and walks from behind the counter, making her way to where he's standing and gives him a hug. He doesn't move. Not even an inch. But Jana doesn't give up, she just holds him tighter, his arms hanging limp at his sides. I watch the emotions flicker over his face before awkwardly returning the embrace, patting her a few times on the back.

"Hey, Miz Fox," he mumbles, looking down to where her head is pressed just under his chest. I almost laugh at how funny her tiny, barely five-foot self looks next to his giant frame, but then I remember it's Maverick and I don't need to waste one second of my thoughts on him.

"You want some pie, Q?" I ask her quietly, not wanting to draw Maverick's attention.

She pulls back and gives me a smile, one that actually doesn't look forced. Bringing my thumbs to her cheeks, I wipe her eyes and return her smile.

"Pumpkin?" she asks excitedly, the bubbly and happy tone back in her voice.

"Would I make you anything else?"

She laughs and shakes her head. "Love you, Leighton."

"Love you back, Quinn."

Ignoring the silent storm brewing between the Davis brothers, with a clueless but chatty Jana stuck between the brooding duo, I take Quinn's hand and pull her over to her table. I say her table because she's usually parked here every chance she can get between her shifts at the auto shop. Walking over to the case holding the slices of pumpkin pie, I grab the thick one I had specially left for her and deliver it.

Right when I open my mouth to ask if she needs anything else, I hear the chime of the bell and the sound of more voices. Giving her a wink, I head back behind the counter, meeting Jana with a smile.

The next few hours pass with a roomful of townsfolk chatting, kids laughing, and more than a few trips to the back to refill the emptying cases of pies. Luckily I'm so busy I don't have time to pay attention to what was going on with Maverick, but the glances I do steal always seem to lead my eyes directly to his. Quinn and Clay stick to their table, letting people come to them with their fake sympathies. Jana makes sure to keep their sweet teas full, and a few times Clay signals for another slice of apple pie, smiling at me gratefully when I set a fresh plate down in front of him. Maverick doesn't make a move to join them at their table, nor does he take a drink any of the times Jana offered. He also never touches a plate of pie, not even after Jana brings the cookie dough pie out from the back, like I told her she could. Something I damn sure notice. He just stands there. A scowling man in black with his back leaning against the lavender wall, one booted foot on the floor and the other against my beautiful wall, and those damn thick arms crossed over his chest.

I also refuse to admit to myself just how good that imposing man in black looks in my space.

"I'm going to go do a round and collect some plates. Are you good?" I ask Jana before picking up the bucket we use to collect the dirty dishes that need to be washed.

"Yup, you know I could work this place in my sleep."

"That you could. You could probably run it better than me."

"About those other pies—" she starts.

I roll my eyes but don't acknowledge her words.

She giggles her little pixie bell laugh behind me as I use the swinging door opposite to where I know *he's* watching me. Just the same way I've known that his eyes haven't left me all night. I should be able to ignore it, but after our interactions earlier, it just pisses me off that he's here trying to throw his intimidating bullshit around in *my* place.

Making quick work of my lap around the room, I scoop up as many of the dirty plates and forks as I can before retracing my steps and walking through the kitchen doorway. The tub just hits the counter next to the sink when I feel him. Like a physical touch, the raw energy that only Maverick Davis has ever seemed to bring about in me, makes my skin break out in awareness. I look down, cursing the goose bumps that dance across my arms.

Ignore him, Leigh. Just go about your business and act like he isn't there. He wants this, to get a reaction from you, so do not give it to him. Do not play his games.

Pep talk or not, I have to force myself to steady my hands as I lift the dishes one by one out of the bucket before rinsing them and placing each one on the tray that will pull them through the washing system. Each plate I pick up I remind myself to keep ignoring him. For whatever reason, he keeps seeking me out, but I'm determined I'm not going to bite.

When the last dish is placed on the cart, I'm left with no other excuse to keep ignoring him. With a deep sigh, I turn and lean against the sink, crossing my arms and moving my eyes right to his. I'll be damned if I'm going to let him see how he affects me.

Maverick smirks. "I was wondering how long you were going to pretend I wasn't in the same room."

Quirking one brow, I give an exasperated huff. "Oh, I wasn't pretending. I just have nothing to say to you, Maverick."

"Yeah, that much was made mighty clear, darlin'."

"It's Leigh. And can we not do this? I don't know what you want from me right now, but just use your big boy words and let me know so that we can move on from whatever this is," I snap heatedly while pointing between us.

"Noticed you had Clay and Quinn's pies out tonight."

"Well, aren't you a smart one," I quip.

"Noticed you had the old man's too," he drawls and walks a few steps away from the closed kitchen door.

"Do you want a gold star?"

"Bitchy doesn't suit you," he responds, ignoring my question as if I hadn't spoken.

I stand up a little straighter as he takes another step closer, leaving just a couple of feet between us.

"Also noticed you seemed to forget one," he continues, taking one more step until he's close enough that I have to tip my head back slightly to look up into his eyes.

"I didn't forget anything," I retort, leaning off the sink edge I had been pushing my body into and rolling on to my toes so I can try to close the intimidation gap he's trying to create by using our height difference against me. "How was I supposed to know that you would roll back into town, tonight of all nights?"

I watch his eyes heat and that storm brew once again within them as he clenches his jaw. My eyes desperately want to move to the corner of his jaw to see if the same flex would be visible that he always used to get when he would clench, but I force them to stay trained on his face.

"Bullshit, Leighton. You knew I wouldn't stay away when Quinn wanted me here."

Throwing my head back, I laugh, the nerves he has flowing through my body firing so rapidly I feel light-headed. "Yeah? What about when he got sick the first time and she asked you to come home? What about the second, third, or even the last time? Where were you then, Maverick? Seems to me that I hit the nail on the head. Don't use your sister as an excuse. So what? You're home now—are we supposed to kiss your fuckin' buckles and throw out the red carpet? Famous rodeo star Maverick Davis is back, so time to bow down? News flash, bucko, while you weren't here I've been making sure to ease some of the pain for them, and tonight is about *them* since we all figured you would continue the coward's way and stay gone."

He grows tense with each word I all but shout in his face, but he remains silent.

"You want *your* pie?!" I yell, my voice coming out more like a high-pitched screech. My ears roar as my heart picks up speed with my anger and I feel like I can actually hear the blood rushing through my veins. "You want *your* blasted pie?" I knock him in the gut with my shoulder hard enough to make him shuffle back a step as I push past him and walk over to the fridge that's closest to my office. The one that I keep all my special pies in. Wrenching the door open, I grab the closest cookie dough creation before slamming the door back.

When I turn back around, he's still standing in the same spot, but instead of that raging anger, all I see is shock. Yeah, soak it in because I'm not the same little weak girl you used to know. My boots hit the floor loudly with each hard step I take back toward him, relaxing my face to offer him my most insincere smile.

"You want your pie, Mav?" I ask again, this time hiding my anger behind a sticky-sweet voice and a little smile.

He doesn't speak, and honestly, I'm not sure I'm capable of giving him a word in anyway. Without a second thought, I bring my arm back before I swing it forward and slap the whole pie into his face.

"There's your goddamn pie, you good-for-nothing jackass!"

Turning on my heels, I take huge gulps of air before

bringing both hands up and slamming them on the door. It swings open and I step into the main room with my head down as I inspect the amount of ice cream splatter that is now peppering my arms and torso. Apparently I wasn't thinking the whole pie-in-the-face thing all the way through or I would have realized I would probably end up wearing a good bit of it too.

With a sigh, I look up, ready to search for a clean towel to clean myself up when I notice the silence around me.

Oh, well . . . shit.

Every single person in the room is looking my way. All of the conversations in the whole room have completely stopped. I chance a look in Quinn and Clay's direction and feel a blush heat my cheeks when I see them both fighting a losing battle with their laughter.

The second Quinn's head tips back and her throaty laugh rings out in the silence, it breaks the shock keeping the rest of the room silent, and before I know it, everyone is joining in.

I drop my head, letting out a rushed exhale, feeling the adrenaline leaving my body. My hands shake when I reach out to grab one of the clean rags from under the register, and as I wipe at my shirt and arms, I do my best to keep my blush from growing.

"That's one way to knock a layer of stubborn off that boy's head," I hear Marybeth Perkins call out, her cackle following her outburst. "Wonder who the pup is now!" she oddly adds. My God, that woman is crazy as it comes.

"You forgot the plates," Jana giggles and walks past me into the kitchen.

Looking back over at Quinn, seeing her laughing even harder now, calms my racing heart. Seeing her like that makes my humiliation worth it. If she's laughing, she won't be crying. Bending over again, I reach behind the stack of rags, move a few things around before reaching my goal.

"Oh, hell, little girl," I hear Angus Todd bellow when the glass jar hits the counter.

"You first, old man," I call, pointing in his direction with a smirk.

He grumbles and puts on a good show for the crowded room, but still stands from his seat. He stomps toward me, adjusting his suspenders and patting his rounded belly. "Give it here, wild one, and let me show you how it's done."

"Let's see if you're singing the same tune when I'm the one standing at the end of the night and you have to call Sheriff Holden to come cart your tail back home."

Pulling his old Stetson off his head, he carefully places it atop one of the pie cases, then runs his meaty hand through his gray hair before picking up the jar of moonshine. With a smile I hand him one of the disposable shot glasses that I keep hidden with the jar.

He's still grumping when he takes my offering and pours his shot, throwing it back and letting out a sharp hiss. "By God, girl. Don't stand there looking happier than a pig in shit either. Never told us you were offering hell water. Where in tarnation did you get that?"

I shrug my shoulder, wink, and take the jar back with a laugh. With this crowd, when the moonshine comes out, it goes quick. Luckily, I have it stockpiled for times just like this. I pour shot after shot from the huge jar. Quinn walks up next and gives me another appreciative laugh before throwing her own shot back, not grimacing half as much as Angus did. Clay steps up next, and I pour his shot before getting one for myself.

"Cheers," I toast them both, looking from Quinn up to her brother.

He gives me an odd look before looking behind me. I don't even have a second to question him. A tan, thickly muscled arm reaches over my shoulder, and the shot is pulled from my fingers. I yelp when I'm turned around by a firm hand on my shoulder and look up in shock at Maverick's pie-covered face, well . . . . what splattering of pie is still left after what looks like a few angry swipes of his hand to clear his face. His hat is long gone, and those raven locks of his are a mess of rumpled waves and streaks of pie.

His rage-filled eyes never leave mine as he brings the shot up to his thick lips and takes it in one quick flick of his wrist. For a split second I see a flash of mischief swirling just below the surface. Had I been thinking straight, I would have heeded that as a warning. He throws the plastic shot glass on the floor, and with a speed quicker than any man his size should ever move, he bends his knees, closing in on me, and hooks his hands right under the swell of my ass to lift me off the ground with that firm grasp on the tops of my thighs. I yelp out my surprise as he keeps lifting me until I'm left with no other choice but to grab on to his shoulders. The second my hands touch his very tense shoulders, he moves his hands down my thighs, forcing me to wrap my legs around his waist.

When I feel the hardness of his erection against my center, my eyes widen even farther and I let out a very audible gasp of shock. Using it against me, his mouth crashes down on mine. I feel us bend slightly as his hands travel back up to my ass, flexing deep, and pulling me tighter against his erection. Without a thought, my mouth opens and my fingers move to push into his hair, holding me in place where he clearly wanted me. I feel the bits of pie sticky between my fingers, but I just burrow them in deeper. The warm burn of the moonshine hits my mouth first as he slowly lets the shot he just took pour into my mouth. Instinctively, I swallow, not even minding the burn of alcohol. When the last drop hits my mouth, his tongue dips out and sweeps in with no hesitation.

At the first touch of our tongues, I feel his muscles jump under my hands at the same time awareness like I've never felt before starts zapping through my nerves. I should be pushing him away, but that one touch destroyed any possibility of rational thought.

The world around us just fades to nothing.

I forget about everything that has ever happened between us.

My anger. His anger. It all just vanishes and it's as if he never left.

Without conscious thought, my body moves on its own. My hooked ankles tighten behind his back and I rub myself slightly against the bulge hiding behind his jeans. My hands move through the soft hair at the nape of his neck, deepening the hold I have on him. The hands holding me to his body tighten even further to the point I'm sure I'll have two huge handprints on my ass.

A groan rumbles from his chest as he deepens our kiss. Our tongues tangling together in a dance that holds so much promise. His mouth feasts off mine as he gives one more flex of his hands, pushing me harder against his erection. Just when I'm seconds away from arching my back and shamelessly begging him to take me, he lifts his head with one final closed-mouth kiss against my bruised lips.

I watch him through hooded eyes and I see the moment he puts his walls back up. I feel bereft, even with his arms still around me, holding me to his hard body.

"Can't remember pie ever tastin' like that when your mama would make it, darlin'," he tells me, his voice thicker, more rough, than ever.

I stare at him, mute as he runs his hands from the hold he had been using on my ass and down my thighs to my knees, prying my legs from his body. When my feet hit the ground and the fog in my brain lifts, his words finally reach my short-circuited brain. Even though it feels like hours have passed during that kiss, I know it wasn't but a minute, if that, but the anger he had managed to quell inside me comes screaming back with a vengeance. I can't believe that I just lost my mind, here, in front of *everyone*, and his words make it painfully clear that this is all just some big joke to him.

"You son of a bitch," I say with a gasp. My hand flies out, but before it hits his cheek he grabs my wrist.

"You're playin' a dangerous game. You sure you're ready to find out what happens when you keep pushin' me, Leighton?"

"I hate you," I fume, my anger building higher when I realize he's just taken the upper hand I thought I had.

He bends, bringing the tip of his nose to mine. His words for my ears only. "You don't. Would be better for you if you really did, but darlin', you wouldn't have come that close to comin' just from a kiss if you hated me." His voice drops impossibly lower, his next words just barely reaching my ears. "Tell me, would you have screamed my name?"

Oh, no, he did not. "I was not about to come!" I scream as fury pulses through me, only to snap my mouth shut when I hear the hushed whispers behind us.

My eyes widen when his lips, swollen from our kiss, twist up into a devastatingly wicked smile. He looks behind me before moving his mouth to my ear. "We'll continue this another time," he says before stomping through the crowd and out the front door.

For the life of me I can't tell if it's a threat . . . or a promise.

8

MAVERICK

"Let It Ride" by Brantley Gilbert

My lips burn as I rush into the muggy heat outside. It could be snowing and I still wouldn't be able to shake the heat burning through me.

Grabbing my shirt, I roughly pull until the buttons give and I'm able to yank the soggy material from my body. I use the shirt to scrub what's left of the pie from my face and neck and then toss the shirt into the bed of my truck. The climb up into my seat is painful when my jeans tighten even further against my straining cock.

What the fuck was I thinking back there? If I wanted to slide back into town without making a big deal out of my return, I just blew that all to hell. I can't even explain what came over my body. One second I'm taking a pie to the face and in the next I've got so much desire for her slamming through me, I couldn't *not* kiss her. It felt like we had been at the end of a long run of verbal foreplay with only one way to proceed.

Together.

"Fuck!" I shout and slam my hand against my steering wheel.

I grab my pack of smokes from the cup holder, but when I see it's empty I crush it in my hand before throwing it on the floor and dropping my head back against the seat.

It was all so simple ten years ago. Cut all the ties to Pine Oak so that nothing and *no one* was waiting for me here, tempting me to return. I would always have my brother and sister, but they would come to me, and I knew deep down, they wouldn't give up this damn town to chase me.

But Leighton would.

She thought I didn't notice, but she did a shit job at hiding her crush on me. But I also knew that if anyone were likely to follow after me, it would be her. She would have given up everything for that. No matter how much I truly did want her back then, I knew I had to cut the ties that connected our hearts. I couldn't ask her to choose between the life I was fleeing and the one I was running to. So I did the only thing that made sense to a desperate kid at the time. I made sure I hurt a young—too young— Leighton James so badly that she wouldn't ever think of me the way I knew she had. I killed whatever she felt for me with words that I wish to God I could take back.

It took me a long damn time to realize that I had really hurt her to prevent her from being the one that hurt me. I knew it would happen. I had been fighting the way I felt about her for too fucking long. Lusting after a girl too young to be lusted after. She made me actually think about sticking around the one place I had been desperate to leave.

I craved her.

Hell, I craved her before I even knew what those feelings meant.

And that was long before she looked like the walking wet dream she is now. She looked good back then, but now . . . fuck. She took what I always thought was perfection and amped it up tenfold.

If I were a better man, I would have just said good-bye back then and left her without pain, but I learned way too early that if you let someone get close enough, they would strike you hard enough to draw blood. And I was done letting people get the first slice at my skin.

How many times had I lain in bed and imagined what it would be like to have her in my arms? How many times had I stroked myself dry with the thought of taking her body? How many times had I regretted leaving town without ever feeling her lips against my own?

And now that I've held her in my arms, felt the fire of her desire for me still burning deep, I'm not sure I could walk away this time if I tried. I know damn well if I would have let myself feel this years ago, I wouldn't have left, and the worst part now is I'm not sure if everything I've been chasing—everything I've lost—is worth knowing what I've been missing.

Turning the key, I fire up my truck and back out onto Main Street, taking the empty roads back toward the ranch. The last place I want to go, but I know it won't be long before Clay is hot on my trail and I'd rather face him without my cock about to explode in my pants with just the memory of what Leighton feels like about to come apart in my arms.

"Fuck," I exhale slowly.

"Ahhh," I groan deeply, feeling the pressure leave my balls as my come shoots from the pulsing cock between my fist. I reach out and use my free hand to steady my body as thick jets of my come shoot over the wall in front of me. My head falls forward as my abs clench with the powerful force that just ripped through my body.

The steam from the shower continues to float around me.

Moving my fist slowly, I continue to ride my release. When the last drop falls from the tip of my cock, I release my shaft and step back into the spray of the shower. Picking up the soap, I continue washing my body and silently pray that I can keep my cock down now that I've given in to the thoughts of Leighton wrapped around me.

As I'm stepping out of the shower a little while later, temporarily sated and praying that will be enough to keep me from going at Leigh again, I hear the sounds of a slamming door echo through the house. I stand on the rug in front of the shower as drops of water run down my skin. The echo of boots slamming against the stairs hits my ears, and I step forward to press the button on my phone that will light up the screen. I laugh to myself when I see the time and look away from where my phone is resting next to the sink to wrap the towel around my hips. I figured he would have been right on my heels, but he managed to hold off an hour before coming home. Right when I finished tucking the towel at the side of my hip, his fist slams against the door, all but shaking the wood on its frame.

With a sigh of acceptance at what I'm sure will be one hell of a showdown between Clay and myself, I turn the knob. "I don't want to hear it, Clay," I start before the door has even cracked, but the second I started pulling the door open, he pushes hard and the knob is ripped from my still-wet hands.

"I don't really give a rat's ass what you want, Maverick."

Before I can blink, I've got a fist coming toward my face and there isn't fuck all I can do to avoid it. Shock has a hold on me, and it doesn't matter a lick that my reflexes should have been able to block the punch because I'm held stock stupid.

"Goddammit!" I bellow when pain shoots out from where the punch landed on my jaw.

"Yeah? Did that hurt? I hope to hell and high water that it did. I should have done that a long time ago!"

Grabbing hold of the counter behind me, I blink a few times to clear the wetness the punch brought to my eyes. Taking a deep breath, I look up from where my hands are clutching the sides of the counter and over my shoulder, taking in the blazing mad blue eyes before me.

Not Clay. Leigh.

"Feel better?" I ask on a deep, exhaled breath.

Silence follows my question. I wait, knowing another outburst is sure to be coming.

"Dammit!"

I push up on the counter and straighten my body when the curse bursts out, and step forward to reach for the vicious hand that just about rendered me stupid.

"Whoever taught you how to punch did a shit job. Did the damage, just not only to me."

She looks up, those eyes that were throwing daggers my way just seconds before are filling with tears. She allows me to take her wrist and I turn her hand over to see her purpling knuckles.

"I did damage," she smarts.

I feel my laughter bubble up my throat, "Yeah, you might actually have done just that." I look down at her hand, accessing the damage she did to herself. "Not broken, darlin', but you should remember how this feels when you get the urge to tap this hard head again."

"I hate you," she whispers without conviction.

"No, you don't. Come on, Leigh, let's get you some ice."

I don't drop her hand and she doesn't pull back as I walk out of my old bedroom and down the stairs to the kitchen. Pulling out one of the old stools by the island, I wait for her to sit before laying her hand on the counter in front of her and turning to grab a bag. I feel her eyes on me when I walk to the freezer and fill the bag with some ice. When I turn, I watch as gravity wins over her tears and they silently roll down her cheek.

"You're right. I don't hate you. I wish I *could* hate you, but I don't think I ever will be able to."

I kneel and place the bag on her outstretched hand. Without thought, I reach up and thumb a tear off her cheek.

"I wish it could have been anyone but you," she continues, looking at the floor. "I wasn't even picky. I would have taken anything, anyone, to feel just a sliver of what I felt when you were around. But, no, just like back then . . . my stupid, stupid heart still beats wildly for the one person who never wanted it."

"Lei—"

"No, Maverick. I don't even know what I'm sayin'. You've had this attitude, this freakin' wall up, for so long that I shouldn't be surprised. I'm madder at myself for letting you get the best of me, pulling my focus from Clay and Quinn. If you really are here for them, then you need to do just that. You leavin' this time will tear them up if you just run off again without a backward glance. You don't understand this because you weren't here, but they all felt the void of you hard, real hard."

"Leigh, look—"

She shakes her head. "No, really, Maverick. Whatever you're about to say with your silver tongue is nothin' I want to hear. I knew how you felt before you left, and regardless of whatever that was back at the PieHole, I think it's safe to assume that things haven't changed in the handful of hours you've been back in town. We need to just put it behind us and move on, for your family. I'll keep my distance and I would appreciate it if you did the same. Honestly, Mav"—she pauses and I watch her chest move as she pulls in a deep breath—"I survived the sting of your rejection back then, and while I'm stronger now, I don't think I could handle your emotional punches again. I'm sorry that I hit you, that was wrong, but let us just chalk up today as the mess it was and move on . . . in separate paths."

She finally meets my gaze, her blue eyes even brighter with the wetness of her emotions coating them.

"I'm not leavin'." Out of everything she just said, the only thing I can even get past my lips is that. There is so much that I need to tell her, but I'm not even sure where to start. I just know I need to address her claim that I'll be hauling ass out of here because if she truly believes that, it doesn't matter what else I say to her. She'll be waiting with the rest of the town, guessing when I'll be kicking up dust like the last time I left.

Her lips open and close, but no words come out. I can see her mind working in overtime as her brow furrows and her eyes search mine. I stand tall and drop my guard, letting her see the honesty and truth behind my words. Her eyes widen when realization hits. I continue to stand there as she studies me.

The years drop away from us.

The pain inflicted and the pain consumed, vanish.

The helpless feelings I battled with daily, the ones that drove my need to escape, are gone.

For the first time in my recollection, I feel somewhat whole. My breathing speeds up as my nerves fire with an overwhelming need. There isn't anything spoken between us, but with the connection of our gazes, we might as well have spoken our deepest thoughts.

I step toward her the second she jumps up from the stool, the wood crashing to the ground in her wake. In a split second, everything falls away. The anger, the helplessness, and the lost feelings I've been struggling with. Gone. And in its wake, a feeling of need so strong it knocks the breath from my chest, takes over, and I know I have to have her back in my arms.

"This can't happen," she says with a gasp when my arms wrap around her to pull her closer, her words breathy against my lips. The soft cotton of her shirt rubbing against my naked, overheated chest.

"It can." My arms snake around her narrow body to pull her closer.

"This is a mistake," she slurs, her mouth opening and our tongues sliding against each other.

Her words fuel my movements and settle a determination over me that demands I prove her wrong. This is far from a mistake. This is a lifetime of want combusting in a split second of affirmation that proves just how wrong she is.

With her still in my arms, I turn, placing her ass on the counter. Just like back at the PieHole, everything else wrong in my life slips away and only my desire for her is left. Everything I ignored years ago floods through my system, mixing and mingling with the new feelings seeing her again after all this time brought forth. It's too soon, but in the same breath, it's ten years too late.

Her hands move sluggishly up my chest, around my shoulders, and then her dexterous fingers push into my hair. Her thumbs stay resting against my face as those very fingers tighten against the short hair at the nape of my neck to pull me closer. Her movements signaling to my brain that she's giving in to what our bodies so desperately want.

She shivers in my arms and I use her distracted state against her. Deepening our kiss while I move my hands from where they had been resting against her hips, up her torso, pushing the fabric of her shirt up as I go. The second my calloused palms hit her rib cage, she squirms, wiggling her hips on a low moan. I step closer, feeling the heat of her through the barrier of my towel and her shorts, and when I press my thumbs against her pointed nipples, she jumps in my arms, connecting our bodies, hip to hip.

We break apart with heaving breaths. Her glazed eyes hooded, her cheeks pink with arousal, and her lips swollen from my kisses. She looks stunning. I give a slight jerk of my wrists, indicating my intentions, and she silently lifts her arms, allowing me to pull her shirt free of her body.

"Jesus." I harshly groan at the first sight of her blood-red, lace-covered tits.

My head drops and I open my mouth to give a soft bite against the sensitive flesh at the top of her bra. The red material against her creamy skin makes my cock swell painfully against the towel tied hastily at my hip. I bring my hands up, cupping her heavy breasts, while I give her one long lick over the top of her left breast and up to her collarbone. My hands squeeze each globe roughly as I bury my nose in her neck, continuing my tongue's wet path up to her ear.

Resting my lips to her ear, I take a second to enjoy the trembles that are vibrating from her quivering body. Her panted breaths echoing off the wall turn into a sharp gasp when I curl my fingers into each cup and jerk down. The tiny straps over her shoulders snap as her breasts spill free.

With my mouth still at her lips, I grab her heavy, naked breasts and squeeze, her hard nipples pressing against the center of my palm while I continue to play with her.

"Touch me," I demand and smile when I feel her body jolt beneath me.

"Mav," she says with a moan, her hands coming to rest right above my towel, on each side of my hips, making my skin burn beneath her touch.

I shake my head, my lips rubbing against her ear with the small movements. I let my tongue snake out and lick her lobe. Moving my hands slightly, I pinch her nipples between my thumb and pointer finger at the same time I pull her wet lobe between my lips, biting softly before sucking the tender flesh hard.

She cries out harshly.

Releasing my hold on her tits, I bring my hands up and cup her head, forcing her to look into my eyes. "Touch *me*, Leighton," I demand again, this time harsher and the undeniable meaning laced in my words. I wait for her to comply, moving so that my forehead is resting against hers, our rapid breathing mingling between our bodies. Our eyes not losing the connection held between bright blue and murky green.

"This is wrong," she whimpers, but her actions betray her words.

I feel her hands slide from my sides to the center of my abdomen. Her touch branding me as she fingers her way over each ridge and dip before moving down to where I want her touch the most. Her fingers curl into my towel and I back my hips up slightly to help her movements.

She gives a hard tug, pulling the knot from its fold, and then drops the cotton to the ground at my feet, her eyes still holding mine. This time the indecision that had been swimming in the beautiful depths is now replaced with solid desire.

"Tell me you want me," I command, my voice strained as her hands move down my torso, her fingers tracing the deep V until she is wrapping them around my straining flesh. Her tentative movements as she slowly caresses the hard flesh in her hands make me lock my knees and clench my gut. Her long and slow touch makes the coil of pleasure tighten.

"I—I want you," she pants, her hands tightening around my shaft, learning what I like by the cues she is drawing from me.

"Tell me you've always wanted me," I continue, not releasing her face, but moving my lips closer to hers so that I can feel the heat of her breath hit my mouth. My words come out in a low, rough garble of desire.

She nods, but that isn't good enough. I need her words to gain back some of the control I feel slipping from my fingers.

"Give me the words, darlin'."

"Maverick, please."

She tightens her grip, dancing her thumb over the bead of wetness coming out of the tip of my rigid cock.

"Tell me now, Leighton. Tell me it's always been me."

Her eyes widen and I watch as one lone tear falls from her lid. Her tear confuses me, but not enough that I stop. Her silence continues and I thrust my hips, my cock moving through the loose hold her hands have around me. Her eyes close for a beat, and when she opens them I see that the last of her indecision has vanished.

"It's always been you."

"Try again," I continue, baiting her to get what I need. "It's always been you, *Maverick*." With my last command, I crush my lips to hers. This kiss is hard and bruising, but full of the promise of what's to come if she gives me what I crave.

She rips her mouth free and screams, "It's always been you, Maverick, God help me, but it's only ever been you!" She drops my cock, her chest heaving, to grab my face and pull my lips back to hers.

I have no idea why I pushed her. Why I made her confirm what I knew deep down, but with her words, everything that had been weighing on my mind for almost two weeks vanishes and I feel the most all-consuming peace flood through my body, leaving an uncontrollable need for her behind.

It doesn't matter to my brain that there is so much unknown floating around outside of our heated embrace. The only thing that matters is this . . . us . . . right here in this moment, as I pull her off the counter to remove the rest of her clothes, tossing them along with her boots onto the floor. I don't give a shit what the consequences of our actions are.

My earlier thought comes rushing back: it's too soon, but in the same breath, it's ten years too late.

And yet it can't be too late, when it feels so right to have her in my arms.

9

LEIGHTON

"I Wish I Could Break Your Heart" by Cassadee Pope

My skin is burning.

I'm on fire. Every inch from the top of my scalp to the tips of my toes is alive with a power I've never felt before. My nerves are taking on a life of their own. When Maverick finishes pulling off each of my boots, he tosses them blindly behind him before he grabs my hips roughly and lifts my body effortlessly up into his arms. My nerves explode with each sweep over my flesh.

It feels incredible.

What am I doing? What are we doing? This has regret written all over it, but Lord help me, I can't deny that it feels so right to be in his arms—regardless of the fallout sure to come after.

His tongue presses into my mouth, swirling with my own, and I whimper. His straining erection makes contact with my bare naked center as he places one huge hand at the base of my spine, using the pressure to pull me even harder against him. His thick shaft spreads me wide, nestling between my lips. The second my sensitive center meets his hard velvet skin, he moans deeply and thrusts, hitting my clit roughly. My mouth falls from his as I drop my head back. He moves the hand that had been squeezing my ass up my back until his fingers are tangled in my hair and forces my head back, his harsh breathing once against just a hair away from my slack mouth.

"Are you protected?"

His words sound foreign. My brain struggles to understand him as his thick, hard cock keeps thrusting through my wetness. I know if I look down our bodies, the sight that would meet me would make me shatter completely.

"Leighton," he says, more urgent now, "are you protected?"

"Wha?" I gasp, rolling my hips when the tip of his cock hits my clit again.

"Birth control, darlin'. Are you on it?"

I vaguely feel my head moving, confirming that I am, in fact, protected, but when he gets the green light he had been waiting for, all rational thought flees. With quick and impatient movements, he pulls his hips back, moves his hand from my hair and down to my hips—mirroring the hold of his other hand as he lifts me from him and slams me back down over his hard cock, impaling me completely.

He growls deep in his throat.

I scream loud enough to wake the dead.

His head falls forward, forehead to my sweat-slicked chest.

My head falls back, forehead to the ceiling.

His fingers painfully squeeze my hips, lifting me until I almost lose our connection, before pulling me down roughly again.

My fingers curl, my nails breaking through his tan, tense shoulders, my walls contracting as he hits a part so deep within me I fear I might split in two.

His warm tongue gives a long lick up my neck and I feel my core clench around his width again. Lifting my head, my eyes going from the ceiling to the blazing emerald orbs of his hungry gaze, I will my fingers to release his shoulders, but when he starts thrusting rapidly into my body, I search for purchase while a string of gibberish flows from my lips.

My back hits the wall and he stops his movements to frame my face with his hands, forcing my mouth to his for a hungry kiss. My hands drop from his shoulders and wrap around his back, the muscles tensing under my hands. Our kiss is nothing short of brutal, his hard shaft still buried deep, and I know he could stay still, just like this, and it would be all I need to push me over the edge.

But with an animalistic sound vibrating against our connected chests, he rears his head back and looks into my eyes. The heaving breaths coming from his slack mouth reach my nipples, the sweat from his chest making it feel almost like a physical touch. He doesn't move, just continues to search my face and I whimper when my need hits a fever pitch, squirming against the wall to try to make him move his hips.

"Fuck," he says with a groan, the word coming out in a long, low tumble between his lips.

"Please," I whine, needing him to move, desperate for *more*.

"Fuck!" His bellow rings out around us. His hands move from my face, down my neck, and he takes each of my breasts roughly in his hands, bending his head to pull one of my nipples between his lips. I feel him hollow out his cheeks as his tongue rolls over the sensitive peak, then he sucks hard.

My fingers contract against his tense back, my nails scraping against his skin, as my head hits the wall behind me hard. The pain against my skull instantly forgotten as it mixes with the pleasure his mouth is bringing me. He releases my nipple with a hard snip of his teeth before those rough hands of his curl under my ass.

"Hold on," he warns, making my eyes snap open. I see his lips, plump and swollen from our kisses, turn up into a devilish smirk before his fingers flex, his hips pull back, and with a wink he takes me in a way that makes my body feel as if he's branding himself into me. The grunts and groans coming from our mouths mix together and echo off the walls. My hands scrabble for purchase, desperate with the fire blazing up from my center—each hard thrust into my wetness making it burn so hard I'm half convinced that he's taking me to the point of no return. My body wound so tight that it feels like I'm going to explode, the feelings too intense and powerful that I feel tears filling my closed eyes.

And then I break.

A million flashes of bright light fire and swirl through the darkness behind my closed eyes, spiraling in a dizzy speed.

My throat becomes hoarse as I scream his name over and over.

I lose the ability to breathe as my climax rages through my body, making my chest burn and my head spin.

My last thought before I feel my consciousness slip away and I feel him spill deep into my body is that if I die right now, it would be the most beautiful death there ever was.

I awaken with a jolt.

My body is sore and screams in protest as I sit up. I look around, search through the darkness, and try to figure out where I am.

And then I see him.

Maverick.

He looks so peaceful. One arm thrown over his head, his face turned toward me. Like this, asleep, he looks like the old Maverick. The one that wasn't fighting a war with his own self to escape some invisible prison. He doesn't look like the warrior that he's since become. The one that never showed emotions. The one that would jump on the backs of beasts capable of killing him with one wrong move and not even think twice about it.

His strong jaw is relaxed and his full lips part slightly, soft snores coming through. I hold my breath, waiting to see if my sudden movement registers through his deep sleep, but he just continues to slumber.

A small part of me wonders if he will still be so relaxed and peaceful when he wakes and realizes that we slept together. I know the last thing I feel right now is calm; full-blown panic is more like it. It's like some weird daze settled over me and fogged out any rational thought.

Lust.

Pure and simple.

Well, not so simple, since now I have to deal with the fallout.

I know deep down that this was a long time coming. We had been building toward it since he rode back into town. Our emotions too strong to deny the explosion our anger was sparking.

I shift, moving slowly to the edge of the bed, while keeping my eyes on his face. He doesn't stir. I stand, letting my breath out slowly when my chest starts to burn. I'm not sure how long I was out.

The only thing I *am* sure of in this moment is that I need to get the hell out of here.

I look around the room, embarrassingly just now realizing that we must be in his old bedroom. The full moon is illuminating the room through the open blinds and I easily spy the dark duffel bag thrown on the floor at the foot of his bed. I grab the first thing my hand hits, a soft T-shirt, and pull it over my naked body. The hem hits me almost to my knees so I stop my search. I would rather be barely covered than risk him waking up while I'm trying to make my escape.

My foot hits a weak spot in the floor and a loud creak echoes around me. My eyes shoot to his face as my breath is once against stalled in my chest. He rolls, one muscular arm coming out and searching. I panic, again, and quickly turn to grab the pillow off the top of the bed and place it in his path. He, thankfully, wraps his arm around it and turns his head into its softness. Letting out the breath I had been holding, I make my way to the door again. Right when I silently close the door behind me, I hear his gravelly, sleep-roughened voice moan my name.

The sound alone makes me want him again, but I know this was a mistake and returning to his bed would make things only worse. But even knowing without a doubt that it would be a mistake, a very big part of me wants to turn around anyway. It takes everything I have in me, but self-preservation wins and I rush down to the kitchen as silently as I can.

One look at the clock above the oven confirms that not even two hours have passed since I arrived at the Davis ranch. I'm sure that had I been here any longer, Clay and Quinn would have returned—but I'm fairly confident that they're still at the PieHole. Especially since I pulled out the rest of my moonshine stash before I stormed from there with the bats of hell chasing my tail.

I grab my discarded clothes, ignoring the mess around the kitchen, and run to my Jeep. I toss my clothes and shoes in the passenger seat, my boots slamming against the door, and with shaking fingers I turn the ignition and slam my bare foot down on the accelerator. I hear the gravel ping against my undercarriage, but the fear of waking Maverick keeps me focused. I turn the wheel, speeding through the circular drive in front of the Davis family home and down the long lane that will put me back onto the main road.

In all my determination to get out unnoticed, I failed to see the porch light flicker on and the tall, very naked man that filled the open doorway. Which really is a shame, because had I been paying attention, I would have seen the look of promise-filled determination that took over his features. I had unknowingly awoken the sleeping dragon, and there wasn't anything that would be powerful enough to stand in the way of the hungry beast that had been hiding for so many years.

It might have taken more than ten years, but I finally got my wish—Maverick hadn't just noticed me, but he also realized what he had missed out on by denying us both what we had always been destined to find.

And nothing would ever be the same again.

10
MAVERICK

"Amarillo by Morning" by George Strait

"**W**hat's gotten into you?"

I continue to spray the inside of Dixon's stall before picking up my pitchfork and shoveling in the hay that I had brought down from the loft this morning, ignoring my sister's repeated questions from behind me. A place where she's been standing since she got down to the barn fifteen minutes ago. Comically trying to intimidate me with her stubbornness.

"Maverick! Stop ignoring me and tell me what the hell crawled up your ass."

"Nothin' to tell, Quinny," I snap back, using her old nickname that I know gets under her skin like nothing else, in a vain effort to cut off her insistent questioning.

I should know better than anyone that when Quinn gets her mind on something, there's no getting her off of it no matter what name you call her.

"Don't you 'Quinny' me, Maverick Austin Davis. You've had a burr stuck up your ass for two weeks now. The same burr, I might add, that has decided to root itself deep in my best friend too. Now, I might be off the mark here—however, I seriously doubt that I am—but I do want you to clue me in on why you both are actin' like petulant little brats."

With one last flick of my wrists, I toss another pitchfork full of hay down into the stall, checking briefly to make sure I've finished, and turn to face my sister. I place the pitchfork's handle against the stall door and cross my arms over my chest—mirroring her stance—and wait for her to continue, because Lord knows she isn't done.

"I mean, Jesus Jones, Maverick. You hadn't even arrived back long enough for the mud on your tires to dry and you were creating an epic storm in your path, but it's more than that and we both know it. What happened when she left the PieHole and came to find you? After, I might add, that insane kiss that you plastered on her in front of THE WHOLE TOWN! I mean, seriously, what has gotten into you!?" By the time Quinn finally shut her damn trap, she was red in the face and pacing back and forth. I could hear Daisy, Quinn's horse, getting agitated in her stall. Not because of Quinn's screeching, but more so because she wasn't getting the attention she loves from her. Those two have been thick as thieves since the day Daisy was born.

"Are you finished?" Ignoring her, I take a step back and reach out toward where Daisy is sticking her head out, huffing deep exhales in exasperation to be noticed, and give her a sugar cube from my pocket.

Quinn pins me with a death stare. "I don't know. Let me think."

My lips twitch and I have to fight the smile that starts to dance at the edges. I wipe off the wetness that Daisy left behind before pulling my favorite Stetson off and wiping the sweat from my forehead into my damp hair and shoving the hat back in place. I should have left this damn hat behind when I left Vegas, but it's been with me every step of the way since I started on the circuit; hell, it's been with me even years before that. Regardless of the fact that it's nothing but a reminder of the future that I no longer have in front of me, this damn thing has too much mileage with me and memories to go along with it for me to just throw it away.

"She did come to you. I know it. She had the fires of hell lighting her ass; there's no way that she would leave the PieHole—early, no less—and just go home." Quinn's voice breaks through my thoughts, bringing my attention back to her.

"Are you askin' me that or tellin' me?"

"Oh, shut up," she snaps, and I lose control of my lips, a smirk replacing my normal stoic mask of indifference. "Tell me what you did, Mav."

"For the last time, Quinny, what makes you think that I did anything?"

"Because!" she screams. "I know her and she wouldn't do anything without analyzing it from every angle. Leighton doesn't run off the handle, but you . . . it's your MO to do just that—run off all half-cocked and without thought of the consequences."

"Damn, Quinn, tell me how you really feel, darlin'."

Her opinion of me shouldn't bother me, but fuck if it does. She's wrong, but she's also so very right. Look at me, a few weeks back and already the hard shell of indifference that I've been able to wear like a shield is cracking. She's not going to let this go, and even though she's the last person I want to talk about that night with, if anyone knows what would be going through Leighton's mind, it would be my sister.

"Look, don't tell me what happened, okay? It's pretty dang clear neither of you wants to talk about it, but Maverick, I'm begging you not to do this to her. I don't feel like fixing the mess you stir up when you leave again."

"How many times do I need to tell you that I'm not going anywhere?"

She looks around, taking in Dixon's now mucked stall, before giving me a sad look of resignation. "Look at you, Mav. You've been back for two weeks and not once have you made the move to make this *stay* something of permanence. Your duffel bag is still packed. You wear it, wash it, and repack it. You haven't been down to the shop. Clay says, while you might keep busy, you damn sure aren't doing anything but keeping yourself busy with bullshit work around here that's better left for the hands. You're here, but you aren't. Hell, you might as well just be a new hired on the ranch. Except at least those guys actually want to be here. Drew even said all you do is the grunt work. The bullshit not even the young bucks eager to learn want to touch."

"Now, Quinn—"

She puts her hand up, shaking her head. "You say you

aren't leaving, but everything you've done so far since Dad's funeral screams temporary. You didn't even wait for the ink to dry on his will before you were talking to Clay about a buyout."

"Don't bring him up, Quinn."

"Someone has to. Look, I get it, you want nothin' to do with *him*, but, Mav, *he* isn't Davis Ranch. Not anymore. The ranch is us. Clay, me, and *you*."

"How did we get on this shit?"

"Well, you won't talk about Leigh, so might as well just move right on to some more bullshit centered on you."

"Fuck, Quinn! I didn't talk to Clay about a buyout because I was leavin'. I just don't want anything that has to do with the old man."

"I get it. I really do. It's about time you accepted that what happened in the past sucked, but it's over. Clay and I both had our own challenges in gettin' over the hurt that Dad put on us, but he wasn't the same man that pushed you away from us. Not at the end, anyways."

Her words tip the aggravation over our conversation to the tipping point, and before I can control the burst of anger that fires through my system, I let out a string of profanity that would make a sailor proud before punching my fist through the drywall.

"You better know how to fix that, Maverick Davis!"

Fists now balled on my hips, I take a few heaving breaths before turning toward the angry voice shouting at me and waving. "I'll see to it, Drew."

"You do that, son," he calls back before clicking at his colt, Stoner, and taking off at a quick gallop.

"I don't know how to talk to you, Mav." Quinn's voice is quieter now, and the break I hear in it cuts me to the quick more than her loudest shout. "I just know you're hurting. You were hurting before you came back, and now it's not just you that's fighting something inside of yourself."

"Come here, Quinn," I demand softly and open my arms.

She runs to me without pause, and suddenly she's just my kid sister again, not the fiery, feisty woman standing before me a moment ago demanding answers. "You're gross," she mumbles against my sweat-drenched shirt.

"Yeah, darlin'."

"Please talk to me," she begs, her slim arms tightening around my torso as she hugs me tighter. "Please."

I bend down and kiss the top of her head. With a sigh, I give in and tell her what I know she wants to hear. "I'm just goin' through some shit, Quinn. I'm not goin' anywhere, I promise, but I also don't know what to do now that I'm back. I don't want to run the ranch, and Clay knows that. The horses—that was Clay and Dad's thing. Not mine. I'm keepin' myself busy, but I'm also tryin' to figure out what to do with myself now that my rodeo career is over."

"You always loved the horses, Maverick." She leans back and looks up into my eyes.

"I loved ridin' them, darlin', but all the bullshit that comes with breedin' the next Thoroughbred champion, that wasn't me. The old man wanted me to be part of that and I guess that's part of why I have no interest."

"There's more to the ranch than that and you know it, Mav."

"Yeah, sweetheart, and none of that is of interest to me.

Clay has it handled. Drew runs this place like a well-oiled machine. I'm just pickin' up the slack until he hires another hand."

"And then what?"

"No clue, darlin'. Guess we can figure out that together. I might not want to take an active role in the current workings here, but I'm not going to leave."

"What about a new role here?"

She steps out of my hold and I drop my arms. She dusts some hay off my shirt and gives me a smirk. "You don't want anything to do with the *old* Davis ranch, but I think we all agree—Clay will too—that it's a new era for the ranch. Dad didn't want to branch out from breeding the prize winners. He was so stuck in his ways. I think that, with your help, Clay can finally make the changes that he's wanted to do for a long damn time."

"First I'm hearin' of this, Quinn."

"Reckoned as much. Look, don't write off the ranch because of the bullshit you're still holding on to as some sort of armor. I'll let Clay know that we all need to sit down and have a family meeting. He's down at the shop doing payroll, but we'll figure out something. Let's go to Bucky's in town. A little business over the best damn barbeque in town is just what the doctor ordered."

I open my mouth, but she interrupts me before I can agree.

"Keep an open mind, big brother. You might not want to hear it, but it's time we talked about what happened with Dad after you left."

"Not talkin' about him."

"I'm afraid you don't have a choice."

"Just leave it."

She shakes her head, her long black ponytail whipping over her shoulder. "The last thing you need is for me to 'just leave it,' but I'll tell you what . . . I'll put off talk about Dad for a little while, not forever, but you're going to have to tell me why my best friend is actin' like an angry bull."

Motherfucker.

She's got me and she knows it, if her raised brow and smirk are any things to go by. There is only one thing that would get me to talk about that night, and if it means I can put off the talk I have no interest in having, that would be it.

"We slept together, okay? In the end, she ran out on me so I'm not sure why she's actin' like the wounded party here. Nothin' else you need to know."

Her jaw drops before I've finished speaking, and I swear it looks like her eyes might bug out of her head. She looks like a frog that had its air supply cut off for too long. Wide-eyed and gaping.

"You . . . you did *what*?" she gasps softly.

"You wanted to know what happened. We slept together. Happy now?"

"You slept together?" Her mouth is still hanging open like a puppy dog in dire need of some cool water.

"Jesus, Quinn. Don't tell me you need more details, because that's not happening. I don't know what she's pissed about. It happened and we're both grown adults. She snuck out while I was sleeping and she's been ignoring me ever since, so I would guess she wants nothing further to do with me. That's all of it." Just the thought burns my gut. She's running scared, I just know it. No fuckin' way she isn't, after what I felt between us that night.

"She's been ignoring you?"

"Are you going to repeat everything I say?"

"She snuck out while you were sleeping?"

"I guess you are," I deadpan, picking up the pitchfork again before walking around her to put it back in the tool room.

"Holy shit," she finally whispers after a long silence.

I shake my head, hanging the pitchfork back up with the others, and make my way to the tack room. I make a note for the ranch hand that took Dixon out earlier that his stall is ready for him after he's done for the day.

"You . . . she . . . finally. Oh, my God! What does this mean?" Quinn calls out to me.

I toss the pen down after making the list of what he and Dixon still need before leaving the room and planting myself in front of my sister.

"Holy shit! Did you guys talk? I mean, this is pretty big—for her, at least; I don't know about you. You're probably used to this kind of thing, but not Leighton. Oh, my God. I can't believe she didn't tell me."

"Don't you think that maybe she didn't say anything because, like me, this is a weird as hell chat to be having with my sister?" I ignore her jab about me being used to this. Little does she know how wrong she is.

"WEIRD?! Do you have any idea how long I've been waiting to *have this chat*?"

I take a step back, and with a laugh, hold my hands

up. "Did the devil just jump in your body? You sound like you're about two seconds from your head spinning on your shoulders."

"Don't act like a smart-ass now, bucko! This changes *everything*." She starts mumbling some gibberish under her breath, and I can't help the smile that grows as she starts throwing her hands up between words of nonsense.

"Seriously, little sister, I think you should just drop it. This changes nothing."

"Delusional. Both of you. Idiots, I swear. That girl . . ." She pauses in the midst of her rant and looks at me with wide green eyes that seem to know more than she should. "You really have no clue, do you?"

"Yeah, darlin', I'm pretty sure that's correct since you're makin' no sense."

Quinn sighs and plops down on a bale of hay. "Okay, big brother. I'm about to go against every written rule in the best-friend bible right now, but I feel like that is completely acceptable to clue you in here. Lord knows one day, maybe after the birth of your first child, she will forgive me for this."

"Uh, who's having a baby?"

"You are . . . well, maybe. If we can get your head out of your ass, that is. And, of course, you're going to have to grovel and shit, but this hypothetical baby has just been waiting to be born and I will not let you two keep my future niece from me."

"What the hell are you goin' on about?"

"Do you know how long I've been waiting for this little princess? No, of course you don't. Completely. Clueless."

"Seriously, Quinn. Who is having a baby?"

"No one!" she screams, looking just about as crazy as she sounds.

"Do you need some water? Maybe you should sit down for a little while, hell-raiser. I think the heat's gettin' to you."

She looks around before pointing up to one of the many vents in the ceiling of the barn.

"This place has air-conditioning, Mav."

"Right. Okay? So you're normally crazy. Got it."

"I'm not crazy!"

"You also aren't sane, darlin'. You're talkin' some crazy shit."

"Now you listen here, Maverick, and you listen real good. I don't want to know what happened that night. I know enough and what I know explains oh so much. For as long as she's been alive, Leigh's only wanted one thing. You. Of course, you put a mighty big wrench in those dreams before you left town, but not once did she give those dreams up. Sure, she might have tried breaking all the chains that connected her heart to yours, but when those chains proved their unbreakable strength, she was forced to build a wall around her heart and climb over it. Sealing it away from everyone else while that damn heart continued to remain tied to you. Even after all these years, I know that like I know the sky is blue and the grass is green."

"I think you're reading too much into this," I say with a grunt, crossing my arms and leaning back against the stall post, but fuck if her words don't hit me hard.

"I'm not and you know it. She's scared. I get it now. She never, not once in her life, found someone else strong enough to break that wall down and sever those chains to you, no matter how open she was to searching for someone that could. And I would guess she just realized that no one ever will."

My stomach knots, and as much as I would love to deny what Quinn said, a big part of me knows she's right. I've felt the same way through the years. The tug my heart felt whenever I would think about her telling me that I would always feel the absence of her, that night in the trees.

I pushed Leighton away because deep down, I knew she was it for me and if I admitted that, I wouldn't be able to get out. I struck with words sharper than any physical touch, knowing damn well that I was pushing her away so that she wouldn't be able to keep me here. Staying here would have killed me, even though leaving her did the trick all the same.

All I had wanted, my whole life, was to be the best damn cowboy the rodeo had ever seen, but all it took was once glance in her direction and none of it mattered anymore.

All she had to do was walk into a room and I forgot it all.

I forgot because she became the only thing I wanted more than my need to chase my dreams. The only thing I craved more than escaping.

For one split second, before I could change my mind, I allowed myself to become what I always feared—Buford Davis—and I used my words to cause enough damage to ensure that I would never have the one thing that would keep me in this town and away from my dreams.

Her.

Only now I know that those dreams meant nothing without her to share them with. I gave up one thing to chase the other, and right now I'm just praying I'm not too late to fix the mistakes of my past.

"Fight for her, Maverick," Quinn whispers.

I look in her eyes, let her words sink in, and speak the truth. "Workin' on it, honey."

11

LEIGHTON

"Why Ya Wanna" by Jana Kramer

"**T**hat's the sixth pie today that you've thrown in the trash, sweetheart."

I look up at Jana, blowing a loose blond strand of hair that had escaped my ponytail out of my face. "It didn't taste right," I grumble, more to myself than her, feeling the need to defend my crazy actions.

And that's just what I've been doing. Acting like I'm bat shit crazy all because some man has my mind all screwed up.

"Oh, I'm sure that isn't the case. You could make them in your sleep. Why don't you take off, beautiful girl? I can finish up here and get the fridges prepped."

"That's not going to happen."

"And why not?"

I look up with a smile, the first one I've had come naturally all day, and laugh at her sassiness. "I already filled the fridges for Monday's stock."

Jana throws up her hands. "Well, honey child, what are you still doing here then? We closed hours ago!"

"Better question would be why are *you* still here? You know I love being here. It's the best place around to think." I laugh, moving to the sink to wash my pie-filled hands and gather the cleaning supplies to scrub down the countertops.

Truth be told, there was nothing wrong with that pie, or any of the other ones. I just didn't realize—again—that I baked another one of Maverick's favorite pies until after I'd pulled it out hot and steaming from the oven. I had been doing it all day. I would be elbow deep in something off our normal menu, then next thing I knew I was looking at a cookie dough pie with no memory of making it.

I couldn't shake him, and it was pissing me off. He was back in my mind deeper than he had ever been before.

Jana pointedly turned away and started folding towels. "What else am I gonna do?"

"I'm pretty sure that Bart would be more than happy to give you some suggestions," I joke, knowing damn well that her man would be happy to see her home early on a Saturday night. "You ready to marry that handsome man yet?" I laugh at the old joke that never seems to get old when it comes to Jana and Bart. She's been putting off marrying the poor man for so long I'm not even sure why he keeps asking, but ask he does. I think we're up to eleven times now he's asked her to be his wife.

"That man is probably already passed out in front of the TV. You know he spends his Saturdays catching up on those stupid shows he misses all week. And I already told you, I'll marry his cranky butt the day you take a vacation!"

"Nothing wrong with daytime television, Jana. And I don't need a vacation." I continue to giggle to myself. She might joke, but I think she continues to tell him no because she likes telling people she's living in sin. Every time I ask her when she's going to finally marry her man of the past fifteen years, she comes up with another off-the-wall excuse.

She grumbles for a second, but clearly decides to drop our constant fight over me taking time off in favor of keeping the mood light. "There is plenty wrong with a fifty-five-year-old man that makes sure and records every episode of *Days of Our Lives*."

I laugh hard at the vision of old Bart watching his weekly soaps. The best part, he still refuses to use the DVR. He's been setting the timer on his old VHS player to record them on tape. Funniest thing I've ever seen was when one of them didn't tape and he went on and on about some man named DiMera, or something like that. Of course, it could have been because his overalls came unhooked in the middle of his rant and he ended up in the middle of the PieHole with his pants around his ankles and his hot pink boxers with red lips all over them.

I turn to face Jana and put my hands on my hips, using my best bossy voice. "Go home. We closed two hours ago."

"I'm aware. I'm the one that's been sitting here for one of those hours watching you mumble under your breath about a certain tall, dark, and handsome cowboy," she jokes, her hot pink lips turning up knowingly—which is impossible because I haven't breathed a word of *that night* to anyone. Not even Quinn.

"I have not." I gasp, my face heating.

"Oh, you most certainly have been."

Do not ask. Do not ask. Do not . . . "What have I been saying?" Shit, why couldn't I keep my mouth shut?

"I think a better question would be what are you gonna do about it?" she asks.

"Do about what?"

"Your broken hooha."

I drop the bottle of sterilizer I had been using and gape at her.

"I might be old, but I know a thing or two. You aren't broken just because you had some good lovin'."

I will the kitchen floor to open me up and swallow me whole, just so I don't have to suffer through this talk with my fifty-plus-year-old employee. "This is so embarrassing. Can't you call it something different?"

"Oh, hush, you. Now tell me, why do you think your hooha's broken?"

I know my face isn't just heated now; it's on fire with one hell of a blush. "This is so not a conversation that we're going to have."

"Have you tried to play with yourself? You know, given yourself a little bean lovin'? That should show you that all is in working order. You know Bart, God love him, throws his back out at least one night a week, so if you need some tips, I'm your girl. I've got it down to a science."

I cover my ears with my hands and let out a little

screech. "Oh, my God, we are so not talking about this. You have no boundaries. You know that, right?"

Jana shrugs. "That's fine with me. You don't even have to talk, just listen. You know the town's already talking, so I've had plenty of time to think about this; let me see if I have it all right. You stormed out of here right after that handsome thing gave you one hell of a kiss. Now, I might not know a lot, but all I had to do was look at the stubborn set in your shoulders and I just knew you weren't going home. My guess is that you chased after him and you guys did a lot more than argue, right?" She finishes with a wag of her brows.

"Jana," I warn. "Boundaries."

"Boundaries, my tail. Don't you dare ignore me, missy. I've been waiting for this to happen for way too long. You have never, not once, been this out of sorts over a boy and we both know why. Even that fancy New York man that came blowing through town wasn't able to get this kind of reaction from you, and honey, all he had to do was look at a woman and boom. So get over whatever ridiculous embarrassment you're feeling and tell me about it."

"I better not regret this," I mumble to myself, ignoring her jab about Trenton, a flame that flickered for all of two months before I realized his candle would never hold up to the brightness that Maverick's still burned. "Yes, we slept together. Yes, the earth moved. No, I haven't talked to him since and don't plan on it. I'm too busy dodging town gossip thanks to that damn kiss. Yes, my hooha, as you so lovingly put it, is most definitely broken. Even I can't get it to work because HE BROKE IT!"

She starts laughing just as I finish. I should have known I would regret telling her all of that. She holds her hand up when it becomes clear that she can't control her hilarity and just points behind me.

I spin.

Then die.

"Now, I highly doubt I broke anything, but I would be more than willin' to check, darlin'."

Oh, my God. Kill me now.

"You—you—don't you say another word!" I try to steady my voice even as I feel my face turn a bright shade of red. If this could get any more mortifying, I'm not sure how.

He holds up his hands and I turn to Jana, only to see her walking through the swinging back door, purse in hand and shoulders still shaking with silent laughter. She doesn't pause in her stride, just keeps going until all I see is an empty hallway. I use the sudden silence around us to attempt to calm my frazzled nerves.

"Looks like it's just us now."

"I said no talking!" I yell, still peering down the hallway as though Jana might pop back up and save me from this mortifying scene. I can't believe her. Well, I guess I actually can. The sneaky woman knew exactly what she was doing. Hell, she probably let him in before she started in on her questions.

Wait a minute. "How did you get in here?"

"Front door was unlocked, darlin'. Not a soul in sight, but it wasn't hard to find y'all since you weren't exactly whispering."

"You didn't hear anything." It's a statement more than a question.

He laughs, the deep and rough sound echoing around the empty room, pinging off the walls, and shooting straight into my body before settling between my legs and waking up the one part of my body that's been completely dormant for the past two weeks.

Maverick looks good. Too good. His jeans faded in all the right places. I'm sure if he turned around, the view would be just as nice. Well, maybe not, since I'm currently graced with a view of the healthy bulge between his legs. The faded denim around his crotch doing nothing to conceal his growing arousal, instead only highlighting it further as the material continues to tighten around it.

"Eyes up here, Leighton."

I shiver, loving the sound of my name out of his mouth. God, some things never change. Even though I know it isn't wise, I let myself soak up the pleasure. Even if it's just a second's worth, it's something and after a decade of nothing—well, anything is better than that.

It isn't easy, but I remind myself of all the reasons why this needs to stop right now. I give myself a little jolt, hoping to fire up my stalled brain, and narrow my eyes at him. The pleasure leaves my body as the stubborn self-preservation returns.

"Why are you here?" I'm proud of the cold note I've managed to muster in my voice, even as my insides are already on fire with his presence.

He unfolds his arms, the corded muscles moving beneath his skin with the movement. Lifting one arm, he points at me, confusion painted all over his face. "What just happened? One second you were an open book, givin' me it all, and then just like that the shutters came down and you're actin' like I'm some stranger."

"You might as well be," I mumble under my breath.

He takes a step forward, his booted foot coming down with a heavy thud. "That isn't goin' to work," he says, twirling the finger that is still pointed in my direction in my face. "I might be a lot of things, but a stranger ain't one."

"You've been gone a long time, Maverick. We don't know each other anymore, so by definition, that would make you a stranger."

"You make a habit out of opening your legs for people you don't know?"

I gasp at his harsh words.

"Fuck," he says with a grunt, taking off his black Stetson and resting it on the stainless steel worktable next to him, his thick raven locks sticking up in a million different directions. "Look, I didn't come here to fight with you. I apologize for jumping the gate with sarcastic bullshit that you don't deserve. But we need to talk."

"Wow, did you practice that little speech in front of your mirror?" I cross my arms and fist my hands at my sides, hiding behind the protective stance.

"Don't be a bitch, Leighton, it doesn't suit you."

My cheeks flame. "You're right, I'm sorry," I respond. "Look, it's been a long day and I just want to go home and crash. Can we just do this another time?"

"I don't think so. I gave you some time, but I'm done waiting around while you just ignore me. I called, you haven't responded. I stop by your house, you don't come to the door. You ran out on me, Leigh, not the other way around, and I want to know why."

"Are you serious right now?"

He nods, but doesn't say anything else.

"That night . . . what we did . . . it was a mistake."

"Wrong."

I jerk my head back at his forceful and quick denial.

"Oh, no, it was. We were caught up in the emotions of the day. We weren't thinking clearly and things just got out of hand. From what I've heard, you had a lot on your mind before you even crossed over the county line, and when you add in why you were even back, well, it makes sense that you weren't exactly of sound mind. I let my anger get the better of me and, to be honest, my hurt fueled my actions. We both are guilty of letting our emotions power the lust that brought us together. But now we need to forget about it and move on."

He's silent a beat before he throws his head back and lets out a boom of laughter that brings goose bumps to my body. It had been so long since I heard him laugh like this that I was immobile by the sheer beauty of it. The deep rumble vibrating from deep in his chest was causing his whole body to shake with his hilarity.

It was beautiful.

He was beautiful.

And I was in big trouble.

12
MAVERICK

"Run" by Matt Nathanson

I couldn't even explain to myself how I'd ended up here, in the PieHole kitchen after hours facing the woman who'd rocked my world two weeks ago and then disappeared, but I was done waiting for her to come to me. Just being near her eases that knot of tension that I've carried around for longer than I care to admit, telling me that this was the right move for me.

Just like that. Clarity floods my system.

After Quinn left, I'd worked around the barn for a few more hours doing stupid labor that no one wants to do without being told. By the time I left there wasn't a single stall out of the twenty that were in the main barn that didn't look perfect. A lot of good the busywork did me, though. I kept replaying the conversation with Quinn over and over.

It wasn't the first time I felt soul-shaking regret over

how I left things with Leighton all those years ago, but it was the first time that I was determined to do something to fix it. To make sure that regret was no longer allowed to cling to me like a parasite that wouldn't stop sucking its host dry. I was done with regret. However, it wasn't until I walked in and saw her that I realized I would do just about anything to turn back time. Now I didn't just want to repair the damage I had inflicted—I needed to more than I've ever needed a single damn thing in my life.

Not even my drive to leave town as a teenager had been this strong.

I continue to laugh at her last mouthy bullshit as my eyes roam over her body. Her long legs are bare and the frayed strings from her cutoff shorts just teased at the top of her thighs, the little white strings against her smooth tan skin making it look like silk. She shifts, and those strings dance across her skin and I groan, memories of our night together slamming into my mind. I know what those thighs feel like now. I don't just have to wonder if they would be as soft as they look while hugging my hips tightly and welcoming my hard thrusting.

Nope. I know exactly what she feels like and it's fucking branded into my skin.

I have to force my eyes from her legs. It isn't until I get to the logo of her bakery right above her breasts that I'm able to stop thinking about bending her over the table and getting those legs back around my hips. The heavy fullness of her chest makes the black cotton stretch tight; the flour sprinkled all over the fabric distracts my mind and finally gets me to focus.

She looks like a complete mess.

One hell of a knock-me-on-my-ass beautiful mess.

Thoughts that I've missed this for so long fill my mind; the regret I've been so determined to stop feeling comes back. I could have had this, but instead I threw it all away because I wasn't strong enough to stick around.

She gives me a look of absolute impatience and frustration when I finish the slow drag of my eyes up her body. Her looks might have rendered me speechless but it's this right here, *her*, that has my heart speeding back up as the feeling of contentment fills my body.

Her blond hair is in a messy ponytail gathered at the top of her head. Her flawless skin is completely free of any traces of makeup. She looks so much like she did ten years ago. Young and full of so much beauty inside of her that it just radiates from her every pore.

The color is high on her cheeks and I can't tell if it's from anger, embarrassment, or maybe—hopefully—some arousal. I just know that being around her makes me feel alive for the first time since being forced off the circuit. I don't feel like there is some big unknown missing in my life. That missing piece I've been searching for since I was old enough to start putting it all together.

The same piece I've felt was missing since the day I hightailed it out of here. I assumed that it was something I would find out on the road. I think deep down I always knew that missing piece was hiding in the one place I was so fucking determined never to go back to.

So no, I didn't just want to clear the air between us, but

I needed it with a fierceness that I still don't completely understand.

I'm finally able to calm my racing thoughts and focus back on her. She's standing there, her arms loose at her sides, shock holding her features hostage. I probably look like I'm as insane as old man Croyers, and that's saying a lot, since he talks to trees and drags around his rocking chair on a leash.

"We need to talk, darlin'. It's time." She shakes her head, but doesn't retreat when I move toward her. "I've got a lot I need to say, and if you don't want to talk, fine . . . but it needs to be said, Leigh."

"You aren't leavin', are you?"

I shake my head.

She takes a deep breath before giving me a small shake of her head. Resignation clear on her face. "Do you want some coffee?"

"Yeah, darlin', make it strong."

Silently, she turns and walks through the kitchen door and into the main room of her bakery. I follow. She lifts a finger and points to the table in the back corner before walking to the front windows. She takes a second to look into the streets and at the townsfolk that are milling around before she pulls down the shades. I'm sure that she has them there to block the sun during the day, but they effectively block the view into the bakery from anyone that is out on Main Street tonight. I could have told her it was pointless. Gossip started burning like wildfire the second I parked my truck next to her Jeep and walked inside. This town, it misses nothing, and they've been waiting to see what would happen next after that kiss.

I watch her as she moves back behind the counter and preps the coffeemaker. It takes effort, but I pull my eyes from her ass and look around the room.

I hate that I wasn't here to see her become the woman that she is today. It's clear in every inch of space in here that she built her bakery with pride and love. I knew from Clay that she was doing well, but judging by this place that's a big understatement.

"Here. Black." She thumps the full mug down; hard enough to make a loud bang against the table, but with enough care that not one drop escapes the top. She's still pissed and isn't afraid to let me know it.

I lift the purple mug and place it to my mouth, breathing in the strong brew before taking a sip. The burn down my throat is welcome as I get my thoughts together. She sits down on the opposite side and places her hands around a mug of her own.

I take another sip before placing mine down and clearing my throat.

"I'm sorry."

She jerks slightly and narrows her eyes.

"There's a lot of shit I've done in my life that I regret, Leigh, but I never let myself dwell on it because, at the time, I knew it was necessary in order to get what I want. To get where I wanted to go. To get out." I look down at my mug, composing my thoughts before giving her the rest. Knowing that the rest is one of the most important things I could say tonight. "I noticed you. You were wrong—God, so wrong. I've always seen you, Leighton. Standing there, that night, and letting you think that I *didn't* see you as the beautiful girl you were back then was one of the hardest things I've ever done. It fuckin' killed me, but I knew it had to be done because if I hadn't made sure you hated me in that moment, I wouldn't have left, and darlin', I had to leave. I wouldn't have survived under his iron fist. So I made sure that I crushed the one person I knew deep down in my bones had the power to keep me grounded in Pine Oak until the day I took my last breath. And darlin', that last breath would have come a lot quicker if I wouldn't have left when I did."

There's a red-hot flash of anger before she lets a frustrated bark of disbelief out. She opens her mouth, only to snap it shut again. She's always been so expressive that it's clear to see a war is raging between fury and hurt right now. I watch her struggle, her eyes showing me what her mouth can't vocalize—which side of her war won—as they wet with emotion. She blinks back her tears, not allowing a single one free, as she bites down hard on her lip. I hate knowing that I'm hurting her right now, but I need her to hear this. My chest already feeling lighter from just the little I've said. I might be a fucking mess in my head right now, but feeling the stranglehold on my chest lighten after a decade of guilt and regret is well overdue.

"I was so focused on gettin' out of here that I never imagined that there could have been another way. A way to chase my dreams and not hurt you, but back then all I could see was a young girl with a family that loved her and a future that you had to realize on your own. I saw a sixteen-year-old girl unaware of the power she held and fuck if it didn't terrify me. I took the coward's way out and hurt you before I would allow myself to be vulnerable enough for you to hurt me. I struck knowing that I would be able to leave with no ties other than Clay and Quinn and even they understood why I was runnin', so those ties weren't tied tight. They lived that hell with me. So while I might have gotten what I was chasing, I accomplished it all alone because I pushed everyone away."

"Why the hell are you telling me this? What does it change, Maverick? Not one damn thing!" she yells, a burst of resentment that lasts only a second before my words sink deep. Her hand on her chest as she still struggles to hold her emotions in check, her anger starting to replace the sadness.

"Because in order to explain the shit swirlin' inside of me, I have to start at the beginnin', and darlin', that's you."

"I don't understand. I thought we were going to talk about . . . well, that night?"

"We will," I vow.

"Maybe we should just skip the past and focus on that then. I'm not sure what you're hoping to accomplish by letting this all out now, but you made your choice when you left, Mav, and I'm not sure if it's best to go back down that road again. No, actually, I know it isn't."

I laugh, the sound just as foreign to me as it was earlier in the kitchen. "I need to get it all out, Leighton, and honey, you need to hear it. After that, where we go from here is up to you."

"Where we go?"

"That's what I said," I respond, picking up the mug and taking another deep swallow.

"I think the only place we're goin' is home after this talk."

"Then I guess it will be up to you if we are goin' to end up in the same house or go separate ways, but you'll make that call with all the information."

Leighton wrinkles her nose like she's smelled something unpleasant. "I don't like this."

I smile, a small one, but genuine all the same. "Yeah, darlin', and neither do I, but like I said, it's time."

She drops her hand from her chest, takes a calming breath, and picks up her mug to take her first sip since sitting down.

I plunge ahead before she can change her mind.

"You know, in my head, I planned everything out, but it wasn't until I had been gone about a year or two when I realized how much I fucked up. I climbed the ranks quick. Made a name for myself in that time and knew I was on the right path—but fuck, I was lonely. Don't get me wrong—I didn't have trouble finding temporary ways to try and fill that void, but it always made me feel even more alone—so after a while, that shit stopped too. I haven't been with another woman in damn near five years, Leigh, and even before that it wasn't much. Focused on my trainin' and ridin'. I was so fuckin' alone. On the top of my game, ridin' the beasts that made me feel like a fuckin' god, but even in a sold-out arena, I felt like I was in a room all by myself. I can still remember the exact moment that I stopped lettin' people—anyone—close to me. Quinn sent me a picture of you two on graduation night, two years after I had left, and it was like a punch to my gut when I looked into your smilin' face. I knew that, while I might have it all, I had nothin' because I didn't get to see that smile every day. I fuckin' missed that smile, Leigh. I felt that emptiness like I had never before that night."

Her mug hits the table, and dark liquid spills out and over her white-knuckled hand. Leigh mumbles a curse and gropes blindly for a napkin from the dispenser on the table, her gaze trained on me. I keep my eyes on her coffee-drenched fingers before opening my mouth to continue, needing the time to get in control of my emotions.

"The night Quinn sent me that picture I stayed on the bull for twelve seconds before I let my ropes loose and jumped off, but it was like I had a death wish. I looked that beast in the eye for a whole solid beat of my heart before he started to charge. I didn't even rush to climb out. I took my sweet ass time. By the time my trainer was bendin' over and heavin' me over the top rail by my vest, that pissed-off bull was about to spear me. I didn't care. I felt nothin'. That was the night I told my sister to never send me another picture of you again."

I clear my throat and finally look up into her eyes. She's so still that I have a feeling she's trying her hardest not to show me what my words have made her feel, but the tears she had been so determined to keep locked away fall freely now, betraying her will to hide from me.

"I might have been the king of the rodeo after that, but I did it with a dead heart that no one came close to touchin'. Years passed and I didn't feel a thing until Clay called and told me he needed me to come home. The old man was gone and he needed me back here to make some decisions about the ranch. Before I got his call I had spent almost two weeks so drunk I couldn't even tell you what my name was, but that call stopped it all. For the first time in a long damn time I didn't see nothin' but dark emptiness in front of me. I didn't feel the chokin' reminder of regrets unchangeable. It was like a sign that it wasn't too late to fix things. I didn't know what I would be comin' home to, but I knew that I damn sure wouldn't spend another day regrettin' the mistakes of my actions. Not when I have the power to do somethin' about it now. A chance."

"Mav," she starts before clearing her throat, twisting the dampened napkin in her fingers, "I'm not . . . I don't really know what to say, Maverick."

"I get that, darlin', I put a lot on you tonight, but you needed to hear it so you understood why I wasn't goin' to allow you to call that night two weeks ago a mistake. I fucked up and I hurt you so I deserve your anger, but I'm not goin' to allow another regret to happen in my lifetime when I can do somethin' to prevent it. I let it all hang out, gave you all the bad and ugly. It's up to you where we go from this point."

Leigh stares at me for a moment, mouth agape, then sputters, "You're asking me to just make a decision like that based on a fifteen-minute conversation as you give me some Cliff's Notes breakdown on your life for the past decade?"

Leaning back in my chair, I have to will myself to stay

calm even though it's clear by her snippy tone that she's pissed. "Not a Cliff's Notes breakdown, Leighton, and you know it. I'm explainin' things the best way I can."

"You fuckin' left, Maverick. Clay and Quinn knew why, but even they didn't give me much. There wasn't a day that went by that we didn't feel the void of your absence. You can't just explain that away easily. You admit you hurt me on purpose. Do you even have any idea how *bad* you hurt me? You can't just decide that now, after ten fuckin' years, that you're willing to . . . to what? To be with me? It's insane!"

"You don't think I know that?!" I yell. She jumps at my outburst but doesn't speak. "Fuck." I stand, pacing the tight space between tables before looking back over to where she is still sitting, coffee mug still held tightly in her hand. "I'm not hidin' shit from you. I'm tellin' you what I need to for you to understand why I hurt you and why I've regretted that night since. I'll give you the rest, but I can't do that until I understand it myself, and right now I'm strugglin' to just get through this."

"You're a mess," she tells me in a tone that is strong and true, the vulnerability that she had shown earlier either gone or hidden.

"Yeah." I laugh without humor. "I'm a fuckin' mess, but I'm workin' on it."

"That's good, Maverick. I'm glad you're working through it. I hope you find the peace you need," she tells him sincerely.

I shake my head. After everything I put her through and she still gives me that. "Another day, darlin'. Let's leave that for another day. I've got my own shit to work on, but I need to fix things between my family too."

She nods, a sad smile playing across her lips. "They missed you."

I swallow through the lump clawing up my throat. "Yeah." What I wouldn't give for her to admit that she's missed me too.

"I need to clean this up," she says to the table, and I know she's looking for a way out. Doesn't take a genius to tell she's trying to get out before I see the emotions she's working so fucking hard to hide from me.

I push back from the table, and her eyes tilt up to meet mine. "Two weeks ago I rolled into town unsure of what I would find and at the end of that night I realized that when I ran from this town to escape the hell I had been livin', I lost the only slice of heaven I've ever felt. I felt it again that night, Leigh, and I'm tellin' you right now, I'm not givin' that feelin' up without a fight. You need to process all this shit I've put on your lap tonight, but you also need to realize that I'm here now. Settled in for the long run, and it's gonna last a lot longer than eight seconds. You better believe I'm ridin' this out with you until you buck me off. And darlin', there hasn't been a ride I've ever been more prepared for."

I bend, press my lips against her shocked and slack mouth before dropping my lucky hat on her head and walking through the doorway to the kitchen and out to my truck. As much as I would love to end this night with her in my arms, I know the best thing I can do is leave and let her do what she needs to do. Quinn was right earlier today when she said Leigh doesn't make a move without analyzing every angle; that's something that has never changed. I've given her all the facts she needs and now the ball is in her court.

I was halfway back to the ranch, smile still on my face and my mind feeling a whole hell of a lot lighter than it was earlier. I might be off the circuit, but I'm gearing up for the ride of my life.

13

LEIGHTON

"What Hurts the Most" by Rascal Flatts

That didn't just happen.

Nope.

That definitely didn't happen.

I lift my hand, hitting the heavy felted brim of the hat on my head. With shaking fingers, I grasp the crown of the hat to pull it off my head. My free hand trembles as I rub the edges of the brim. I don't know how I know, but I have no doubt that this hat is special to him. It's so well worn that even an idiot could tell it's got a long life behind it. I place it down on the table behind me, before standing from my seat.

I hadn't moved for so long after I heard his truck fire up that my back instantly protests and my feet scream after finally getting comfortable after a long day. I make quick work of cleaning up our coffee mugs and the rest of my mess, wiping down the table before throwing the rag in the basketful of used linens I had ready to take home and launder before Monday. Ignoring the emotions raging through my body. So much conflict. Sadness, regret, and a whole lot of deep-seated anger. All of them swirling around, making it impossible for me to tell which one is strongest.

I can't even think about what Maverick said tonight; instead I keep my mind focused on closing everything out properly, checking that the front door is still locked before grabbing the till out of the register. I had planned on working through the books and readying a deposit for Monday morning before I opened up, but after Maverick's appearance and talk, my mind is not capable of handling anything more than the drive home. I lock the till up in the safe in my office with a sigh, knowing that this means I'll have to come in and handle it tomorrow while we're closed or it will just mean more work on Monday.

With my purse over my shoulder, I take one more pass around the kitchen to make sure all the fridges are shut tight and the ovens are off, and grab the laundry basket from the doorway between the kitchen and the main room. My eyes go directly for the lonely cowboy hat, still resting against the table where I left it.

I should leave it. I should just walk out the doorway and pretend that I didn't know it was there and let Jana deal with it Monday when she opens. Instead, my feet carry me to the table, and my hand wraps around the crown before I place it with reverence onto the top of my head instead of on top of the soiled laundry inside the basket.

I shouldn't care about getting it dirty, but damn if I don't.

Juggling the basket, I walk out the back door before locking it and head to my Jeep, refusing to acknowledge the warm feeling traveling down my body from where the hat rests. I can smell him, just as strong as if he were right before me. Having a piece of him near me does nothing but amp up the very big part of me that wishes I had all of him.

Damn, I'm really in big trouble.

"What are you doing?"

I jump, the rocking chair I had been sitting in jolting under my sudden movement. I have to squint my eyes to see through the darkness that I just realized had settled around me. When I sat down earlier I had been so upset and confused over what Maverick's talk had made me feel. I couldn't understand why, even through the anger I felt, all I wanted to do was rush to him and force him to make sense of it all.

With his hands. And his mouth. And other things.

"God, Q! You scared the shit out of me." I wheeze, clutching my chest.

"I reckoned as much, since you almost took the chair down jumping like a baby."

Still breathing deeply, my heart rate racing wildly, I reach up and give her my middle finger.

"Yeah, yeah . . . I get that enough from the guys at the shop. You're gonna have to try harder if you really want me to feel like you really mean it."

"What are you doing lurking in the shadows, anyway? Did you walk over here?"

She laughs, the sound a feminine, deep, husky rumble, her normal voice hoarse like she's got a cold. It's the kind of voice that would make a 1-900 operator millions. "Well," she starts, breaking me out of my thoughts again, "I drove, which you should have seen, being that I forgot I had my brights on and the damn things were shooting right in your face before I realized you were sitting here in the dark. If that wasn't a big enough clue, I had been calling your name since I jumped out of the truck again—something you should have heard."

"Oh," I mumble sheepishly.

"Yeah, oh."

She knocks my knees as she pushes past me to sit in the chair next to mine. I close my eyes when I realize my mistake, her gasp echoing through the still night air around us. She's standing in front of the rocker paired with mine, the dirty-laundry-filled basket sitting on the table between us, but that's not what causes her reaction.

It's the lone hat sitting on the chair that has caught her attention.

"What is that doin' here?"

"What is *what* doin' here?" I hedge, looking up to see her staring at the hat like it's a snake about to strike.

"Don't play dumb with me, Leighton Elizabeth James. I'd know that hat anywhere. Especially since it's the only hat that has ever, in almost fifteen years, sat on top of my brother's head."

My heart jumps and I jerk my head toward the hat in

question. Seeing it in a whole new light now. I knew it looked familiar.

No way.

There's no way that this hat is *the* hat. Maverick's hat from when he was a teenager.

"You're reading too much into it, Q. It's just a black hat. You just think that because all he ever wears, regardless of the time of year, is a solid black Stetson." My voice is just as weak as my argument.

And she knows it, judging by the smirk on her beautiful face. "Then turn it over, why don't ya?"

"No."

"Turn it over, Leigh."

"Leave it, Quinn."

"If you're so sure it's *just a black hat*, then what's the big deal? Prove me wrong."

"I don't need to prove you wrong, but while you're here, why don't you take it home with you and give it to your brother. He left it at the PieHole earlier when he came by for some coffee. Like I said, reading too much into nothing, Q."

"Fine," she snaps. "If you won't check, then I will."

I have to will myself not to react, but it's so damn hard. Especially when I feel the overwhelming need to slap her hand away when her fingertips are just a breath away from the felt.

Do not react, Leighton.

Don't you dare.

"Mav would kick your ass if he knew that you put it down like this. Don't you know the old superstition that if you place the hat opening down, all the good luck that has been collected will fall out?"

"That doesn't even make sense, Q."

"Doesn't have to make sense, it's just the cowboy way. Never, ever, rest a cowboy's hat with the opening down. You place it with the opening facing the sky so that it can continue to 'catch luck' . . . and while I'm at it, don't ever put it on your bed."

I frown at her, for a second forgetting what she was even doing. "You've been spending too much time with your ranch hands."

"Seriously, Leighton, you would think that you weren't even born and raised in Texas. Everyone knows this stuff."

"If you say so."

She lifts the hat, her gentle hold easing some of my anxiety over her just touching it, which is absolutely ludicrous. I hold my breath, looking away from her face and out into the dark front pasture between my house and the road down the long drive. The moon hides behind the clouds, casting nothing but different shades of darkness, and not allowing me anything to focus on.

Quinn makes a noise but doesn't speak. I refuse to look at her, but I feel her walk farther down the porch to where I have another table. I hear the soft connection of the hat against the wood, inwardly cringing and fighting the urge to put a towel under it.

"You never really thought that whole infinity symbol thing through, did you?" Her voice rings out in the darkness.

My eyes shut.

My throat closes.

Her meaning clear.

"I mean it's an honest mistake for a fourteen-year-old girl to make. Never thought instructions on its directional flow would be important, did you?"

She stops talking.

My heart continues to pound.

Her meaning crystal clear.

"I guess it all worked out, since he thought you meant to stitch the number eight into the liner. You were always the one that cheered him on the loudest. I still remember the day you begged your daddy to take us to the rodeo over in Clareview. I almost thought you would jump down the bleachers when he didn't get bucked off. Of course, we joked that it was his new hat with the lucky eight that made that ride possible."

My throat burns.

My eyes water.

Her words a hushed reminder of a stupid girl's dreams.

"When I saw him five years ago out in California, we went out for drinks at a bar near the arena," Quinn continues, a little softer now. "Rowdy as all get out, it was. Some drunk cowboy itchin' for a fight knocked Mav's hat off and the first thing he did was jump up from his stool and grab his hat off the dirty ground. You should have seen the care he took in making sure it wasn't damaged. He placed it—opening up, mind you—on the table before laying the jerk out with one punch to the jaw. I saw the same faded stitching before he placed the hat back on his head. I would have known those jagged stitches anywhere. The same ones made by the solid red thread you rode your bike almost twenty miles outside of Pine Oak to get at the neighboring town's Walmart. The same ones that you spent three days perfecting inside the hat you spent two whole years' worth of allowance on. The same ones that you spent another two days cryin' over when you realized you put that infinity on there vertically and it just looked like a crooked eight. All of that inside the same hat he's worn since the day you gave it to him, Leighton."

My chest hurts.

My throat hurts.

The pain from my sobbing burning through them both.

Quinn doesn't speak until I can get myself under control, her hand reaching over from her seat and holding mine the whole time. It isn't until I had just lifted my shirt up to wipe my eyes that she says another word.

"Go look in the hat, Leighton. Don't argue with me. You go on and do it while you feel like you do right now. It's important that you do this now, while I'm here."

I look over, my eyes fuzzy with tears, and nod my head. Finally, one of the emotions I felt warring inside of me since he left the PieHole earlier comes to the forefront: sadness. The last thing I want to do is go look at that stupid crooked number, but she's right—it's better that I do it while she is here because once I see those stupid red lines, it's going to remind me of every painful memory I've worked so hard to forget.

"I'm right here, Leighton," she reminds me softly.

I stand from the rocking chair, my body stiff from too

many hours in one position, and walk over to the hat. I hear her move, the sound of my screen door creaking as she opens it.

The second the porch lights turn on, the one directly above the table Maverick's hat is resting on acts like a spotlight inside of the opening. It wasn't the faded red stitching that she promised would be there that catches my attention, though. It couldn't be ignored, but it also didn't bring the pain I thought it would.

No, it wasn't the crooked stitching of that faded failed attempt at a romantic declaration that broke me into a million pieces. Had it been that alone, I wouldn't feel like someone had just punched me in the gut.

"That was the last picture I ever sent him, you know," Quinn whispers from behind me, telling me something I already know to be true, thanks to Maverick's own admissions earlier. She reaches down into the hat and pulls the well-worn picture from where it had been shoved behind the sweatband. You could tell that even though someone had taken the time to protect the photograph with a layer of lamination, it had been handled—often judging by the worn edges—many times over the years.

When Maverick spoke of this picture earlier, I had assumed that he'd gotten rid of it. He spoke so strongly about how it affected him that I never imagined he would have held on to it, let alone placed it somewhere meant to be close to him. It was because of that alone that I broke into a million painful pieces. I would gladly take the anger back if it meant I didn't feel like I had lost everything I ever wanted all over again.

Quinn doesn't speak again, but she doesn't need to. Her point was made, and after she moves to pull me into her arms, she does what she's done my whole life: picks up the broken pieces of my soul and helps me find a way to get them together again.

14

LEIGHTON

"Whiskey Lullaby" by Brad Paisley and Alison Krauss

Denial was the first thing that happened after discovering the significance behind Maverick's stupid hat. I spent a solid day—my day off work—going over all of the things that it *didn't* really mean. Cowboys are a superstitious bunch; everyone knows that, so I had convinced myself that it was nothing more than that. I came up with every excuse I could, but in the end, I knew deep down that I was casting lies to protect myself from pain.

By the time my Sunday had come to a close, though, that denial had quickly turned to anger. That anger was a powerful thing, and even Jana gave me a wide berth that day. I kept thinking about his stupid hat, that ridiculous crooked eight, and that damn picture. Every single time one of those would enter my thoughts, I ended up with a plate thrown against the kitchen wall. I was sure we would lose customers that day, but it seemed like everyone was itching for a show because we were packed all day—which, of course, just pissed me off even more. He did this. He made us the focus of this town's rumors. Just by being back he had cast a spotlight on us while the towns-folk waited for more things to whisper about behind our backs.

I skipped the third stage completely. Realization that I seemed to be on the grief train dawned when I docked at the depression station. By the time I realized what was going on, I was begging for the anger to return. At least with that, I could still breathe without pain.

The pain of what could have been.

But what wasn't.

And what now might never be.

So far, the deep depression that had settled over me hadn't left for one aching second. Not even when I was asleep. I would wake up with tears streaking my face, gasping for air. It had been two days since that heaviness had settled over me.

I worked through it yesterday, keeping to myself and avoiding everyone. I could tell Jana knew something was wrong, but she didn't call me on it. For once, she left me to my thoughts, coming back into the kitchen only when she needed to restock something we were out of. She allowed me my solitude in the kitchen while she worked the floor and dealt with customers, something I was grateful for.

But today I just don't have it in me. I can't fake my way through the day again, and to be honest, I just can't find the will to get up from the bed. For the first time on a weekday since the PieHole opened, the closed sign would stay hanging over the purple door. It didn't escape my notice that even when Buford passed away, the sign was flipped and the door opened, but all his son has to do is come riding back into town and everything had been overturned on its ass.

I sniff, rolling my body so that the sheets let my arm free, and grab one of the tear-soaked tissues balled next to my body, wiping my nose before reaching out and grabbing my cell off the table next to my bed. Earl starts purring from his spot above my head, laying one large paw on my nose when I turn again, thinking that it was finally time for his mama to give him some attention.

"Stop, baby," I thickly say through the lump in my throat, swatting away his paw.

He gives a hiss of irritation that I've had the nerve to scold him before moving to the end of the bed. He gives me a look, his yellow-green eyes blinking once before he curls, lifts his leg, and licks himself.

My eyes water when I think that even Earl, the only faithful man that I have left in my life, has turned on me. It takes me a solid minute to calm down before I pick up the phone and call Jana.

"Good mornin', beautiful girl," she hums into the phone, her voice clear and cheerful despite it being only six in the morning.

I open my mouth, take a deep breath, and proceed to give a fake cough performance of a lifetime.

"Oh, good heavens, honey!"

I give a few good throat-clearing noises before I take the coward's way out and lie through my teeth. "Hey, Jana. I was hoping I caught you before you headed in. We're going to stay closed today. I've got something nasty and since I started feeling bad last night, I don't want to chance that this could be supercontagious. Which means all the pies I prepped yesterday are being tossed. I don't feel well enough to make more." I pause and give a few deep coughs. "We're just going to close for the day."

"Honey, I can take care of things at the PieHole. All it needs is a good scrub and I can make up some new goodies before we even open the door. Don't you worry about a thing. You get yourself all rested up and I'll handle it all."

I clear my throat again, this time more to ease the claw of emotional guilt that's taken a choke hold on me. "Jana, let's just take the day and keep things closed. You're always after me to take a vacation, so looks like I'll finally take one."

"A vacation isn't when you're home sick, Leighton, baby."

"And I'm not leaving you to run things all day by yourself, so if you insist on going in, I'll just have to leave my bed to come too."

"Nonsense. You get yourself better and don't you even worry about a thing. I'll take care of it all. If you don't start feeling better, you call Doctor Baker, you hear?"

My mouth had just opened to argue when I hear the click of her disconnecting our call. The guilt taking a life of its own and only amplifying the fog that has been hanging over me for the past two days.

Blinking away the tears, I look over at the hat that is still sitting on my dresser—opening side up, stupid Quinn.

How could he do this?

How could he admit that everything I've ever thought, all the pain that has followed me around, has been a lie? Because of him I've been unable to move on, judging every man before giving them a chance, always finding them lacking of the high standards in which Maverick had me measuring them to. He ran off, leaving to live the high life, without a thought to the lives he was leaving behind.

He escaped.

And I stayed.

If he truly did feel for me—still does feel for me—like he says, how was that even possible?

I never had the urge to leave Pine Oak like he did, but I would have for him. For me, I would have given anything to have him be mine. For him, he would have given everything to get out. I thought we were destined to be together, but he wanted only to run.

And I still don't understand why.

I knew he had dreams of being in the rodeo. Hell, almost every little boy in Texas does, but I always thought that deep down he would join his brother on the ranch and that his rodeo career was just something he did for fun.

I roll over in bed and look out my bedroom window, the sun starting its climb high in the sky. Earl comes back up and curls his big body into mine before he starts to purr loudly. Without looking away from my window, I reach down and start to pet him, wishing that the pain of my confused heart would ease.

- ★ -

"This has to stop, Leigh," Quinn exasperatingly huffs. "You look like—"

I glance up from the wrench I had been twirling around my hands, waiting for her to stop eating and get back to work, knowing this will be the first thing she forgets to pull under the truck with her. I lift a brow at her. "Finish that sentence and I'm going to beat your head in with this." She holds her hands up and sticks her tongue out before taking another bite of the strawberry rhubarb pie she had just grabbed off the counter I placed it on when I got here—the second one since she just finished eating one straight from the tin rolling back underneath the truck she's been working on since I walked into her shop an hour ago. "Shouldn't you be workin' instead of eatin' another pie? I swear, if you ever paid for the crap you keep beggin' me to come over here and bring you in the middle of the day, I would be a millionaire."

"And I would be living out of a cardboard box behind the building."

"At least you wouldn't go hungry," I joke, a small smile lifting my lips.

"Ah, I've missed that," she says through the full bite of pie she just shoved in her mouth.

"Missed the pie? You just ate a whole one not even ten minutes ago."

"Smart-ass," she says with a pout, taking another bite. "I meant your smile. I haven't seen that much this week."

I stop my movements, looking up from the wrench in my hands and into her emerald eyes.

"Do you want to talk about it?" she asks when my silence persists.

"Not really, Quinn."

"I think you need to."

I give up on my avoidance and place the wrench down on her tool bench. I let the silence continue before leaning against the counter in front of where Quinn is sitting and meeting her knowing gaze.

"I'm not really sure what you want to hear, Quinn. I was sad. Then I got confused. Which turned into anger really quick, and now I'm back to sad. I'm all over the place and half of the time I don't even know what to do with myself. It's almost as if I'm stuck in some weird purgatory that just won't let me escape."

She swallows her bite, looking just as sad as I feel before speaking. "You know, I think that's the same thing that Maverick told Clay and me a year or two before he left."

My brow furrows. "What?"

"That he was in a purgatory that wouldn't let him escape. A pain-filled world that wouldn't stop striking him down."

"Quinn—"

She jumps off the counter she had been resting on and walks over to where I'm leaning. "I hate seeing you hurting, Leigh. It cuts me so deep I feel like I'm the one bleeding right along with you. No matter how painful it was helping you heal after Maverick hurt you, that didn't even hold a candle to how I felt when I would climb into his bed as a kid and hold him tight as he cried in his sleep. I never told you this because I knew how much you hurt back then, but I was glad he left. He needed to, because honest to God, Leighton, being here was killing him."

I don't speak, thoughts rushing through my mind so rapidly I can't even make sense of them.

"He's always felt things so much stronger than Clay or myself. When our mom left, that void hit him so hard. He was so close to her and then one day she was just gone. When you add that to all the pain our father put him through, he couldn't win for tryin'. He wasn't interested in the ranch like Clay was. He wasn't interested in the shop like I was. The only thing he was interested in was the one thing our father hated almost as much as he hated our mother. When he told him that he wanted to ride, Dad beat him so bad he had to go to the hospital. Told them that he got hurt during ridin' practice. Can you believe that?"

"Quinn, I don't think you should be tellin' me this." And I didn't. It seemed like a betrayal to Maverick, and even though I didn't owe him that, I shouldn't be learning the secrets they've kept buried within their family from his sister because she was trying to play some sort of match-making game.

"Probably not, but that doesn't change that I'm going to. I didn't tell you this back then because I knew he *had* to leave, Leigh. He had to. If he hadn't he would have either killed our father or died trying. There was too much pain there. Maverick never was the same after Mom left, but when he told Dad that he wanted to leave the ranch the old man had worked to grow for his boys to take over—for the rodeo, of all places—it killed the only thing good left inside of him back then. Dad would never forgive him for running off with rodeo dreams in his eyes. Just like Mama. Mama ran off chasin' the buckle just like Mav."

"What? You mama wasn't a rider, Quinn."

"Not of horses or bulls, but she loved herself a cowboy, and a cowboy with the lights of fame in his face was the only thing she cared about."

I gasp. "You never told me that, Q."

She drops the now empty pie tin and looks up at me, sadness and anger swimming behind her gaze. "Because it's better to say your mama ran off because she couldn't handle being a mother to three kids and the life of a rancher's wife than to admit she's nothin' but a slut with dollar signs in her eyes."

"Jesus, Quinn."

"Yeah, I know. Look, I'm over it, I just wanted you to know there's a lot more behind Maverick than what you know. I understand you're upset right now and I'm not saying that you shouldn't be, but I think you need to get over yourself and cowgirl up. You aren't a quitter and honey, he's home . . . do something about it. It isn't too late for you two."

I make a mental note to talk to her about her mama later because it's clear she has no interest in continuing that conversation right now. She's as stubborn as a bull when it comes to something she doesn't want to deal with. Quinn is an expert at avoidance.

"It's been ten years, babe. We aren't the same kids we were back then. We were shaky friends at best and regardless of what he's said a lot of hurt is standing in the way of taking that friendship to something further. I love you for your optimism, but I'm not sure that it isn't too late." My mind quickly brings up the memory of our stolen kiss in the field between our families' properties, the one that even now—ten years later—I haven't told a soul about. We were so much more than shaky friends.

She studies me for a second, not giving anything away with her expression. "I understand that, but Leighton, I want to say something to you and I need you to really think about it. Don't make a split-second decision, but really let it sink in, okay?"

"Okay," I respond hesitantly.

"Can you honestly tell me that since he's been home, you don't feel like that piece of you that's been hollow since he left isn't starting to feel like it's mending a little? You've dated, sure, but you've NEVER let that piece find a way to heal. My brother comes back home and not even twelve hours pass before you two are pulled back together. Regardless of what happened to fuel that, when two people are meant for each other sometimes their souls make the moves their brains are too busy analyzing in order to allow it to happen. You both use your pain as a shield to keep people out, and because of that, you're fighting against the one person that has the power to heal every second of that pain. Stop fighting. You're allowed to be hurt over his actions, Leighton. You should. But when you are tied to another person right down to your souls, you don't give that kind of connection up without making sure you have all the facts, and honey, you don't. Let him give you the full story. If you feel like what he's done in the past is unforgivable still, then at least you can make that call with all the facts."

"You make it sound so easy, Quinn."

She laughs, the sound lacking any humor. "It's not, Leigh. It's gonna be hard and I'm sure painful, but just think, if the end means you two are together, or you finally have the closure you need to move on, well . . . either way, you can leave that purgatory you say has you held captive. But if you end up with him, just think about how sweet that is going to be when you come out on the other side."

She gives me a sad smile, grabbing the other rhubarb pie I brought over before she walks out of the work area and into the break room where the fridge is.

Could she be right? Is opening myself up to this kind of pain worth the payout that might be waiting for me? Or what if I open myself up again, only to have my heart smashed all over when Maverick feels like this town is suffocating him again? Better yet, will I regret it if I don't try?

I guess the better question at this point is, who is going to run first? And will that person be running toward something, or away from something else?

With my mind spinning from everything that Quinn told me today, I do the only thing that has ever been able to help when my thoughts are a maelstrom of confusion.

I rush back down Main Street and I bake.

15

MAVERICK

"Should've Been a Cowboy" by Toby Keith

Sitting across from Clay in the old man's office is making my skin crawl. I hate being in here. Judging by the tension rolling off Clay, he hates it just as much as I do, but there's work to do and this is where it needs to happen.

"This place could run itself blind, Clay. You don't need me on the breedin' end. Hell, neither of us would have to do a damn thing but show up when buyers do and collect the checks and this ranch would continue to thrive."

He pulls his white hat off, scratching his messy hair before placing the hat back down, shadowing his face once again. "I hear what you're sayin', Mav, but what you're askin' means I would need to sink a ton of fuckin' money into something that I have no interest or fuckin' time to handle right now."

"I'm not askin' you to handle shit and you know it. I own just as much of this ranch as you do now. You also know I don't need your fuckin' money to make it happen. I wouldn't want that money even if I did. I want this for me because it's somethin' I believe in, but it's also some-thin' that's mine without *him* all over it. I'm askin' you for land you don't need and I'm askin' for your blessing to find my own way with somethin' that makes me happy."

"Fuck!" he bellows and looks up to the ceiling. "What are you fuckin' up to, little brother?"

"Hell, Clayton . . . I'm just tryin' to find my feet when they've been knocked out from under me. I'm tryin' to find my way while I make some good memories to re-place the nightmares that hide in every corner around this fuckin' ranch. I'm just tryin' to get back what I lost when I couldn't see past the horror show that was our childhood."

He pulls off his hat again, tossing it onto the desk. I watch it spin a few times before settling with a gentle rock. Seeing the sweat-stained band on the inside of his Stet-son makes me think of my own that I had left behind with Leigh. I feel like I've lost a limb being without it, but I'm fuckin' prayin' that by leavin' it behind, I've given her enough to find her way back to me.

"The land you're asking for, Maverick . . . shit. If you fuck this up and hightail it back outta here again, this will make that night in the middle of the woods look like a fuckin' paper cut compared to the damage this will do."

It takes one hell of an effort not to blow my top at him; instead, I take a deep breath before answering. "I've told you every day since I got back in Pine Oak, Clay. I'm not leavin'. I'm here to stay, and God willing, I'm here to get back what I lost."

He makes a noise deep in his throat and shuffles some papers around on the desk. "I figured when you told me you would come back, you would actually help around here."

"There's nothin' good for me on this ranch except you and Quinn. I can't be here without thinkin' the old man is goin' to come out and bash my head in because I'm not walkin' straight. I'm tryin' to prove to you I'm stickin' around, but I can't do that here, on this property."

Clay looks up, his eyes more sympathetic than I've seen since I got back almost a month ago. "He's gone, Mav. Can't hurt you from the grave."

My chest vibrates, the sound far from a laugh. "That's where you're wrong, brother. He's left his mark all over this damn place. Just being here, in this house, around the barn, the training fields—it's all him. All I do is walk two fuckin' feet and I'm relivin' some bullshit in my mind. I don't want to run, but to prove I'm stickin' around I have to do it away from the Davis ranch."

"Is that all this is about?"

I knew he would see right through me to the bigger picture. Clay's always been fifteen steps ahead of the rest of us. "What else would this be about?" I respond, playing stupid and avoiding the rest of the topic at hand.

"Leighton."

I feel my brows rise slowly and I allow my lips to turn up. "What about her?" God, just hearing her name settles me. I've been coming out of my skin for days. Not just because of her silence. Everything I've told Clay is the truth; I can't stay at the Davis ranch and stay in Pine Oak because *here* makes me feel like a caged animal again.

"She's been through a lot, Maverick. I'm your brother, and because of that, you get my loyalty . . . however, I love that girl like she's a sister, and brother or not, I will lay you the fuck out if you hurt her again."

I lift out of the chair, but before my ass was even an inch off the old leather seat in front of my dad's old desk, Clay holds up his hand to halt my movements.

"Sit the fuck down and listen to me. I understand why you left, Mav. I get it. I know you needed to. That being said, you were so single-mindedly focused on getting the hell out of town that you might as well of been blind as a bat. I can't change things with Dad. I can't change what happened with Mama. I can't give you your career back. But I can give you this. You aren't the only one who carries scars. You need to learn to forgive Dad, if anything to just let it go and be able to move on. You need to forget about Mama. You did what you could, but she didn't want us then and she's never gonna change. You also need to give Leighton everything. One thing us Davises are good at is hidin' the pain. So you want *her* land—you need to talk to *her* about it. I might own it, but I only bought it from her so I could keep her close. She was going through so much and I couldn't let her leave Pine Oak. We couldn't lose her too."

He adds the last part almost as an afterthought. His words hushed and hard to hear, but I did hear him and the thoughts running through my mind are anything but nice.

"Tell me, you and Leigh . . ." I let the unasked question hang in the air.

He looks up from the spot on the desk he had been lost in thought focusing on. "Are you fuckin' kiddin' me?"

"It sounds like there's something strong between you two."

"Yeah, you're damn right there is."

This time I do come up from my chair. Clay does too and before I realize, we're chest to chest next to the desk, both of us breathing harshly.

"I will kill you if you touched one hair on her head," I say with a growl.

"Let me ask you something, big man . . . who do you think was there to pick up the pieces after you stomped all over her that night?"

My anger spikes. Just thinking about my brother with his hands on Leighton makes me want to kill him. Rationally, I know I have no right to feel this way. I knew what I was doing that night, and in doing so, I knew I was breaking her heart, but I never thought about who would happen to be there *after* I left.

"Clayton," I seethe.

"You don't fuckin' get to be pissed. You left. I told you I understand why you did. We *all* understood it. You were meant to ride, Mav. Even if you hadn't felt the need to escape this town, you were born to ride. Even knowing why you left, it doesn't fix the fact that you went out like a tornado set on destroying everything in the way. You fucked up and because of that I had to come in and fix it all. You gotta lot of balls to sit here and be pissed because we grew closer after you left."

"How close?"

He pushes back with his chest, but I don't budge.

"I'd kill for that girl. Even my own damn brother. Hurt her again and I won't even think twice about it, Maverick."

"How. Fuckin'. Close?"

Clay's jaw sets, the hard clamp of his teeth making it flex rapidly. His green eyes turn cold as his lips thin.

"You really want to do this? Fine! You destroyed what little confidence she had in herself. She was already insecure about everythin', as you know, but her beauty shined through even as she was still comin' into herself. She's always had something about her. Even when she was just a young'un, that girl screamed forever and that scream was always directed right at you. You were so busy tryin' to find a way out—to get away from Dad, chase some bullshit with Mom, and to ride—the only thing you loved at the time, that you didn't even see that. Or anything else—here at home. Out with friends. With the attention from girls you didn't want. I only saw you at peace when you were ridin' *or* when you were with Leighton. You really think, knowing that, I would move in on her the second you left?"

His words knock some wind out of my sails. The truth I had been avoiding. The pain knowing that one of those things that already brought me peace is gone and the other might never be mine is a very real reminder of the stakes I'm up against to finally be free of the pain that haunts me.

"You gotta focus on one thing at a time, but I'm proud of you for putting that focus where it matters. I can honestly tell you, you fix this shit with her and you two finally live out what you've always been destined for, I have a feeling she will be all you need to face the rest of what is haunting you."

"I never should have pushed her away," I tell him, voicing the one thing I've known deep in my gut since the day I left. "I should have been stronger."

He takes a deep breath, and clamps his large palm on my shoulder. "You are one of the strongest men I know, Maverick. You could have done things differently, but we both know you did what you had to do in an impossible situation."

"You stayed," I whisper. It's one of the biggest things that's fucked with my mind over the years. I took the coward's way out, and in doing so, I left my siblings to battle the beast alone.

"Fuck, Maverick!" Clay yells, startling me from my thoughts. "When you think back to what it was like growing up here, really fuckin' think about it, I want you to see it clear. Yeah, he was a son of a bitch, but he didn't treat Quinn or me like he did you. You were the closest to Mom, never cared about the ranch, and when she left, he held some sort of blame on you for always having her love . . . what little she was capable of giving. When he found out you were ridin', all that did was remind him that his wife ran off with a rider. Everything you were, just bein' you, set you up for his hatred and fury. He was a sorry fuckin' drunk back then, but he only put his hands on you. I didn't need to leave because by the time you were gone, he didn't do anything but drink himself to the grave until it finally came to collect. Ten years is a long time, Maverick, and by the time he was too sick to turn it around, the guilt of his mistake-filled life killed him faster than the bottle did."

I take a deep breath, my head swirling with my brother's words. "You forgave him?"

He nods. "Had a lot of time to talk to him before he died. He wasn't the same man, brother. When I tell you that regrets are a powerful thing, I say that knowing that they can very well be strong enough to kill you. Do what you can to make peace with yours."

I throw up my hands. "What do you think I'm doin'? I left here with anger ridin' my back and I came back with the same partner ridin' along. I'm workin' on it, but I've done a lot of harm and I'm not sure if it's too late."

He gives me a look of sympathy before pulling me into a hug. I wrap my arms around him. He pats my head like he used to when we were little and I'd come seeking his comfort and love. "It's never too late, baby brother, long as you're still breathin'."

16

LEIGHTON

"Rise Up" by Andra Day

It was dark by the time I left the PieHole. After Quinn left, the only thing I could do was think.

And boy, did I think.

I thought about a little girl who would follow around an equally little boy imagining what would happen when they got older and had little kids of their own.

I smiled when I reminisced about that little girl, a few years later, realizing that when that little boy was hers, they would have everything.

I recalled the time that teenage girl, awkward and insecure in her own skin, thought she was the most beautiful thing on the earth when that boy, now a teenager too, would give her some attention.

I mourned the day that teenage boy stopped giving that teenage girl his smiles freely—until one day he stopped smiling altogether.

I remembered the day he stopped seeking her out to sit in the middle of the wildflowers behind her house to just look at the clouds. Holding her hand and talking about what his life would be like when he was a famous bull rider.

I laughed, humorously, when I thought about the dreams that teenage girl had about joining the teenage boy while he made those cloud-whispered dreams a reality.

I gasped with pain over the memory of the day that teenage girl witnessed why the teenage boy no longer stood with his shoulders stretched with pride and strength.

I relived the pain the day that teenage girl saw the teenage boy's father hit him with a riding crop.

I felt the heartbreak like it had just happened when that teenage girl decided to throw caution to the wind and try to get those smiles back. The day she decided that she had to get him back before he left forever.

I cried remembering the words of the teenage boy when he broke and destroyed the teenage girl's ability to believe in dreams.

I had to sit down when I remembered the loneliness the teenage girl felt long after the teenage boy had left.

I couldn't breathe when I felt that loneliness amplify as the now young woman experienced when she lost both her parents, wishing and praying that the young man she missed deeply would return and help her heal.

I smiled through the tears when I thought about the young man's family helping her heal instead—even as she continued to long for him.

I replayed the years the young woman spent building

new dreams around her business. Opening her heart only a few times, but never letting another young man close enough to touch it.

I watched a slide show of years pass by as the young man and woman grew older. The woman now seeing him only at a distance, but feeling the void that the losses through the years created in her soul.

I looked at the woman's reflection in the oven built by her new dreams with tears streaking down her face as she recalled the last month of her life. A turmoil of emotions since the man had returned to her and revealed things she never knew.

By the time I had climbed into my Jeep to head home, I knew that if I wanted to move on with my life—truly move on—I had to do it knowing that I had tried. All of the pain I had relived during the hours spent baking still raged strong, but when I remembered how I felt in that man's arms, new hopes filled my heart.

I left feeling a sense of determination to move forward with a newfound strength that I found at the bottom of the barrel of my emotions.

I had nothing to lose but everything to gain.

With that in mind, I knew that the first thing I would do when the sun started to wake would be to go to him. Regardless of what happened after that, at least I would know that I tried, and gave it my all. I had let go of a lot of the pain I felt through the years in the course of a few days, and now it was all riding on what happened next. I would either be free of it all, or I would be using that residual pain to move on.

Either way, by tomorrow morning I would be facing Maverick again. I couldn't tell if I was excited as hell, or terrified down to my bones.

Or a little bit of both.

When I get back to the house, I feed Earl and go directly into the shower to wash the clinging emotional weight off my body. I have no idea what might happen when I finally sit down and talk to Maverick. He said he felt something that night we were together, but I also know that the only reason that night even happened was because we were both riding high on our emotions and maybe a little of the power of feelings long suppressed. A small part of me couldn't forget the fact that he didn't even recognize me when he first saw me, so a little nagging part in my mind wonders if he even realized it was *me* that night we were together or if I was just another way to use something—*someone*—to forget.

I know it's stupid, but I guess it's part of me trying to set myself up for every possible situation that I might face tomorrow. Using the darkness of tonight to cast out my fears and concerns to better prepare me for whatever might come. I don't want to go to him with my mind already set on failure, not when so much is riding on this.

Given what Quinn told me today, I know there is a lot about him and his life I don't know. It breaks my heart that as close as I've been to the Davis family, I had no clue it was as bad as it was for them. Their mama's departure was something that was wildly debated all over town, but

I never knew the real reasons behind it. I knew Buford Davis was a hard man. With my own eyes I had witnessed him hit Maverick once, only once. Never did I even think it could have been so much worse than that—the reality, though, makes it so much worse than it had been and it had already been hard to stomach. I had heard him more times than I care to count emotionally throwing punches at everyone, but I never once saw the things she talked about.

It was the unknowns that worried me the most. I know Maverick is more complicated than I ever could have dreamed. Those unknowns are what kept us apart. All I can do now is hope that I know what to do once it all finally comes to light.

I step out of the shower, drying off before throwing on panties and an old faded T-shirt. I brushed my hair out before braiding it and finishing up my nighttime routine. I feel so much better after that long shower, almost as if the water cleansed my doubts and revitalized my confidence.

But my stomach is still in knots over the heaviness of this past week catching up with me—the fog that had settled over me the past few days has lessened my appetite so much that now I don't even feel the hunger pains I know I should have. I can't even remember the last meal I had. I might feel better about what's to come, but that doesn't mean my belly isn't a ball of nerves.

Walking out of my bedroom, I grab my Kindle off my dresser and head to my favorite chair in my library. Sleep isn't going to come easy tonight, so I might as well keep my mind occupied with a good book. Escape to the fantasy that always helped me forget about the things around me. I hadn't made two feet out of my bedroom before the sound of my doorbell is echoing through the house.

Earl barrels past my feet, weaving between my legs in his hurry to get to the front door. I swear, it's moments like this that have me convinced he has some sort of species confusion and thinks he's canine. I drop my Kindle to reach out and steady my swaying body against the wall. Instead of picking it back up, I leave it in place when the bell chimes again.

Earl turns his head, his beautiful eyes looking at me with impatience, and his long bushy tail swishing behind him as if to tell me to hurry so he can meet whatever new friend is waiting for him. Yes, because it's so hard to believe that whoever it is, is there for me.

"Yeah, yeah, I'm going as fast as I can, baby," I tell him, stepping around him and placing my hand on the knob, waiting for him to move so I can open the door. I end up having to push him to the side with my foot, his furry body making the slide easy against the hardwood, and I smile when he gives me a hiss of irritation for taking his spot away.

That smile dies when I look up and see the shadowed person standing on my front porch.

"Evenin', darlin'," he drawls, his accent thick and his voice a low rumble.

The earlier determination I had over moving forward fizzles out as the fear over the unknown bubbles back up. I stand there, struck immobile as he leans against the open screen door, one long arm braced against the frame. It takes me a second, but I finally click my brain back on.

"He—hey, Maverick."

"Mind if I come in?"

I jolt, feeling my cheeks heat with my lack of manners. "Uh, yeah."

I step back, losing my footing when I topple over Earl. My arms windmill as my eyes widen. I hear him hiss, but before my ass hits the ground, Maverick moves with a swift grace someone his size shouldn't be able to master.

"Whoa, there," he rumbles, holding my body up with his hands clamped firmly against my biceps.

My hands fist the fabric of his button-down shirt, the dark blue material at eye level stretched tight against his muscular build. I force myself not to think about how easy it would be to curl my hands into the slots between the buttons and pull it apart.

My body hums, being this close to him making it come alive.

And my stupid broken hooha suddenly rights itself and screams with ecstasy.

"Nice shirt," he whispers huskily.

I look up from the top button I had been studying, loving the hint of golden skin that is peaking out the top, and meet his stormy green gaze. Without his ever-present hat, I'm graced with a clear view of his face.

His very expressive face.

"Did Quinn get that for you?"

"Huh?" I ask, confused.

"The shirt, darlin'. Did she get that for you?"

I look down and groan. I take a second, remembering when I got it, and then answer him. "No, Maverick. I bought it for myself."

He's silent and I look up. His eyes still reading the print on my shirt. It doesn't take much to realize just how well worn and loved this shirt is. Since the date is printed on it right next to the bold print announcing which rodeo event it was from, he's going to be able to tell a lot by how faded it is for something that's only a year old.

"How, Leighton?" he asks thickly.

"What is it you want to know, Maverick? That could be askin' a lot of different things."

"How did you get that and I didn't see you?"

"I didn't want you to see me. I knew that Quinn and Clay were heading to Vegas for the World Finals. You were at the top of the rankings to win again and I didn't want to miss it, so I went with them. Bought the shirt before I left." I swallow the lump in my throat, remembering the pride I felt for him as he rode. I was screaming his name before I realized what I was doing that night. I could have sworn, even with the roar the crowd was making, that he had heard me too, because right when he climbed off the dirt floor, he looked right toward the section I had been sitting in.

His expression darkens. "You were there?"

"It was the only one in Vegas I made it to. I flew home that night."

"Why didn't you come see me?"

"I saw you, Mav. You didn't want me around, something you had made clear, but that didn't mean that I didn't still crave seeing you . . . even if it was only for eight seconds in a crowded arena."

He drops his head, his chin hitting his chest, and I try to back up when his thick black hair tickles my face. The light from my living room makes his hair shine, and I feel my palms itch when I remember just how soft those strands feel when I'm running my hands through them. His fingers tighten around my arms when I make another move to back up.

"I wish you would have let me know you were there," he whispers.

"Would it have made a difference?" I ask honestly.

He looks up, his eyes bright but full of distress. "I'm not sure."

I make an attempt at a shrug, but his hold on my arms makes it hard. He stands taller, letting go, and I have to tip my head back to hold the connection between our gazes.

"What are you doing here, Maverick?"

"I know it's late, but I've got a lot I would like to speak to you about, if you don't mind." He takes in a gulp of air. "I know I said I'd let you be to figure out what you want to do, but damn if I can let you be, Leighton."

I sigh. "Do you want something to drink?"

"If you've got anything strong, I'll take that—if not, sweet tea."

I nod and turn to walk through the house to the kitchen. I can feel his eyes on me and I have instantly fidgeted with the hem of my shirt. With him here, in my home, I'm very aware of my lack of clothes. But the shirt is long and covers me completely.

Grabbing two shot glasses and the bottle of Jameson, I walk back into the living room and see he's standing by one of my picture-framed-filled bookcases. He doesn't turn to acknowledge that I've returned, but instead continues to study the photographs.

"I was going to come out to the ranch in the mornin'," I tell his back.

He turns, his eyes rounded with shock at my admittance. I give him a weak smile and shrug my shoulders.

"I wanted you to know that. I feel like it's important that you know I *was* coming to you. You kinda stole my chance to make the next move, I guess, but I was comin'. You were right when we spoke last. It's time."

His eyes close and he stands stock-still, breathing harshly, for a long while. "How come you aren't married?" he softly asks, breaking through the silence that had settled around us.

"I'm not sure that's very polite to ask a lady, Maverick." His topic change is confusing, but I'm thankful that he accepted what I told him for what it was—admitting to him that I was ready for whatever is about to come.

One thick shoulder comes up in a shrug, but he doesn't speak. I busy myself with opening the liquor and pouring two heavy shots. I knock one back before dropping the glass and refilling it. When I look back up, he's studying the frames again.

"Marriage doesn't really interest me anymore," I tell him honestly. "I'm happy with my life the way it is."

He turns and looks at me. "Are you? Happy, that is?"

What a loaded question that is. "I've got a very profitable business doing what I love. I have good friends and a roof over my head. I live a simple life, Maverick, but it's a busy one doing what I enjoy. It's fulfilling and I get to spend my days bringing people joy with my pies."

"That doesn't answer my question, Leighton."

"Are *you* happy?" I ask, trying to flip his probing back around on him.

"Not in the slightest."

"Oh." His blunt, abrupt answer catches me off guard, and I shift my feet and motion down to the coffee table and full shots. "Uh, you asked for something strong."

Out of the corner of my eye I see him move before his arm stretches through my line of sight. He bypasses the full glasses and wraps his long fingers around the bottle of Jameson. The top is tossed down on the coffee table before I hear him take a swallow from the bottle. I don't look up; instead, I take both of the glasses before drinking them down as I turn to the kitchen.

Looks like we're drinking from the bottle tonight.

When I walk back in the room, he's still standing where I left him, sipping from the bottle.

"I've missed you," he says gruffly. "Not a day went by that I didn't think about you. I always thought that you would be married with two point five kids by now. You used to always talk about how much you couldn't wait to be a mama. I avoided asking my family, though. I didn't think I could handle it if they told me you were. Made no damn sense to my mind, but I knew if I heard you were married it would have been painful as hell."

"Maverick—"

"I don't think you're happy, Leigh. I really don't. I think you're far from it, and that hits me harder than a punch to the gut. For a woman who always talked about how much she couldn't wait to be just like her own mama, a rancher's wife with a huge family, it's a cryin' shame. But the selfish part of me, the one that lived with a life of what-ifs and regrets, that part of me is damn glad you aren't."

I swallow the thick lump in my throat. "Please, Mav." God, I need him to shut up.

"No, just . . . fuck!" His sudden outburst makes me jump a foot. I watch him take the bottle and swallow deeply. He takes a few more pulls before I get his eyes again. "I fucked up. I know it. You know it. Everyone fuckin' knows it. I need you to understand why I'm standin' here about to beg you to look past all of that and give me a chance to find out what it feels like to find happiness. To give us both that chance, Leighton."

The silence stretches out around us. His normally strong and proud mask slips, showing me the pure desperation he feels while he waits for my next move. Finally, I nod and hold my hand out, pointing at the bottle so he knows what I want. The heaviness of today on top of the emotional roller coaster of this past week is taking a toll on me, but I made the decision today to be strong, and by God, that is what I'm going to be.

17

LEIGHTON

"Yours" by Russell Dickerson

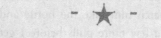

When Maverick sits down on my couch, Earl doesn't waste a second before jumping up into his lap. Maverick startles for a beat before hesitantly petting my big beast. Earl's purrs fill the silence around us and I curl my legs under me and lean back in the chair next to the couch, watching Maverick's hand as he strokes Earl slowly.

I take another big gulp, only to sputter through it when the burn goes down wrong.

"You all right, darlin'?"

I cough a few times. My eyes watering profusely. The alcohol starting to warm my body. "I'm fine."

He nods. "This might take awhile. You should probably pace yourself."

I roll my eyes and take another large swallow, this time managing not to choke on it, and look back at Maverick pointedly.

He smirks. "Or not."

"It's late. Instead of lecturing me on my drinking habits, why don't we get this over with so I can once and for all try to make sense with the confusion running through my mind."

I feel bad when his shoulders slump slightly and he sighs. That came out snappier than I intended, and I instantly wish I could force the words back in. It doesn't do us any good for me to start this on the defensive. I made the decision to see what happens next, with an open mind, and getting frustrated with him will get us nowhere. Earl lifts his body up, his large paws against Maverick's chest, and sniffs his chin before giving him a rub of his whiskers. Leave it to my furry baby to know when someone needs a little comforting.

Traitor.

"You know, when Clay called me about the old man dyin', I was in a bad place. I was in such a bad place that every mornin' when I woke up and looked in the mirror, I started seein' Buford lookin' back at me. I would be just as drunk and angry as I was when I passed out the night before. I hated that so much—becomin' him, I mean. I hated it so much that I would spend the day keepin' myself drunk in order to forget that image. I couldn't break the cycle. I was so damn lost, angry because of it, unable to get over the hump to see a way out. All it took was one call from Clay and I felt somethin' I hadn't felt in a long damn time. Hope. Stupid as it sounds. I know I could have come back without that call, but it was like a rope danglin' down to where I had been sitting at rock bottom." He's so lost in his thoughts, just petting Earl and looking off into the distance, not focusing on anything. I give him the time he needs, knowing that there's more to come.

"I used that to help drive me. Motivate me to put down the bottle and see, for the first time, that I hadn't lost everything. Instead, I was given a new chance to right everything I *thought* I had lost. So there I was, finally sobering up, but even with all that ridin' me, I was still nowhere near leavin' that bad place I had been stuck in. The second I got into Texas, it was as if the hope had disappeared. A feeling of dread over returnin' to Pine Oak had joined the drive. I couldn't stop thinkin' about everything that happened before I left. What I did to you was a big part of it. By the time I got here I was feeling so sorry for myself that I used that and my anger with Buford to turn me back into that person I hate. Him."

I pause, remembering the snarling hellion that had flown at me outside the church the day of Buford's funeral. "You were grieving, Maverick. You were justified in your emotions."

"I wasn't grievin'. Not him, at least. I thanked the good Lord the day I found out he died."

I nod, understanding his words a little better than I might have otherwise, thanks to Quinn. It doesn't matter that Buford had worked hard to try to right his wrongs when he faced his own mortality. Sometimes it really is just too late. Buford did what he could to gain a semblance of respect from his oldest and youngest children—but whenever Maverick's name would come up, he just kept saying that it was a lost cause and to let it be.

What if that's the case here too? Are we a lost cause? Should I just let it be?

The silently asked questions make me pause as my heart speeds up.

"That man hated me, Leigh. Always did. I don't have a single memory of him *not* hatin' me. I didn't find out until I had been gone for about four years that he didn't just hate me because I was my mama's favorite. He didn't hate me because I didn't love the ranch. It wasn't because I wanted to ride. He hated me because when Mama left, she left her bastard son behind. When she left *me* she left *him* with a daily reminder of her infidelity. When it became clear that my callin' was ridin' and not ranchin', I might as well have signed my own death certificate. I found out after my first big win that my biological father was another rider that she had caught the eye of when the rodeo came through Austin. There I was, his bastard, followin' in my real father's footsteps."

He reaches out, leaning over Earl, and my shock-filled eyes drop to his outstretched hand.

"Bottle," he commands.

I mutely hand it over, watching his throat work as he swallows.

"He beat me, Leigh. It wasn't so bad when I was a real little young'un, but when I stopped ridin' around the sheep—things got bad. After that day that I started learnin' the ropes and ridin' the stationary barrel over at Triple R ranch, there wasn't a day that went by that he didn't put his hands on me. I never understood what I'd done wrong. I couldn't figure out how to make it stop.

I hid a lot of how bad it was from Clay and Quinn, but even so they understood that why I left had everything to do with runnin' from him. I knew that it had to be done because every single day that went by, he was breakin' me further. That was when I started trainin' harder and focused on one thing—usin' my talent and gettin' the fuck away from Pine Oak."

I swipe at the wetness under my eyes and keep my silence, letting him say everything he needs to say. Having him opening up like this, letting me in, and showing me a part of him that I know brings him pain has me nervous that one sound or movement might break the spell. My heart continues to break with each word he speaks, but even through that, understanding why he left goes a long way to ease the pain I've carried around like some stupid scar since.

"I found my mama, you know. What a mistake that was. She was so strung out on booze and drugs. She had no clue who I was. She thought I was someone lookin' to score some ass for a couple bucks. It took me almost nine hours to get her coherent enough to even hold a conversation that made a little sense. The second she realized who I was, she just put it all out there. How I was a mistake from one night of fun. She got that taste of the high life and couldn't think of anything else. Stuck around, but even I'm not sure how she did that and still managed to bring Quinn into this world. The second Quinn was in school, though, she was gone. I still can't wrap my mind around the woman I saw as my mama bein' the same one wasted out of her mind on the streets.

She's done so much damage to herself that she might as well be a vegetable."

"Where is she now?" I ask, my throat thick with emotion. He gives a little jolt of shock, almost like he had forgotten I was there. His silence continues as he looks into my eyes, and I silently curse myself for speaking and halting his train of thought.

"In California," he tells me in a sad tone. "She requires constant care now and will remain at the long-term-care facility until she dies. Last I checked she had a grocery list of health issues that wasn't getting any shorter. The doctors are shocked her body hasn't shut down yet, but for whatever reason, she's still breathin'."

My mind fires and I know instantly, without a doubt, that he is the one taking care of her. Even after everything she did to him and his siblings, he can't let her go. "Do you still see her?"

He shakes his head, his blazing green gaze holding me captive. "I haven't been in a year or so. The last time I was there she had to be sedated, she got so upset. All I did was walk into her room and it was like she had seen a ghost. She went insane, Leigh. I decided it was too much, her seein' me, so I keep my distance and make sure she's comfortable."

"I'm sorry, Maverick." And I was. I hated that this was the reality for him and his family. "Clay and Quinn, they don't know all of this, do they?" I ask.

"No. What good would it do? They don't need to see her like that anyway. It's not somethin' I'll ever be able to get out of my mind."

"You should probably let them make that call on their own, honey."

He had looked off in the distance again, but the second the endearment slips from my lips, he jerks his eyes back to my face, studying me. "Maybe. Something to think about," he allows.

"Do they know? About Buford not being your real dad?"

He shakes his head. "They're all I have left, Leigh. Admittin' I'm not their full biological brother would change things. I just know it."

I shift my body before reaching out and taking his large hand in mine. "It wouldn't change a damn thing. They're your family, regardless of the fact that you don't share the same father. I honestly think . . . well, I think it would help them let go of their own pain from the past."

His hand turns, shifting so our palms touch, and his fingers contract against our hold. "I'll add that to the list to think about. How's that?"

With a small smile, I nod.

"You gonna help me with that?"

I feel my brows turn in. "Help you with what?"

His eyes crinkle, a tiny smirk forms on his full lips. "Dealin' with that list when the time comes."

"Yeah, Maverick." I sigh. "Even if I'm just there as a friend to turn to. If you need me, I'll be wherever you need me."

Once again, the silence grows. His eyes continue searching mine, but this time he doesn't look pained—instead, a look of reverence is shining through the bright green depths. I know what is likely to come next, and I'm not sure how I'll handle it. I just know I'm ready.

"Maverick?" I ask, breaking the silent tension. He raises his brow for me to continue. His grasp on my hand still held in his tightens. "Why didn't you just tell me this? You say that you knew how I felt about you, but why was hurting me the only answer? You could have just left . . . you know, without doing that."

He continues to look into my eyes while petting a now sleeping Earl with one hand and sweeping his thumb against the sensitive skin at my wrist with the other. I take a deep breath and try to calm my racing heart, waiting for him to speak.

"No other answer I have could ever make sense of what I thought was my only option back then. I knew that what I felt for you was strong. I was drawn to you, just as you were to me. My whole damn life you were the only one that ever made me feel like I wasn't lost. You came into a room and I didn't feel trapped. You were completely clueless about how I felt, but even without any indication that I returned your feelings, you never hid how you felt about me. I knew if I gave in to the pull I felt to you, I would be here forever, and with Buford around, I couldn't stay. I also knew that on the off chance I got out and was able to keep you in the process, you would have followed me without thought. You would have given up everything you were meant to become and I couldn't let that happen. I was ashamed and felt weak because I had allowed Buford to treat me like that for so long. I didn't think I was worthy of you. In my head, it was better for you to hate me and let me go than to look at me like a coward and one day resent me for stealin' you away from the future you always wanted here in Pine Oak."

"I can't pretend to understand how you came up with that logic, Mav, but you were young and I reckon just trying to find your way out of what you felt was an impossible situation. I can see that now. It doesn't make it hurt any less, but I get it. I never would have looked at you as weak. Ever. I honestly don't think I could have ever resented you, but I can also see why you would think that possible. To be honest, who knows what would have happened?"

It breaks my heart even more knowing that he felt the same pull to me, but left because he didn't feel like he had any other choice. He had been abused for so long that survival mode had kicked in and became the only thing he could focus on, and because of that, it cost both of us so much.

"I should have stayed."

My eyes shoot to his from where they had drifted while I thought.

"Maverick—" I say with a sigh.

"No," he interrupts. "I should have stayed. I should have been strong enough to stick it out. Things could have been so different. For both of us."

"Or we could still be right where we are right now. You can't let yourself think that way because you honestly don't know how our lives would have gone if a different path had been taken. We can't dwell on what could have happened if things were done differently, Maverick. Nothing can change the past. I understand now why you did the things you did. I know that wasn't easy to tell me, but thank you for explaining. I'm not sure that knowing that back then would have changed things. I do know that I would have wanted the best for you—just like I do now—and I really do think you leaving to chase rodeo gold was the best thing you could have done for yourself. Even if that means admitting you did the right thing pushing me away."

He rakes his hands through his hair. "Do you know how hard that is? To just accept the way things went when you know there were mistakes made? To not dwell on the things we wish we could have done different in life?"

I give him a small smile, his eyes going to my lips instantly. "Yeah, I know how hard that is, but it's those mistakes and what-ifs that help mold us into the people we become. It's because of those things you try not to dwell on that you're able to make new decisions for your life as you grow."

He lets go of my hand. I pull it back into my lap, still feeling the warmth of his touch. He picks Earl's big body off his chest and places him on the cushion next to him before standing. My eyes follow his movements. He stops in front of me and holds out his hand. I take it without question, shivering when our skin touches again. My feet hit the rug, and when I expect him to drop my hand, he doesn't. Instead, he brings our joined hands up until they're folded between us. His other hand comes up to my jaw, tipping my head back so I'm looking into his eyes. He's so much taller than I am, but with the way he's bending down, our faces are just a breath away from each other.

"I can't fix the past, Leighton. I can't erase it, no matter how hard I wish I could. Hell, I can't even promise that I'll ever be able to forget it. The only thing I can do is to make sure that each day I live is worth somethin', from this day forward. I could spend the rest of my life stuck livin' for nothin', or I could work my ass off to make sure that I make up for my past mistakes, so I can make sure they become mistakes I learn from and finally find a way to live for *everythin'*."

My breath falters, and had he not been holding me up, I would have collapsed. My hand, held in his, tightens. The other, which had been limp at my side, reaches up and tentatively pushes up his chest until I curl my hand around his neck. His eyes darken. I lick my lips and I feel his arousal jerk at my stomach.

"I'm terrified." My voice comes out as a whisper.

"Me too, darlin', me too."

He closes the distance between us and presses his lips to mine. He doesn't move to deepen the kiss, but instead just holds his mouth there. Our breaths mingling as we stare into each other's eyes. He peppers my lips with a few more closed-mouth pecks before lifting his head, keeping our faces close while he waits for me to speak.

"You're asking a lot, Maverick. You're asking me to forget the past, everything that happened, and take a giant leap of faith. I want to, I do, but—"

"Baby," he starts, looking into my eyes. My heart picks up speed at the endearment he's never used with me. "All I'm askin' is that you give me a chance. Give *us* a chance. It wasn't our time back then, but we wouldn't be back together like this if it wasn't meant to be now. I can't promise that it will be an easy ride, but stick with me and I'll show you that I'm pretty damn good at holdin' on for the long haul."

"What happens when it's time for you to leave again?" Just thinking of him taking off makes my heart clench in despair.

"Leighton, I'm not goin' anywhere."

"You say that now, Mav. Can you honestly say that the urge isn't there? After everything you've just told me, I wouldn't blame you if it was. Plus, ridin' is in your blood. You can't just give that up."

His eyes flash. "Darlin', my last ride was almost two months ago. Too many blows to my head over the years and doctors said I wasn't fit to ride anymore. Even if that wasn't the case, I wouldn't be able to leave you behind. I've had one night with you and I have a feelin' that even forever will never be enough. I've had a lot of time to think about what comes next. Tryin' to find a new direction in my life now that ridin' is no longer an option. It didn't matter which direction I could think of goin', you were always right there with me."

Is he sticking around because he has nothing left to chase? Does he really want to be here, or is this just a fall-back plan now that Buford is gone? My mind races as I try to analyze his words, looking for a hidden meaning. He's telling me everything I've ever wanted to hear, but it feels like it's too good to be true.

Maverick's eyes crinkle as he runs his fingers over the crease between my eyebrows, the one I get whenever something is troubling me. "Stop thinkin' whatever it is that's goin' through your pretty little head, Leighton."

"Why are you staying? Can you tell me that you would have come back had Buford not died?"

He lets out a sigh, his breath fanning against my face. "I was lost, Leigh. I had just been told I could no longer have the only thing I was livin' for anymore. I kept myself angry and drunk, not thinkin' about anythin' because I didn't allow myself to get sober enough *to* think. Would I have come back without his death? Honestly? Not as soon as I did, but I would have come back. I made sure the life I had been livin' was so full of trainin' and ridin' that I didn't give myself time to think about anythin' other than the competition. I wouldn't let myself think about what I was missin' out on. But once the ridin' was gone, and once I crawled out of that bottle I had been swimmin' in, well, darlin', the only thing I had left was to look at the regrets I wished I could take back. So it might have taken me a little while, but I still would have realized that what was missin' was you."

He's telling me everything I want to hear. Things I would have given into just like that, with no thought, years ago, but a decade of pain has the doubt still lingering.

"We don't even know each other anymore." He smirks devilishly, and memories of our one night together flood my mind, making my cheeks heat. "Don't say it. Don't you dare. I'll amend that. We don't know each other well enough anymore to even know if we're compatible." That smirk turns up a notch, his perfectly straight white teeth flashing at me. "Jesus Christ," I grumble. "We don't know each other as the adults we've become is what I'm tryin' to say, Maverick Austin Davis, get your head out of the gutter. We can't make a decision this big based on the fact that we're combustible between the sheets."

"Best I remember there weren't any sheets involved."

I lift my hand and slap him lightly against his pec. He laughs. A carefree expression takes over his face that I haven't seen since we were younger. Long before the innocence of a child's mind vanished and reality took hold.

"You didn't even know who I was when you got back in town," I whisper. I can't help the sadness I still feel over that. I might have brushed it off with Quinn, but deep down that hurt more than I care to admit. I would have recognized him in a dark room, and the fact that he couldn't do the same, even after all he just admitted, hurts.

I watch his eyes work. Their hold on me paired with having him this close almost make me forget what I just said. He struggles with his words, I can tell because his mouth parts a few times before closing, as though he's working out what to say. His brow furrows, his lips thin, and he swallows thickly, all the while just looking into my eyes.

"You have to understand, Leighton, when I tell you I was in a bad place . . ." He trails off, his hold on the hand between our bodies tightening almost painfully. His eyes continue to search mine. "I was blinded by that. I had so much anger burnin' inside me. Not just about being called back for his funeral, but also because I had been strugglin' for a long damn time drunk, angry, and a whole lot scared. I didn't know what was comin' next, and for someone that always knew what he was doin', flyin' off the handle filled me with fear. Too many emotions fightin' for the top spot inside me and I couldn't see a damn thing past that. Like I said, it blinded me. I've got no other excuse for that, darlin', but I can tell you now—had I been in my right mind, no damn way I would have been able to step into a room and not realize who was standin' right in front of me."

My lips pinch, and I have to fight myself not to fly off with a smart-ass comment. I almost win. Almost. "Yeah, well . . . I don't exactly have the same little boy body that I did when you saw me last, so I guess it makes sense that it was easy to forget me when that was the last memory you had."

Anger flashes bright across his face, and his nostrils flare. "I told you I'm sorry and I regret what I did to you back then. I explained to you why I hid my true feelings for you behind those harsh lies, but if you are going to keep holdin' that between us, we're gonna get bucked off before we can even climb in the saddle." His tone is low but lethal.

"I'm sorry," I hush, looking down in shame.

"Don't be sorry, Leigh. You're allowed to be mad still. I haven't proven to you that I can be trusted in what I'm sayin', but I mean it—if you can't find a way to let it go, we don't stand a chance."

I nod, afraid to look back into his eyes.

"You say we don't know each other anymore, but you'll always be the same girl I've always wished was mine. Your hair is still the same color of the fields when the wheat is blowin' in the wind. Those eyes look just like the blue-bonnets that grew behind your house—so deep blue they almost look purple. I've never seen another person with eyes like yours. When you're mad, you still bite your bottom lip and pull your brows in. It almost looks like you're just thinkin' hard, but you always used to do that when you were tryin' to keep from sayin' somethin' you couldn't take back. Your freckles still refuse to go away, even under a layer of makeup. I could keep goin', but judgin' by the way those eyes I love so much are waterin', I'm thinkin' you're wantin' me to shut up." He laughs deep in his chest, the vibrations tickling against my hand.

"You forgot to mention, I grew . . . well, I grew up."

"Yeah, darlin', you did, but you're still just little Leigh to me. I want *you*, Leigh. I want what's inside of you that has always pulled me in and made me feel like I was the only man in the world. I want the peace that you bring about me, calming me all the way to my core with just a glance. I want your laughs, your tears, your smiles, your snores, and your moans. I want everythin' that I didn't dare think I deserved to hope for when I lost you because I was too focused on my own selfish pride. I want to know that everythin' I did in the past, all those regrets, don't mean I lose you all over again. I want you, regardless of what the outside looks like, darlin'. I promise you, I will make sure not one damn day goes by that you don't know without a single doubt that I'm here fightin' for you . . . fighting for *us*. I want you now, same as I wanted you then, because it's our time to have what we were always meant to have. Each other."

"This scares me so much, Maverick. If I let myself believe that you're being honest with me . . . I'm givin' you the power to crush me again."

"God, sweetheart, I know, but you aren't alone. Give us a chance, Leigh. I hear you, darlin', I do. Come on and go for a ride with me and let me show you how good I am at makin' sure nothin' bucks us off. We'll take the time to get to know each other as adults and see where it goes from there. Take the time so that you can truly see what I'm tellin' you is the truth."

"Are you asking me to go steady, Maverick?" I laugh, swallowing down the emotion climbing up my throat at his words, trying to lighten the mood, but the seriousness in his expression makes me trail off until I'm left just staring into his eyes.

"I'm askin' you to give me a chance to make you mine. I'm prayin' you'll give me that so I can prove to you that I deserve to, how did you put it? Go steady."

This is it.

This is everything I've ever wanted from him and as frightening as it is to give him the power to hurt me again, I know if I'm the one to turn this away this time I will never be able to move on. I'll always be stuck living with doubts, wondering what my life would have been like. There's a reason that, for ten years, I have always held on to the hope that one day I would have another chance with the only man I've ever loved.

I have to try.

I have to open myself up and knock down the walls I had built to protect myself from feeling pain again because if this truly does pay off, I know with the same certainty that the sun will rise in the east and set in the west and that what we will have together will be the most beautiful kind of love that ever did exist.

"Oh—oh." I clear my throat. "Okay, Maverick," I whisper softly.

He's quiet for so long that I have to wonder if he even heard me, but then I see his throat working and the emotions flying behind his eyes.

"Okay, darlin'," he finally says, and without warning, takes my mouth in a kiss meant to brand my soul. Deeply he takes my mouth, his tongue moving slowly against mine in a hypnotizing dance. When he pulls back, I struggle to open my eyes. Both of us are breathing heavily.

"I'm askin' this, prayin' you tell me to stay, but know I'll respect whatever you want, Leigh. This is the beginning of us and I don't want to rush you. I've got all the time in the world to feel myself inside your body, but tonight I really just need to be near you. Do you want to be alone tonight? You have my word, if you let me stay, I will be a complete gentleman. I just need to know this is real and you're really here, willing to give me another chance, Leigh."

"Stay," I tell him without hesitation, and my heart that was already thundering from his kiss further picks up speed. He nods, his dazzling smile reaching all the way to his eyes, something I haven't seen in a long, long time. He gives me a small, brief kiss before releasing his hold on me to look around the room. He grabs the remote from the table before sitting back on the couch. Earl gives him a one-eyed glance before going back to sleep. He gives the cat one long stroke before holding his hand out for me. I shuffle my feet forward and lift one very unsteady hand to his. His lips twitch, but that smile doesn't dim in the least, before he just pulls me silently down to the couch. I curl into his side, resting my head against his chest. His arm wraps around me and pulls me even tighter against him.

It feels like heaven.

That was the last thing I thought before a peace unlike anything I had ever felt washes over me and I fall asleep in his arms, the loneliness that had been dragging me down for so long lifting with each beat of his heart under my ear.

18

MAVERICK

"Good-bye, Earl" by Dixie Chicks

I'm afraid to move.

I've been awake for a handful of hours, but fuck if I'm going to move an inch and ruin this moment. She might have agreed to move forward and see what comes of it, but I know that acceptance comes on shaky grounds.

I've spent the past two weeks or so racking my mind, trying to think of how I can prove to not only my family, but Leigh as well, that I'm not going anywhere. To find a way to make Pine Oak the home I never thought it could be. I know now, with Leighton in my arms, that "home" won't be hard to find anymore.

Quinn says everything I've done since returning screams temporary, and honestly, now that I'm forced to really take a good look at things, she's right. I might have been thinking about how to make my own way here, but I've been doing it while keeping my guard up.

I came back unsure of what I would find. How I would feel. A lot of that had to do with me still struggling to find my place after losing my rodeo career, but I know a big chunk was because so much uncertainty was floating around the air. I could feel the unfinished business slap against my skin the second I crossed the county line.

Now however, after my talk with Clay today and the woman in my arms tonight, I know I'm headed in the right direction. I don't think I'll ever feel like the Davis ranch is home, not when I've felt truly at peace only with Leighton.

It wasn't until the other day that I realized I didn't lose everything just because I couldn't ride anymore. In that moment, everything became clear. I didn't feel lost. Everything started to click together.

I'm on my way to having it all again, and hopefully, God willing, I'll have it with this girl always by my side. This is my second chance at everything, and I'll be damned if I fuck it up.

I know I still have to prove to everyone that I mean what I say. When I tell them I'm here for good, they don't have to worry that the urge might strike to flee. By putting down steel-enforced roots, there will be no way to deny I've come home for good.

I'm sick of living with my mistakes.

It doesn't escape my notice that the one place I've been too scared to come back to is the one that finally made me feel like I have a purpose again. The dust around me has settled and I can finally see the clear path that's been waiting for me. I thought I had lost it all when I was told I couldn't ride anymore, but if I play my cards right I won't have lost a damn thing.

I will have gained everything.

There's no doubt in my mind that this is where I'm meant to be.

I let out a deep but content breath, and Leigh shifts in my hold. Her body curling more into mine as she hikes one bare leg up and over my hips. Her full breasts pressing against my ribs. I fight a groan when she connects with my still-straining erection.

When she had fallen asleep last night, I moved only enough so that we were both stretched out on the couch, not allowing any distance between us. Her back to the couch and her body pressed tight to my side. She had hardly moved all night.

My arm had fallen asleep somewhere around one in the morning.

My neck had started feeling like someone was stabbing it around three.

My back was screaming in protest from not being able to move.

My cock had been hard since I walked into her house and her wildflower scent curled up my nose, branding my senses.

I was in pain, all over.

And I had a smile on my face the whole time because fuck if that pain didn't feel like the most beautiful thing in the world. I had my little slice of heaven back in my arms and there was no doubt that I would fight to keep it right here.

I look up at the ceiling fan above us, the blades moving slowly, but just enough to fill the room with a nice gentle breeze. There is still so much left to prove to Leigh. She might have said she's giving us a chance, but I know part of her is still waiting for me to jump in my truck and hightail it outta here.

I hope that the plans I've set in motion with Clay help prove to her that I'm here to stay. I want her to know I'm doing all of this because I want to be here—with her—and not for any other reason. Not just because my rodeo career is over. Not because my siblings want me home. Not because the old man is gone.

They might have jump-started getting me here, but they aren't the reason I sobered up and hit the highway.

She is.

She was my compass when I was lost without direction.

She was the pull I always felt to come home but never had the balls to try, knowing that it might be too late.

She was my biggest regret, but she will be my biggest accomplishment—God willing.

I close my eyes, a smile on my face, and the only girl I've ever wanted in my arms. My thoughts don't have anything to do with rodeo fame anymore. I don't see myself as a lonely cowboy that had pushed everyone away. I'm not consumed with fear-driven anger. There's no more wall to keep out the things I had always been too afraid to hope for.

No, not this time.

All I can see now is a blond-haired, blue-eyed woman that still, after all this time, looks at me like I hung the fuckin' moon. I see fields of bluebonnets, children laughing, and a happiness that I never thought possible. The crushing weight of the anger I've carried around for so long falls to the wayside when I feel her small arm curl around my chest, pulling herself closer into me.

I truly had been living for nothing, but right now I know I have a shot at everything.

Finally.

- ★ -

I come awake with a jolt. I had been in that space between consciousness and sleep when I realized I didn't feel Leighton's body against mine anymore. The panic that rushed through me in that moment was powerful enough to feel like it could have stopped my heart.

Coming up to a sitting position on the couch, my body screaming in protest the whole time, I look wildly around the living room. There's no sight of her. I scan the room, searching, my heart pounding wildly. I hunch, my elbows on my knees, and look down at my socked feet on her rug. I don't remember taking off my boots last night.

I hear movement and look up from the ground, not moving my body. Her large cat—at least I think that thing is a cat, I didn't want to offend her last night by asking—struts into the room, coming from the back of the house. It looks at me with its odd yellow-green eyes. I feel like it sees right through me. We continue our staring contest, the only movement from the cat/beast coming from the hairy tail swooshing behind it. I watch the feline jump on the coffee table before walking to the edge, stopping when its face is right in front of mine, just continuing to stare at me.

It's creepy as fuck.

"You're awake."

I nod, not wanting to look away from the beast in front of me and give it the upper hand. I'm also not entirely sure it couldn't claw my face off. Best to keep my eyes on this thing. "This is a house cat?"

I hear her laugh softly; then, to my shock, the couch move a bit as she settles behind me, climbing right over the back of the couch like it's the most normal thing to do. Her comfort around me eases some of the trepidation I had felt when I woke up alone. I feel a little guilt that I instantly thought the worst when I didn't see her in here, but let the thought vanish when I feel her move behind me. Her legs spread as her knees roll across my back. She shifts, I feel it in the moving cushions, and I wait for her to settle. When she leans forward, though, you could have blown me over in shock. Her chin hits my shoulder, one arm wraps around my torso, and the other reaches out toward the cat/beast.

Her actions and her comfort with me show me that she meant what she said last night about giving us a chance. She isn't holding back. If I had to guess, she feels the need just like I do to be as close as possible.

"His name's Earl and he's my sweet baby. He eats too much, hogs the bed, and sometimes snores, but I love him. He's just curious about the big man in his space." The smile in her tone relaxes me completely and I lean back into her. She drops her hand from the cat and wraps it above her other arm, holding me to her tightly.

"You named your cat Earl?"

Her soft giggles tickle my cheek. "What can I say? I was going through a Dixie Chicks stage."

I turn my head so that I can see her face. My arms going around her spread legs to wrap them around my body. I'm completely surrounded by her. We're so close that I have to remind myself not to rush this and fuck her right here on the couch. "You do know what that song is about, right?" I joke, rubbing my hands up and down her smooth-as-fuck legs.

Her face lights up with silent laughter. "Yeah. Well, you can thank your sister for that one. She thought it was a great way to remind me that men are stupid or something like that."

I can't help it. I laugh, loudly, when I think about my sister helping to name a cat after a man named Earl that did some shitty things to women and ended up being murdered by those same chicks. "Is that so?" I ask, the smile present in my tone. "Well, if it's all right with you, darlin', I'm goin' to have to ask that you leave black-eyed peas off the menu indefinitely."

Those eyes of hers are bright and happy. Her lips pull in for just a second before she loses her ability to keep a straight face. I watch, spellbound, as she throws her head back and laughs. Her wavy hair, no longer bound by the braids she had in last night, moves with her as she continues to giggle.

God, she looks beautiful.

"What time do you need to be in at the bakery?" I ask, having to clear the lump of emotion from my throat before I speak. It's way too early to be telling this girl I love her, even if I want to, but fuck if it almost doesn't just come out. I guess, considering I've felt that way for her my whole life, it shouldn't be too soon, but now isn't the time.

"Jana's got it covered today. I called her twenty minutes ago and asked if she would mind opening by herself and closin' down after lunch. I . . . uh, I thought maybe . . . well, I thought maybe I should stay home today."

"Hey," I say softly when she looks away. She looks back at me, clearly feeling some sort of embarrassment. "What's going through your mind?"

She shrugs. "It feels silly now. I didn't even ask if you had plans today."

"So ask me, darlin'. I know I haven't got the best leg to stand on here, but I want you to be able to tell me what you want without worryin' I'm going to shoot it—you—down."

Silence ticks around us while I wait for her to speak. "I, well . . . I just thought we could spend some time together today. I should have asked you first before assuming that you weren't busy. You probably are. Busy, I mean."

It takes me a second, but I shift our bodies so that she's still straddling my body between her legs, only this time she's sitting in my lap. Her legs folded on the couch, spread wide around my body. Her ass resting midthigh. After guiding her arms up and around my neck, I place mine on her hips, then I pull her forward so that her center is right above the hard ridge of my cock. I couldn't have stopped the deep rumble of pleasure that vibrates from my chest if I'd tried.

Her eyes widen and her fingers push around my neck into the curly hair that is way past needing a cut. I feel her give a little tug, whether it's subconscious or not, and I vow right then and there that I won't cut my hair again until I feel her do that while I've got my head between her legs. Just the thought of her using her hold on my hair to keep my head where she wants it makes me feel like I might come right then and there.

"Let's get something straight right now, sweetheart." My voice is thick with gravity while I speak, but in the position she's in, I have her full attention. "If you want to spend the day with me, all you gotta do is tell me. If I'm busy, I'll do what I can to change that. If I can't, I'll do my best to free myself up as early as I can. All I have to offer you is my word, which isn't something I give without thought, but I'm giving that to you now, Leighton. I've never broken my word once in my life, darlin'. We're both findin' our way here, but we will do that together and without holdin' back. We've lost too much time already because of my bullshit . . . so yes, in answer to your question, I think spending today together sounds real damn good."

"Okay, Mav," she responds, her cheeks pink and her breath coming in harsh pants.

"I've got some stuff I want to talk to you about anyway, but I would rather do that after you've gotten dressed and I'm not fightin' myself not to fuck you right here on the couch in front of this big cat/beast that I'm not entirely convinced hasn't been fuckin' sizin' me up for his next meal."

She giggles.

I take a playful swat at her delicious bottom. "Go get dressed, darlin'. We'll grab somethin' to eat and then I've got some stuff I want to discuss with you."

"That sounds serious," she hesitantly says, the light-hearted expression on her face clearing.

"Hey," I whisper. "None of that. Shit!" She jumps in my lap when my voice rises. "Sorry. I'm tellin' you this, and I really want you to understand what I'm sayin'. I'm goin' to do whatever it takes so that I never see that fear in your eyes again. Yeah, I have somethin' serious I want to talk to you about, but I promise you it's not anything that will cause this heart harm. Trust me to take care of it and you."

"Okay, Maverick. I trust you." Her words are so soft that I almost can't hear them.

"Not completely, but you will."

Her fingers tighten again, tugging on my hair. The tiny bit of fear I had seen cross over her expression clears. She looks at me now with the love I hope to hear her one day confess to me, completely open and unguarded. She allows me to drink in my fill of what she's showing me before closing the distance and pressing her lips to mine. The touch is brief, but no less intimate.

"I trust you, Maverick, but that doesn't mean I'm not scared. I'm working on it, but it's going to take a little more than one night for me to be able to stop worrying that this is all just some dream that I'm going to wake up from only to find you gone again. I just need some time to let myself believe you're really here and offering me everything I ever wanted."

I nod, pressing our lips back together. "That's all I'm askin' for, but I'm tellin' you right now that if this is a dream that we're ever going to wake up from—no matter what, I'm still goin' to be right here, right where I belong. Where I've always belonged."

19

LEIGHTON

"Next Boyfriend" by Lauren Alaina

Maverick didn't tell me much about what we were doing today. All he said was to wear jeans and my boots. It was days like this that you forget summer had already started. It had been a mild May for Texas standards. Even now, with June already halfway over, the temps were still comfortable. It was only a matter of days until we started feeling triple-digit temps, though, and when that happens, I wouldn't be caught dead in jeans.

I throw on a tank top, pull on my favorite jeans, and make quick work of pulling my boots on. I can feel the anxiousness to get back to where Maverick is waiting as my heart kept thundering. I didn't want to be away from him. I know, logically, that I shouldn't feel this intense about him already, but he isn't a man I just met. Sure, we've been apart for ten long years, but when he touches me those years fall away and I feel like the same sixteen-year-old that knew with everything she was that he would be hers forever.

It would be so easy to let my thoughts linger with those fears, doubts, and concerns that had been swimming in there for the past month. It damn sure would be easier, but he isn't the only one who's sick of living with regrets.

This is our second chance. He might have been on to something last night when he said it was our time to take what we weren't meant to have ten years ago. We were meant to come back to each other, I know that deep in my bones, and I'm going to make sure I give this every chance to succeed.

I smile to myself and stand in front of the mirror that is on the back of my bedroom door. "My God, we're going to have a beautiful future," I tell my reflection, letting that declaration fill my body with the knowledge that I'll do everything in my power to make it happen.

I'm all in.

No more looking back. It's time, together with Maverick, to start living for everything.

Maverick's voice calling out through the house makes me smile. "Did you get lost, darlin'? I know from Quinn that you women think you need to spend hours on end in the bathroom doing whatever it is that has you comin' out lookin' just like you did when you went in, but you could knock me on my ass without all that, and Leighton, I'm pretty sure your cat/beast is tryin' to figure out which part of me is gonna taste the best, so please hurry, darlin'."

I snicker to myself. My thoughts going from funny to X-rated with one beat of my heart. "I could probably tell

Earl which would taste the best, if you want me to help him out," I call back before I can stop myself from letting my erotic thoughts out.

I hear a crash in the distance. Silence follows, but not for long. Right when I'm about to open the door and go investigate what is going on, it's pushed open and a panting Maverick is filling the space. His chest is heaving. The now-wrinkled, dark blue button-down that he's had on since he showed up last night is untucked and hanging at his sides, the stark white undershirt pressed tight against his chest. When I'm finally able to move my gaze from its fixation on the bumps his abs make against that white shirt, his expression looks wild.

Wild and out of control with a little bit of panic mixed in.

"Are you okay?" I question, trying to shake the lust-fueled thoughts from my mind. I take a step toward him and he finally comes out of whatever trance had him glued to the spot.

"You can't say shit like that to me, Leigh."

"Uh, shit like what?"

"If you say shit like that, I'm going to forget that I'm supposed to be a gentleman and take things slow. If I let myself forget that, I'm not going to be able to hold back anymore."

I appraise him, dragging my eyes over every mouth-watering inch. "How much slower can we take something that's been building for twenty-six years?"

My words seem to only egg him on. His chest still heaving, but now I can hear the force of his breaths leaving his lips. "Darlin', I'm hangin' by a thread here. I went years without wantin' or needin' another woman. All you have to do is breathe and I feel like I'm goin' to come out of my skin with my need for you. You have no idea how much I want you. I just need you to work with me here. I don't want to screw this up between us by rushin' you to the bed."

Oh, wow.

Logically, I understand what he's saying. I do. Hearing him admit, again, that he hasn't been with anyone in years does something powerful to me. That being said, I wasn't kidding either. You can't rush something that's been more than two decades in the making. "I appreciate that, Mav, I do. But you can't make decisions like that without talking to me. For fifteen years, even with the ten that you weren't actually present, I always wanted you. I've been with two other men in that time and even they couldn't break through the part of me that only wanted to share that with you. So, while I get what you're sayin', I want you to hear me when I tell you I'm sick of wastin' time."

His eyes close and he drops his chin to his chest, looking pained as a groan escapes his lips. I hear him mumbling, but with the way he's standing, I can't make out what his words are. I shouldn't push him, but the memories of our night together a few weeks back have made it impossible for my body not to crave him when he's near.

"I don't want the first day of our ride together to make it look like I only want one thing from you, Leigh. I let the desire I have for you take the lead that night, and as much as I want and need that from you again, you have to let me prove to you that I want more than just to fuck you raw."

"I'm not really sure what to say to that," I tell him, my voice coming out thick and hoarse with want.

"Darlin', give me today. You want to keep pushin' my buttons, do it, but until the day I know you've given me all of you with complete trust with your heart, I'm not goin' there—no matter how much I want it."

I stare at him. "We're not going to have sex?"

He shakes his head.

"Even if I want to?"

He shakes his head again.

"Even if I tie you to the bed and make you?"

His eyes darken.

"It might be hard, to get you on the bed and tied up and all. I mean, you've got almost a foot on me, but I could probably figure it out."

A noise, deep in his throat, rumbles through the air.

"I really want to feel you inside of my body again, Maverick Davis."

And that's what breaks him.

He pushes from his spot with a shove against the hold he had on the doorknob and frame. I don't even have a second to pull a full breath into my body before it's knocked right out by the force of his large frame colliding against mine.

One large hand pushes into my hair to hold my head where he wants it, the other hits me right on the ass, flexing. His mouth crashes against mine in a bruising kiss.

I can't get close enough to him. My hands push up and under the unbuttoned shirt. I drag my nails up his cotton-covered chest and around his neck. With little effort and one hand, he pulls me up his body until my legs are locked behind his hips.

He doesn't move from our spot in the middle of my bedroom. He just continues to kiss me with so much power that I'm half convinced I might melt right here in his arms. It's the most intense, insane kiss I've ever experienced.

When he pulls back, long minutes after he took me in his arms, I'm drunk with pleasure and half a rub against the bulge pressing against my jean-covered center away from coming. His hooded eyes looking deep within mine while pressing his forehead against mine.

"Not until I have your heart, baby."

With that, he presses his lips back to mine briefly before helping me detach myself from his body. No words are spoken, but the expression on his face is full of carnal desire. There's no doubt in my mind that by walking away and denying himself what we both want that it's costing him greatly.

I want so badly to run after him and tell him my heart is his, just so he'll take me right here and now, but I know that I still have the tiniest bit of fear still inside me that he's going to leave again, regardless of what he tells me. I'm not sure what it's going to take to convince myself otherwise, but I know until that doubt is gone, I won't be able to give him all of me.

And it looks like that means I'll have to do without all of *him*, for the time being.

Lord have mercy.

An hour and a whole lot of heated glances and stolen kisses later, we're in his truck and headed out to the main road. He hasn't spoken much and I'm a little worried I've made him mad with my failed seduction attempt. I look over at him, his Stetson now back on his head, and wish I could see his eyes clearly. Judge what's on his mind.

We were close as kids. We grew apart, but we were still as close as teenagers can be when one is secretly in love with the other—or I guess, now that he's opened up to me, both are secretly in love with each other. His moods were never hard to gauge with one look into his eyes, but what was going on in his mind has *always* been a secret. I realize the only way I'm going to know for sure what he's thinking is to ask. It almost comforts me knowing that part of him hasn't changed, regardless of how annoying it still might be.

Don't be a baby, Leighton. Communicate. Tell him what's on your mind.

Easier said than done. I look back over at him, his forearm flexing as he steers the truck. The only way we're going to move forward is by doing it together and without constantly fearing the next unknown move. I know this, but damn if I can't get my mouth to move.

"I'm sorry," I tell him long minutes later, softly, but loud enough to be heard over the hum of his large tires against the asphalt. There. I did it.

He looks over, reaching off the steering wheel long enough to tip his hat up, giving me his eyes. "For what?"

"I shouldn't have pushed you."

He looks back at the road, not speaking.

"I just want you to know that, while I'm sorry I pushed you, I don't regret it or what I said. I want you to know that. I mean, I understand if you aren't ready."

I see his shoulders move as he gives a few silent chuckles.

"Well, you don't have to laugh at me. This is hard enough to get out as it is, cowboy."

"I'm not laughing at you, darlin'."

"Then what's so funny?" I snap, losing my patience and throwing my hands up in the air.

His shoulders continue to move. "It's funny that you think I'm not ready. I've already been inside you, darlin', and I was ready to get back in there the second you came around my dick. It has not one damn thing to do with me not being ready."

"You don't have to be crude."

"I'm not, Leigh. I'm being honest with you. It's not that I'm not ready, it's that *we* aren't ready. I want you to believe me when I tell you that I'm here for good, and until I can prove that to you, I'm not taking it there. I don't want to build what we're starting with a foundation of just sex, even if it's the best sex I've ever had."

"Such a charmer." I laugh. "I hear what you're saying,

but how are you going to judge when we hit this invisible point of acceptance in our relationship?"

"No clue, Leigh. I reckon we'll both know when we get there. It might be a week, might be a month, hell—it could take less or more than both of those, but until I stop seein' you glance at me with worry that it might be the last time in your eyes, I'm goin' to keep tryin' to prove to you that I'm here for good."

20

LEIGHTON

"Poison & Wine" by the Civil Wars

"**Y**ou know, we could have just walked."

Maverick laughs, his hand tightening around mine. He doesn't speak, but the silence is comfortable. I've had a smile on my face since he parked his truck and demanded I don't move until he comes to open my door. My smile might be a little manic, but I can't help it. This Maverick—the one I've had since I opened my door last night—is the one I thought I had lost forever. There is no longer a guard up, keeping him from everyone around him. The heaviness he's worn since his late teens isn't anywhere to be found.

He really is giving me all of him.

And all of him is beautiful.

"We could have, but where's the fun in that?"

I look over my shoulder at his truck, the one that was

perfectly clean when we left my house, and my smile grows when I see the amount of mud stuck to it.

"It's been a long time since I went muddin'. Quinn and I used to go all the time, but then things at the shop picked up for her and the PieHole kept me busy . . . we just hadn't found time. I forgot how much I loved it."

"I have claw marks on my arm that tell me a different story, darlin'," he says with a laugh.

"Oh, hush. That ride just took me by surprise."

His deep, bellowed laughter rings out around us, and I feel like my heart might explode. When was the last time I saw this? His unabashed hilarity. I don't even care that I'm the butt of his laughter. I would gladly get back in the truck, take the trail, and scream all over again.

And boy, did I scream.

I completely get why he's laughing.

Saying I was taken by surprise is a *big understatement.* You would have thought I was about to come out of my skin the first big mud hole he hit. And true to his words, when I look at his forearm, there are bright red nail marks present.

"You done, cowboy?" I smile.

He holds up his other hand, his shoulders still shaking. I just lift a brow and wait for him to stop, my smile growing as the seconds tick by.

"Do you have any idea what you do to me?" he suddenly asks.

I shake my head.

He closes the distance between us. "Darlin', if that's the kind of reaction I get from a surprise ride through the mud, I can't wait to see what happens when we really get dirty."

My jaw drops. "Maverick, I'm going to need you not to say stuff like that when you've made it clear you're not going to do anything about it."

His free hand comes up and cups my jaw, his expression shifting. His eyes darken, as his smile turns mischievous. "Soon," he whispers with promise.

"Yeah, yeah."

"Promise me, when we get there, I'll get those claws back while you scream like that again. This time in my ears, though."

I groan, a little annoyed and a whole lot turned on. Shifting my feet, I try to ease some of the tension between my legs. "You have *got* to stop talking like that."

One side of his lips turns up and he winks. "That's not a promise I'm willin' to make."

I narrow my eyes. "Then do something about it."

"I'm workin' on it, darlin'. You keep puttin' these thoughts in my head, though, and I can't help but use them to build this up so it's the best damn ride you've ever had."

"*God*," I say with a gasp. "Stop."

"Come on," he chuckles. His eyes still hold the passion I had just seen blazing, but his tone is playful rather than seductive. When he turns from me, he has to pull my arm softly to get my feet working again, my mind still thinking about the possibility of other surprise rides we will take together.

I have no doubt the claws will come out and he'll get me screaming again.

It takes me a second, my mind still fuzzy, but when we stop walking a few minutes later, I realize where we are. I know, if the trees weren't blocking my view, I would see my house just to the west of where we're standing. A few hundred acres in the other direction is the Davis ranch.

And in the middle of it all is an achingly familiar field that I know still blooms bright in the spring with the most beautiful patch of bluebonnets around. My father had planted them years and years ago, a gift for my mother when she mentioned how much she wished we had them closer to our family land.

With spring over, now the field waits with weeds and grass, for the next time it'll be painted in stunning color. If I close my eyes, I can see the beauty that will be back next year.

It's one of my favorite places in the world.

Or it was, long ago.

When I'm finally able to drag my eyes from the patch of land spread out before us, and look at Maverick, he's so still. His eyes roaming over my face, waiting with rapt attention to see my reaction to where he's brought us.

"Do you know why I brought you here?" he questions, his serious tone breaking me free from the trance my memories held over me.

I swallow thickly. "It's been a long time since I came out here, Mav."

He drops my hand, then lifts up and removes his hat. When he pushes his hand into his thick hair, I take the time to really look at him. By all accounts, he looks relaxed, but I know better. The dusting of stubble covering his jaw can't hide the way it's ticking as whatever's going on in his mind plays out. I don't need to see his eyes to know he's working through the words he wants to say. After a few silent seconds, he squares his shoulders and places his hat back on his head.

"Do you remember coming out here with me?" he asks softly.

I nod. "Of course I do."

"I think the last time we were here I had just turned fourteen, maybe fifteen. Quinn had come home around lunch after spendin' the weekend at your house. I remember because I had just taken a bite of my sandwich when I got the old man's hand against the back of my head. He knocked me so hard just for askin' if he would take us to the old drive-in movie place on Buckley that night that I saw damn stars go off in my head. I was used to bein' on the receivin' end of his anger, but I still haven't got a clue what set him off that day. Quinn had just walked in a few minutes before talkin' about how beautiful the fields over here looked now that the blue- bonnets had started bloomin'."

"Mav." I try to stop him, hating to hear how bad things had been for him.

"Gotta get it all out, Leigh."

I nod, taking the few steps toward him to grab his hand.

"I knew two things in that moment. My head hurt like a bitch, but I didn't feel a thing when I thought about this field. About you. I dropped my food in the trash and slammed the door behind me, tearin' ass out of there without even speakin' a word. Something inside me had to get here. I just had to. Couldn't explain it to you if I tried."

"I remember that day." I'd noticed him wincing in pain a few times but hadn't wanted to bring it up, worried about breaking the spell of him just being with me. "You were so mad."

"Yeah." He grunts. "I *was* until I got here and you were just runnin' around lookin' up at the sky with the biggest fuckin' smile on your face. Your hair was a lot longer back then and I swear to God you looked like a fuckin' angel with it dancin' behind you. I might have been mad, but when you stopped and gave me that smile, the rage racin' through me just vanished."

I think back to that moment, the same one that began our weeks of sporadic meet-ups in the same spot. He always looked like an enraged bull when he would ride up on one of their four-wheelers, but the second he sat his butt in the dirt, it was almost as if a calm had taken over him.

"I can even tell you how many times I came back to this very spot," he tells me, looking away from me to point behind his shoulder. When his eyes meet mine again, they don't look nearly as troubled as they did minutes before. "Come on." I get a small smile before he guides me a few feet behind him.

He looks around for a second before he drops to the ground, pulling me down with him. We sit, much like we used to, with the wildflowers surrounding us. I don't wait for him to speak; instead I drop to my back, look up into the sky, and let the years fall away from us. He clears his throat and I feel him moving to lay next to me, placing his hat on the ground next to him before taking my hand in his. I don't take my eyes off of the clouds. Even back then, I didn't take my eyes off of the clouds. Part of me always thought that if I did, he wouldn't keep talking.

"This was the first time I ever told anyone about ridin'. The first time I vowed, out loud, to leave this town and be the best damn rider the rodeo had ever seen. You didn't say a thing, but when I said I would be leavin', you held my hand so tight I almost checked to see if it was broken. Each time we came out here, you would change. You started lookin' at me differently. I think I knew, even then, that you would have done just about anythin' to help me make my words a reality. You never said anythin', just let me get it all out, but I could see it in your eyes. If I would have asked, you would have left this town with me. And you wanted me to ask."

I blink wildly to keep the tears from escaping at his words.

"Just started middle school, not even old enough to know what the hell you were thinkin' about, but still you would have done that."

"Yeah," I respond thickly.

"The last time I came out here, do you remember what you said to me?"

I shake my head, trying to recall the worlds of a love-drunk teenager.

"You said"—he pauses, and then looks over at me— "Maverick Davis, you're going to be the best rider in the whole entire world and I'm going to be there for every single ride yellin' for you so loud they'll hear me back home."

I have to close my eyes; the battle I had been winning with my tears is lost, and I feel them roll down my cheeks and into the dirt under me. "You didn't come back out here after that." My words sound just as pained as that teenage girl had felt when he never came back out to the wildflower field.

"I didn't. That was the day that I realized I had to do whatever it took to make sure you were able to find your own dreams and grow without me draggin' you down the dark path I was stuck on."

"You changed so much after that spring. That boy I knew was gone in just a blink of an eye."

He moves, and I turn my head to see him leaning up with his elbow on the ground, looking down at me with regret in his eyes. "It was one of the hardest things I ever did. I know now that I could have gone about things differently, but to a desperate kid, that was all I could see. No matter how much I wished differently, I couldn't tear you away from this place. Not when you loved it so much. I had to let you find yourself."

"Why did you bring me back out here?" I sniff, trying to rid my mind of those painful memories.

"Because even though this place eventually didn't hold the same feelings as it did at first, it still is a place that I look at fondly, knowin' how close we were at the time. I sat here and made plans for my future. I looked up at the sky while we were side by side, flowers all around us, and each word out of my mouth I used over the years as a promise I was unwilling to break."

The hand not holding his weight comes up. He brushes

his fingertip across my forehead, moving some of the hair in its path. "It only seemed right that I bring you back to the same place I made all those grand plans years ago and give you new ones. New dreams for a future that, this time, we'll be buildin' together. Tell me, why did you sell this land to Clay?"

"What? I don't understand." His question makes my mind pause, still stuck thinking about his reasons for bringing us here.

"When you sold him your land, why didn't you keep this part of it?"

I sit up and his hand falls, the piece of hair he had been playing with landing in my eyes. I roughly swat at it and then turn my head to look down at where he's still lying. He holds my gaze, but moves to sit as well.

"You have to understand, while this place was always special for me because of you, it also held a lot of memories of my parents. In time, all it did was remind me of everything that I had lost. This is the first time I've been here in almost eight years."

"Why?"

I let out a puff of air. I feel another tear fall, but he reaches out and brushes it away before I can.

"When they died so suddenly, it felt like I had lost everything. One car accident and poof, they were gone. I had been taking classes online, working to get my business degree, with plans of helping Daddy around here. Of course, that all changed when they were gone. I wasn't really in a good place, but it was because of that loss that I was able to find my new path. During that time I realized being here, running the ranch and all, wasn't what I wanted. And to be honest, it was too painful to come out here and not only remember them . . . but you as well. I just couldn't hold on to it, but I also didn't want it to be gone. I knew Clay wouldn't sell it to anyone else. So, I guess, in my haste to forget, I got rid of all those memories at once."

"When did you open the PieHole?"

"A few years after they were gone. When I was in the kitchen, the smells of Mama all around me, I didn't feel so alone. It was my way to make new memories without having the pain of the old ones."

"So," he says, reaching out to grab the hand closer to him. "You sold it, but you did it in a way that you could still hold on to it?"

My smile wobbles, his words washing over me. "I guess I did. I didn't do it with that in mind, but when you put it that way, yeah . . . I guess so."

"I'm glad that Clay made sure this wasn't lost. I know your parents meant a whole lot to you, Leigh. I'm sorry I wasn't here to help you through their loss."

I shake my head. "It was a long time ago, Maverick. Don't carry that on your shoulders."

"It was, but I know you don't miss them any less because that time has passed."

He squeezes my hand and looks from my face to the land around us. I use the break in our heavy conversation to get ahold of my emotions.

"I talked to Clay for a long time yesterday. I realized that I've been tellin' y'all since I got back that I was here to stay, but I hadn't done shit to make y'all see that. I knew he had this land, he told me when he bought it, but it wasn't until yesterday that I realized he did that to help me just as much as you."

"How do you figure?"

"He made sure you didn't leave. I think he knew that our time was going to come and he did what he could to keep you here . . . while I made my way back to you."

"I think you're reachin'," I tell him smartly.

"Nah, darlin', it all makes sense now. You'll see. Tell me, where do you see us in a few years?"

Well, if that isn't a loaded question. "Honestly, I haven't let myself think that far in advance, Mav. I'm still wrappin' my head around the fact that you're back in my life—in the way I've always wanted you to be."

This time his smile doesn't hold the heavy sadness that our chat had created. His eyes dance. "Why don't you let me help paint that picture for you?"

"Give it your best shot, cowboy."

"I asked Clay to let me buy this land from him," he lets out in a rush of words.

My eyes widen. Of all the things I thought he would say, that definitely wasn't one of them.

"I know that ridin' like I did isn't somethin' I can do anymore, but the rodeo is in my blood, Leigh. When I was forced to sit back and look at my life now that ridin' was gone, I knew I couldn't give it up completely. My hope is that, with your blessin', I'll be able to keep that part of my life, but this time I'll be doin' it with you by my side, sharin' this new part of my life, every step of the way."

"I'm really not following you, Maverick." And I'm not. I have no idea what he's talking about. "What does buying this land from Clay help?"

"I want to start instructin'." His words are so full of pride and excitement that I can't help but feel the same buzz tingle over my skin.

"Instructing what?"

"It will take awhile, but eventually I plan on openin' up a school of sorts. I want young men to have a place to learn when they've got big dreams and even bigger talent, but no way of makin' them a reality. I talked to Clay about it and even though he's hesitant, I know he can see the same vision that I do. So this is me, puttin' down roots that will never be unearthed, but doin' it in the only place I ever felt like I could truly call home."

I look around, seeing in my mind the land around us. There is so much property that I have a hard time seeing exactly what he does in his head. "Right here?" I ask, pointing to the area around us.

"Not here. This is our place and I won't give that to anyone else. On the other side of the land you kept, there's almost two hundred acres. I would buy it all back from him, but this part would be untouched. The rest will eventually be a training camp of sorts. Intimate with low enrollment. I'll have some dorm-type housing built around the main training areas for the folks I'll hire and those that enroll. They'll be able to learn it all, different areas built for each field offered and a personal trainer for each. The biggest planned for the buckin' bulls to be kept for riders to train."

"You want to build an arena?"

He laughs. "Not quite as big as you're used to watchin' me ride, but to those ridin', it damn sure will feel like it."

"What about you?"

"What do you mean?"

"In all of those plans, where will you call home?"

His chest rises as he pulls in a deep breath. "The long answer, I'll have somethin' temporary out on that land while it's being built. The short answer, wherever you are."

I'm at a complete loss for words, and it shows. "Wow," I finally say. "This is a lot to take in."

He laughs softly. "Yeah, it is. I want you to know, none of this will happen without your blessin'. Either way, I'm not goin' anywhere. If you don't want this on the land that your daddy used to work, just say the word. I'll look some-where else in Pine Oak, but no matter what, it's happenin' in this town. Steel roots, darlin'. I'm not goin' anywhere except wherever you go with me."

"Here," I whisper. I close my eyes, trying my best to see what he's explained, but the only thing I can see is him, smiling up at me while he builds his new dream. "You belong here, Maverick. I know Daddy would agree with me if he was still here, but I couldn't think of any-one else I would rather bring life to this place again. Build your dream, honey." The rush of utter certainty fills my body. I know without a single doubt in my mind that this man is meant to be mine, and with the same conviction, I know he feels it too. His words and actions proving to me that his heart is in this just as much as mine is.

He moves quickly. His hands coming up to pull me to him. Our mouths connecting. "*Our* dreams, darlin'. Ours." With those words, whispered against my lips, we sit in the same field where old dreams were once talked about, and make new ones.

21

MAVERICK

"H.O.L.Y." by Florida Georgia Line

"**C**ome on then, cowboy. Show me where these new dreams of ours are going to be."

For the first time since we drove away from her house, I feel the nerves disappear. I've worked myself up so much for this talk with her that I had been close to puking before I could even get the words out. But I shouldn't have worried, not with Leigh. This girl might need to analyze most of the shit in her life, but just like it used to be between us, she's never needed much to follow me with her whole heart.

And I'm going to make damn sure she doesn't regret placing that kind of trust in my hands.

I stand, grabbing my hat off the ground on my way up, and dust the damp dirt off my ass. I should have thought this through a little better. It had rained yesterday, a lot, not only giving us some great mud on the trails—but since

I didn't bring a blanket to sit on, our asses are now dirty and wet. Not that Leigh minds, though. She stands, looks behind her, and giggles.

The sound goes straight to my crotch. With her attention not on me, I grab the uncomfortable thickness and adjust myself quickly, not taking my eyes off her ass. When I look up from the wet spot our sitting made on her jeans and meet her gaze, I know she caught me, though.

"Need some help?" she asks with a wink.

"Not yet."

She rolls her eyes, but holds her hand out for mine. I take it and let her lead me back to the truck. Once she's settled in, I walk quickly to the driver's side and climb up.

"I'm gonna head over and grab one of the four-wheelers from Clay. Do you want to come, or do you want me to pick you up after?"

She smiles, wide and toothy. "I'm with you, cowboy. Lead the way."

The engine turns over with a loud roar and I drive us back through the muddy trail, making sure to hit each deep rut on the way. The sounds of her excited squeals make my face hurt from smiling so damn much.

Fuck, this girl.

When we pull off the road and onto the drive that will take us up to the main house, I don't feel even an ounce of the normal trepidation that I used to. I don't feel the clawing need to be anywhere *but* here. Not with her by my side. With that in mind, I reach over and grab her hand. She looks over from where she had been looking out her window and gives me a big smile.

"You still don't like being here?" she asks, knowing without words that this isn't a place I enjoy being.

"It's not so bad when you're with me."

What crosses over her expression is nothing short of rapture. She loves knowing that her presence calms me and isn't afraid to show that to me.

"And when I'm not?"

"I hate every second of it."

She clears her throat and I look away from the drive and at her profile. Her lips are rolled together, and that little space between her brows is wrinkled.

"What is it?"

"I was thinking, now that I understand why you don't like being here and all, why don't you stay at my place? You could stay in the guest room if you wanted your own space, but at least you wouldn't be *here*."

Her last word comes out harsh, like she is seeing this place through my eyes and can't stand the thought of being here any more than I can.

"Darlin', if I'm at your house, I'm not going to be in a damn guest room."

"Oh." She gasps. "Well, that's fine too . . . I mean, if you don't need your space and all."

"The last thing I want from you is space, Leighton, but you're askin' me to move into your house. That's not somethin' that should be offered without really thinkin' about it."

"I don't want you here," she venomously shoots back. "I want you with me."

"One day at a time, sweetheart. There isn't anything in

that house that's mine except for a duffel bag I still haven't unpacked. We don't need to make any decisions like that right now." I say the words, but my chest tightens at the thought of her wanting me in her house. Not just because she knows why it's hard to be here, but also because she *wants* me with her.

She huffs and crosses her arms, the movement pushing her chest up. I lick my lips at the swells that are exposed from her low neckline. Why the hell did I say we wouldn't be fuckin'? Oh, yeah, because I had some grand idea that when we were there next time it would be because she gave me all of her.

Stupidest smart move I've ever made.

"You're in my bed tonight," she demands, her tone leaving no room for argument.

"Yes, ma'am," I quip.

"I mean it, Maverick. If you aren't in my bed, don't think I won't find a way to tie you up like I said I would. I. Don't. Want. You. Here. And I don't just mean tonight, cowboy."

God, she's beautiful when she's pissed. "Darlin', calm down. There isn't anywhere I would rather be. I'll be there tonight. We can talk about the rest later."

"Good. And you're bringing that duffel bag with you. It's time to unpack." One arched brow goes up, just daring me to argue with her.

I laugh, shaking my head with a smile, and jump down from the cab. I look up when I hear my name and give Clay a nod. I know he can't see into my truck, not with these black as hell window tints on them. I keep my eyes on him as I walk, waiting to see his reaction when Leigh gets out. His stoic expression watching my every movement.

"Where have you been?" he calls out right when I open her door.

"With me!" Leigh jumps out of the cab with a bounce, waving to Clay.

Clay doesn't even have a chance to react before a flash of black hair and pink clothing is knocking him over in a rush to exit the house. "Shut the hell up, you hooch! You better get to talkin' right this second!"

I don't look away from my brother, wanting to see with my eyes how he feels about Leigh being with me. I know what he said yesterday, but something inside of me needs to know that he is happy with us together. By the time Quinn is about to reach Leigh, he has a big grin on his face. I get one nod before he stomps off the porch and heads toward us.

Quinn slams into Leigh so hard that they both fall to the ground. One second I had my hand resting against the small of her back, and in the next I was left with dead air and two grown women laughing on the ground in front of me. The gravel can't feel good against Leigh's back, but you wouldn't know because she's got one big damn smile on her face.

"You sneaky bitch. I called you last night and you said you were just going to read before going to bed."

Leigh giggles and looks up at me. "I had a change of plans."

I smile down at her. Our eyes communicating so much, but no words needed.

"I'll say. A big brooding change of plans."

"He wasn't brooding."

Quinn sits up. I can't see her, but judging by the blush that's covering every exposed inch of Leighton's face from the roots of her hair to the top of her chest, my sister must be making some sort of crude gesture.

"Don't you dare," Leigh whispers firmly.

"Don't I dare what? Comment on what must have happened to make him stop brooding?" She laughs mischievously.

"Quinn, shut your mouth," she hisses back.

"Fine. Fine, mouth is shut." Quinn climbs off the ground and holds out her hand to Leigh, helping her up.

I was about to open my mouth and ask her where my hug was, but she turns around the second that Leigh was standing, and the expression on her face has me snapping my mouth shut.

"You know what I want," she tells me with a hard tone.

"Uh," I mumble.

"You *know* what I'm waiting for," she continues, wagging her brows.

What the—clarity strikes, and I have to bite back a laugh. The conversation I had with her in the barn when she was trying to figure out what was going on between Leigh and me comes back in a rush. "How about you let me worry about that now and leave it alone knowin' that there's a greater chance of you gettin' what you want if you don't scare my girl off before I even have a chance to take us there."

"I'm not sure if that's good enough."

Weird as hell, my sister is. "It's gonna have to be."

"What are you two talkin' about?" Clay asks, breaking into our little huddle.

"Nothin' worth repeatin' right now," I tell him, my eyes still on Quinn so she knows to keep her mouth shut.

"You said your girl." Quinn gasps the words out, her eyes wide as she looks between me and Leigh. "You said . . . holy shit! You said YOUR GIRL!" She screams the last part and leaves her mouth hanging open.

Leigh giggles again, but doesn't respond to Quinn.

"Did you know about this?" Quinn continues, glaring at Leigh.

"Uh, yeah . . . seeing that I'm the girl in question, I would reckon that's a good guess, Q."

"You knew and didn't tell me!"

Leigh steps closer to me, wrapping her arm around my back and digging her fingers into my side. I look down and see her wink, returning the gesture and pulling her closer to my side with one arm over her shoulders. Her other arm comes up, Quinn's wide eyes following the movement, and rests it against my stomach. I feel my abs clench with just the smallest touch from her.

"We're tellin' you now, Q."

"Ohmigod. Ohmigod. Oh. My. God," my sister mutters under her breath, eyes even wider. "Clay," she says with a gasp, reaching out blindly behind her to find him, not looking away from the two of us. "Clayton!" she screams when her hand can't find him.

"Jesus, Quinn, take a breath," he grumbles, grabbing her hand before she can slap him.

"It's happening," she breathes.

"You are the weirdest person in the world," Leigh says, laughing.

"I knew one day this would happen. I just knew it."

Leigh squeezes my side, but I'm too busy rolling my eyes at my sister to give her my attention.

"You're happy for us?" Leigh asks. Something in her tone makes me finally look away from Quinn. When I look down and bend so that I can see her face, I know this is a question that isn't being asked lightly. She really does want to know if Quinn is happy. How she has to question that with the way Quinn is acting is beyond me, but I keep my mouth shut and tighten my hold. She needs this, for whatever reason.

"God, yes," Quinn breathes. "You have no idea how happy I am. For both of you," she adds, looking away from the girl in my arms and back into my face. "So damn happy for you."

I know the last part is meant for me and me alone. I clench my jaw when the burn of emotion hurts my throat. Damn, that feels good.

"Just in case anyone is wondering how I feel, I just want to add, it's about time."

We all three laugh, the girls both a little wobbly, when Clay finally speaks, his deep voice washing over all of us.

Yeah, that feels real damn good.

After leaving Clay and Quinn, we grab one of the four-wheelers and head out. Leigh knows how to ride, but even though holding on to me isn't necessary, she still keeps her arms wrapped tight around my stomach. Her head resting between my shoulder blades feels almost as good as her hands rubbing against my torso.

Because the Davis ranch is so big, it takes us a little while to reach the line that used to separate the two ranches. Since Clay doesn't use this part of our property anymore, and there are no longer animals being housed on the old James ranch, the gate had been taken down, but I would never forget the line that took me to my sanctuary.

A little while later, accompanied by some squeals and laughter coming from Leigh when I hit the gas on the uneven earth we're riding over, we pull up to the part of the property I had been telling her about earlier. It doesn't look like much now. The old barn is still in good repair, even if it hadn't been used in years, but it would need work. I would never allow that piece of her past to be torn down, so it's a big focus in what I'm hoping to create here.

She climbs off, giving me a squeeze around my middle before doing so, and looks around her with her hands on her hips. Her face looks serene as she takes it all in. I imagine she's seeing what it used to be as well as what it will be. Her daddy was a damn fine rancher and you can see that in how well this place has stood with little to no maintenance over time.

"I want to turn the barn into the mess hall of sorts. I'll have to gut it, add a kitchen in the back, but I want to be able to keep a part of your parents here when we build this thing."

She looks over, her eyes wide. "We?"

"Yeah, darlin'. This is just as much a part of you as it is me."

Her hand comes off her hip and she reaches out for me. "It means a lot that you said that, Maverick, a whole lot, but honey, this is all you."

Grabbing her hand, I swing my leg over the back of the four-wheeler and jump down onto the grass at her side, keeping her hand firmly in mine. Her head tips up and she continues to smile at me. "Thought that I made it clear, but there isn't anything I do from this point on that isn't about the both of us."

"You did. I was just sayin', well, I didn't want you to think you had to do things a certain way because this used to be my family's land. There aren't any expectations from me. I'm still going to support you in this one hundred percent."

Pulling her into my arms, I wait for her fingers to push into my hair, wishing my hat wasn't on so she had more room to play. With her head tipped up and her body pressed to mine, I feel like the luckiest bastard on earth. That's all it takes, her in my arms and that smile trained on me.

"I don't think you'll ever know how much that means to me, Leighton."

Her face softens and the smile I love so much grows a little. She doesn't talk, but her eyes tell me what I want to hear. She's happy, damn happy if I'm reading her right. I vow right then and there with a small kiss to her forehead that not one day will go by without me making sure she always feels like she does right now, every single day.

22

LEIGHTON

"Heartbeat" by Carrie Underwood

I can't believe the difference that just one day has made.

Last night I made a promise to myself to see this out. To open my heart up again and move forward. Of course, I also made that promise not knowing if I would be moving forward with or without him, but standing here right now in his arms, I'm the happiest I've ever been in my life.

And it's all because of him. Well, maybe not *all* because of Maverick. Knowing that Quinn and Clay support this and are happy for us goes a long way in my mind, solidifying that I'm in the right spot—at his side. Seeing the man that Maverick has grown to be and knowing why he was the angry teenager he was back then also made me realize that, had we had our chance then, we might not have been strong enough to make it through the troubles that haunted him. Don't get me wrong, I know he's still holding on to that pain, but the wounds aren't as fresh as they once were.

He's stronger.

I'm stronger.

Together I just know we'll be unbreakable.

This, right here and now, is our time. The only thing holding me back from believing that without any doubt is the knowledge that he's still got to let go of all that pain he holds deep inside him because, until he does, I'm not convinced he won't leave when things get too hard to handle emotionally.

He knows that too. Everything he told me last night attests to that. The only thing I can do is to promise that I'll be there to stand by his side and help him every step of the way.

Starting now.

"Come on, cowboy," I softly say. "Tell me about your plans."

He gives me a crooked smile before pressing another kiss to my forehead. His arms leave the loop they had been making around my body, turning me so that I'm tucked under one arm and curling one large hand around my shoulder.

"Like I said, the barn will serve as the mess hall, but also will be a place for everyone to hang out and talk shop. My hope is to make it half kitchen and dining, with the other half having couches and an entertainment center. They can watch footage of themselves that will be filmed in order to learn what they need to improve on, but they'll also be able to watch movies and shit."

"And shit." I laugh. "So basically, a living room and a kitchen all in one giant barn?"

"That's right," he answers with a smile in his voice. "On the left side of the barn, where there isn't as much land, we're going to have some small cabins built. Since I want to keep this exclusive in a way, the plan is to have no more than five or so riders here at a time. Each will have their own bedroom and bathroom, but they will all share one cabin. The other cabins will be built more like small houses for the instructors and staff to have to themselves. I think, going off the land I want to dedicate to that, I'll have almost ten cabins in all. The riders' bein' the largest in size."

"Wow," I respond, looking at the area of land that he had pointed to and having no problem envisioning what he is saying. "What kind of staff will you have on hand?"

"I'm hopin' at the least, three instructors other than myself. Each with a different specialty to offer the riders. Since we're goin' to focus on bull riding exclusively for now at least. That might change as time goes on. They'll have a cook, as well as a doctor on hand. The doc will help with everything from medical needs to teachin' them how to use their body as a tool."

"You've really thought this through," I praise, looking up at him.

"Yeah, darlin'. Like I said, steel-enforced roots."

My stomach flops at his words.

"Tell me more," I request with a wobble to my voice.

Maverick spends the next half hour walking me around the land, explaining where he wants to build things. His patience explaining to me what each "training area" will focus on, and why, really helped me understand the magnitude of this endeavor. I honestly didn't realize just how big these steel-enforced roots of his were, but hearing about it while visualizing his plans left me with no doubts that something this grand wouldn't be happening if he wasn't in it for the long run.

"So, there will be two arenas for ridin'," he continues. "One for practice and the other to emulate a champion-level ride. They'll use everythin' they've learned while here in that arena. We'll judge them just as they would be if they were on the circuit ridin' for the big purse. They'll be graded on everythin' from chute procedure and ridin' skill to dismount technique. They'll be filmed each time they jump on the back of a bull in this arena, so by the time they leave here, they'll ride just as effortlessly as they breathe."

"God, Mav. What you're doing here is amazing. This place is going to be something else."

"I hope so. I've started to put some feelers out, see who I can pull into this place with me. I'm excited, Leigh, and darlin', that's not somethin' I've felt about my future for a long time."

"I know you are. I can't wait to see you bring this vision to life. It's going to be beautiful, I just know it. You're going to have so many people flocking to Pine Oak to be trained under 'The Unstoppable' Maverick Davis."

His face turns serious, and I feel my smile slip a little.

"Honest to God, Leigh, hearing how much faith you have in me—in this—means the world, but I'm tellin' you right now, if I don't have you by my side every step of the way, all of this"—he trails off and looks around us before I get his attention again—"all of this means nothin' if I don't have you. Everythin' I want for my future is built around ours bein' interwoven. I don't want to do this without you. Do you understand that?"

I nod, not trusting my voice to talk.

"It's not just me that I'm building this for. I want it here, on your family's old ranch, not just because of the peace this place brings me, but because this is the first step in *us* mergin' our lives together."

"I'm not sure what to say to that, Maverick. Part of me wants to scream that it's too soon to be making decisions that mean forever, but an even bigger part of me knows that nothing we ever do will be too soon. Not us. I'm not saying that I'm not nervous—I am—but I know that something that feels this right couldn't possibly be wrong. I'm scared, but a lot of that fear is because of how much I care about you. I'm not lost when I'm with you. I don't feel the aching loneliness anymore. My heart beats strong and true again. Everything I've ever wanted, Maverick, that's what you're offering us here. So I guess what I'm trying to say is yes, even though I'm so scared of that future, I'm going to be here every step of the way."

He bends and takes my mouth in a slow, burning kiss, tipping his head just so in order not to have his hat knocked off. When I feel his tongue trace my bottom lip, I open with a gasp. Our tongues tangle together, and I feel tingles fire through my nerves when his hands curl around my body, holding me close to him. My own hands fist in the soft material of his shirt, desperate to find something to hold on to when my legs start shaking.

When we break away with a gasp, I look up at his full lips and feel a tremor rock through me when I see how bruised and swollen they are. All from our kiss. Judging by how his focus is also on mine, I have no doubt that they look just like his do.

I feel like I've been branded.

I *hope* I've been branded, because there will never be another man for me, not now . . . not ever.

After our talk, we spend some more time walking around the land. Seeing my old place in a new light now that I have a good picture of what Maverick is planning in order to build his training school.

I wasn't in a rush to leave, though, something that I made sure to voice to Maverick. His answering smile told me he was feeling the same way. This time together has been something we both needed. From his own admission, I know we had both been feeling the oppressing weight of our loneliness. But together now, there is a happiness filling the air that can't be denied. I know for me, that's not a feeling I'm in a hurry to have interrupted, and I'm pretty sure he feels the same way.

We take some time before heading back to his truck to jump on the four-wheeler and race through the property. I don't feel the heavy sadness that used to hang from these pastures like a thick fog. They might have lost the meticulous standard of perfection that my father held his ranch to over the years, but even with the overgrown blanket of time, they still hold the footprint of my parents. Now with

Maverick here with me, and the knowledge that he's going to be breathing a whole new life into this land, I can't wipe the bittersweet smile off my face.

My daddy would be so proud. Not just of the plans that Maverick has for this place, but also because of the man he has become. He always loved Maverick, just as much as he loved Clay and Quinn, but like his daughter, he had a soft spot for the middle Davis boy. After overhearing a conversation between him and my mama, I know, even though he never voiced his thoughts to me directly, he was very aware of his only daughter's crush on Maverick. I'll never forget the words he had whispered to mama. He said, *"It's bigger than life, how she feels for that boy and I couldn't be happier about that, but he's got to figure out his own heart before he can accept hers. Mark my words, honey, it will happen one day. I just know it."*

I wish he were here to see that finally happen, but I know somewhere up there he's smiling his toothy grin down on us.

Maverick drops me off at my house after we go back for his truck. Quinn isn't there, thankfully, so I'm saved another tumble to the ground with her excitement. She hadn't called either and I'm equally thankful that she's giving me some time to wrap my head around the new status between her brother and me.

Clay's truck is there, but he didn't come to talk to us this time. Clay's stretched thin, another thing that Maverick told me, but something that I also knew from Quinn. Before Buford died, Clay had been spending a lot of time at the shop with her. Helping her find new ways to grow the business there, not that they needed it, she was as swamped as my bakery was. I know Clay had hoped to get both the shop and the ranch running in a way that he could oversee them from behind the scenes as the owner, but that hasn't happened yet. He's still very much the workaholic he was, only this time the weight on his shoulders is so much heavier.

Maverick left almost an hour ago, telling me that he would be back after he "handled some shit." I'm not sure what shit he needed to handle, but I was a little relieved to have time alone. So much has happened in such a short time that my head feels like it might literally start spinning. Not that I'm complaining. Still, it's nice to have some quiet for my thoughts.

Add to that, Maverick telling me that he was taking me on a date tonight, my spinning mind has kicked into overdrive. The date itself is a big deal because he's not only showing me he's serious about us, but he's going to be showing the whole town. And with a town like Pine Oak that thrives on the next biggest gossip story, we're going to be talked about for a long time. It isn't just the story of us that they're so fascinated about, don't get me wrong, they are—but it's also him. His departure from Pine Oak was talked about for years after the fact, but with him coming back *and* coming back somewhat famous—okay, a lot famous—he is sitting under a giant neon sign of attention.

And that terrifies me.

Our relationship is new. We're new. Even with our very long history. It's a given that with the attention he brings with him, every single second of our relationship will be stalked, whispered about by most, and analyzed by many.

I hate that.

I hate knowing that this time between us will be subjected to so much talk while people watch us with a hawk-like focus, hoping that they get to watch the fireworks.

Even though I know that we have the support of the town, I would be a fool not to be nervous. With so many people watching your new relationship, there is a lot more added pressure. I just hope that with their excitement to watch little Leighton James finally get the boy she's always loved doesn't encroach on what we're building.

He didn't tell me where we were headed tonight, but with a town this size, there aren't that many options. Unless, that is, you wanted to drive outside of town to one of the more populated areas. It wasn't like we were in the middle of nowhere, but we were more than an hour from Dallas and a good thirty plus to get to another major city.

Unless he plans on our first date being at the diner, nothing glamorous there, we were going to be driving for a while. I couldn't think of anything else that he would pick for our first date. Well, there was always the Chicken Coop, a popular local bar aptly named since there are a whole lot of chicken wire pens around outside. Don't get me wrong—I love it at the Chicken Coop, or as locals like to call it, the Coop, but it would make for a very rowdy night.

"Well, Earl, how do I look?"

He looks up from his spot in the middle of my bed and blinks at me.

"Yeah, that's how I feel too, baby."

I decided to go with something casual, that way regardless of where we ended up tonight, it should work for any situation. Be it a nice restaurant or a crowded bar.

The white lace sundress was one of the nicer ones I owned. Depending on the shoes I paired it with, it could go from fancy to casual in a blink of an eye. Tonight I went with my favorite pair of brown cowboy boots. My hair was hanging in loose curls, and aside from mascara and some lipstick, I didn't have any makeup on. Some Alex and Ani bangles on my wrists were all that was left.

It was 100 percent me, but it was also a far cry from the kind of women I know he's spent the last ten years seeing. Of course, those girls were more worried about catching the eye of a rider than they were about modesty. Self-doubt had been keeping me company since I got out of the shower and tried for almost an hour to find something to wear, but in the end I knew I would never be anything other than the woman in the mirror before me.

"You look beautiful, Leighton."

I screamed, jolting in place before spinning to look at the man now standing in my open doorway. "Jesus, Maverick. You scared the crap out of me."

His shoulders shake, but other than a few deep rumbles, he doesn't make a sound. His eyes roam from the top of my head to the tips of my boots, not missing an inch as he takes his time. The zap of arousal from his commanding gaze is so powerful it feels almost tangible.

I shift my feet, feeling the thin silk between my legs grow wet with the excitement his appraisal gives me. "If you keep looking at me like that, cowboy, the only ride we're going to have tonight is me on top of you."

His eyes close and he drops his head back. I smile to myself, not even caring if I'm egging him on. He's got his formfitting Wranglers on, this pair a deeper denim than the last. He's switched the button-down for a plain black T-shirt, his muscles straining the sleeves. His black cowboy boots have a layer of brown dust covering them, but other than that, he looks like he took a lot of time and care in looking good. Not that he has to put much effort in that.

"I wouldn't be upset about that though, in case you were wondering," I add with a wink.

When he brings his gaze back to mine, his Adam's apple bobbing as he swallows hard, I smile, knowing my skin is flush with the need I feel.

"You've got no idea how much it kills me to say this *again*, but not until I have all of you, Leigh. Not a second before then."

I want so badly to scream that he already has my heart. That he's always had my heart. He narrows his eyes and looks at me as if he knows what's going through my mind. He moves, taking the few steps needed to bring him right in front of me and looks down. Even with his hat on and the dim lighting in my room, I can see the fire blazing from his brilliant eyes.

"You're almost there, I know it, darlin', but until I no longer see any fear in your eyes, I'm not makin' my move."

"I'm not scared, not of you."

One corner of his mouth tips up. "You are."

My hair tickles my shoulders when I shake my head, denying what he's saying.

"Leighton," he says with a groan.

"I'm not scared of you, Maverick. Am I scared of the feelings I have when it comes to you? Yeah . . . but that's something that will never go away. I don't care if we're eighty years old, rockin' on that porch while our grandkids scream around us, I'll always feel it," I whisper, and reach up to cup his now-shaven cheek. "The feelings I have for you are so strong that I almost can't breathe because of them. Honey, that would make anyone scared, and that will never change. I've felt it my whole life, only I don't see it as fear. I see it as me always knowing that what we have together is the biggest kind of love two people will ever share." His eyes close and I feel his jaw work under my palm.

"Leigh," he thickly breathes, sounding pained.

"Take me out, Maverick. Stop looking at it as something negative and get used to it."

"What you're sayin'. . ." He pauses, his jaw once again ticking under my hand. I give him a smile and push my hand back into the hair that is just long enough to curl under the edges of his hat.

"No way, cowboy. You'll get those words the second you're back inside of me with your naked body moving on top of mine and I can feel your heart beatin' against my chest and not a moment sooner."

He groans, the sound low as it echoes around us. I roll up to my toes and give him a brief kiss before leaving him standing in the middle of my bedroom. I should feel bad about pushing him, but he never had to wait for my heart, that has always and would always belong to him. He needs to realize that. Even if my words that he's never needed to wait for my love bring him shock.

It shouldn't, though. Not when that love's always been his to have.

23

MAVERICK

"Stay the Night" by Jordan Gray

The whole drive out of Pine Oak I've been replaying her words in my mind.

She didn't say the words, but the meaning was clear.

She loves me.

Fuck me, her admission leaves no room for doubt—she's always loved me. Even after I purposely hurt her deeply, that love never died. God, what did I do to deserve this woman? And more important, how did I ever live this long without feeling what her love could do to me? I feel as if every broken, hollow inch of me has been healed, and fuck, she hasn't even fully said it. It was implied, no doubt about it, but if I feel this rush of healing power just from her alluding to it, what will happen when I finally hear those three words from her mouth?

"You're thinkin' pretty loud over there," Leighton quips. I reach over the console and take her hand, lacing our fingers together. Her hand flexes and moves so that the hold is tighter. After she stills, I bring our hands up and press my lips against the smooth skin, breathing in her scent.

"You've given me a lot to ponder, darlin'. No doubt my thoughts are loud when I've been repeatin' your words since you walked out of that girly as hell bedroom of yours."

"Girly as hell, huh?" She laughs.

"Leigh, the only place that has more purple than that might be the PieHole. Hell, I'm startin' to think that cat/beast of yours wasn't tryin' to figure out how to eat me whole the other night, but instead tryin' to tell me man to man, he needs some more testosterone in that place."

I see, out of the corner of my eye, her throw her head back. Her fingers tighten around mine as she lets out a loud belly laugh.

"It's not that bad," she gasps between laughter. "Just a little purple."

"Just a little, she says," I mumble.

"Okay, so maybe a little more than a little. I like it, it made me happy."

"Made?" I question.

"Well, it still does. I'm thinkin' a little update wouldn't hurt."

"It's you, Leigh. Don't change a bit of that. I'm just pullin' your leg, anyway."

I hear her shift, her arm moving, but she doesn't let her hand slip from mine. "I meant what I said about wanting you at my place, Maverick. I don't want you back at *that* place." When she pauses, I glance over and see the look of disgust on her beautiful face. Before I can open my mouth and address it, though, she continues. "The second I said it, I knew that's where you belong. The hell with the timeline that a normal relationship might hold, we are far from normal and you know it. I want my house to feel like a home again. No, I need it to. I'm starting to realize I stopped feeling like that long before I lost my parents. After all, they say home is where your heart is."

"God, Leigh."

"I mean it, Maverick. No expectations. If you still want to bring in something temporary while you're building our future, then do it, but until then you're under my girly as hell roof."

I take a quick second to close my eyes before focusing back on the road, her words washing over me. "I told you earlier I would be there, Leighton. I just want you to be sure."

"I know what you said, but you also said we would figure out the rest later. I don't need to figure anything out. I know where I belong, I know where you belong, and that place is one and the same."

"What was that you said earlier about being too soon?" I hedge, pissed that I'm actually giving her an out. Even if it's an out I pray she doesn't take. I don't think I could stomach it if she realized it wasn't somethin' she wanted somewhere down the road. "I have to know you understand what you're sayin' here. Full disclosure, darlin', it makes me feel like the king of the fuckin' jungle to hear you say you want me in your home, but playin' devil's advocate here—you have to look at this from every angle."

"Yeah," she snaps. "And every angle begins and ends with you."

"What happened to thinkin' things were happenin' too soon?"

She snorts. Not even a ladylike one either. Deep, throaty, and full of fuckin' sass. And it shoots through me from heart to crotch.

"Let me break this down for you, cowboy. Twenty-six long as hell years. Sixteen of those I spent weavin' dreams all centered on you. Ten of those I spent prayin' those dreams would find their way back to me. I might not have realized what I was doin', but not once in all that time did I ever come close to finding the kind of contentment I've felt since you blew back into town. Even through all the emotional punches I got slapped since that moment with you did the contentment dim. Deep down, with you back, I knew that the past twenty-six-years were going to finally be worth something. We were rushin' to this point before our minds had even had a chance to realize what Fate had in store for us. There is never going to be a minute that ticks by that could be too soon when we have a past as deep as ours, drivin' us blindly to where we were meant to stop."

"You came to this conclusion pretty quick, Leigh. Don't get me wrong, what you're sayin' is somethin' I fuckin' want, but it's only been a day since you really understood everything that happened. Everything I did, why I did it, and most importantly, why in doin' all that I stole ten years from us."

"Yeah, but it wasn't you that stole that time. You had no control over the life that you were born in. The pain *you* felt that meant those ten years were stolen. And, Maverick"— she pauses and squeezes my hand hard—"those years were stolen from you too."

I swallow the lump in my throat and tighten the hand steering the truck. God, this girl brings me to my knees.

"You said we would talk about this later, but the hell with that. Later just means more time gone, and I won't let any more time get stolen when we are finally getting our chance. I want you with me. If *you* feel like it's too soon, then get your temporary home in place. I'm tellin' you now, though, it would be a waste of time and effort when you know just as well as I do that you only belong in one place."

I pull the truck onto the shoulder, no longer content to have this conversation when I can't look at her. After throwing the truck into park, I turn my head. It's not fully dark out, so it's no trouble to see her clearly, and what I see is like a punch to the gut. Her chest is heaving with each harsh intake of air she pulls through her lungs, the harshness of her releasing it coming out like a pant. The color on her cheeks is high, but not because she's embarrassed. No, this is because she's on a tear. A tear to make me see what she believes true with unquestionable certainty.

"I'll unpack the duffel, darlin'," I answer hoarsely.

Her whole face lights up with those five words. I shift and regard her chin as it wobbles and she pulls her bottom lip between her teeth. Jesus Christ. Giving her that, what I wanted just as much as she did, undoubtedly was the right decision. I feel it with the pressure that I've always had around my chest easing up. I believe it when I see her curls bob as she gives me a curt nod. I feel it when she moves, pulls herself over the console, and brings the tip of her nose to mine.

"Head over boots, cowboy. Head. Over. Boots."

They're not the words she alluded to earlier, but they might as well be. I move quickly, shocking a squeak out of her that quickly turns to a moan when I haul her over the center console and into my lap. We're a mess of tangled arms and tongues a second later. My hat is knocked off my head when she pushes both of her hands into my hair, pulling me so hard that our teeth knock together. My heart hammers in my chest. I'm vaguely aware of the sounds of traffic passing by us.

What I wouldn't give to lay her down and sink into her body, and that need just amps up with every slide of her wet tongue against mine. I'm not sure how much longer I'm going to last, not when I feel like denying my need to be inside of her might very well kill me.

My hand moves down her back, and when I hit her hip, I realize that with her position half on and half off the console, it would be so easy to sink my fingers into her body. The scent of her arousal is swirling around the cab, and I have to squeeze my eyes tight when I feel my balls pull up and the wetness from my cock wetting my boxer briefs. I curl my fingers in the soft flesh at her hip, praying that I'm strong enough to resist what I crave.

She whimpers and I'm honestly not sure if it's from my hold on her body or because she's feeling the same need I am. It kills me to do it, but I break away from her mouth with a groan. Her eyes are still closed when I lean my head back on the headrest and stare at her. Without opening them, her tongue comes out and licks her red, swollen lips. The sound that escapes her mouth after that is nothing short of sensual.

When she finally opens her eyes the fear that I've seen in them since I got back home a month ago isn't anywhere to be found. Pure, unadulterated love is shining bright.

I'm going to get those damn words out of her. She might believe she wouldn't give me them until our bodies are naked and fused tight, but I know I won't make it that long.

Even if it kills me, I'm getting them before that.

When I watch her shimmy back down to her seat, the skirt of her dress riding up and giving me a glimpse of her white panties, I really do think I might die before then.

- ★ -

"What's wrong?" I question when Leigh returns to our table after a quick bathroom break.

"Nothing," she mumbles at the table, not looking me in the eye.

"The fuck, darlin'?"

"It's nothing, Maverick. Just leave it alone and let's finish our dessert."

She picks up her fork and takes her sweet-ass time getting a bite of the chocolate cake that had arrived while she was gone. I wait, silently, hoping for some sort of a clue to why her mood went from blissfully happy to sullen in a span of five minutes.

I open my mouth to press harder for answers, but when I hear the sound of catty giggling behind her, I shift my attention to the duo of women coming from the bathroom. They're looking at the back of Leigh's head, snickering and whispering to each other, but they're doing a shit job if they think it isn't obvious who they're talking about.

"You know them?" I ask her with a bite in my voice.

She straightens her shoulders, and even though she's trying to put on a brave front, it's clear as fucking day that she's trying her damn hardest to become invisible as they get closer.

Looking back at them, I can't help but notice the differences between them and Leighton. We're in a fancy Italian place just outside of Dallas, but it isn't fancy enough for the shit they have on. The blond hair on both of their heads is just about the only thing they could come close to having in common with Leigh. The shit they have on is just as tight as it is short, their sparkly dresses leaving nothing to the imagination. I steal a glance down and see the ridiculously high heels they're prancing on. They look like hookers, but judging by the amount of diamonds dripping off them, they're more likely just rich sluts.

To my complete shock, they walk right up to the table and stop.

"Can I help you?" I question, annoyance fueled by my worry over Leigh making my words come out uninviting and harsh.

"Are you—" thing one starts to say, but her irritating

as fuck giggles start back up again and she just ends up smiling.

"What my friend here, Tamera, is trying to ask is, are you Maverick Davis?" The other one cuts in, leaning forward a bit so her ample cleavage pushes together even farther. "*The* Maverick Davis?"

Leigh makes a noise that sounds a whole hell of a lot like a whimper, the sound so low I almost miss it.

What the fuck?

"I am," I respond, not looking away from Leigh until the chick opens her mouth again. The sticky sweet voice is as high as a mouse.

"I'm Veronica, by the way," she continues. Like I give a fuck.

Not wanting to do something to embarrass Leigh, especially when I'm not sure what's got her upset to begin with, I bite my tongue and answer politely. "Nice to meet y'all."

Thing one, whatever her name was, moves closer, pushing into Leigh and making her fork clatter onto the plate. Her head shoots up at the sound, looking around the restaurant with wild eyes before stopping on my face.

"Fuck this," I grumble, tossing my napkin on the table and leaning back. "Excuse me, but could you have a little respect?" The chick rolls her eyes, not moving an inch. I look from her to her friend and then back again. "Back away. Now."

This time she moves, but barely, and only because her friend pulls her away.

"We just wanted to stop by and give you this," Victoria, Vicki, whatever her name was says, holding out a piece of paper. I stare at it, but only when she starts to jam it into my face do I reach up and take it. "We weren't sure how much time you had here in town, but if you want to have some fun, we would love to show you how a real lady can rock your world." When she says the last part, she looks down at Leighton like she's some sort of diseased animal.

"A real lady?" I ask incredulously. Leighton's eyes narrow as she regards me. I look from her up to these bitches and raise my brow. "Are you trying to imply that my woman isn't a *real lady*?" I seethe. I hear Leigh gasp, but fuck if I know what's gotten her heckles up now. I don't look away from them, hoping like hell they can see how pissed I am.

"Well," the giggling one says, still fuckin' giggling, and looks down at Leigh. "I mean, look at her."

She can't be serious. I glance at the other one, Vanessa or whatever, but get only more pissed than I was when it's written all over her face that she thinks the same. Opening the paper, I see a hotel name, room, and a phone number written down. I blink a few times, not even believing the nerve of these two.

Leaning back in my seat, I shift my scrutiny and scan my eyes over Leighton's face. I can't tell if she's pissed, but she is definitely upset by their words.

"Let me ask you, what makes you think I don't already have a real lady?"

Their lips curl in disgust. Both of them roll their eyes with a huff. It almost looks like something they coordinated in advance. Vapid bitches.

"She's wearing old, dirty boots and something that I bet

she bought at the discount mall," the one closer to Leigh says smartly with another roll of her eyes.

Vanessa bats her ridiculously false eyelashes. "I think what Tamera means is that you're clearly used to women more like us and we didn't want to leave without making sure you knew that you have options. We would hate for someone like you to end up with, well . . . options is what we wanted to give you."

I lean forward, pulling my wallet out and snagging a few bills. More than enough to cover our dinner and leave a more than generous tip. Flipping their proffered paper around between my fingers, I look up and smile. Leigh remains silent, and I know she recognizes my fake sincerity.

"In my book, *ladies*, my princess always wears boots. You two have no clue what type of women I'm used to, but let me assure you, it has never been the type of woman that would rather look like a two-bit whore than a . . . what did you call it? A real lady? A real lady wouldn't be caught dead outside the house wearing something a hooker would have in her closet. A real lady doesn't have to show off her body, because all she has to do is smile and men will drop at her feet to give her the world. This woman, *my woman*, is as real as it gets and you two would be lucky to have just an ounce of what she does."

I stand, towering over them, and reach my free hand out for Leigh. She takes it with no hesitation and I pull her into my body. Her soft curves pressing into my side dims some of my anger. With the paper they had given me between two fingers, I reach forward and sink it to the bottom of my water glass.

"With all due respect, you can take your offer and fuck right off."

They sputter and gasp. I pick my hat up off the chair that I had hooked it on before we sat down, and place it on my head. Turning at the same time, the people at the tables around us start clapping. I ignore it, but Leigh just presses her head into my chest. Leighton keeps pace with me all the way out of the restaurant, even though I know, in my anger, it can't be easy. I help her up into the truck, pulling the seat belt across her body silently. Right when it clicks into place, her tiny hand folds under my chin and tips my head up.

"I lov—" she starts, tears in her eyes, but I interrupt her instantly when I realize what she is about to say.

"Don't you dare give me the words I want and have the memory of this moment tainted with that bullshit you just had to sit through. You hold them tight and let me get us home, baby. Let me get us *home*."

I don't even waste a second before pressing my lips to hers. The contact is harsh with the quickness that I move to erase the space between us. Everything that just happened in there vanishes. I feel her wet tears move between our faces and I move my hands to the back of her neck, pulling her closer. I take a deep pull of air through my nose, our closed mouths still pressed tightly together, and with her words banging around my body, I feel like I might add some fuckin' tears of my own.

We're both breathing heavily when I pull back. Moving my hands, I clear the tears from her cheeks with my thumbs. "You're going to give me all of you?" I breathe.

She opens her mouth, my eyes moving to watch her lips open. "I . . ." she begins, but stops and closes her mouth, getting me to unglue my attention from them and back to her blue gaze. "Yes." She clears her throat. "Yes, Maverick. I'm going to give you all of me."

We don't look away from each other, what just happened inside only adding to this moment so we're both feeling nothing but raw emotion. With a kiss to the tip of her nose, I release my hold on her and back up.

"Let's go home then, darlin'."

Her smile wobbles and her gaze brightens, all the clouds that had started to brew inside of them while in the restaurant clear. I shut her door, and with my heart about to race out of my chest, I round the truck and climb in. She reaches out this time, grabbing my hand, and we jump back on the road . . . headed home.

24
LEIGHTON

"Head Over Boots" by Jon Pardi

How did I just go from devastated to on top of the world in just a blink of my eye?

After hearing those girls talk about how they couldn't believe that the famous Maverick Davis, rodeo star, was with such trailer trash and they would make sure and give him what he really wants, I was blown away. I thought that taking the high road when I walked out of the stall, letting them see that I was in there and overheard them, would be the end of it. Sure, they hurt me with their words, but I was more upset with myself that I allowed them to get a reaction out of me.

By the time I got back to the table, I still couldn't shake what I had overheard. I looked across the busy restaurant at the handsome man who had brought me there and thought, what *is* he doing with me? He could have anyone. It was only natural to feel a bit of insecurity after the things they had been saying. I hated putting a damper on our night with the path my mind had taken. I had almost been able to shake off their words, doing my best to move on and put it behind me.

That was, until I heard them laughing behind me.

I should have known better than to think those dark thoughts. There is no room for the bullshit they actually made me think about myself when I have a man like Maverick at my side. His words to them, both of them, filled my heart full to bursting. The venomous tone that he took left no room for argument, not even from me.

I knew before he had even tossed his cash on the table that I had to tell him I loved him. I had to get the words that I meant with every fiber of my being out—the ones that I've always felt for him. It wasn't just him standing up for me back there. He indisputably did, but the way in which he did not only proved to those women that his heart only beats for one person—he showed me too. He single-handedly erased the pain he had formed when he turned his back on us years ago and in turn filled it with the new memory of him creating and solidifying a bond I know will never be broken.

As simple as that.

This is our time, finally, and I wasn't going to waste another second of it.

My princess always wears boots. His words echo through my mind, and I feel myself smiling at them all over again.

I take another peek at him, the darkness in the truck giving me only a shadow of his large frame, but I can see his face clearly in my mind. The way that he looked at me when I started to tell him that I loved him, *that* expression was something love stories are written about. His eyes burned bright, for me, and the fierce power of adoration within them whipped around us like a physical touch. I have never seen him look so vulnerable. He left no room for doubt to linger. That look obliterated it wholly.

For the thousandth time in the past thirty minutes of our drive I open my mouth to say those words again, but I snap my lips shut before I can get them out. Part of me, the selfish and needy part, wants to wait in the hopes that he will beat me to it. However, that part will never win. I won't let it.

I think back to everything he's told me about his life growing up. How that ache his parents had created with their selfishness had forced him to leave when he wanted to stay. To wait for us. He spent his whole life not believing in love, and I'll be damned if I let him go another day without feeling it and knowing it was given to him freely.

"You're thinkin' pretty loud over there," he jokes, giving me back the words I had spoken to him earlier in the night.

I hum my acknowledgment and grin, knowing he can't see it, but enjoying the easy banter that had returned after the tumultuous end to our date.

"We're almost home," he continues.

"I like hearing you say that, cowboy." Oh, boy, do I ever.

"I know, darlin'. You made that pretty clear earlier."

"And you?" I ask, leaving the question hanging in the air between us.

He's quiet for a while, the hum of his tires just barely

audible over the beat of my heart. I know I'm pushing hard, but I wasn't kidding when I told him I didn't want him to stay on the Davis ranch. Not now, not ever. The second the thought of him under my roof took root, I knew with crystal clear certainty that was where he belonged.

"I can honestly tell you, Leighton, that there isn't anywhere else I would rather be. That is a fact I guarantee to you will never change."

"That's good," I breathe lamely.

He snickers low and deep. I reach out, content with the silence, and lace our fingers together, wishing the big console separating us was gone so I could feel him against me.

Soon, I think.

Very soon.

- ★ -

Maverick's phone had started to ring about ten minutes from the house. He looked at the display, but put it back in the cup holder between us, taking the hand he had let go back within his grasp. It hadn't even stopped ringing a full minute before his phone was once again going off. He gives me a squeeze and then let go of my hand again, checking the display, but continuing to ignore it.

"Do you need to get that?" I ask, looking down at the phone's display.

"He can wait."

"It seems pretty important," I drone when it starts ringing for the third time and the same man's name showing on the screen. "I don't know who Trey is, but it seems like he really needs to talk to you."

"Not as important as what's about to happen, Leigh. I don't want to take any more time than what it took to get here. Not when I'm this close. He can wait."

I feel my brows pull in, confused at the last bit. "This close? This close to what?" I question, thinking he means our approach to the house.

Flicking his blinker on, even though we're the only vehicle on the road, he turns his truck onto the drive that leads to my house. I continue to look over at him, his profile outlined in the illumination by the lights that line my porch, and wait for him to answer me.

He stops his truck, pulling in right next to my Jeep, with a heavy foot on the brake before shutting it off. Without even looking in my direction, he jumps down in a hurry. The sound of his door clicking shut in the silence around us makes me jump. I vaguely hear his phone start to ring again, but with the way that my heart is galloping against my ribs, I hardly hear it. All my focus is on him. His pace is brisk as he walks around the front of his truck, the whole time I feel like I'm the prey being hunted. I can't see his eyes, with the lights now at his back and the hat casting his face in the shadows, but I can feel the burn of his stare like a physical touch. Branding me with promise.

The force with which he flings opens the door has it banging firmly against his side, but he just shoulders it and continues with his mission, reaching over to unbuckle my seat belt in silence. His breathing is harsh and rushed through his parted lips, mirroring the same sounds that my heaving chest is making.

There is so much carnal desire sparking between us right now. The goose bumps that dance across every exposed inch of my skin make me tremble. The anticipation of what's to come makes me weak with need. This is so different from our first time together. We've come so far in just a short time, but it feels like we've been building up to this moment for years.

I guess, in a way, we have.

After the metal of my now unbuckled seat belt bangs against the truck's frame, he doesn't make a move. He continues to regard me, not touching any part of me, but still I feel my body's response as a wave of heat washes over me from head to toe. It's so intense, the need I feel deep inside me, that I shiver and let out an audible moan.

That sound is what breaks him. He makes a noise deep in his chest, almost animalistic in nature, and reaches out to twist me with his hands on my hips, turning and lifting me right out of the high truck with ease. My hands shoot up to his shoulders at the same time that my center slams against his. Just when I lock my feet behind him, right above the swell of his fantastic ass, his hands move. Going from midthigh, moving underneath my dress, until his long, dexterous fingers are pushing under the band of my panties. He flexes both of his hands against my ass, causing me to shutter as he shoulders the door shut.

"Oh, God," I breathe.

"Hold on," he demands, flexing his hold again while stomping up the steps to my porch.

One hand leaves my bottom and he folds his knees, effortlessly bending to move the mat and grab the key before standing quickly. The move pushes his erection harder into my desperate body, the friction rubbing against me perfectly, and I cry out with a low moan of pleasure.

"Fuck," he hisses through his clenched jaw.

Knowing that he's feeling just as desperate for me as I am for him does something dangerous to my body. Knowing that he is so close to the edge spurs me on, and I'm no longer a docile participant in this. My hands move, slowly caressing and massaging the tense muscles under my palm. He grunts when my fingers leave the cotton of his shirt and I look up into his hooded eyes. At my wink, the only clue that I'm up to something, his lips part and I see the spark of need light his penetrating gaze. Bending my head, I run the tip of my nose along the strong column of his neck, starting right behind his ear until I feel the material of his shirt. I breathe him in, his hardy scent making me hum in pleasure while I rock my hips.

This time he doesn't hold back the delicious sounds. The throaty and deep rumble vibrating against my hard nipples makes me only rock against him harder. My head spins, dizzy with my hunger for him. When he takes a step into the house, jostling my body enough to give sharp friction against him, I open my mouth and bite down on his neck. Not enough to break the skin, but just hard enough to get a reaction from him. He stops in his tracks, instantly.

"Goddamn!" he bellows, using his hold on me to roll my hips harshly against his. "You're so hot, even through my fuckin' jeans I can feel your heat, darlin'. Keep ruttin' against me and you won't be the only one that comes fully clothed."

I release the hold my teeth had, licking the spot with my tongue before trailing it up to his ear, nibbling on his lobe before whispering into his ear. "Then hurry, cowboy."

He doesn't need any more encouragement from me. The second my words are out, I continue to lick and kiss down his neck, and he starts walking again, faster this time, if that's even possible. I'm not aware of anything else around us except for the overwhelming need that I feel for him. This last month has been a whirlwind of emotions, all of them building to this, us coming back together—but this time it's fueled by the love we both have for each other, making it more powerful and all-consuming than I could ever imagine.

No longer willing to waste another second, I hunch my back and give myself a gap between our bodies to drag my hands from his shoulders and down to his stomach. When I pull his shirt from his pants and push my hands under the material, his abs clench under my touch and he grunts. Encouraged by his reaction, I quickly bunch his shirt up, knowing he can't remove it without dropping me, but I get it far enough up that I can still tease him further. Drive him just as mad as I feel.

I have his shirt as high as I can get it. I peek my eyes open slowly and try to focus through the lust-filled haze that's floating around us. Right when he steps into my bedroom, I turn my head and bend my neck, taking his nipple between my lips with a wet suck. The words that leave his mouth are completely inarticulate. Just a garble of sounds that escape in a rush.

And then, I'm flying through the air with a breathy

gasp, landing in the center of my bed. My hair completely covers my face and it takes me a second to recover from the shock of his toss before I can move my arms and start to push my hands through the tangled locks, parting through my curls to see Maverick. Nothing could have prepared me for the sight that met my eyes when I finally cleared my vision, though.

No, there wasn't a thing in the world that could have prepared me for what Maverick Davis looks like when he's let go of his fierce control. To see him let his guard down while everything he has kept locked deep inside him was finally able to break free, creating an almost tangible electricity around the room that whips, rolls, and pings across my body with just the heated connection of our stares.

It is the most beautiful thing I have ever felt in my life. He no longer has an air about him that screams lost, wounded, and withdrawn. He, standing in the middle of my girly bedroom, looks like he has found the purpose for his heart. And that purpose is me and me alone. I feel the sob clawing up my throat before I can even do anything to stop it, the sound choking me the second it bursts through my lips.

He grabs the shirt that's still bunched under his arms and with a grunt, pulls it over his head and throws it somewhere to the side. His chest heaves as he prowls to the end of my bed, the bronze tan of his skin looking darker in the muted light the moon casts through the open windows.

When he is close enough, his hands make quick methodical work of pulling off my boots and socks, letting them fall to the floor. I push off the bed and scoot to the end, wrapping my fingers around the heavy buckle on his belt. I glance up, through my lashes, and wait to see the flash in his eyes before I pull the thick leather through the loop. My hands push between his jeans and the thin layer of his boxer briefs, dragging them down his thick thighs.

His nostrils flare, the only warning I get before he pounces, moving with the strength and agility only an athlete can master, and even with his jeans around his knees, he has no trouble maneuvering my body to get what he wants.

What he needs.

What I need.

What we crave.

25

MAVERICK

"The Only One Who Gets Me" by Charles Kelley

I'm on fire.

The blood that is rushing and roaring through my overstimulated and deprived body makes me feel like I'm seconds away from exploding. Literally, it's as though Leigh keeps sparking new flames through my body. Fuck, I almost came in my pants when she bit down on my neck. But somehow I held back. Kept my control. It wasn't until just now that I knew holding that control was futile.

I almost trip, the pants stuck on the top of my boots, resting right at my knees. I'm not even sure if I'll be able to stop long enough to get them off. The only thing I can see right now is her.

Leighton's hands slip under my arms and I feel them press against my back. Almost like a ripple effect, all the muscles start to spasm and constrict. I've never, not in my whole fucking life, felt something as powerful as the two of us together. Not even fully naked, and my chest is so tight it's hard to breathe through the emotion that is building there. My heart feeling like it's beating for the first time. Pressing my forehead to hers, I close my eyes and try to calm the wild thumping.

I've never given anyone this part of me. Not a single person would have ever gotten it. This part of me, the part that was made for her, has been locked up and guarded so tight that I feel complete and utterly vulnerable. The unnerving feelings that brings forth leave me defenseless with the enormity of this moment.

It's the most beautiful kind of terror a person will ever experience.

Her hands start to roam, soothingly, and I open my eyes to gaze down at her. Her face is soft and her eyes are full of love. The gates have been opened, and what she's giving me in this moment is everything I was always too afraid to dream of. I knew, every day that we were apart, that if I never had this, I would be lost forever. Nothing would ever be able to bring me back.

Slowly, I roll to my side and sit up. My boots hit her wood floor first, followed silently by my socks, and then the heavy clang of my belt buckle hitting the floor. With my elbows on my knees, I exhale loudly and drop my chin to my chest. I was so lost with my mind, attempting to regain just a sliver of control over my body back, that I didn't even hear her move. One dainty hand presses against the middle of my back seconds before her soft body curves against my side, rubbing in soothing circles while I get my bearings. Her lips press soft kisses all over my shoulder and bicep. My cock jumps with each press of her mouth against my overheated flesh.

Lifting my head, I look over my shoulder. Her eyes are closed, the content pleasure that she feels from just touching me, though, is still written all over her face. I continue to watch her, leveled to the fucking ground with how beautiful she is right now.

"Leigh," I say hoarsely. Her lids slowly lift and she looks up at me almost like she's drunk and can't focus. I clear my throat. "Come here, baby."

She moves quickly, her leg swinging over mine, and then she settles her ass in my lap. Words aren't spoken, but we move synchronized, both of us knowing what the other wants without voicing it. Her dress is pulled over her head by my hands while hers work on unsnapping her bra. By the time the white dress had fluttered to the ground, my lips were wrapped around one of her nipples as I took the other and squeezed gently with my hand. My other hand went behind her back to pull her chest closer to my face. Her hands start pushing through my hair, running from the top of my head to the base of my neck. Switching my mouth to the other nipple, I move my hands to her hips and press down. She lets out a low whine when the hardness of my cock presses against her panties. Even though the barrier isn't much, I want it gone.

Releasing her tit with a loud pop, I look down our bodies. Her flat stomach tightening with each roll of her hips. The desperation to feel more evident in her heavy pants.

"Lift up, darlin'," I huskily request of her.

Her legs tremble against my thighs and I look up at

her. She has her bottom lip pulled in and her teeth biting down on it hard. Her wild eyes begging me for what she wants. My hands go to her panties and with more help than I thought she would be capable of, she helps lift each leg so I can drag them down and drop them to the pile of clothes on the floor.

With her still lifted up, I lay back and hook my finger in my boxer briefs and pull them past my ass. She follows the movement with her eyes, and thank fuck she did, because I'm so hard I can't get them over my cock. Her hands come out and gently, so fucking gently, she lifts the band and helps free me. I pull them the rest of the way to my knees, but with her legs still spread around me I have to stop. My cock standing straight up and the sight before me has me so fucking turned on it twitches once before slapping her in the stomach softly.

Even though the light from the moon gives us plenty to see clearly, I need more. I don't want to miss a second of this, and fuck me, I'm going to make sure I have the clearest images burned into my brain for the rest of my goddamn life.

"Hold on," I huff, taking her in my arms and standing. Her pussy opens and wraps around the thickness of my cock. I look down, seeing the angry red tip peeking up at me. I almost forget my intention at the sight.

With a groan, I kick my briefs down my leg and off before walking back to the doorway and flipping the switch to bring her overhead lighting on. The harshness of the bright lighting makes me blink a few times, but when I focus back on the woman in my arms I'm beyond pleased that I took the time to turn the light on.

She's the picture of desire. The hunger I feel for her amps up. The itch just under my skin starts to simmer when her hands roam across whatever part of my body she can touch. However, the demand I feel to sink into her body takes a backseat as we continue to study each other. It turns into something new, something indescribable, licking up my spine and making me gasp when it becomes too much to bear. We're as close as we can be without fusing our bodies together, and with her heart beating just as wildly against my sweat-slicked skin, I realize what this new need is.

And I know the second I get it, I will never be the same again.

Walking back to the bed, I lay us softly down onto the mattress. Keeping our bodies together, but this time closing my eyes and taking her mouth. She opens immediately, a sigh of happiness escaping her lips and letting my tongue in. I kiss her deeply and slowly, pouring everything I feel into that kiss. Our tongues tangle, gliding against each other with slow sweeps. I feel her hands shaking as she runs them up and down my back sluggishly. Her legs trembling around my hips until she's no longer able to keep them locked tight, letting them fall against the mattress, and opening up her pussy even more for my thick cock. I groan, feeling her wetness coat me as I start to glide through, thrusting slowly. Each time I rub against her clit, she whines. With one more sweep of my tongue, I pull back and look down at her, my eyes widening when I see the tears falling from her eyes and down to the bed.

Her sobs are silent, and despite the tears, she smiles up

at me. Her arms move, and then I feel her hands frame my face. She blinks a few times before knocking the air out of my lungs with her words.

"I love you, Maverick Austin Davis. I loved you then. I love you now. I'll love you always."

There it is. All of her. And finally, with that, I've found all of *me*.

"I, *God*," I breathe, closing my eyes while her words wash over me before opening them again. "I love you right back, Leighton. Loved you then. Love you always."

Her breath hitches, more tears fall and fuck me, they aren't just her tears.

"I'll never let you go again." She hiccups.

"I never want to go."

Lifting my hips, not looking away, I sink into her body. Each inch that enters her makes her moan a little louder. When I'm all the way in, my balls tight against the wetness running from her body, I take her mouth again. This time there is no slow buildup—I take her like a starved man. My hips go from lazy rocking to forceful thrusts. Her tits bounce between us until I press our bodies even closer, hitting her cervix with how deep I am. When I feel her walls ripple against me, I tear my mouth from hers with a groan seconds before her head pushes into the mattress and she screams my name.

I hiss through my teeth when her pussy becomes impossibly tight, then she starts to come, her walls flexing, releasing and squeezing my own climax to the edge. My thrusts become frantic, the slapping of our wet bodies connecting, echoing loudly. My spine feels like it's being cranked tighter each time I drive into her tight, wet body, but I'm selfish and I want more.

Reaching between our bodies, her eyes widen and her swollen lips part. The second I roll my fingers over her clit she screams a loud, jumbled mess of words completely incomprehensible.

"Give me another one, Leigh. Come on my cock again and let me give you every part of me."

She whimpers, shaking her head. "It's too much, Mav. God, it's too much."

"It's never too much, darlin'," I wheeze when she gets even tighter. "Baby, God, give it to me. Let me love you good."

"Oh, my God. Oh, my *GOD!*" She starts to moan, shaking her head and arching her back. "You're so deep," she continues, the words a struggle to get past her heaving breaths making me take her even faster than before.

I drag my cock out, the tip resting inside of her quivering body, and wait for her eyes to focus on my face. When I feel like I might pass out from denying my body what it needs, she gives me what I want.

And I give her the only thing left.

"Never going to let you go. Not another day apart, Leigh. You and me, forever," I vow, pushing in to the hilt and emptying myself inside of her body with a loud shout. My stomach starts clenching tightly and my whole body shakes. I wrap my arms under her and squeeze her tightly, not letting go even when I roll so she's on top. Her arms stay under my back, just as needy as I am to stay connected. I feel our combined wetness start to fall from where I'm still hard and buried deep, but I'm in no hurry to move an inch.

Everything I've always wanted.

Right here in my arms.

26

LEIGHTON

"Drunk on Your Love" by Brett Eldredge

I want to wake up this way for the rest of my life.

I've been awake for hours. Well, not hours, but it feels like it. I woke up with my body pressed tightly against Maverick's. Our naked bodies a tangle of legs and arms. He didn't even stir when I slid from the bed to use the restroom. There wasn't even a twitch when I returned, bringing myself back to him. I didn't press as close as we had been, but I couldn't stand to be far, so I kept my head on his outstretched bicep while curling my arm over his body. With this new position, I was able to keep us connected by touch and still be able to look at him clearly. To study the man that is finally mine.

And that's where I've stayed for what feels like hours, just watching his handsome face while he sleeps peacefully. He looks so youthful. His dark eyelashes curling against his cheek, his mouth parted ever so slightly, and even in his sleep, they're curled into a content smile.

His strong and angular face is now sporting the shadows of his stubble. The sight alone makes my palms twitch with the desire to feel the roughness. With the sheet riding low on his hips, I can see the generous ridge between his legs. I know, because I peeked when I got back in the bed, that even though it looks like he's hard, he's not. My mouth watered when I saw his sizable soft cock resting against the tan skin of his legs.

My core throbs just thinking about how talented he is in bed. Of course, when you're working with something *that* awe-inspiring, I'm half tempted to never leave this bed. It seems silly to call a man's penis beautiful, but I can't come up with a better word for it. My train of thought makes it impossible to hold in the soft giggle that bubbles up. If you had asked me a year ago if I would be lying in bed next to Maverick Davis, thinking about the beauty of his penis, I would think you had lost your mind. However, now that I know just what said penis is capable of, I'm tempted to see if we can cast a mold of it and bronze the damn thing.

I wiggle, rubbing my legs together, when my mind shifts to last night and just how well he can work that part of his body. My need for him cranks up. Surely one more peek won't hurt anything. I shouldn't feel guilty about it. Not at all. Anyone in my position would do the same thing.

Having enough with the inner debate going on, I throw caution to the wind and lift the sheet to look down his body. I've worked myself up so much one more glance might very well send me over the edge.

My eyes trail over the perfect rows of his abs. Each of the bumps and dips that lead to the deep V above his hips is so well defined, even in his slumber. Again, my fingers itch to feel the hot steel of his muscles. Continuing to peruse the Adonis in front of me, though, I'm pretty proud of the self-control I have to hold back. However, when I get to that beautiful package between his legs, expecting to see it slack against his skin like it had been before, I gasp. It's no longer resting against his leg, nope. The second the sheet was lifted the rest of the way off his crotch, that beautiful penis might as well have been a neon arrow pointing to my hand—in the air—holding the sheet from Maverick's body.

I gasp.

He chuckles.

I scream.

He laughs louder, the roughness in that sound shooting right through my already amped-up body.

"Darlin', you keep lookin', and it was only a matter of time before he said good mornin' to you," he drawls, his voice even deeper. The rough grit of his sleepy voice doesn't do anything to cool my body off.

His voice sounds like a wet dream.

His chest moves and I shoot my eyes to his face. "I said that out loud, didn't I?"

"You did," he confirms.

"Well, I meant it," I defend, refusing to feel embarrassed over my appraisal of him.

"Get over here and tell me good mornin' the right way," he says with a laugh.

I roll my eyes, my smile growing all sorts of wonky at his request, and make a big production of moving closer. Not happy with my slow movements, he reaches out to grab me around the waist, pulling me up and on top of his body. My legs open and his very much awake, beautiful cock, is right back where I want it.

"Good morning." I beam, resting my arms on his chest, careful not to dig my elbow into his skin and remind my body that we aren't as desperate for him as we feel.

"It sure is," he quips, grinning right back at me.

"I need to jump in the shower. I wish I could stay in bed all day, but I need to be at the PieHole by ten. We don't open until noon today, but I need to go and make sure we don't run out of pie since I took yesterday off."

"I reckon I need to get a move on the day too, darlin'. I've got a duffel bag to go get," he adds with a wink.

"That makes me really happy." I sigh, my voice full of the dreamy wonder that I feel.

"Yeah, Leigh. Me too."

Moving my hands, I kiss the spot right above his chest. "What are your plans for today?"

His fingers start tracing lazy circles up my spine and I shift, making the part of him that I swear is way too talented hit my needy center. We both groan.

"I've got a future to build." His fingers move back up and I lose them briefly as he makes a soft drag over my shoulders, my skin burning in their wake. Then he takes my face in a gentle hold. Lifting his head off the pillow so that we're nose-to-nose. "I'm meetin' Clay for a late lunch in town. His lawyer is comin' and we're gettin' all the paperwork and legal bullshit out of the way so I can buy the land back. It's going to take some time to get all the plans in my mind designed before we can begin buildin', so it's just the formality that needs to happen quickly so I can get this off the ground." He's silent for a beat before I see his face grow serious. "If you can get away, I would like you there."

"Me?" I ask, confused, searching his face for a clue.

"Our future, remember? It won't just be my name on that land, Leighton."

My jaw slacks until my mouth is hanging open silently in shock.

"Fuck, you're cute."

"Are you sure? I mean, this training school, honey, that's yours."

His eyes narrow. "It's *ours*. Just because you aren't gonna be the one runnin' it or workin' it doesn't change that. I'm buildin' this for us—our future. We're startin' our lives together and I want you to know that with no doubts to where I stand when it comes to you."

"I trust you, Mav," I respond, slightly troubled that even after last night he still thinks he has to prove something to me. "I thought you knew that, honey," I say with a sigh.

"I do, Leigh, I really do. This isn't just about that. It means a lot to me that you're part of this. I want everyone to see what we're buildin' here and know that it's forever. I want to give us a solid start, but I want that start to be somethin' that's built on an unshakable foundation. One day, I'm gonna give our kids that foundation, and they're goin' to know their parents built it—together—with their love, merging all the parts of our lives. This land, the memories we shared on it, and us. It will be visible in everything we're buildin', Leigh. Bits and pieces from our past mixing with the people we became while we weren't ready to be us. It's so much more than just leavin' no doubts, darlin', so much more. It's *us*."

"You're going to make me cry," I speak on a rush of air.

"You'll be there?" he asks again, his face softening with the wetness gathering in my eyes. His thumb presses against my wobbly chin as if trying to ease my emotional heart.

"Yeah, honey, I'll be there." After that, I would give him the world if he asked for it.

"Good." He smiles.

"You hungry?" I question, blinking furiously to clear my eyes, and changing the subject before I end up ugly crying all over him. "I can make you something after I shower, before I head out."

"Starved." His eyes darken, the bright emerald turning murky. That grin turns dangerous and I feel my belly clench.

He moves so quickly, sliding out from under me and standing from the bed in one quick movement. His arms are reaching down to pull me up and over his shoulder before my mind has even registered that I'm no longer straddling him. He stomps to the bathroom, my position over his shoulder giving me one hell of a view of his hard, round ass. Each step he takes makes it flex in the most mouthwatering way.

My God, this man is perfect everywhere.

The bathroom hadn't even had a chance to fill with the

steam from our hot shower before I was crying out my second release, coming against his tongue. Only then did he stand and gave me the most devilish grin. My heart racing from the whirlwind of leaving the bed and being at his mercy.

"Thanks, darlin'. That was the best breakfast I've ever had."

Even with my sated body, feeling like I'm incapable of lifting even a finger, his words have me throwing my head back and laughing harder than I have in years. Well, that was until my laugh turned into a high-pitched, toe-curling scream. There really is no better way to wake up than with this man. Especially when that wake-up comes with his hard body pressing me against the shower wall as he takes me in the most deliciously hard way.

Yeah, I want to wake up this way for the rest of *our* life.

- ★ -

"Someone looks like she woke up on the right side of a cowboy," Jana observes, wagging her brows rapidly when I walk into the kitchen of the PieHole two hours later. My legs still feel weak from Maverick's very energetic good-bye against the front door ten minutes ago, so I almost fall on my ass when she speaks. I had been so lost in my thoughts, I don't even think I realized she was standing there.

"Hi, Jana. Yes, it's a beautiful day. I'm doing great, thanks for asking." I respond smartly, pushing the images of Maverick's good-bye from my mind, and grabbing my favorite apron off the hook of my office door before going to the sink to wash up.

"Don't you be a smart-ass, Leighton dear. Give an old lady something to think about here! Come on, details, missy."

"You really don't understand boundaries at all, do you?" I laugh, moving from the sink to start prepping for today. First up on the list, cookie dough pie, I think.

"There is no such thing. Boundaries are for the boring and the young, too dumb to realize how short life is. Now tell me, how's that broken hooha of yours?"

I hang my head, hiding my smile, and trying my hardest not to laugh at her. It would just encourage her. Which, if I'm honest with myself, doesn't take much. The smallest reaction, even if it's just breathing, will just incite her impossible behavior. I swear she gets more outrageous as the days go by.

"I'm guessing, with that blush you're sportin' now, you definitely fixed that broken hooha," she muses to herself, clearly not needing an active participant for this conversation. Good, maybe she'll move on and go get everything outside of my kitchen ready for the start of our day.

Of course, my relief is short-lived when I hear the back door bang open.

"Who had a broken hooha?" I hear and look up to see Quinn walk through into the kitchen from the mouth of the hallway. "I saw you pullin' up and decided to come over," she says with a shrug, answering my unasked question before walking over to the fridge closest to her and pulling out a pie. With her shop just down the street from the PieHole, this is a normal occurrence, something I would have been anticipating had I not been lost in the Maverick lust fog.

"Hey!" I snap, throwing my hands in the air and narrowing my eyes at the pie in her hand. "Sure, Quinn, help yourself."

She sticks out her tongue, grabs a fork from the cutlery station, and starts eating from the center of the chocolate chip cherry cream pie that she just grabbed. I should have better hidden the featured pie for today. Or, at the very least, realized this could happen and made an extra to cover the one she'll devour in seconds. Her eyes close in bliss around the prongs. She points her fork down toward the pie and then lifts her thumb up. Guess that means the new recipe I had created for the nonbake selections is a go.

"So," she says, ignoring my annoyed glare, "what was all that about a broken hooha?" She finishes her question just like Jana had, wagging her brows in a dramatic fashion.

"Oh, no way! There is no way in hell that I'm having this conversation with *you*! Do you see what you've done now, Jana?" I complain, huffing at both of them.

They both laugh at my expense, clearly loving the fact that I'm uncomfortable talking about this with them. I mean Jana is one thing, but Quinn? There is no way that she wants to hear about her brother's sex life with me. Scratch that; she's just as shameless as Jana. There is no way *I* want *her* to hear about my sex life with her brother.

"Oh, come on!" she whines. "You have to give us something. There has to be some bonus here, being your best friend. I get the scoop the whole damn town is desperate for. The way everyone is talking you would think the two of you are two steps toward the altar! Hell, just this morning Elliott Parker came to pick up his new F-250 and he didn't even want to talk about the lift I specially ordered and installed for him. The same lift I told him might not be available for *months* but that I was able to get in three days. Did he care? Nope. All he wanted to talk about was you and Mav. You betcha ass I'm going to be getting some details *from my best friend* if this is what I'm going to have to put up with from now until forever."

I blush. "You're being ridiculous."

Quinn's cheeks get red, not from embarrassment, though. Stubborn as a bull, my Quinn, and she hates when I don't give in to her. "It will happen. I'm going to be hearing all of this, Leigh. You guys are like Romeo and Juliet. No, that's not right—they had that whole-families-that-hate-each-other thing. And they died and shit. Whatever. You two are the town fairy tale, yeah, that's it. They're not going to stop. I just know it. Not even after you guys finally get married. Mark my words."

"I would love a good wedding," Jana adds wistfully.

"No one is getting married!" I yell, still looking incredulously at Quinn.

"Yet," they both add simultaneously before dissolving into uncontrollable laughter.

"You keep it up and I won't let you be my maid of honor," I shoot back at Quinn. She stops laughing, looking over in my direction with wide eyes. I sneak a peek at Jana, seeing the same shocked glaze in her eyes that have taken over Quinn's. Hell, I didn't think they would take me seriously. Like I would ever think of excluding Quinn. I open my mouth to tell her that very thought, but stop dead when I feel the hard body press against my back.

Warmth settles into my skin for just a beat before it's zinging and zapping every nerve.

"Who's gettin' married, darlin'?" the deep voice asks, lips poised right at my ear. Chills dance down my skin like a steady rainfall in response to him being this close. My body's reaction to him is something I hope I never get used to.

Instead of looking sheepishly shocked, the brazen duo is fighting with everything they're worth to hold in their laughter. Something they're failing miserably at.

Oh, the hell with this. Tossing the bag of berries that I had just grabbed off the workstation back down, I salute the ladies in front of me with one proud middle finger before turning to face Maverick.

"No one. Especially not you."

He staggers back, dramatically, like I just punched him. His hands going to his heart playfully, and I forget every ounce of my embarrassment I had felt earlier now that I'm faced with a playful Maverick Davis. He continues to sway on his feet before leaning back against the wall behind him. Has there ever been a time, even when we were young and carefree, that I had ever seen him this lighthearted? No, I'm pretty sure I haven't, because this is something I never would have forgotten.

"Say it isn't so, darlin'," he wheezes after he finishes his dramatic fall against the wall, eyes crinkled at the side and a wide smile on his face. "You wound me."

"Holy shit," Quinn whispers behind me.

Jana giggles.

I just stand there, mouth hanging wide, feeling like

something in my chest had shifted with this sight of him. His elated grin doesn't leave his face when he stands to his full height and walks back over to me.

"Hey," he says with a wink, reaching out with two fingers to close my slack jaw, his grin growing knowingly.

"Hey," I parrot lamely in response, still feeling winded.

"Miss me?"

I laugh, the sound coming out more like a wheeze. "I just saw you not even a half hour ago."

"Well, I missed you."

"Oh, my God, Jana," I hear Quinn sputter. I'm sure she thought it was said low and for her ears only but nothing about Quinn is soft; it comes out just as if she were yelling it. That girl doesn't have a subtle bone in her body.

"I see it, sweetheart," Jana says with a sniffle.

Those two are all it takes for me to snap out of whatever spell playful Maverick had me entranced with. I roll my eyes teasingly at him and watch as his smile grows.

"What are you doing here? I thought I was meeting you at two over at the diner."

"You are. I just had something come up that I didn't want to do without you."

"Uh," I lament. "Okay?"

He looks over my shoulder at the girls behind me and tips his hat before grabbing my hand and leading me to the office. He doesn't shut the door, so if privacy was something he wanted by moving us here, he won't get it. Not when I can hear them both rushing around the kitchen to get closer. Thank God we don't open for another hour; judging by the sounds they're making, I'm going to have a mess to clean up, and if I know Jana, she wouldn't leave her post outside this door until she had all the juicy details her heart could handle.

"You know they're going to stand there like the busybodies they are and listen to whatever it is you dragged me in here for, right?"

He chuckles. "Reckoned as much." He turns back and shuts the door softly before returning to my side. "I should have known. Now we have our privacy from their ears and eyes. Which is good because I didn't really feel like kissin' you the way I want to in front of my baby sister."

Oh. Wow.

His pulls me into his arms, his butt resting against my desk, and kisses the strength right out of my legs. When he pulls back, I have to take a moment to get my brain to turn back on. If he hadn't been holding on to me, I would have melted into a puddle.

"Remember those calls I got last night?" he asks in a low tone. Even though the door is shut and I know we can't be heard, he obviously isn't taking any chances. My mind is still knocked drunk by his mouth, so I have to take a second to process his question.

"Uh," I hedge, trying to clear my mind in order to think back to anything that happened last night outside of him and me between the sheets. Or in the shower. Or against the door.

He groans, clearly reading my face. "Right, you'll remember if you think what happened before all *that*," he jokes. "The calls I got when we were on our way home? Those were from Trey. He left a message, one I got this mornin'. I listened to it when I got in the truck, but decided to come here instead of headin' over for that duffel bag. Wanted to call him back with you."

"Okay?" I drag the word out, confused why he would need me to be with him to call some man back.

"Darlin', Trey was one of the best trainers when I was ridin'. Not only that, but he's my biological father's brother. We got close and he was able to give me parts of his brother that I can't ever get back now that he's gone. He's a big part of my life, Leigh. Trey's still there, but he was callin' because he was offerin' me a spot to train next to him on the circuit."

My eyes widen, what he's telling me registering and wiping that love-drunk feeling right out of my mind. Words escape me. He had opened up to me the other night about his biological father not being alive anymore. He never got a chance to know him so he hadn't felt like it was a big deal. I've worried since about how he was coping with never having a chance to know that part of him, but with this new knowledge about an uncle, I feel as if maybe he has been able to know that part of him. Not directly, but clearly this Trey means a great deal to him. I want to be excited that he got that offer, especially since it means he's close to that part of his family, and it clearly shows that the men he had traveled and lived with for so long know he's an asset to the sport even if he isn't riding anymore. I want to be supportive if this is something he wants. But I would be lying, because just the thought of him leaving fills me with dread.

He kisses my forehead, looking down at me knowingly,

with love in his eyes. "It's okay to not be happy about that call, Leighton. Don't hide what you're feelin'."

I try to choose my words carefully before I speak. "You know I only want what is best for you. I won't lie and say that it doesn't fill my belly with lead thinkin' that you got an offer that could pull you away from me, though. I just want you to be happy, honey, and if goin' to your uncle is what you need, I'll support that."

He reaches out, not lifting his bottom off my desk, and grabs both of my hands, pulling me between his spread legs. "I came here after hearin' his message because when I call him back, I want it to be with you. I'm gonna have him in my life regardless. I knew what I would tell him before I got here, but I wanted to do this with you. Together, darlin'."

He doesn't wait for me to speak. He shifts, dropping one of my hands to pull his phone from his back pocket. I watch, my heart in my throat, while he presses the screen a few times before ringing fills the silence around us. He keeps hold of the phone but doesn't let go of my other hand, his thumb continuing to caress it soothingly.

"Well, I'll be!" the disembodied voice booms through the speaker after the click of the call connecting. Maverick's shoulders shake as he turns the volume down on his phone's speaker. "About time your sorry fuckin' ass learned how to return a call."

"Got my girl in front of me, Trey, do me a favor and watch your mouth," he says in lieu of a greeting.

"My apologies," he mumbles. "You get my message?" If he was shocked at Maverick's claim to having his girl with him, he didn't show it.

"I got it, Trey. You didn't have to call fifteen times last night to leave it, though. I would have called you back with one missed call and no message."

"That might be so, son, but have you ever known me for being patient? I was too excited to wait. Not only is it a great opportunity for you, but I knew you would be happy to get that call."

Maverick's face gets soft and he squeezes my hand. I swallow the hot saliva pooling in my mouth. No matter what, I will support him and stand by his side. I will not break down and beg him to never leave. Part of us moving forward, together, means blind support no matter what.

"Well, Trey," he starts and my hand involuntarily flexes within his hold. "I appreciate the offer and for the faith you have in me to even offer it—"

"Of course I've got faith in your sorry ass," Trey interrupts with a gruff chuckle.

Before panic can fill my system, though, I feel like a slide show of our lives starts playing through my mind. Rapidly, zooming through those memories, until landing on the ones of us since he returned. In that moment, without him even voicing it, I know there is no way that he's going to accept. The clarity of that knowledge beating back the panic.

Even though I know with everything I am that there is no way Maverick would be accepting, the words from a man I've never met feel like a punch to the gut. I cock my head and study Maverick, waiting for him to talk. Raising my brow and mentally beating the doubt back, knowing in my heart that he wouldn't leave.

"Like I said, it means a whole lot to me that you have that faith. You know how much I respect you and I wouldn't be the rider that I was if it hadn't been for your guidance through the years."

"Shit, boy. I might have been guidin', but the rider you are has nothing to do with that. It's in your blood, son. You were born a rider and there isn't anyone else that I want workin' alongside me. I knew you wouldn't turn this down," the man speaks again, interrupting Maverick. I'm starting to think that's normal, since Maverick doesn't seem to be offended or annoyed. But I am.

"I think you should let him finish," I snap. "Sir." I add the last part in a rush as an afterthought, not letting my manners slip just because I'm feeling emotional. Maverick's whole body starts to shakes with hilarity.

The phone is silent between us after my annoyed rush of words. Maverick leans forward and gives me a quick kiss before speaking again. "Like I was sayin', Trey. I appreciate the offer, but I'm going to have to say no. You know I'll always be here if you want to shoot the shit and talk shop, but I'm home now. Where I want to be. When Doc told me I couldn't ride, it was the best news I could have gotten . . . a blessing in disguise. Damn sure didn't see it then. Couldn't see what was right in front of my face long before I got bucked off that last time. I've lived my life being driven by anger, fueled with a whole lot of regrets, but I'm done with that life, Trey. I know we talked about ways to get me back out, to keep me where I thought I needed to be, but I can honestly tell you with no regrets, everything I need is right here in front of me."

Trey doesn't speak for a second, clearly not happy with the rejection of his offer because he grumbles some unpleasant words before speaking again. "I hear ya, Maverick. I respect that, and even though I wish I had your skills by my side, I'm happy that you're not still drownin' in your own mind's bullshit anymore. I know my brother would be feelin' the same way."

My big, strong man bends, pressing his forehead to mine. "Nah, I might have been lost for a little while, but I had a good guide to bring me back. I've got some shit I'm startin' here that I have a feelin' you're gonna want to chat about. I'll give you a call next week. See if you can make some time to come out and meet my girl."

The rest of their conversation is brief, but by the time he stops talking I have tears rolling down my face. Not sad ones, but pure happiness is leaking from my eyes. The magnitude of his decision is something that can't be ignored. Two months ago, when he rolled back into town, I never would have believed that he would stick around Pine Oak. I would have been crippled the second he even mentioned the call and the offer that came with it. However, that was before I felt how powerful our love really was. Before I knew the truth that pulled him from my life to begin with. And long before I accepted that it was the right move, no matter how much it hurt. Even being torn apart for a decade, I know that it really was our destiny taking a driver's seat, making sure that we were ready when our time finally came.

That time is now.

I believe in our love, the future he's building for us, and

most important, him. There is no place for doubts or fears when you have a connection as deep as ours. We didn't know it then, but these bonds were always unbreakable. It was just a matter of time before they snapped us back where we belonged.

Together.

27

LEIGHTON

"Yeah Boy" by Kelsea Ballerini

After Maverick's call, we left the office to find that Quinn had already left to head back to her shop. When he shut the door on her eavesdropping, she must have gotten bored. Or maybe she remembered that she runs a business and actually went back to it.

Jana didn't ask any questions, just gave me a knowing smile before leaving the kitchen to get everything ready to open at noon. She doesn't ever cross those boundaries she couldn't care less about if there isn't sex involved in the gossip anyway. Silly woman.

The day went by too quickly after I was left alone in my kitchen. I spent the vast majority of my time before Maverick was due back to getting ahead on my prep for the week, meaning I would have some extra time to spend with him. It's been so long—if ever—that I went out of my way to make so much overage that I had almost ran out of refrigerator space, but it's important to me that I find a balance between work and my new love life. By the time Maverick had come back to get me, I had enough done that I could have taken the rest of the week off if I wanted to. As tempting as that sounds, I can't just abandon the PieHole because my heart has found its reason to race again.

I felt like I was in a daze during the whole meeting with the Davis boys and their family lawyer. Maverick, though, hadn't stopped smiling, not once since leaving the PieHole hours before. Of course, I didn't know that for a fact, since we weren't together the whole time, but that smile was still on his face when he walked back through the kitchen doorway, and it hadn't left once during our lunch meeting. I had my head so far in the clouds that I almost signed my name on a bunch of documents with no clue as to what I was actually signing. It took me longer than the men would have liked, but I read through each and every page. Every noise I made had Maverick's hand rubbing soothing circles on the inside of my thigh, a place he had placed his hand the second we sat down.

Jana has given me my space since I got back from the diner earlier, and thankfully Quinn hasn't been back yet. She will be. It's our thing for her to join me at some point before closing. For the first time, I'm not full of my normal excitement at anticipating spending time with my best friend. I love her, but I also know that her normal quirky self won't stop until she is satisfied that she knows more details about my relationship with her brother than anyone else. Including myself.

I'm sure she already knows everything that went down at the diner earlier. Even without him confirming it, I know Maverick picked that spot with care. He could have, and probably should have, had that meeting back at the ranch. By moving it to the one place in Pine Oak that would guarantee the quickest flash of gossip to spread, my man was making it a point for us to be seen—together, as a couple. They might not know what his plans are as far as the big picture, but then none of the specifics matter. Not when the fact that both Maverick and I were purchasing land—together—and to anyone watching, he was making the biggest public display to prove our commitment. I could have told him it was pointless, I know where his heart is, but a small part of me is giddy with happiness that he purposely wanted people to know how serious we are.

I thought Marleen Day, best friend of Marybeth Perkins, was going to swallow her tongue when Clay mentioned his jealousy over his brother getting pie whenever he wanted it now that he was living with "the best damn baker in Texas." And of course, Jimmy Lane, one of the diner regulars, looked like he was about to have a heart attack when Maverick joked that he was going to have fun eating that pie off said baker. Then there was Jimmy's best friend, another regular, Terry Long, who couldn't help but mention that it was about damn time Maverick had his pie and ate it too. I would have been embarrassed, but when I saw the looks on the faces of Joellen Heely and Tracey Hawthorn, two of the biggest sluts in town, when they heard all that—it was worth it. In the end, once everyone inside the diner realized what was going on, it started a domino effect that went on and on until I was finally able to get back to the PieHole.

Once I'm back in the solitude of my kitchen, though, my mind just won't shut off. Good thoughts, but still, I'm ready for the novelty of us to wear off so the town will stop acting like we're the most incredible thing since sliced bread. I can't help but wonder whether the overexuberance and near-frantic excitement we're encountering are helping my mind still the anxiousness I've felt over of us moving so quickly. Not doubt, just stress because of how much things are changing. I've never done well with change. There have been so many huge changes in my life in this short time, I should be a mess, but I'm far from that. If it were anyone other than Maverick, I *would* be a mess with things moving as rapidly as they are, changing so dramatically. Any other man—or any other relationship, rather—it would be too soon.

With him, though, I feel like it's about time.

We just decided to give us a try, but even though it's been only days, it feels like years. You don't spend your whole life wanting something you know you're meant to have, living without it for ten years, and not grab hold with everything you are when you finally have it. Knowing that Maverick has always felt the same way, I imagine that even the lightning speed in which we are moving is too slow for him.

Even though we wasted so much time, I know without any doubts that time was needed. My heart breaks for Maverick, knowing the pain he felt—the pain he lived— that pushed him to leave. I don't hold that against him, not now. The time that we lost built him into the man he is today. We had time to discover ourselves. We both had other relationships—a term I use loosely for him—but it's because of all that I know we're finally ready for us. I believe with everything in my heart that had I been given him when we were so young, me full of naïveté and him full of pain, we might not have been strong enough to last. It's a sobering thought, especially since I know we were made for each other. I could choose to dwell on what we lost, but instead I prefer to focus on what we will have.

I know Maverick feels the same; his warp speed is a testament to that. He, like me, is very aware that in a different life, we would be married with kids by now. Hell, if he had his way, I bet he would have me barefoot and pregnant tomorrow in an effort to start making up for that lost time.

I step away from the fridge after placing the last pie I had just finished inside, fanning myself with my hand at the thought, and look around to see if anyone had witnessed my hot flash.

Alone, thank God.

With the heat still high on my cheeks from just the thought of being pregnant with Maverick's children, I plop down on the tall stool next to my prep station and stare off into space. Now, that's something that I know is too soon to be hoping for, but now that the vision is in my mind, I can't clear it. God, our children will be beautiful.

"What are you daydreamin' about?"

Startled, I look up, glancing at Quinn before looking at the clock. "You're done early?"

"I was missing some parts for the lift on Tucker Hillstorm's son's truck. I figured, I can't get the rest of my shit done without those parts, so I might as well come bug you some more."

"Uh-ha," I smart, feeling my brow arch. "And did these parts go missing before or after all the gossip firing through this town hit your shop? I have to admit, I expected you earlier than this."

"I may have put it behind some stuff I know won't be moved so that I could claim they were missing if Tucker asked someone else while I was gone. And that may or may not have been right after some juicy whispers started to hang in the shop's air."

I toss my head back and laugh.

"You would have done the same thing," she says defensively.

"If what? You stopped avoiding relationships long enough to be the center of those whispers?"

"Hey," she laughs. "I'm not avoiding relationships. I'm just picky."

"Quinn, seriously? The only person that is more afraid of a relationship than you are is Clay. He's so phobic about it he's still driving three towns over to hook up with chicks. Look at you! All I have to do is say the word and you're cringing."

She narrows her eyes.

"Relationship," I throw her way, enunciating the word slowly.

"Shut up!"

"Re-lay-shun-ship!" I yell.

318 - Harper Sloan

"Whatever. I'm not afraid of them. I just haven't met someone worth my time."

"What about Travis? Or Michael? Or Brett? Or—" I start laughing even harder when she holds her hand up and throws daggers my way with her eyes. "You haven't met anyone worth your time because all you're willing to give them is a sliver of you. You can't know what they're worth when you aren't willing to try. Mark my words, one of these days you're going to fall on your ass over a guy, and I, for one, can't wait to see that happen."

"Well, until then I'm going to just enjoy falling on my ass with guys for a whole different reason."

I roll my eyes. "I swear you have a man's mind. All you think about is sex."

"Speaking of—" she starts, and I hold my hands up immediately.

"Don't you finish that thought unless you really want to know. You're my best friend and I've never kept anything from you, but you're also his sister. Awkward doesn't even begin to touch that one."

She huffs impatiently and lifts off where she had been leaning to walk toward the fridge. Luckily, she picked the fridge that I keep stocked just for her and Clay's random drop-bys to raid my stuff. "You're the only one making it awkward. Just because he's my brother doesn't mean I can't high-five my girl for getting some much-needed dusting on her meat curtains. Plus, aside from the fact he's my brother, there isn't anything awkward about it. I've known you just as long as I have him."

"Did you . . . I . . . meat curtains?"

She shrugs.

"I've been neglecting you. Is that it? Are the guys down at the shop corrupting your mind again? We need to have a girls' night of pampering so you remember what it's like to think like a girl."

"What's wrong with meat curtains? Is vagina better, Leigh? Pussy. Love tunnel. They're all the same thing, just a little more pizzazz."

"Hooha!" Jana yells through the open doorway leading into the main floor. I hear snickers following her bellow.

"Right, and hooha," Quinn adds with a nod.

"Don't encourage her," I yell toward the doorway. "Okay, I get it. You are apparently a wealth of knowledge for vagina terminology. Should we talk about your brother's big huge cock now?"

She shrugs again, bravely. "You aren't going to shock me."

That felt a whole lot like a challenge. Quinn and I have never had boundaries when it came to dating, men, or sex, but I know her, and she might *think* she wants to know, but doesn't.

Well, Quinny, challenge accepted.

"Oh, Q, let me tell you, that man has a monster in his pants. I'm not even sure how I'm able to walk. Don't even get me started on the things he can do with his tongue, though. They should be illegal. Just this morning, he took me so hard in the shower that I feel like my insides are permanently branded." I finish and bite down on my tongue to keep from laughing at her expression.

Her face, the normal tan glow, is pale, and she is frozen

still. Fork in hand halfway to her mouth with cherry filling falling onto the floor.

"Perhaps"—she starts on a gulp—"I can be shocked after all."

I wink, turning to finish cleaning up the mess I had made with the last pies of the day. I should have known better than to think she would have been mortified into complete silence, though.

"You should probably be more careful if his big giant monster cock permanently branded you," she mumbles through a full mouth. "That can't be safe for your lady parts, and Leigh, I need you to protect those parts better until I get my niece."

I turn, woodenly, and look at her like she's lost her mind. "I'm not even sure which part of that to touch first."

"Probably the big giant monster cock," she snickers.

My eyes widen. "You are something else."

She beams.

"I'm not sure that's a positive thing." I laugh.

"Whatever. Don't keep things from me. I don't like it."

"Okay, okay. All joking aside, though, things are amazing, Q. I feel like I should pinch myself and make sure I'm not dreaming. All of those fantasies I've had all these years of being his—they pale in comparison to what the reality of being loved by him feels like."

She abandons her pie on the counter, grabbing a napkin to wipe off her hands and face before walking over and enveloping me in a big hug. "I'm so happy for you guys. I really am." And then she pinches me so hard on my side that I scream. "There, not dreaming," she adds with a laugh.

I join her, laughing at her crazy antics. I love her special type of crazy. She goes back to her pie, content in the silence, while I finish cleaning and closing down the kitchen. The only chatter coming from our back and forth trying to decide where to go when we close tonight.

"What about heading to the Coop?" Quinn asks when the dishwasher noise finally settles to a dull hum.

"That sounds good. Let me text your brother and see if he wants to meet us there. Last time I talked to him, he said he was going to have dinner with Clay."

"I passed them on the way here. I think they were going to that new pizza place just outside of town."

I fire off a text to Maverick before going about my business. Quinn is so used to my routine at closing that she silently starts to help. When Jana locks the door behind the last customer, we're able to knock out the rest of closing in ten minutes. By the time we were done I still hadn't heard from Maverick. I wasn't worried, though, knowing that he was spending some much-needed time with his brother.

"Let me send Mav another message and just let him know to meet us at the Coop, then we can head out," I tell Quinn, my face in my phone.

"Are you comin'?" Quinn asks Jana.

"Honey, I wouldn't miss this for the world. You better let that handsome cowboy know he's on designated driver duty," she adds with a hoot.

- ★ -

Let it be known, you should never trust Jana when she mentions needing a designated driver.

In the two hours since we got to the Coop, she's been making sure my drinks are never empty, between her bouts of line dancing and loud belly laughs. I lost count a long while ago.

"Why issshhhhhh everyone looking at me?" I slur, leaning into Quinn. At least, I think I'm leaning. Everything's been spinning for the past hour. We just got back from another dance-off in the middle of the crowded dance area.

"Because you're drank?" she hoots.

"Did you just say I'm drank?" I giggle, picking up my Corona. I'm a little too eager, though, and end up missing my mouth by a mile, spilling my intended mouthful all over my chest, causing Quinn and Jana to erupt in laughter.

"Are you trying to start a wet T-shirt contest?" Quinn wheezes through her chuckles.

I look down, and sure enough, my black bra is showing through the wet front of my white shirt. Shrugging, I decide that taking another hardy swallow is more important than worrying about it, the whole point of the black bra under the white shirt is a fashion statement, right? I'm totally covered in alcohol and loving it. After placing my glass down, I pick up one of the pigs in a blanket off the plate in the middle of our table. I love how the Coop has the best finger foods and apps. Technically, these aren't even on the menu, but when you grow up with the owner, you get what you ask for. I think it helps that Quinn and I have spent the past five plus years getting drunk and rowdy so they know it's best to give us food throughout the night, to soak up all the alcohol.

When I take a bite of the little wiener covered in buttery dough, my mind starts thinking about other "wieners"— bigger wieners—and every other thought vanishes.

"Hey Jana, can a monster penis break my hooha?" I ask, suddenly completely serious.

Quinn chokes, a spray of her beer flying from her mouth. "You!" she screams. "You can't just say that. Give a girl some warning."

"Well? Can it?" I continue as if Quinn didn't just cover everything—and me—in sticky beer.

"You could probably bruise your uterus," Jana muses, giving it an actual moment's thought.

Quinn screams in outrage and looks at me like I've just committed the gravest sin. "Don't you dare fuck things up and keep my niece from me!" Of course, she picks the one time that the bar noise and music aren't at their loudest to scream that, gaining wide-eyed shock from the surrounding people. "What?" she snaps at them with a slight slur. "You've never heard of big dicks breaking things? My brother is too busy breaking her shit to give me that baby!"

"What baby?" I ask, confused.

"The one you're going to make with my brother," she says slowly, as though explaining something to a child. "He understands the seriousness of this."

"Uh, no . . . we aren't makin' babies anytime soon, Q." I look around, seeing that now the people around us aren't even trying to act like they're not listening.

"Yet. Which, I might add, I'm not too happy that I'm being forced to wait."

Jana breaks in. "Sweetheart, you gotta let them have some fun first. Once those babies get here, they'll have to use all these stored-up humpin' memories until they can sneak away, trying to find time."

"You two are insane," I say, gasping. "We won't need to sneak away and find time. There isn't anything better than being loved nice and good by Maverick!"

"Until he breaks your vagina!" Quinn yells over the table.

"My vagina is not broken," I fume, tossing the fry I had been about to eat at her, hitting her in the middle of her forehead.

"Then why are you walkin' like you have a stick rammed up your butt?"

I frown, trying to remember if I actually have been, but it's hard to focus on that with all the beer swimming around my brain.

"I'm not walkin' funny. I've just been well used by a monster!"

"You don't have to brag about it," she grumbles.

"You're the one that keeps bringing up your brother's beautiful penis."

"Uh." I hear someone clear their throat, but keep looking at Quinn. She's not even paying attention to me, though, instead being held up by Jana while she struggles to stay on her stool because she's laughing so hard.

"Darlin', I'm not sure I would refer to my *monster* as beautiful."

I jerk my head around, and momentarily forget what I was doing when I see the two handsome men standing behind me. The Davis boys are a sight to behold, so similar in build and looks, but my heart goes wild for only one of them.

"And call it a cock, not a penis, Leigh! Men like to call it manly things like that."

Maverick looks behind me at his sister's vulgar words and just shakes his head, a vaguely pained expression on his face.

"Is it better if I say your cock is beautiful?" I ask in a serious tone, looking between Maverick and Clay, waiting for one of them to answer.

"Are you drunk, baby?" Maverick smirks at me.

I nod.

"You want to keep getting drunk or go home?"

"That depends," I whisper huskily, crooking my finger so he'll bend closer to me. "Do I get to ride my cowboy in both scenarios or only one?" Apparently I'm not as quiet as I had thought because Quinn and Jana start laughing loudly.

Maverick never answers me. He pulls me to my feet before sitting down in the stool I had been on and pulling me into his lap. Of course, judging by the hardness against my bottom, I have a feeling that I'll be riding my cowboy soon enough, no matter how much I have to drink tonight.

And I can't wait.

28

MAVERICK

"Save a Horse (Ride a Cowboy)" by Big & Rich

"**S**top," I scold, slapping Leigh's hand away playfully from my belt for the fifth time since I climbed into the driver's seat. We haven't even pulled out of the Coop and she's so worked up I half expected her to jump me in the parking lot.

"Please?" she whines.

"If you get your hands anywhere near my cock right now I'm going to wreck my truck."

She makes a sound of protest before huffing her hands over her chest and pouting out the window.

I've never seen Leigh drunk, but the playful, uninhibited side of her is something else. She was definitely feeding off the attention that our group was getting tonight. She's always been the quiet one, never shy to have fun, but she definitely didn't seek out the spotlight. Instead of allowing myself to get pissed that I missed watching her grow into her confidence, I thank my lucky stars that I get to spend the rest of my life experiencing every facet of her personality. We've known each other our whole lives, but in a lot of ways we're strangers.

I glance over, realizing I haven't heard from her in a few minutes, and seeing her slouched over sleeping like the dead, that gorgeous mouth hanging open slightly, I smile to myself. Clay warned me at dinner what we would find when we got to the Coop. Apparently the girls love going out to have a good time, and when alcohol is in play, they get a little rowdy. It was my decision to wait a few hours to head over. I wanted Leigh to have some girl time with Quinn, but a big part of me couldn't wait to experience drunk and wild Leighton James.

And I wasn't disappointed.

By the time we left, three hours after Clay and I got there, I was more than a little turned on. The drunker Leigh gets, the more handsy she is, apparently. But the more handsy she was, the wetter that white shirt kept getting. Hell, at one point I was mildly concerned that she couldn't even feel her lips anymore. She would just dribble her beer all over her. Don't get me wrong, I fucking love watching her cut loose, but I don't need the motherfucking punks in this town seeing her like that.

I pull up to the house, Leigh now snoring and drooling against the window. Turning off the truck, I look down at my still painfully hard cock and apologize for him not getting to have fun tonight. I was looking forward to finding out what drunk sex with Leigh would be like. Something tells me, judging by how hard the booze has hit her, it wouldn't be a fun time.

I drop to the ground and shut my door. She doesn't even stir, so I run up and unlock the door with the key that's now on my key ring. Earl gives a hardy meow before walking back into the dark house, clearly not impressed enough to stick around. I can see her still passed out from the porch lights reflecting into the cab. Even a mess, she still makes my chest feel like I'm about to have a heart attack. The power she holds over me is something indescribable.

I walk over to her side of the cab and ease the door open, planning to scoop up my little sleeping angel and bring her inside the house.

"Yeeeeeawwwwwwkkkk!" Leigh jumps me the second I click the door lock.

The next minute, though, I'm convinced I really am having a heart attack. The second her door clicked, moving under her passed-out slumber, she jumped and attacked. Second winds have nothing on my girl when she remembers what she was after before passing out. She moving so quickly that she brings us both down to the grass next to my truck. I've fallen harder, so a buck twenty-five woman bringing me to my ass is nothing, but it's the power behind her actions that knocks the wind right out of me. I'm fucking powerless. Powerless and loving every fucking second.

What was that I thought about her being a submissive woman during drunk sex? Fuck, could I have been any more wrong?

"You taste so good," she hums against my neck, her tongue licking hot paths from the collar of my shirt up to trace the shell of my ear. I was hard before now, but her actions are making my cock painfully so. "God, every inch of you tastes like an orgasm in my mouth."

My hands grip her hips, trying fruitlessly to guide her fumbled movements and keep her from doing permanent damage to my crotch. Her fingers curl into the gap between my buttons, and she leans up long enough to rip the shirt open, not even wasting time to pull it all the way off before her nimble fingers are pushing up underneath. My hands end up empty when she moves from my hold before I can even register it, but when I feel her hot breath against my stomach, I lift my head up to look down my body.

She's kneeling next to me, thankfully in the grass and not on the gravel that's on the other side. Her mouth is kissing softly across the skin right above my belt, her fingers making quick work of the leather. I push her hair over her shoulder, about to come in my fucking pants at the sight of her aroused face.

Fuck me, she wants this. Desperately, if I had to guess.

"Lift up," she commands, and I comply. She shoves my jeans down, taking my boxer briefs with them. The second my cock springs free of its bindings, though, she abandons my pants.

"Fuckin' hell!" I bellow into the darkness around us when her mouth takes my cock deeply. Not even gagging when I hit the back of her throat. When her hands come into play, one playing with my balls and the other working in tandem with her mouth on my cock, my eyes cross.

The ability to hold my head up is lost, and I drop back down and look up at the stars painted in the sky. The groans of her getting turned on just from my cock in her mouth become a sound track of lust. Between her noises and her mouth, I have to squeeze my eyes tight and clench my ass, the need to come overpowering.

"Get up here and fuckin' show your cowboy how you ride," I grunt, praying that I don't lose it before I can feel her hot pussy surround me.

I keep my eyes clenched and my hands fisting the grass under me, because I know that seeing her astride me would undo me completely at this point. Control? What's that? I had almost gained just a smidgen of it back when I feel her straddle my body, but when she drops hard down on my shaft, what little control I had managed to find evaporates.

My eyes snap open of their own volition to witness a sight I will never forget. I had been so lost in trying not to come that I completely missed her stripping down to nothing. There she was, with the moonlight bright on her pale skin, bouncing on my cock. With each vigorous shift of her hips, her tits sway. Her hands brace on my knees behind her, thrusting her chest into the spotlight, and making my mouth water.

"Your penis is so beautiful," she says with a moan. Even though I'm seconds away from blowing my top, hearing her say that makes my chest move with a laugh. Her head, which had been thrown back in pleasure, lifts, and she glares at me. "Don't you laugh at me, cowboy."

"Wouldn't dream of it, darlin'," I thickly rumble.

She moves her hands, still rocking against me, and brings

them up to squeeze her tits. My eyes falling to watch her pleasure herself. She gives her heavy breasts a few flexes of her fingers but then moves to pinch her nipples harshly. Her moans pick up volume. I say a silent prayer of thanks for being in the middle of nowhere because seeing her fuck herself on my body in the wide-open space of her front yard is a vision I hope to have branded in my memories forever. I feel my cock swell, her tight pussy making it impossible to do anything but pray I can last.

"You're so big," she whimpers, her even rocking faltering slightly.

My hands take her hips again, helping to steady her. Her hands drop her breasts as she falls to brace herself with them on either side of my head. The heavy weight of her huge tits leaves them rocking between our bodies, making my cock twitch, earning a squeak from her. I lick my lips, wishing I had the ability to flip her over and get my mouth on her tits, but I'm powerless to the woman taking what she needs, bringing us both to where we want to be.

Her lips move to mine, not moving to kiss me, as her breath ghosts over my parted mouth. 'Hold on, cowboy," she coos, the only warning she gives me before she starts bouncing, faster this time. Her tight heat swallowing me whole with every slam against me, moving her hips up rapidly until I can feel her tightness trying to suck me back in at the tip. She speeds up even further, her wetness running from our joined bodies down my shaft. There is nothing I can do but hold her hips tight while she shows me what it's like to be well and truly fucked.

When she drops one last time, squeezing my cock in

a vice grip, I'm powerless to hold back. My back flies off the ground, hands off her hips, and I groan out my release while kissing her roughly. With each pulse of my cock, she whimpers in return, swiveling her hips while riding out her own orgasm.

"Can we do that again?" she whispers against my lips, after our movements still to just a slight rustling.

I fall back, pulling her with me, and roar with laughter.

"Darlin', you just sucked me dry with your tight pussy. I'm gonna need to rest a bit before I can fuck you properly and show you how much I loved that ride."

She smirks and then to my utter shock throws her head up to the sky and starts singing Big & Rich's "Save a Horse (Ride a Cowboy)."

One Month Later

"Can I ask you something?"

Leighton looks over, stopping her puttering around the kitchen. "Of course you can." She smiles, but it looks worried.

It's been a month since we signed the deed for the land. Things are moving quickly, and construction is slated to start next month. As for Leighton, she won a big award for the Texas State Fair in Dallas the week after we signed the deed, and she hasn't slowed down since. Her Taste a Cowboy pie, some mix of cream, fruits, and bacon, of all things, won best tasting. She's been doing a few different county fairs since, not that her business needs to hype, but

I know it's something her mama used to love, so she does them for her.

We've been so busy that the time we do have together is usually stolen in between our schedules and sleeping. Not that I'm complaining; we've settled into our new lives together effortlessly. There isn't a second that passes Leigh doesn't make sure I know how much she loves me. Even if it's just a shy smile before driving to the PieHole. I might not be taking her out on extravagant dates, but I make sure she knows that her love is returned in spades.

Even with all that, though, I can't help but feel like there is just one piece left in a puzzle I've been working on for almost thirty years. The last one needed to fill that tiny empty spot I've never been able to satisfy.

"Why did you give so much of yourself to Buford?"

Shock flashes, clearly not expecting me to ask that. "What do you mean?" she hedges, walking around the island to sit at the kitchen table next to me.

"Clay told me you were there after he got sick, that you were there when he passed. I know that must not have been easy for you, with the PieHole and all, stopping your life to take care of him."

She reaches out and takes my hand, pulling it to her lap while shifting her chair so that we're right next to each other. I look up from the cat/beast I had been petting and give her my attention.

"You have to understand, Maverick, I didn't know everything that was behind you leaving. I knew Buford was a big part of it, but in my head he was still your father. When he got sick, all I could think of was what if that was you? What if you were out there on the road, sick and unable to care for yourself? No matter how much I wanted to hate him for pushing you away, even before I knew the magnitude of it, I looked at him, and I saw the man I was missing more and more as time passed."

I nod, understandingly, the heartbreaking reality that she was there and using him to replace me, in a way. "Do you think it's wrong that I can't forgive him?"

She's silent while she searches my face, whether it's so she can attempt to see where I'm headed with my questions or to choose her words carefully, but with a small shake of her head she breaks the silence. "I don't, honey. I know that it's been drilled in our heads that it's best to forgive, but some sins can't be washed away. What Buford did to you was wrong, so wrong. Your whole life was changed because of one hateful man. I've had my own issues with the forgiveness I had so easily given him after you told me everything, but in the end, I know I can't change anything by hating a dead man. I think what you really need to ask yourself is if holding on to all of that is worth the price you're paying."

Confusion pulls my lips into a frown, my brows wrinkled, and I feel myself start to protest before I even know what I'm going to say.

"Let me finish," she says, her free hand coming up to smooth the skin between my eyebrows. "You trusted me with the truth of your past, and that is something I will never take for granted. I will hold those truths inside until the day I die, but I think you need to tell Clay and Quinn. They didn't have it as bad as you, I would never even hint that, but they struggled too. I think you need to be honest with them about your mom, your relationship to Buford, all of it. I'm not saying it will be easy, but to leave it all behind you and forget it all, you have to let it go, and by keeping it bottled up between us, you're making it impossible to ever leave it behind completely."

"What good could telling them the truth do?"

"Honey," she says with a sigh, "Buford was a hateful man, but when he got sick a lot of that hate dissipated. I'm not saying it was gone or that it excused everything he did wrong in his life. Clay might have forgiven him for the past, but he will never forget. He gave Buford his forgiveness, but I think it was more for himself. He had carried a lot of anger around for a long time, and between Buford's hard hand and your mother leaving him, he doesn't trust easy. He has so much love to give, but because of the crap he's holding on to because of his parents, I fear he will never give it to someone lucky enough to have it."

She looks down, covering the hand she is still holding before lifting it to kiss against my knuckles. Not letting go, but giving me some of her love knowing that this conversation is hard.

"And then Quinn," she breathes. "My best friend has a heart so big but she keeps it hidden away. I've watched her harden herself from the sting of rejection her whole life. She won't let anyone get close enough to her because she is terrified of feeling that wound again. She used to burn so bright that the sun couldn't even keep up with her, but all it took was her opening her heart up a few times for that brightness to dim. It's been a long time since I saw her let anyone in. That fear rides her. She's damn good at hiding it, but it's there."

My chest hurts hearing about the struggles my siblings have hidden from me. "I thought that I would spare them the same pain I had felt, Leigh. In my head, I thought that if I was gone, maybe the old man would be different to them. It kills me to know that they've been suffering. Why don't they show me this?" My throat constricts and I have to blink back the emotion that wants to fall free.

She stands from her chair and I hold my hands out for her to sit in my lap. Her arms go around my neck and her forehead hits mine lightly. Her eyes are full of love, but I see the sadness swimming wet. "They both watched you suffer at Buford's hand. They lost *you* because of his abuse. That isn't something they could have ever let go. I have no doubt that they haven't told you everything for the same reason you're keeping your truths from them. To protect you."

"God," I breathe, closing my eyes.

"I'm not sayin' it will be easy, baby, but you need to give them all of it. Let them have the chance to find their own peace with the truth. They've made peace with Buford— let them make peace with the reality of your mother too. The only thing you can do is be there for them, but I don't think you will ever be able to put it behind you while keeping this from them."

Her body shifts as she rests her head on my shoulder, giving me the silence for my thoughts but keeping herself close in support. My mind swirls and my heart pounds. I know she feels the rapid beating because she brings one of her hands to my chest to rub soothing circles.

"I don't want to hurt them more," I whisper hoarsely.

"Honey," she cries softly, leaning up to look at me, "don't you think that by knowing the truth it might be what they need to heal?"

"What, Leighton, the truth that I'm not really their brother? The truth that our mother was more interested in fucking cowboys and doing blow than her own children? How do I even justify keeping that from them? This pain that kept me away from all of you for too long, driving me to a life of regret and torment . . . how would giving them my reasons and truths do anything but crush them? What part of that would help them heal?"

Her hands come up, swiping at the tears that I can't hold back. I close my eyes and try to calm down.

"Look at me, my handsome cowboy," she softly demands. I inhale a deep breath before opening my eyes and focusing on her. "First of all, you are their brother. The fact that you don't share their father will not mean a lick of shit to them. They love you, and that will never change. Second, your mother doesn't deserve you keeping that from them. What she does deserve is to come face-to-face with the children she abandoned. She doesn't deserve the peace that comes with Clay and Quinn not knowing her sins. They made their peace with Buford so that they could put it behind them and move on. His death was the best thing that could have happened to them. By giving them the rest, you're allowing them the ability to finally get some closure on it all. You aren't crushing them, honey, you're healing them. You have to trust them to be strong enough to ride that out."

I look away, glancing at Earl as he gives me a pissed-off

look for pushing him from my lap to make room for Leigh. As hard as it is, I know she's right. For the most part, she knows them better than I do. I haven't been around long enough to see the sides of them that she's describing. I don't doubt the truth to her words.

Now that I'm forced to see what they haven't wanted me to see, it's as clear as day. If giving them this heartbreak means they can heal, the only thing I can do is make sure I'm there to give them the same support I get from Leighton—love—and if that means they have a chance to find what I have with this woman, I have to give them every chance to accept that love when it comes looking for them. I didn't have this for so long that I felt the void of that loss burning in my gut daily. I don't want that for them. I don't want a life of loneliness for them because they're too afraid to let someone get close enough. And if telling them the truth about our mother will help get them there, then I reckon I don't have any other choice.

"You'll be there with me?" I question, knowing it isn't even something I have to ask, but needing the confirmation from her to ease my trepidation.

"I'll be with you every step of the way, honey. Forever."

I nod, not trusting my voice.

"I love you," she says softly.

I choke down the lump in my throat, feeling my chin shake, and hold up two fingers. Understanding dawns on her face at the same time I lose my fight, wrap my arms tightly around her, and cry like a goddamn baby into her neck.

29
LEIGHTON

"How to Breathe" by Matthew Mayfield

For the past two weeks, after our conversation about telling Clay and Quinn the truth about their past, Maverick has been struggling. It's not an obvious struggle. He hides it well, but not from me. He'll be fine one minute, and the next, he's just staring off into space. I know it's because his mind is working in overdrive, worried about what the truth will do to his siblings. I hate it, but I know there isn't anything I can do until he gets it all out. I understand his fear in telling them—causing them more pain—but because I'm an outsider looking in, I don't have any doubts that this is something they need to hear to move on with their lives. Just like Maverick, his siblings are built from a formidable mold. It will sting, no doubt, but the Davis kids are born warriors.

"Are you okay, honey?" I ask the silent man looking out our front window. We invited Clay and Quinn over for dinner tonight, so that Maverick could have a chance to talk to them, and he's been a hot mess, pacing the living room for the past half hour. I've given him his space, interrupting his taciturn brooding only long enough to give him a new beer when he was finished, but I can't stand the heavy quiet any longer without at least trying to be there for him.

"Yeah, darlin'," he sighs deeply, and I stand there wordlessly, waiting for him to get it all out. "I just hate knowing at the end of tonight, they might hate me."

"Oh, Maverick." I worry, closing the distance between us to envelop my big, strong cowboy in a hug. "They could never hate you. They might be hurt, but they won't ever turn that on you."

"I hope you're right," he muses.

"I know I am. Don't doubt them."

I feel him nod when his chin moves on the top of my head. I back up, give him a smile, and stand on tiptoes to give him a chaste kiss just as we hear a knock at the door, heralding their arrival.

A couple of hours later, I stand up to clear the table, shooing off Quinn when she stands to help.

"You're being weird," she mutters, rolling her eyes when I swat her with a dish towel again.

"I've got this, Q. Go sit with your brothers."

"Weird," she grumbles again, but complies, going back to the table to sit with a huff.

Maverick and Clay make small talk about the old barn demolition that Maverick is starting tomorrow. He decided to gut the whole thing himself, something I'm happy with because he'll be able to channel his emotions into that project.

"Come here please, darlin'," Maverick calls to me from the table, and my heart sinks at what's coming.

I go to him, drying my hands on the way, and drop the towel on the island before moving to his side. His arm snakes out and hooks around my waist before pulling me into his lap. The nervous flutters in my belly have me fidgeting with my hands, trying to ease the tension radiating from Maverick into me. He reaches out with one hand and places it over mine, stilling my movements.

"Why are you two acting so strange all of a sudden?" Quinn questions sharply. Her eyes are flying between her brother and my face, puzzlement dancing in her tone. "Are you pregnant?"

"No!" I rush at the same time that Maverick lets out a "not yet." I shoot him a glare, but he just winks in return.

"Well, something is wrong with you two." Quinn levels me with her I'm-your-best-friend-and-I-see-right-through-you gaze. "Is your hooha broken again?"

"Jesus, you're something else," I grouse. "My hooha is just fine, but thank you for your concern."

She gets a mischievous glint in her bright green orbs. I rip my hand out from under Maverick's hold. "Don't you dare," I fuss through clenched teeth, pointing at her.

"What? I was just going to say that I'm happy his pocket monster isn't branding your uterus anymore."

"Quinn!" Clay snaps. When I look his way he is obviously trying to stifle a laugh, but clearly having picked up on the nervous energy as well, he's more concerned with that.

She holds up her hands but thankfully keeps her trap shut.

Silence continues, the apprehensive air turning into a deep cloud of foreboding.

I give Maverick a supportive smile. "It's okay, honey," I tell him softly, cupping his strong, clenched jaw. I don't look away, holding his stare. "It's *okay*," I repeat.

I feel his jaw work under my palm. A flash of fear blankets his face, the look gone just as quickly as it appeared. We ignore his siblings and I hope like hell that I'm able to give him the encouragement he needs with my small cues.

"I need to tell you two something. Something I've been keeping from the both of you," he rumbles thickly.

"This isn't easy, so please let me get it all out. I'll tell y'all anything you want to know after, but I just need y'all to let me tell you everything, okay?"

Quinn nods, chewing on her bottom lip.

Clay lifts his chin, his hand coming up to run through his short black hair. A sure sign of his apprehension.

"You two know why I left. Or more important, what drove me out of here with pure rage-filled determination. Buford was a bastard to me—to all of us—but you *know* why I couldn't stay here or be anywhere near that man. I've never hidden my reasons, but when I left I found out a lot about the man who pushed me to leave the people that I love."

I pull his hand into mine and hold it tight, not looking away from Clay and Quinn. I want to be Maverick's shield here, but I also want them to know that I'm here for them as well. I hate the dread I see in both of their faces, especially knowing that fear will quickly morph into hurt.

"Fuck," he hisses, and I feel his forehead against my shoulder. He stays like that for a second before getting whatever he needs to continue. "I found Mama a few years after I left Pine Oak." He pauses when Quinn gasps. I see Clay's jaw flex and his lips thin. They keep their silence. "I'll tell you whatever you want to know about her, but after. Our first meeting was fuckin' shit, but in the end I learned a whole lot I never fuckin' knew. I always wondered why Buford treated me like crap, but never took it that far with y'all. He was shit to both of y'all, to be sure, but not like he was to me. It was my talk with her that had me searchin' out a trainer I hadn't worked with before: Trey Mavericks."

He clears his throat. "I never wanted to tell y'all this. You have to understand, I kept this from you both because I was fuckin' terrified that it would be too painful, but I've recently realized you might need this to put whatever might be hauntin' y'all two behind you forever. Trey, he became the closest thing to family I had while I was gone. Not just because he ended up bein' my trainer for the majority of time I was ridin', but also because he's my family."

"I don't understand," Quinn whispers.

"I'm gettin' there, Quinny," he breathes. "Trey's my uncle. My *biological* father's older brother."

"What?" she says with a gasp.

I steal a look at Clay to see his own shock present with wide eyes.

"When I finally managed to track down Mama, she told

me about her affair. My real father was a cowboy named Trent Mavericks, who's since passed. She named me Maverick after him, but in doin' so she gave Buford a constant reminder that she fucked around on him. Knowin' that, he used his hate for her and her actions as the fuel to hate me, well . . . it made sense. He hated me. Not for any other reason but because of the reminder I was. My dreams of ridin' just made him spite me more. I know there wasn't a thing I could have done to change that."

"Goddammit!" Clay exclaims, standing from his seat to pace, his shoulders pulled tight.

"I love you both so fuckin' much that it killed me knowin' that you might see me like he did. The bastard."

"Mav," Quinn cries, tears rolling from her eyes. "None of that changes a damn thing. You have to know that," she pleads.

Clay turns at her words, his features carved in granite. "Nothin' they did would ever make you less of my brother. I don't give a fuck shit about the blood that runs through your veins. You are *our* brother."

Maverick's grip turns painful, but I don't dare show it. My eyes pinging from both Clay and Quinn, wishing I could ease their pain.

Maverick pushes on, the words spilling out of him now that he's gotten going. "I want you both to know, I never wanted to tell you this, but I know now it wasn't right to keep it from you. Leighton, well . . . she's been here when I wasn't. She knows you both better than I probably do now. She's been my rock workin' through this shit, but more important, my voice of reason. I pray I don't cause you more pain with this knowledge. And maybe give you peace so you can put some shit behind you. I've had a lot of time to come to terms with this shit, but it's because of her that I've been able to put it behind me and start to move on. You both deserve that in your life. I know now in order to move on you have to open your hearts and don't let our fucked-up history repeat itself. Don't live your lives with the anger we were taught."

Quinn is openly sobbing now, her head pulled down into both of her hands. Clay moves to her side, pulling her to her feet before wrapping his arms around her. He looks at Maverick, the silence thick. My own heart is lodged high in my throat, but I don't move. Whatever happens next will tell me everything. If I need to build a wall around my cowboy to protect him from heartache or if I break down like a baby while a family heals.

"Brother," he grunts, his voice even deeper with the heaviness now weighing on him. "Get over here," he commands with conviction, pulling an arm away from Quinn and stretching it wide.

I hurry to stand, almost tripping over Maverick's big booted feet. I whip my head back, watching him climb from his seat, a sob catching my throat when I see one silent tear fall from his sad eyes. He walks past me, catching my hand and pulling me with him before falling into his brother's arms. I give him a squeeze, my gaze holding Clay's. He gives me a bleak smile before mouthing to me "thank you." That was all it took for the floodgates to open wide. I press my forehead to Maverick's shoulder, giving him whatever he needs by keeping me close during this moment.

Quinn gives a sniffle before lifting her head and wiping her face on Clay's shirt. He looks down, some of the harshness leaving his face, and gasps at her. "Did you just wipe your snot on my shirt?"

"Shut up," she hiccups, turning in his hold to face me. "I always knew you would bring my brother home."

I jerk, letting go of Maverick's hand and pulling her close. "I didn't bring him home, Q. He showed me, just like I showed him, where his heart was meant to be. All I did was love him."

Quinn smiles through her tears. "So, Maverick Mavericks, tell me about your father." The heaviness parts. I can feel it like a fog dissipating around us. My beautiful best friend giving her brother the assurance he feared wouldn't come, proving that nothing will ever change between them, and she did that by just being her.

30

MAVERICK

"Trouble" by Ray LaMontagne

"**Y**ou payin' for her care?" Clay questions, his rocking chair moving steadily as he gazes into the dark front yard.

"Yeah," I exhale.

"You should let her rot."

I move my gaze from the nothing I had been focusing on and look at Clay. Really look at him. He's the picture of frustrated pain. A mask I'm all too familiar with wearing. We've been talking for hours, all of us, and I fucking hate that I've brought this to him, but I know deep down Leigh's right. He's never going to stand a chance at finding something like what I have with her if he doesn't move on completely. All I can do is be here for him.

"Clayton." He turns and gives me his attention. I suck in a breath. It's like looking in the mirror. The rage and confusion all swirling around like a tornado inside of him, each one battling for dominance. "Talk to me," I plead.

"What do you want me to say?" he roars, throwing his hands in the air.

"Start with what's on your mind, big brother." Quinn speaks from behind us, walking around our chairs to sit on the wooden porch, her back to the railings.

I hear movement behind me before Leighton's hand slides from my shoulder to rest right above my heart. She doesn't move, just keeps her hand there in silent support.

"I'm still tryin' to wrap my head around that shit, Quinny. I knew she ran around on him. Everyone in town knew she ran around on him. I never, not fuckin' once, thought all that sprintin' she had been busy doin' was the reason Dad . . ." He trails off and then clears his throat. "I never imagined Buford's hate toward you was because of that shit, Mav. Blamin' you for somethin' so completely out of your control. Even now I can't understand it. I gave him my forgiveness and fuck if now I feel like he didn't deserve that kind of peace before he died."

Fuck. "He's still your father, Clay," I say vehemently.

"He's no father of mine." The lethal power behind the words leave no room for argument. He needs time, I know that, and I'll do whatever I can to help him through this.

I look down to my sister. She is just as angry as he is. She hides her hurt with laughter and jokes, but she feels deep.

"He was a terrible father," Clay continues. "I refuse to justify his abuse. I couldn't even before I knew all this shit, and nothing changes that. You were an innocent kid, Mav.

You didn't ask for any of that, but he punished you all the same. I gave him what I thought he needed to leave this earth with some peace. I struggled with that then, but it's nothing compared to how I feel now. Mama should have been here. She should have shielded you. She was never fit to be a mother, though. That shit was clear in the little time she was here, but I can't help the part of me that wants to blame *her* for all of this. The years you suffered because of her actions. The years we *all* lost with you because of them. I made excuses for her. Never once would I let myself believe that she actually *wanted* to leave us. I know better now and I fuckin' hate her for it. Not sure who I hate most, her, him, or myself for not doin' what I could to protect you."

"Not your cross to bear, Clay. I mean that shit. Don't for one second take that on."

He looks at me, his features carved in stone, and I know he wants to fight me on it. "You were just a kid too, Clay," I add, whether he wants to admit it or not. We might have been able to fight back physically, but Buford had done his damage on all of us and it was because of that fear he instilled that none of us fought back against his abuse.

"Do you think she even loved us?" Quinn questions, changing the subject and asking what all of us have probably wondered. Leigh's hand twitches and I reach up to keep it against my heart. Needing her to keep me grounded.

"In her own way, Quinny. I think she did in her own way." I push the words out even though I'm not even sure how many of them are true.

"How can you defend her?" Clay barks.

"How can I not? I know you're angry, Clay. I get it—trust me, I do. You have to remember, I've had a lot of time to get to this point of acceptance. I hated her for a long time too but holding on to that was dragging me down. When I think back to the time that she was actually here, she didn't act like he did. She smiled. She laughed and played with us. That woman is the one I choose to remember instead of the ghost of her that haunted the house long after she was gone. That woman is the one I cling to when I wake up shaking with the nightmare of what she became. I have to believe that she loved us, even if it was a tiny part of her."

"She left us!" he bellows. "She fucking left us with him, knowing what would happen. Don't you even think of defending that, because he was never any different."

I lose Leigh's hand when I stand. Quinn squeaks and quickly moves the legs that she had stretched out in front of her. I stomp past her and stand right in front of where Clay is sitting.

"I fuckin' left you too!" I thunder. "I left you just like she did, Clayton. Be fuckin' pissed. Hate her. Hell, hate me. But remember that she wasn't the only one that disappeared knowing what you were being left with. She wasn't the only one that made those choices and in turn hurt every single person she loved. So yeah, I can fuckin' defend her knowin' that I followed the same fuckin' path!"

My chest is heaving by the time I stop shouting at him. He doesn't move, though. His jaw continues to tick, the only part of him that shows me just how angry he is. Clay's the master of control, but it's slipping.

"You let that anger inside you win, Clay, then you become the very beast you're so angry with. She loved us in her own way. Even if she hadn't had me as a result of cheatin' on Buford, she wouldn't have stuck around. Sometimes the stubborn will to escape and survive is just too strong. In the end, regardless of the bullshit we were dealt, we have each other, and nothin' can ever take that away unless you give it the power to do so. Don't give that to them."

"I wish she was fuckin' dead." His control snaps in that moment and he drops his head. He breaks, and I'm thankful that I'm standing right in front of him. The first choked cry that he tries to hide from us kicks me into action. I bend and wrap my arms around my big brother, giving him the strength I didn't find for almost a decade, praying it doesn't take him that long to make peace with this.

"You don't, Clay. You're hurtin' and confused because it's so fresh. I'm here every step of the way to help you get past this."

I hear Leigh and Quinn talking quietly before their footsteps leave us. I know she's going to be there for my sister while I give Clay my undivided attention and support. Both of them are going to have a hard time, I know it, and all we can do is help them reach the other side. I don't want them to make my mistakes. They deserve the kind of freedom they will find after pushing through the things that have held them back because of our family's past.

"Clay, I need you to listen to me." He pulls back. The bruising hold that he had been clinging to me with easing now that he isn't squeezing me like a vice. "I never wanted you to feel what you're feelin' in this moment, but I know now that I did more harm than good by keepin' it from you. I've kept you from movin' on, even if you didn't realize you were bein' held back all this time. I've spent so many years lost because I felt just like you do right now. We can't change what they did, the people they were, but we can make sure we don't repeat history. I'm here for you every step of the way. I hope that, with time, you'll be ready to let it go. It wasn't somethin' I was able to do overnight, but I tell you that the reward that's waitin' for you when you set that shit free is worth every second of feelin' like your insides are burning. All that pain is worth it when you allow yourself to be vulnerable enough to accept another person's love."

"It fuckin' kills," he says through a heavy exhale.

"Not denyin' that, Clay, but I would live it all over again as long as I knew I would end up livin' the life I have now."

He looks at me, really fucking looks at me. I can't see his face clearly through the shadows, but when he nods, I know he understands what I'm telling him.

"I don't know if I'll ever find myself there, Mav, but I hope you're right."

"You will," I promise. "You damn sure will. One day when we're grumpy old men we'll sit right here on this porch and watch our kids and our grandkids together, Clay. They'll run around these fields knowing a happy fuckin' life built with nothin' but love. Mark my words, brother. Happiness the likes you have never imagined is waitin' for you. I want you to know that kind of contentment. The kind you feel deep in your bones. I hate that I hurt you with the truth, but I did it knowin' that when you get past what you're feelin' right now it will be worth it."

I back up when he moves forward. He's had enough tonight and I have to give him the space to search through all the turmoil boiling inside him. He nods, and I hear him swallow thickly. Then his chest is slamming against mine in a rough hug.

"Love you, Maverick. Nothing will ever change the fact that you're my brother. I can't promise I'll get past what I'm feelin' tomorrow, but I want you to know that no matter how angry I am—none of that anger is directed toward you. You did what you had to do, and no one faults you for that. I'm proud of the man you've become."

I cough, my throat bobbing as I force down the cry that almost came out.

"Love you too, Clayton."

He pulls away and uses the back of his hand to dry his face. "I'm glad you have Leighton. I can't say I'm thankful that this is what it took to give you her, but it does give me a little hope knowin' that you've been in my boots too and still have that."

"We aren't *them*," I tell him honestly. "We're in charge of our own lives. Our own happiness, love, and future. I couldn't dream of leavin' her again, and I know she wouldn't ever leave me. God willing, she gives me babies and I know with everything I am that I would never give them what Buford gave us. I was lost for a long fuckin' time, Clayton, but I will not let them rule my future. We don't live by their mistakes."

"No, we don't," he agrees with conviction.

354 - Harper Sloan

"You'll find your own slice of happiness, I promise you that. Until then, I'm here every step of the way to make sure your path is clear when it comes ridin' into town."

"We'll see," he says with a sigh. "Let's go check on Quinn. I don't want her thinkin' this is going to come between us. She's not as tough as she tries to convince us she is."

He steps past me and walks into the house. I turn and look up at the full moon. It kills me knowing that they're both hurting, but even witnessing that pain, I know Leighton was right in pushing me toward revealing the truth to them. I meant every word I just told him. I know he wouldn't be able to move on with the trust issues and anger that our past instilled in us. It held me back for too long. I wish I had had someone to push this on me years ago. I might have lost years of my life with Leigh because of the woman that birthed me and the man that raised me, but I will do everything in my power to make sure my siblings don't lose that time too.

With a sigh, I push off the railing and turn to enter the house. No, not just a house . . . home. My home with Leighton. She's standing in the doorway, her beast/cat in her arms, and her heart in her eyes. The illumination from the lights behind her cast her in some angelic-like glow. Fuck, I sound like a damn Hallmark card.

"Put him down, darlin'."

She doesn't question me. My tone is desperate. I need this stolen moment before entering the house. After placing Earl on his legs, she opens the screen door and steps into the darkness with me, the door shutting softly behind her with a low creak. She's in my arms seconds later. Her legs come up and she wraps them around my waist with a little help. I drop my face to her neck and breathe her in, taking the strength her very existence brings me.

"I'm proud of you, cowboy," she breathes; her softly spoken words make me tighten my hold. "They're hurting because it's fresh, but you've given them something they've been missing for a long damn time tonight."

"What's that, baby?"

"All of *you*," she answers, and, fuck me, I stand there and have to fight to take a breath through the tightness in my chest.

"How's Quinn?" I question after finally gaining control over myself.

Leigh pulls back and gives me a sad smile. "She wants to see her. Not tomorrow, maybe not even next year, but she wants it all the same."

"If that's what she wants." The last thing I want is to see her again, but for Quinn, I would move mountains.

"Come on, let's go back inside." She drops her legs after giving me a quick kiss and takes my hand to lead me into our home.

Leigh lets my hand drop after a quick squeeze when we step into the living room. Quinn rushes into my arms and hugs me tightly. No words are spoken, but by the time we sit down, some of the melancholy that had settled over all of us has dissipated. Both of them are still shaken up, but by the time they leave we're all laughing after spending hours telling stories about the good memories we had growing up together.

Love is a powerful thing. Now that I've opened myself up to that with Leighton, I know it really can conquer all. The love that Leighton and I share brought me back from the darkest times I had ever been through. The love we both have for my siblings will go a long way while they take the steps they need to truly let go of our past. With any luck, they'll find themselves experiencing the same divine power I get rushing through my veins every time the woman I love is near.

Sometimes it takes hitting rock bottom to find your way again. You have to be lost before you can ever be found. It might have taken me years, but when I hugged them good-bye I knew without a single shadow of doubt that I'm no longer adrift.

Turning from the door, I see Leigh walking back into the living room from the kitchen. She's doing whatever it is that chicks do to put their hair in some ball on the top of their head. Her bottom lip pulled between her teeth as she focuses on her task. The second she sees me leaning against the closed front door, she rushes to finish. A few pieces fall, her thick hair refusing to stay in place. She blows at them until they aren't in her eyes and gives me my reason for breathing. Her smile grows, her eyes brighten, and the rush from her love fills my body with overwhelming supremacy.

"You okay, Maverick?" she asks softly.

"I am now, Leighton. I am now."

Epilogue

LEIGHTON

"Eight Second Ride" by Jake Owen

Four Months Later

"**W**e're out of apple, birthday cake, and cookie dough!" Jana yells through the kitchen doorway.

I huff and look up at the clock. Only two in the afternoon, and I already feel like I've been run ragged. Fridays are normally a little busier than Monday through Thursday, but it seems like today especially has been nonstop since we opened the door.

I was in a sour mood anyway because Maverick's been out of town for the past two days. He has a friend in Wyoming who breeds bucking stock and went out there to talk about his needs for the school he's building. Well, I call it a school, but I think it's more like a training camp. An elite training camp, that is.

As much as I'm supportive and excited that he's making great progress in his plans, I hate when he's gone. We've been able to grab a few calls here and there, but for the most part, I haven't heard from him a lot since he left. When we talked last night he said he wouldn't be home until Sunday. This normally wouldn't be such a big deal.

I'm an independent woman.

Or so I thought.

It took one night without him for me to realize I had lost all ability to sleep without his arms around me. I've gotten so used to his presence that I don't *like* not feeling his dominant energy taking over our home. Even Earl's been pouting. He sat on the other side of my shower door this morning and wouldn't move so I could open it. I had to push it, and him, to get out. I'm completely thrown off my axis and I hate it.

It's been a few months since our dinner with Clay and Quinn. For the first two weeks after, my demands at the PieHole kept me away during the day and past dinner. Maverick made it a point to start his day after I had woken up, even if that meant he got a late start with his own work for the day. I never asked, but I have a feeling that was something he needed after everything that had come out that night. Whether it was reassuring himself that he really was in *our* home or that I was there with him, I'm not sure, but I gave him that without question.

Clay comes over often now to talk. He and Mav talk outside, rocking in the porch chairs long after the sun has set, and I'm none the wiser to what they discuss, but I'm hoping that it's just Clay leaning on his brother, taking the help and support that Mav promised to give him. If they ever need me to be part of that, I'll be ready and willing. There isn't anything I wouldn't do for the both of them.

Quinn, on the other hand, has been more of a challenge. I know she's having a hard time knowing the enormity of her parents' transgressions. With Buford gone, she can't get answers from him. Not that he would have given them. They might have put a lot behind them after he got sick, but she never forgot. My girl, she's loyal to the death, and in that case, she remained loyal to her brothers. She'll never get those answers, not now and maybe not ever, and I think that's something weighing hard on her. Not only that, but she is struggling with wanting to run to the mother she has very few memories of and despite the fact that the new knowledge she has of her brings forth hate and anger.

She's confused. She's hurt. She's afraid.

And even though she has her brothers and me, she's alone.

She's had a fear of commitment since the day she was old enough to stop thinking boys had cooties. It's hard not to, when you're raised like the Davises were. Aside from the one kind of serious relationship she had one fleeting summer, she settles for one-night stands and no strings. Now though, she's seeing her actions in a new light. One cast out from her mother's transgressions. I worry that she is comparing her legitimate fear-driven choices to the ones her mother made.

"And blueberry!" Jana yells again, interrupting my thoughts.

Pushing my concerns with my best friend from my mind, I rush around the kitchen. I bring the birthday cake pies out first, not even looking up in my haste. Jana makes a noise to get my attention, but I just hold my hand up and speed-walk back into the kitchen. It takes me three more trips to bring the other nine pies out. When I place the second cookie dough pie on the chilling rack, I finally look up, blowing a piece of hair out of my eyes.

My heart speeds up and my stomach is suddenly filled with butterflies.

"What are you doing here?" I ask breathily.

"Well, if you would have looked up I could have saved you the trouble of those cookie dough pies," Jana mutters, edging past me and leaving me with the sight of Maverick, glorious Maverick, grinnin' at me as he shovels a huge bite of cookie dough pie.

"I missed you too, darlin'," he says with a laugh, standing from the table after placing his fork down. He licks his lips before bending to give me a deep kiss.

"I thought you weren't coming home until Sunday?" I ask against his mouth before pulling away and looking around at the crowded room, smiling at the familiar faces looking on.

"Change of plans."

"Change of plans?" I repeat, studying his face. He's carefree as can be, but there's something mischievous working behind those green eyes that make my knees weak.

With a wink, he looks over my shoulder. "You good here, Jana?" he calls back toward the counter.

"Hey," I protest.

"Girl, don't you argue with your man," Jana scolds from behind me. "If he wants to steal you away, you let him steal you away. Just don't let him swallow the key. Nothing good ever comes if the key is swallowed."

My head snaps over to Jana with a gasp. "Boundaries!" I yell over the laughter that's now rolling from everyone around us. They're not even pretending not to watch with rapt attention.

"No handcuffs this time, Jana," he jokes.

"Do not encourage her," I hiss.

He holds up his hands, chuckling deeply. "She started it."

"Maybe you'll be the one in handcuffs if you keep this up," I smart.

His eyes darken and he leans closer to me. "Darlin', you want me in handcuffs and you say the word I'll be chained to the bed before you can blink."

"Go grab your stuff," Maverick breathes against my ear, pulling me back with his hands on my hips so I can feel his thickness against the small of my back. I make a mental note to look into buying some handcuffs before walking to my office and grabbing my purse. I check the ovens on my way back out, trying not to cringe at the mess on my workstation.

"Go on, sweetheart," Jana says, breaking into my thoughts and pulling me from the kitchen before I can reach for the cleaner. The woman knows me too damn well. "Don't you dare even think about it. I'm perfectly capable of handling things here."

"I hate leaving you alone to close."

"I'm not alone! You're the one that hired that sweet little Avonlee just last week so we would have another body for nights just like this. Go on and spend some time with that handsome man of yours." She snaps her towel at me like I'm a pesky fly. "Now go on, shoo."

I roll my eyes but know she's right. Avonlee hasn't been completely trained, but there's no better time than the present. She's in good hands with Jana. I purposely hired Avonlee so I would be able to stop working past five. This way I would be able to spend more time with Maverick and hopefully set things up here at the PieHole for a more part-time role for me in the future.

The future that hopefully gives us a houseful of children.

"See you in the morning," I tell her, pulling my purse strap over my shoulder. She doesn't respond, but before I can call her on the weird look in her eye, Maverick is back at my side and pulling me out the doorway.

"Would you slow down, you big giant," I say with a laugh, rushing to keep up with his long strides.

He turns, and without a word, picks me up bride style and continues to march to his truck, my laughter echoing around us. Maverick effortlessly opens the truck door, has me in the seat, and is walking around to his door. The whole time his smile never dims.

"Well, cowboy, you've got me. Now what are you gonna do with me?"

He reaches out and grabs my hand. "Hold on."

He cranks the truck, the vibrations making goose bumps pepper my skin. When he takes off with a jump out of the PieHole's side parking area, I settle back with a smile plastered on my face and enjoy the ride. He revs the engine when we pass Quinn standing outside the shop's bays. Her hands on her hips and a huge streak of black grease across her forehead. She smiles brightly and waves back. Mav turns up the radio, and with some old Lynyrd Skynyrd cranked up, he drops his foot and rumbles through town.

Content not knowing where we're going, but knowing I love the man who's taking me there, I look out the window with a smile on my face. If following him blindly keeps him looking as carefree and happy as he does right now, I would follow him to the moon.

MAVERICK

I pull off into the road, right after the turn-in to our house, and throw the truck into park. It was one of the first things I did before starting construction—adding an additional drive that would take people directly to the main barn. I can still get to everything from our personal property, but this way we can keep our lives separate from the training camp.

Leighton looks over at me in confusion before glancing out the window. I wait, knowing she'll see it without me having to point it out. We had never discussed this, and I know it was a risk without her input, but I have no doubts my girl will understand what brought this about.

All it took was a call to an old friend up in Montana, a former rider like myself that took his passion for welding and made it a thriving business after he left the circuit, and part one of my plans for today was in the works. It was harder than I thought to be home a night early, hiding out back in my old bedroom at the Davis ranch, but seeing Cliff install his work this morning made it all worth it.

I hear her gasp and I look proudly from where she's sitting to the huge wrought-iron arch ten feet from the road, over the gated entrance.

MAVERICK JAMES RODEO SCHOOL.

The large bold letters, with two huge posts connecting them to the black fence below, were created as spotlighting to what is being built behind those closed gates.

"You . . ." She gasps, her head shooting from the gate to look at me in shock before whipping her head back to gaze out the window.

"It's important to me, Leigh, that this is just as much a part of you as it is me. The Davis name, that isn't me . . . not anymore."

"But honey," she starts, her breath hitching, "people are coming for you. Maverick 'The Unstoppable' Davis."

"They'll still get that, darlin'. Doesn't matter that Davis isn't up there, not to them, but it does to me. They wouldn't be gettin' that if it hadn't been for the woman who saved me." She opens her mouth, but I shake my head to silence her. "If you want to argue with me later, you can, but not yet."

She frowns, but after searching my face, she just gives me a curt nod before settling back against the seat to wait.

I put the truck back in drive and move to the keypad in front of the gate, punch the code in, and wait for our path to clear. I drive down the lane, looking ahead and seeing how much progress we've made in the months that have passed since signing the deed to the property. The old barn was finished a few months back, the bright red-and-white paint standing out against the green fields around it. The small bunkhouses that scatter around it were finished shortly after. The medical and equipment buildings were close to the main barn. Each of the training arenas were close to being finished. There were only a few more things left to complete, but for the most part, we're almost ready to start going through the thousands of applicants that had started applying and pick our inaugural class of students.

Once I made news of the school I was starting public, there wasn't a fledgling rider around that didn't know about my training program and want to join. On top of four other instructors that I handpicked, Trey would be leaving the circuit to join me here after the season ended. He had come out to meet Leighton and see the land a month after I turned down his offer, and didn't even give me a chance to get the question out before he was making plans to move to Pine Oak.

By this time next year, we'll have a full staff and riders living here, spending their days learning from the best. There isn't a training school in the United States that can offer the kind of knowledge that Maverick James Rodeo School will.

A familiar rush fills my body when I think about the future. The only thing that gives me more happiness than that is the woman sitting right next to me. I still can't even really believe how much has changed since I rolled back into town angry about what I thought I had lost, only a mere half year ago.

"Where are we going?" Leighton asks, holding on to the

door handle when we leave the road and start bumping through the field.

Instead of answering her, I look over and give her a wink. She just laughs and rolls her eyes. When we reach the fence that separates our property and the schools, I jump out to open the metal gate. We haven't gotten to laying down the gravel for the road, so after I climb back in and pull the truck through, I make a mental note to have them come out sooner than later. If I keep driving my truck through this shit, Quinn will kill me. She's already had to replace my shocks once.

It doesn't take long to get us where I want to be. The same field that has always been so special to the both of us, that holds so many memories. I steal a glance at Leigh, seeing her eyes spark and the happiness she's feeling making them burn bright.

She doesn't wait for me to open her door; instead she jumps down and meets me at the front of my truck, looking around at the picnic that I had set up before coming to get her.

"Are you being romantic, cowboy?" she smarts.

"Depends. Will I get lucky if I am?" I quip.

"Since when don't you get lucky?"

I throw my head back and laugh. "Come on, darlin'."

I would have done this a long damn time ago, but I wanted to wait for the bluebonnets to bloom before bringing her out here again. She doesn't mention it often, but I know seeing them makes her feel like she's closer to her parents. I wanted her to have that comfort when I brought her back out.

"Thank you," she says as she drops to the plaid blanket that I've spread out in the one spot where there aren't any flowers, the brilliant blue that surrounds her painting one hell of a stunning picture. I swallow the thick lump of emotion and bend down to open the basket. I grab the bottle of the champagne I bought in Austin a few weeks back. I couldn't tell you if it's good shit or not, but seeing as it cost me a few hundred bucks, I'm guessing it is. Leigh leans back, bracing her weight on her hands, and gives me a wide smile. "Daddy would love seeing the James name up there."

I make a noise in my throat and continue to pour our glasses before handing her one.

"I know you think it should be Davis up there, Leighton, but it's important to me that I start this new chapter of our lives without it. I used to think that being a Davis is what defined me, but I know now that isn't the case. A name only holds the power you let it. I'm the man I am today because I fought not to become him and it was because of you that I finally had the tools to win that fight. To me, that is everything. It's you and me, Leigh, for the rest of our days."

"Honey, all I did was love you."

"And that love saved me," I tell her honestly.

I let the silence linger as I wait for her to take a sip. I'm half tempted to down my whole glass, but I just swallow a small bit before sitting the glass on the top of the basket.

"Come with me?" I ask, taking her glass and sitting it in the other cup holder on the lip of the basket before standing and holding out my hand.

Her lips curve into a small smile, and she takes my proffered hand to help her stand. I pull her from the blanket and walk toward the end of the field. The small raise in the land gives us the perfect view of the school beyond. You can't see everything, but a good portion of the school's land is visible from the field's higher elevation.

"You know, when I made my way back home, I dreaded every second it took to get me here. I was so fuckin' angry, baby. I couldn't even see past that for one second. Because of that, I didn't see a future for myself anywhere. I was lost, so fuckin' lost, Leighton." I take a deep pull of air, looking beyond us while searching for the right words. She moves closer and wraps her arms around me. "I ran from you and I knew deep down inside me it was wrong before I even left this place. I can't tell you how much it means to me that you were willing to forgive me for that. I will never be able to express how much that forgiveness saved me."

"Honey," she whispers, looking up and tightening her arms around me.

"You saved me, Leigh. You brought me back and showed me that I wasn't as lost as I feared I was. All that darkness and pain around me, you are the reason I beat them back. Trust me when I say this, your love gave me a reason to live again, and I will spend the rest of my life making sure you know how grateful I am to have that gift."

"Maverick, honey, you say that like I was the only one doing the saving. I was just as lost. The loneliness was killing me slowly. All that time we were apart—even with all that distance—it made that bond we've always had so much stronger." She gives her head a small shake and her curls dance around her face. "You think I saved you, but sweetheart, I think we saved each other."

Bending slightly, I pick her up with my hands gripped to her thighs. She doesn't wrap her legs around my hips, but her hands come up to cup my jaw and tip my head back to look up at her. She smiles and brings her lips down for a kiss so full of fucking emotion I have to tighten my grip for fear of dropping her. I feel my hat fall next to my feet, but I continue to kiss her passionately. Our mouths move hungrily as our tongues slide and swirl against each other. The promise of what's to come makes me groan deeply into her mouth, turning my head in to deepen our kiss.

"I love you," she says against my lips after one last wet swipe of her tongue against mine.

I don't respond. Instead I slowly drop her to her feet before falling to my knees. She gasps. I look up at her, the enormity of the love I feel for her making my throat burn. My forehead hits her belly and she stumbles slightly when I cross my arms around her back, pulling her closer with my hands at her sides. I dig my fingers into the soft flesh and squeeze my eyes shut. Praying I get this out before sobbing like a baby.

"I love you so fuckin' much, Leighton. I know if I was ever forced to live without you again, I would never find my way back from that. You're everything to me, darlin'. Everything I never let myself believe I would have, but I thank God every day that I finally have it." I look up, not even ashamed of the tears rolling down my face. "One of these days, our kids will run through these same fields that we grew up on. They'll do that with happy hearts because their parents love them just as much as they love each other. My past will never touch them, and by giving our land both of our names, I'll ensure it. Marry me, Leighton James. Marry me, give me babies, and let our love become something that people dream of findin'."

By the time I finish speaking she's sobbing so hard that if I hadn't been holding her tight, I reckon she would have fallen.

"God, yes!" she cries, her tears falling even faster now. "Nothing would make me happier."

I stand and pull her close. She rolls to her tippy toes and I bend to meet her the rest of the way. Our kiss is slow. The heavy breathing falling from both our fused mouths turns our connection desperate, the need to be as close as possible building between us as our tears of happiness dance together.

That need builds as our frenzied movements tear at our clothes, the silent demand our bodies make fuel us until we're both as naked as the day we were born under the bright Texas sun. I lift her and she wraps herself around me, our mouths never breaking as I take her back to the blanket. Her wetness has me pulling her closer to my aching cock, and before her back has even hit the ground, I'm inside her. We move slowly, her body taking every inch of me. I lift my mouth from hers, keeping my forehead connected as my hips start to move faster. Her cries pick up tempo with each deep drive I take into her tight body, our eyes still wet with emotion.

"I'm gonna take your name, baby," I vow, slamming my hips down.

"Oh, God." She gulps, her whole body trembling as her pussy quivers around my cock.

"I'm gonna take your name and when we have our babies, they're gonna to have it too."

"Oh, God!" she screams, her core squeezing me tight.

"Nothing I want more than to let the world know that you saved me. Gonna show them all that when you marry me, baby."

She jolts, my cock hitting the deepest part of her, and I groan as my balls tighten up.

"You gonna give me that?" I pant in question, feeling my release start to rush through my body.

"I'll give you everything!" she screams, her body once again squeezing me, tighter than before as she starts to come.

I give three more powerful and deep thrusts before I feel my release pour into her welcoming heat.

"You already have," I whisper, taking her mouth again while I lazily plunge myself into and out of our combined wetness. With any luck, those James babies I want so desperately will come sooner than later.

We settle after a few more minutes, and Leighton lets out a happy little sigh as I nuzzle against her. We're in no rush to leave our field. No one will bother us here. Not in our place. With the flowers of our past blooming just as stunningly as our love, I hold my future in my arms.

I was lost once. A rider without the ability to do what he loved. I came home even though it was the last place I thought I wanted to be, and in the process not only did I find myself again, but I also found that my reason for livin' didn't have shit to do with ridin'.

No . . . ridin' doesn't define me anymore. Not when I've got the love of the woman made for me. She gave me *me* back, and in the process, I gained *everything*.

Leigh rustles against me. "Should we get going, baby?" she murmurs, half asleep.

I just tuck her tighter into me and kiss that sweet forehead for all I'm worth. "Baby, we aren't going anywhere. We've got all the time in the world."

ACKNOWLEDGMENTS

To my family—your understanding, support, and encouragement fuels my every move. This journey wouldn't be half as fun without your love. To my girls for keeping me going when I felt like giving up—everything that I do is with the hope that you will see dreams do come true. Never stop dreaming, my babies. To my husband for loving me when I'm a mess, feeding me when I forget, and keeping me sane. I wouldn't be me without you four. To my parents for never losing faith in me, even if it took me a while to find my place in life.

To Felicia Lynn—my best friend, partner in crime, and writing marathon partner. I'm pretty sure it would take me three times longer to finish a book without your reassuring support. I like you, a little.

To Lara Felstein—it seems like forever ago we were working on one of my first books . . . at this point I'm so needy for your brilliant mind, I couldn't imagine writing without your feedback. Clay can't wait to steal your heart forever. ;)

To Danielle Sanchez—the best publicist in the universe. The virtual whip of your messages is almost as strong as the support you give me. No matter what you're

Acknowledgments

there to listen to me and build me back up when I feel like I've crumbled.

To Marisa Corvisiero—thank you for everything you've done to help being the Coming Home series to life and making sure it was brought to life with nothing but love.

Keep reading for an excerpt from book two
in the Coming Home series

Kiss My Boots

Available Summer 2017 from Pocket Books!

1

QUINN

"Middle of a Memory" by Cole Swindell

The aroma of oil and exhaust fumes swirl in the air, mixing and mingling with the scent of metal baking in the strong summer sun. Even with the bays of the garage closed, the shop can't escape the soaring temperatures. Every truck that's brought in gives off waves of fiery heat for what seems like hours while we begin our work.

If you've ever worked under a vehicle that spent any amount of time kicking up rocks on the scorching Texas asphalt, then you know it's about as close to feeling the heat of hell that one chick can take.

And I love every second of it.

Ever since I was a kid, I've been happiest when getting my hands dirty. Most of the girls I knew went to mud holes to find their dirty fun—not me. While they were in the passenger seats of their dads' or brothers' or boyfriends' trucks, laughing and screaming as they bumped along through the holes, I was too busy climbing behind the wheel, analyzing each and every move my truck would make—even before I could legally drive, something that drove my own brothers, Clay and Maverick, insane. But I didn't care. I couldn't get enough of it. I would envision ways to make the truck roar louder, kick up its spray of murky clay and water more powerfully, and take those back roads trails with a supremacy that even the deepest rut couldn't stop.

Of course, it didn't hurt that while I was growing up, my father owned the best auto shop around. It was also the only one around, but that didn't mean it wasn't the best. Davis Auto Works has been *the* place for custom auto needs since 1982.

And it's been my haven for longer than I can remember.

"Q! You gotta second, doll?" Tank bellows from somewhere close to the 2017 Dodge Ram I've been working underneath for the last hour.

Waiting a second, knowing he can't see me, I close my eyes and take a deep pull of my special brand of calming air. The scent of motor oil, chassis grease, and break dust trickles through my system and blankets my frazzled nerves instantly.

"What's shakin' cowboy?" I ask with a sigh, pulling myself to my feet. My hands go to the sides of my coveralls to wipe them clean out of habit, before I realize I pulled them down after lunch to try and cool off. "Damn," I mutter, peering at the black handprints now adorning my faded denim. "I liked these jeans, too."

"Nothing a little elbow grease can't handle, darlin'."

I look up . . . and up . . . and up, finally meeting the dirt-brown eyes of Miles "Tank" Miller. The man is huge, hence the nickname, and, bless his heart, dumber than a box of rocks. He's a handsome devil, don't get me wrong, but even if he wasn't a complete idiot when it comes to anything other than motors, I wouldn't be interested.

I don't date. Ever.

"What do you need, Tank? I need to get this lift finished before five so I'm not stuck here all dang night."

"Got a real shitter comin' in. Man said he wanted every whistle and toot out there. I ain't sure what that meant though, seein' as he said it ain't even runnin'. Not sure you can put a whistle and toot on a heap of broken metal."

It takes every ounce of sweet Southern darlin' I have deep in my soul not to snap at Tank and tell him I can barely understand his broken English, but my brothers' didn't raise a rude little bitch.

"Tank, sweetheart, can you be a little more clear for me?" I roll to the tips of my boots and reach up to pat his beard-covered cheek.

He looks down, blinks a few times, and shrugs one meaty shoulder. "Naw."

Patience, Quinn. Patience. "Did you take his number?"

His eyes crinkle as his brow pulls into a frown. "Reckon I might have."

"How about you finish up fine-tuning the suspension system on the Ram for me? I was almost done, so there isn't much left, just finishing up with the sway bar. I'll go look for that number. How's that sound?"

"Sure thing, Q. You takin' this baby up nice and high. Chester handlin' the engine on this bad boy?"

I nod, but don't bother answering him since he's already dropped down to disappear under the truck. I walk over to the sink in the corner and wash up with some GOJO. I might love getting my hands dirty working with trucks, but I still enjoy looking like a girl—which means I'm anal about washing often to avoid the perpetual black stains most mechanics have on their hands.

Stepping into the back office, I cringe when I see the mess on my desk. Normally, it's kept in what I lovingly refer to as organized chaos, but all it took was one visit by our resident Tank and it looks like an F5 tornado blew through.

"Jesus Jones," I mutter, shoulders dropping in frustration. "How the hell am I supposed to find something in this mess?"

"My guess would be clean it up," a familiar sardonic voice laughs from behind me.

"I do clean! Which you know damn well!" Fake annoyance laces through my words and I spin around, smiling as I face my eldest brother.

"Let me guess, Tank." The corner of his mouth tips up as he smirks at me. I can't see his eyes because of the shadow of his cowboy hat, but I imagine the deep hunter-green is brighter than usual with a knowing sense of mirth.

"The one and only," I drone.

"I just stopped in to handle payroll. I didn't have everything I needed at the ranch, but I can hang around if you need somethin'."

"Now, Clayton Davis, you keep that up and I might think you enjoy tinkerin' around the garage," I say in jest, knowing damn well Clay hates working in the shop.

He takes off his hat, placing it open-side-up on top of the filing cabinet as any good Texan would, running one hand through his thick black hair. "Funny, Quinny."

"I try, big brother. I know you've got your hands full at the ranch, so don't worry your pretty little head over things here. I've got everything under control."

"I know you do, Q. You could run this place hog-tied and blindfolded. But, everything is handled at the ranch. Drew's been one step ahead of me all damn week. It's drivin' me insane."

I laugh at the mention of the ranch's foreman, Drew Braden. He's the only man I know who works harder than Clay. He keeps that ranch running with so much pride you would have thought it was his own family's land—but that's just the type of man he is. He always did say you could tell the measure of a man by how hard he worked. He's been around since well before my father died last year, and he's always treated all of us like his children.

"Still workin' like crazy?"

"Ever since Jill told him she was pregnant. You would think at his age he would know how to wrap his shit up, but I have a feelin' Jill knew exactly what she was doin'."

"You make forty-eight sound ancient, Clay," I giggle, pushing some of the papers around, hoping to find some sort of message from the call Tank took.

"Shit, Q, I'd be freakin' out, too, if I was going to be

a dad—again—years after my grown kids had already left the house. He's old enough to be my dad."

I roll my eyes. "I think that's a stretch, cowboy."

"He had Missy when he was fifteen, Q. And I graduated high school with Missy. Not exaggerating in the least, darlin'."

"Well, even so, that's what happens when you're pushing fifty and get yourself a new bride who probably graduated with your daughter, too."

Clay starts grumbling under his breath about beauty queens, big hair, and gold diggers. Not that I would call Jill a gold digger, but rumor around Pine Oak has it that she married Drew for his money. The man might work at the Davis Ranch by choice, but he's never had to work a day in his life, he's that loaded. His grandfather's grandfather struck it big in the oil fields years ago, and to this day the Braden family is rolling in money from the investment. Not that Drew acts like it; the man still drives the same truck he had when he was in high school.

Finally spying Tank's near-illegible chicken scratch, I grab the torn scrap of paper and move to sink my tired body into my office chair. Clay moves to his desk in the corner—much neater than my own—right as I pick up the receiver to dial what I hope are the correct numbers that Tank wrote down.

Then I see the name.

And everything around me washes away. My vision going foggy until memories long since locked away start slamming into my head. They're so crystal clear that I feel like I'm the same love-drunk eighteen-year-old all over again.

- ★ -

"Damn," a husky voice grits out. "It's just not right how hot you look tinkerin' around my truck, darlin'."

I look up from the oil cap I just finished tightening back on and smile, wide and toothy, before giving him a wink. "Is that why you asked me to change your oil when we both know you're more than capable? You're lucky, I don't normally make house calls."

He reaches up, the material of his T-shirt lifting from his Wranglers, showing off the toned, rock-hard abs and that mouth-watering V at his hips. When I feel the weight of the hood lift off my hand, I let out a squeak, looking up to see him gripping it, returning my wink with a smoldering gaze of his own.

"Busted," he whispers, bending down to press his full, smooth lips against mine. The kiss is brief, but the butterflies that take up residence in my stomach whenever he's around pick up their fluttering until I feel like they might fly right out of my mouth.

I move awkwardly out of the way while he slams the hood down on his brand-new Chevy. I busy myself with washing up, making sure to clean my hands thoroughly, until not a speck of grease is left on them, even if my pretty manicure is blown to hell. The last thing I hope Tate Montgomery is thinking about is the chipped red polish adorning my nails. His grandparents are out of town at a craft show near Austin and my brothers think I'm at Leighton's tonight.

We've got more important things to do than hold hands. Tonight, I hope and pray that Tate makes good on all the promises our heated make-out sessions have been hinting at. I'm ready to give myself to him, pretty red bow intact.

- ★ -

"You hot, darlin'? I didn't think it was that bad since the sun went down, but we can head on in if you want." He points toward his grandparents' house and all I can do is nod. I can see the questions in his eyes, but he doesn't voice them as we make our way inside. "Paw said Gram left a fresh batch of chicken and dumplin's if you're hungry."

He was a few steps ahead—his back still facing me—when he spoke, so I take the time to take a deep, fortifying breath before he turns back around. The last damn thing I want is chicken and dumplin's, but how do you tell your kinda-sorta-maybe boyfriend that you would rather he eat you than dumplin's?

"I'm good," I whisper, my heartbeat roaring in my ears. God, Quinn Everly Davis—cowgirl, up and take the bull by the horns . . . or the man by the balls, same thing.

"Darlin'?" he questions, heat pooling in his denim-colored eyes.

"Please," I croak, the little badass that usually lives inside me long gone, made weak with hunger that has nothing to do with golden fried buttermilk biscuits. "Please, Tate. We've been scratchin' this itch for two years now, and every summer you say not yet. Don't make this another summer where you leave without showing me how much you love me."

"Quinn," he sighs, taking off his white Stetson and running a hand through his chocolate waves. "Baby, you know I love you, but this isn't just any other summer. I'm not going back home when I leave this time. We're both about to start the next chapter of our lives—you takin' over the auto shop and me startin' at Emory. Georgia is a long way away, and we both know we've never tried long distance for a reason. Not sure that's somethin' I can stomach, finally getting' to have you completely, only to lose you."

His words are all it takes for my temper to snap. "We've never tried the long distance thing because of you, Tate. Don't put that bullshit on me."

"Not because I didn't want to and you know it," he growls in return. "Fuck, Quinn, you don't think I've wanted to make you my girl since the first summer my parents shipped me off to Gram and Paw's? You know damn well I have, but it isn't that easy."

"Because I'm not some high society princess?"

He stomps the few feet between us and curls his fingers around the back of my neck with a touch that is gentle but unmistakably dominant. His thumbs, resting at my chin, give me a gentle push of encouragement to look up at him. I don't even bother fighting him. My head moves, eyes travel the strong planes and sharp features of his handsome face until I meet his pleading eyes.

"You know I don't give two shits about what they think, Quinn, but until I finish medical school they've got more pull over me than I wish they did."

I sigh, knowing he's right. The Montgomery family holds the purse strings to Tate's future, and that's a hell of a bind. He's had his hopes set on going to an expensive out-of-state school, and we both know he wouldn't be able to afford it without their help. I know how much it means to him, too—going to Emory University—because it's where his paw attended, so as much as I hate accepting him leaving for school that far away, I'll support that dream.

The silence ticks on while we hold each other's gaze. I pray that he can see the desperation my love for him makes me feel. The need to get as close as two people physically can is almost unbearable. What I feel—this needy fire burning deep in my belly—only becomes more powerful the longer I deny what I crave.

He must see something written in the silence around us because in that moment, the deep, dark blue of his irises swirls and lights up with understanding. And unmistakable lust.

"You sure about this, Grease?" he questions on a whisper, lips quirking with his nickname for me. He's used it since the first day we met, when I was covered in engine grease.

"I've never been more certain about anything in my life, Starch," I answer, the butterflies picking back up to full speed when his smirk grows into a panty-melting smile at the use of my nickname for him—a standing joke about the high society world he comes from back home in Dallas.

"Nothing in this world could make me stop loving you," he murmurs, his head moving down, closer to me, and before I can reply, his mouth captures mine in a deep kiss. I feel him all the way to my bones with this kiss. He's branding himself into my very soul, and I know without a shadow of doubt that I will always feel him there.

There isn't any more talking after that. Moans, grunts, and the sound of bare skin brushing against bare skin, tentatively at first and then more urgently as we move together, are the only things that fill the silence around us. Through the pain of losing my virginity to the only boy I've ever loved, I bask in the beauty of this moment we've been building toward for years, knowing that my life will never be the same. Our future might not be set in stone, but we've come this far with only summers together since we were middle school age. I have no doubt that we have what it takes to make it through him starting his medical school career and beyond. We're not little kids anymore, confused about how we feel. We're on the cusp of adulthood; old enough to understand that our hearts are connected so powerfully, you can almost feel them nestling close together, beating as one.

As one.

Present Day

I gasp when the memory clears, feeling my cheeks wet as I focus back on the paper in my hand. Praying that the name I read wasn't his, but with the shaking of my hand making the paper vibrate softly, I know it's just wishful thinking.

The ghost of heartbreak past apparently is back in Pine Oak.

Tatum Montgomery.

Jesus Jones.